Queen
of
Chaos

Sabrina Chase

Copyright © 2012 Sabrina Chase

Cover art by Les Petersen

ISBN-13: 978-0-9852704-8-3

CONTENTS

Also by Sabrina Chase

Firehearted
The Last Mage Guardian

THE SEQUOYAH TRILOGY:
The Long Way Home
Raven's Children
Queen of Chaos

ACKNOWLEDGMENTS

Thanks to everyone who saw me through this trilogy—the STEW critique group, fantastic editor Deb Taber, detail-oriented proofreader Roger Ivie, and countless beta readers. If there are any errors, they probably warned me about them so it is entirely my fault.

S.Chase

DEDICATION

For the crew of B-17 "The Old-Timer"—Floyd Gast, Robert Effinger, Lloyd McNulty, Norman Pries, Verne Willey, Robert Talbott, John Palmer, John Butler, and Robert Chase. Thanks for looking after my Dad during the War, guys. It just wouldn't have been the same without him.

CHAPTER 1
ENTROPY ALWAYS INCREASES

Moire Cameron stared at the jewel-like planet on her viewscreen. Sequoyah looked so peaceful and serene; the countless islands scattered over the brilliant blue oceans, the three moons playing tag. And here she was, bringing it war. She sighed, and slumped in *Frankenstein's* pilot's chair.

"Nothing but trouble from start to finish," she muttered to herself. "Better if we'd never found it." Better for her, at least. Better for the rest of the exploration team, the ones who hadn't made it back.

She rubbed her face, willing the dark memories and her fatigue away, and glanced at the viewscreen again. The cave—no, New Houston, it had a name now—was well into the night side. Everyone should be asleep except for the night duty folks. Maybe she could get some time to herself. So she could think about Ennis and be miserable.

Moire reached for the comm switch, but before her fingers touched it a pinlight glowed on the board. The display claimed it was a direct, external signal. Someone was on the ball.

"Captain! Did everything go as planned? We were starting to worry." Kilberton did sound agitated, which wasn't like him.

"Yeah, dumped off the ship and the commander just like we planned, no problems. Why, is something wrong?"

"Well, you did have difficulties with *Frankenstein* before," he said, apologetically. "Understandable, since Gren removed half the superstructure and tied the gravitics in knots. How was it in webspace?"

Moire grinned. He loved his pilot-talk. "Like trying to walk with three feet. It helps if you don't think about it too much. Strange thing was it was worse without the crab ship in tow. Gren did what he could, but—" Another pinlight lit up, then two more. "Oh great. I'm becoming popular. I should probably head dirtside—can you scramble up a watch crew? I don't want to leave Radersent with just Perwaty up here."

"How's he doing?"

"Same number of tentacles as when we found him, so I guess he's OK. Hard to tell. Oh, and he'll want someone to talk to. Gets agitated if he's alone too long." And crab sleep cycles were much longer than human ones, so that had taken a good bit of explaining before he caught on that the crew needed it more frequently than he did.

She locked in the orbit and set the auto for the shuttle, then did a shipwide comm to announce it. Moire got out of her chair stiffly, and stretched. She should probably go and tell Radersent herself what was going on. He never questioned or argued with her. A model crewmember. Pity he couldn't breathe their air.

If her only impression of crabs had been from Radersent she would have never believed they would fight a vicious, unrelenting war with humans. Yet they did—and here was Radersent, who had never lifted a pseduolimb against any of them. It didn't make any sense.

She followed the ladder-infested route to the crab's quarters. Nothing was easy to get to on *Frankenstein*, since they had gutted most of the ship. Quarters were bad but storage was even worse, and Radersent's "quarters" were actually a huge sealed cargo container.

Moire peered in the viewport of the door—another custom fitting—and entered the security code. They were still taking precautions with the crab. Trust was one thing, crew morale was another. She wasn't sure if he knew why they were doing it, but he'd never asked any questions about it—which told her, from her experience with the crab, that he'd noticed.

The Created were, as usual, in the human section with Perwaty, the human they had rescued from the sargasso along with Radersent. Ash was asleep, being held by Hideo. She was still recovering from getting shot on Kulvar. The Created were tough but she had lost a lot of blood. Too much. George and Alan were at the communication console, arguing.

"No there doesn't have to be a star! There wasn't one at the Place, and we went there. To get *you*," Alan added, pointedly.

"There does so! Gren said there has to be a...a mass point to make the line or the drive won't work."

Moire came up behind them, grinning. "What's up?"

Alan spun his chair around. "Does there have to be a star where the ship goes?"

"Is Radersent asking about web travel?" Moire asked, raising an eyebrow. Maybe they should be recording all the conversations through the translator, just to make sure. The kids spent a lot of time with the crab, sometimes unsupervised by an adult.

Radersent was just visible in the gloom and murk of his quarters, seen through the large, formerly exterior viewport that now functioned as his window to the human side of the room. He was doing the slow, gentle motion that indicated he was in a good mood. She could tell when he recognized her, because he tilted back his long bony head so his throat-opening was clearly visible and the tendrils to either side radiated out, then back. He never did that for anyone else.

"Small-she," said the synthetic voice of the translator. His name for her.

Alan was still looking at her, expectantly. "You are both right. You have

2

to have a star in the direction you want to go–that gives you your lineup–but you can stop any time along the way." George and Alan digested this information in thoughtful silence. "Tell Radersent that I'm leaving the ship for a while."

"Okay!" George turned back to the cobbled-together crab-human communication and translation device. They really should make a better one, or at least have a spare. Right now it was the only one in the galaxy.

"Where are you going?" Alan asked. Worried, like he always was when he thought she might leave him.

"Just down to the planet. You can come with me if you like, but it's local-night down at D'Accord. The rest of the kids won't be awake."

"We want to go down there!" Hideo blurted. Ash stirred in her sleep and made a small noise.

"You can catch a shuttle later, when it's day," Moire said. "We're going to be here for a while." At least she would be, trying to figure out what to do next with all the different projects.

All the kids, even the now-awake Ash, wanted to come with her. Moire acquiesced. The skeleton crew would be much more willing if they knew the Created weren't on the ship to cause trouble.

She got them all herded into the dropship and fastened in. The problem was they were children, with all that implied, but without the physical restrictions that usually applied to children and that could be exploited to keep them from doing things they shouldn't. They were the same size as a fully-grown adult, stronger, intelligent, and curious. It was a miracle they hadn't blown anything up yet.

"Did you really have shuttles that rolled on the ground long ago?"

And of course, trips were never dull. Or silent.

"Yes. We called them cars."

"Why did they roll on the ground? They would run into things, wouldn't they? Why didn't you have flying ones then?" Ash wanted to know.

"We had to learn how to make flying ones," Moire said. "Remember, this was over eighty years ago. We only just had figured out how to build ships that could travel web space."

"You mean nobody could go anywhere? They were stuck on Yerth?" George was horrified.

Moire grinned. He'd come a long way from not even knowing what a planet was. "Earth, George. It's not a bad place to be stuck. It's a big planet, like Sequoyah."

"Were the crabs stuck too, where they were?" Ash asked.

"That's a good question. I don't know." The kids were silent for a while, pondering the implications of Moire not knowing something.

"You got unstuck though. But...but you got lost, so you couldn't find the right time to go back in," Hideo said. "Is that why you know about the

3

old times so much?"

Couldn't find the right time. That was a pretty good approximation of Einstein's Revenge, from a child's point of view. Couldn't go home, ever. Because home had floated down the river of time and would never come back again. "Something like that."

The cave was still full of gear and shuttles, so she landed the dropship on the cliff top. Two of the moons were up so handlights weren't strictly necessary to see the path to the cave, but she handed them out anyway. "And watch out for splatterplants!" she called after the kids as they raced down the path. "Get any of that goop on you, I'll leave you here!"

The threat was bad enough they at least slowed down. Splatterplant essence was worse than skunk.

Kilberton was waiting for her at the cave, as she knew he would be. He had a seemingly endless supply of questions, about the dropoff, about the salvage plans, but after the first hour she cut him off. "Are there any other emergencies? Anything that can't wait until morning?"

"Well no, but—"

"Then unless there are things I need to know ahead of time, I'm going to get some sleep. Anything that comes up, wake me. And go get some sleep yourself, got that?"

He grinned, tiredly, and waved goodbye. Moire scrounged a pad and a blanket and found a secluded cargo crate to collapse on. She fell asleep in the middle of wondering if she was too tired to sleep.

She was wakened by someone shaking her shoulder and talking rapidly in her ear. Harvey Felden, the old ship steward and now general planetary commissar, by default.

"We gotta do something. They've been patient and all but the construction folk can't cut rock fast enough."

Moire rubbed the sleep out of her eyes and stretched. "What are you talking about, Harvey?"

"Them folks off Bone. It was crowded enough with the Created and all our people, but we don't even have enough shelters. Not unless you want to take the ones we gave the prisoners," he added, looking as if that was a good idea.

"Right. Accommodation for the new people. I'll talk to Kostas about it. Wasn't in the original plan, but maybe he can come up with something." It would take more money that she really couldn't spare, but she owed the Bone people. Waylands had only gotten blown up because Toren had been chasing her. People had been killed. The least she could do was give them shelter before Toren chased them here.

"Prisoners doing all right?"

Harvey shrugged. "Lost a few. One suicide, and one tried to jump Grimaldi when she went to drop supplies."

"I'd count that as suicide too, myself," said Moire.

"Woulda been more, if Kilberton hadn't stopped it. One of the crew that was with us on the rescue–got drunk, snagged a scooter and a rifle and was going down to do some target shooting."

They would have to do something about the prisoners, but shooting them out of hand wasn't what she had in mind. She could understand the motivation of the would-be shooter, and if she could avoid official knowledge of the incident–and it didn't happen again–she'd let it drop. The prisoners were some of the cargo they had taken from the hidden site where Toren had been manufacturing the Created. They'd saved some of the Created still there, but not all. The Toren employees had tried to destroy the evidence of what they had done by destroying the Created still being grown.

Moire unclenched her hands with an effort. The Toren prisoners would get what was coming to them, one way or another. A bullet was too kind. On the other hand, they were using up valuable supplies. She had to figure out a way to stop that.

While she was getting some breakfast Kostas, the big, barrel-chested construction boss found her and greeted her with a crushing hug.

"Hey! Thought you got lost out there or somethin'."

"Nope, just busy," Moire gasped when he let go. "How's the site?"

"Excellent!" he boomed. "I gotta tell you, working without suits or pressure locks–it's hardly work at all! Crew loves it. Hell, they love this place. When ya gonna open it up for colonization?"

"Ten minutes after the war ends, if we win. Toren's going to do its damnedest to take it away as soon as they can find it, remember?"

Kostas looked hurt. "We ain't gonna tell anyone!"

Moire sighed. "Somebody will say something, or send a message that gets intercepted. These guys play for keeps, and they know how to hack too."

"What?"

Oh great, another anachronism. "They can get into comm networks, data nodes, that kind of thing. Eventually your people are going to want to go home, aren't they?"

Kostas gave her the kind of evaluating, sideways glance she'd learned to be suspicious of. His beefy exterior hid a Machiavellian mind. "Maybe. We travel a lot–wherever the work is, ya know? Guess it depends on where home is."

Perhaps she was getting used to the way his devious mind worked, but it only took a moment before the blinding flash of insight hit.

"Say, there's something I wanted to ask you," Moire said, trying for the same level of deviousness. "You know all those people from Waylands we picked up? From Bone?" He nodded. "They need housing, workshops, stuff like that. I know it isn't in the original contract, but I was wondering...maybe we could work something out with your crew? Like, say, a stakehold on the planet?"

Kostas didn't even bother to hide his grin. "Hey, that would be great! Why didn't I think of that?" Then his face fell. "I gotta tell you, though, motivating my people ain't the problem. Hell, they'd work full cycle to get a piece of this, if I'd let 'em. I just don't have enough people here. And I'd need trained folk, not willing hands. We really want to stay, but I won't lie— we can't do the job you gave us and that too. Not unless we got more time than you been sayin'."

Well, it had been worth a shot. "Would they be willing to stay on-planet until the whole question of ownership has been settled? That might give us more time before Toren finds us."

"We get to stay here for good, damn right we will. And you know we'll do the job right if we're protecting our families too. Deal?"

"Deal."

"Hey, you should take a look at what we done so far. That deep site? Slower than we thought. Rock's tough, but that's good. It'll take a pounding—just hard to drill is all. But we did better on the hillside jobs, so the schedule is still on."

Moire nodded, listening, snagging a pistol from the lockbox as they headed out of the cave. More people were gathering, some of her crew and some of the people they had rescued from Bone.

"Damn. How many people do we have here?" It was very crowded. Half of the people there she didn't even know. Bronze hair—why was that familiar?

The man with bronze hair turned, and Moire gasped. The pistol was out and pointed at him before she knew it. His expression of happy surprise changed to one of horror.

"How the hell did he get here?" Moire yelled.

People scattered out of the way. The man—what was his name again? Eng. Peter Eng. He had frozen in place.

"He came with the Bone folk!" That was Harvey, shouting across the cave.

"He's *Toren*," snarled Moire. "Here, on this planet! Who else got in?"

Eng dropped to his knees, hands up. "I'm not. Not any more. The grant ended."

Moire kept the gun steady. "And you stayed on Bone for the balmy climate?"

"I wasn't done with my research," he said, swallowing hard. "I had some money saved. I thought if I...if I could really do a good job on the Bone ecosystem, I could maybe get a job at a university and never have to take a Toren grant again."

Another familiar face appeared in the crowd. Mammachandra, the restaurant and store owner from Waylands. "I can say there is truth to what he is telling. He had an account with my store, and the money that would come by transfer he arranged to go to me. I see the transfer source with this. Yes, it was Toren, but then since four months there is no transfer and before it was every month at least."

"I know he was connected with Toren. What I want to know is, who let him in here? He wasn't with the original group I saw or I would have kicked him out. For all I know he's still their employee and they pay him another way."

She could see sweat on his face now. "I was unconscious, dammit! They found me in the wreckage at Waylands."

"How did you get on my ship, then?"

"There was great confusion," said Mammachandra. "It is not impossible that he was taken by mistake with our wounded into the ship. Still, I am wondering why he said nothing to anyone of this when he woke."

Moire looked back at Eng, who was not meeting her eyes. "I heard some of the crew talking," he admitted finally. "About this place. All my research was blown up along with Waylands. I figured, why not take a look? I didn't really believe it–I would have heard about a biopositive planet like this! But it was real," he said in a wondering tone. "And nobody else knows about it?"

"There's a reason for that," Moire said, gritting her teeth. "Those people who blew up Waylands? And your years of research? *That was Toren. Because they want this planet.* Now do you understand?"

His jaw dropped, and he held his hands out in front of his face as if to block the sight of the gun she held. "Oh shit. Ohshitohshit...."

Great. Now what was she going to do? He might be legit, in which case he was only guilty of very bad luck. If not–she couldn't risk that. At least he hadn't been off-planet, so he couldn't have sent any messages back. Yet.

Moire hesitated, then thumbed the safety and jammed the gun back in the holster. "Here's the deal. I can't trust you. You admit you used to have a connection to the people who are willing to kill everybody on this planet to get it for themselves. But," she held up a hand to stop his protest, "I don't have to trust you. Just so happens we could use a xenobiologist. Plus, this planet has a lot of islands, and some really nasty predators in the water. So we'll do what we usually do with troublemakers here. Dump you off with some supplies and a single-channel comm out in the middle of nowhere. And in your case, a datapad and any research equipment people are willing to lend you and that I approve."

"I can stay?" He had gone from despair to delight. "I can be the first researcher here?"

"You aren't going anywhere," Moire said firmly. "If we win, we can discuss your situation further. And you'd better hope we win, because Toren won't want your inconvenient memory getting in the way of their version of events." She gestured to two of her crew. "Stay with him. Tie him up if he gets itchy feet. Somebody find Grimaldi and tell her to haul him somewhere north of here, and to write the coordinates down this time so we can find him again!"

She looked around at the crowd of people filling the cave, and sighed. "Where the hell am I going to find room for everybody?"

"Space ain't the problem, it's the fittings," Kostas said. "We can dig ya caves aplenty—excavator works great here, no overheating like in an asteroid."

"Could we use ship fittings?"

Moire spun, jumpy, but it was just Carlos Montero, the perpetually foggy repair chief. He blinked genially at her.

"Kostas?"

He looked puzzled. "Sure. But you'd still have to get 'em and install 'em, and that's what takes the time."

"But they are already installed," Montero said, surprised. "In the ships."

"I think he's talking about the salvage ships," Moire said slowly. "But Carlos, we'd have to have people go out there, take the fittings, and then ship them back and install them here."

"Not if they are still in the ship," he insisted. "Take the whole ship, and just put it here. It wouldn't have to be a good one we could sell, either."

Moire stared at him in awe. Sometime it seemed like Montero saved up extra brain cycles being dense so he could come up with brilliant ideas like this one.

"I don't get it," Kostas said bluntly.

"You dig a hole. We drop in an old wreck that has the rooms, corridors, hell, maybe even a reactor for power, and you cover it up again. All it needs is a tunnel in and we have instant hidden quarters. The hull doesn't have to be intact for that, or the drive. We have *lots* of ships like that."

"You do?"

Moire smiled. "Someday, if you are very good, I'll take you to see the sargasso."

Ennis looked around, carefully. One more time. The realization washed over him in an icy wave. He was lost.

The interior of the crab ship must have some kind of reference marking, but it appeared to be something only crabs could see and the murky atmosphere didn't help. To his eye the dark, rough-grained surfaces looked uniformly identical when he turned his handlight on them. The tunnel entrances looked the same too, and to make matters worse the crabs used a three-dimensional hub-and-spoke arrangement for the tunnels and intersections. The tunnels met in a kind of hollow sphere, and since the crabs were masters of environmental gravity, they radiated out in all directions. The gravity changed to match.

He'd been careful. He hadn't gone through any interior doors for precisely this reason. He'd even brought a paint-pen to mark his way. It wasn't until he'd gotten further into the ship that he'd realized the marks were somehow being absorbed by the walls. That far in, he had thought just a little more exploration wouldn't make things any worse.

Ennis snorted, starting to get angry with himself, and checked his suit readouts to try and calm down. Air was good for several hours; the filters not quite as happy. The suit was a working rather than survival suit, so it didn't have much in the way of water. He had to find his way back—not only for his own health, but because nobody in Fleet knew how to work the main airlock door. Nobody else would be rescuing him.

Even if the Fleet ship did show up, weeks before he had any right to expect it, he probably wouldn't notice it this deep in the crab ship.

Ennis carefully sat down to think. This particular nexus had seven tunnel entrances, two with doors. He hadn't gone through any doors, so that left them out. Or had he? What if the door had been open and then shut itself after he had gone through?

What he needed to do was somehow open the doors and look through without losing his position. He had left a tunnel entrance, gone past another on his left, and then looked in the one he was standing beside now when he realized he was lost. The door controls were simple, if you could reach them. He'd added a rope to his toolbelt for that very reason. But these controls were halfway across the nexus.

Throwing the rope with a loop on the end didn't work. The heaviest thing he had was the handlight, and he was reluctant to use it, afraid it would come loose and get lost, but there was nothing else. He attached it to one end and tossed the rope.

It went at a slight angle, then turned sharply at the edge of another gravitational field and hit the side wall. Ennis sighed, hauled the rope back, and tried again. Throwing straight up, the handlight didn't quite make it—but it didn't fall back. It hung there, floating in balance, the weight of the light and the weight of the remaining rope, each being pulled in the opposite direction.

Ennis considered it for a moment, distracted by the strangeness of it, and tugged on the rope. It felt reasonably sturdy, and he realized he might have something he could actually use. Holding on to the rope, he jumped with all his strength, using the rope to pull himself to the null point. The bare end of the rope swayed a little, but still marked his original position. With some awkward twisting and stretching he could then open the door controls by kicking them with his foot.

One of the sealed doors had a short, branching tunnel behind it. The other door's tunnel was long and straight, unusual in this ship. The tunnel he had come in from—had it been straight? He thought so. Ennis twisted around, looking at all the openings in turn. None of them had a straight tunnel.

He dropped back down and cut off a small piece of rope to leave at the entrance to the tunnel, just in case he had made a mistake and needed to backtrack. Ennis hoped the crab ship didn't have some kind of auto-clean function. He waited a few minutes, watching, but the piece of rope stayed put.

As he continued down the tunnel he recognized more landmarks. Every time he had to choose a path, he left another little piece of rope to mark his way. This proved useful when he took a wrong turn a few times. Eventually he arrived back at the big main cavern-entrance, with the airlock door that Radersent had modified for human use. His filters had ticked over into the dangerous side, so he didn't waste any time tugging on the steel lever and lifting the latch cemented into place with the strange goop the crabs used like a universal glue.

The surface of the big door shuddered and thinned, holes appearing in it as it compacted into a web which collapsed against the frame. Ennis shook his head as he went through. He could see it a hundred times and still be amazed at the technology. Melting airlock doors! He closed the door again and jogged around the corner to the outside airlock door and quickly opened it.

And there, sitting like a big ugly brick, was his shelter. It had never looked so beautiful. The air in his suit was getting rather muggy and stale, and he sprinted for the airlock door. Everything was just as he left it, and he pulled off his helmet inside with a shaky sigh of relief. He'd been damn stupid and it had nearly got him killed.

Despite his tiredness he forced himself to go through the suit maintenance and recharging procedures, then allowed himself to rack out. Sleep was fitful and uneven, filled with snatches of dream he could only vaguely recall when he woke. He did remember the one with Moire, chasing her as she ran down the same crab-tunnels, leaving a trail of frozen blood-drops that he had to collect to save her life, but he also needed to leave them so he could find the way back. It was not the one he would have chosen to remember, and he knew all too well what it symbolized.

He woke in a bad mood and unrefreshed. After his near-disaster he was not inclined to go exploring the crab ship again, so he decided to investigate the contents of his shelter. Moire and her crew had provided many boxes and containers, not all of which were food. There was a data drum, he knew, that was a copy of all the vid they had of Radersent communicating with them, and he went searching for it. He found *three* data drums.

10

One bore scorch marks on the surface of the canister, and the contents were encrypted. He gave up and tried the next. It was the vids of Radersent. The third was something completely different. It held clips from what appeared to be an ordinary hand-vid unit, and they were scenes of carnage. He watched them all, startled when he recognized some of Moire's crew. Then there were scenes of large tanks of murky fluid, some shattered. The vid panned, showing one of the broken tanks with a human arm dangling over the sharp edge, but there was very little blood. The viewpoint shifted closer, and he saw a strangely unfinished-looking body, lying in a pool of fluid, an umbilical cord that his hand could have barely gripped completely still attached. Then he knew. The rescue of the Created.

Moire had hinted at it, but had never gone into any detail. He could understand why, now. And when he found the still-shot of Alan, rifle in his hand, staring off into the distance surrounded by dead bodies in brightly colored uniforms, he discovered his hands were shaking with anger.

What had Alan been thinking then? To go back to the place he had been...grown. Where Toren had done such horrible things to him. Teaching him, a child, to kill. Ennis breathed deeply, forcing himself to relax. That hadn't been a smart move for Toren in the end, had it? Alan had used that skill against his teachers. The other Created would to, if they got the chance. He'd seen it himself.

He wasn't sure why Moire had included the vids in his stash, but he did catch one hint about the encrypted drum at the end. There were clips of the crew ransacking the Toren site, and one thing they took was a data drum with similar scorch marks on the casing. Perhaps she was hoping Umbra could decode the files.

In a plastifiber box were happier items from the crew. A picture-cube with stills of the Created children he'd trained on *Raven*, and some scenes of Sequoyah. Madele had included a container of spice cookies and other treats, and he took a cookie to nibble on as he continued looking through the box. He pulled out what looked like some kind of sensor component and considered it in growing puzzlement. What was it? Why was it there? Who would think he would have any use for it?

Enlightenment dawned. "Carlos Montero, the walking out-of-body experience," he exclaimed. No doubt it had made perfect sense to Montero. He'd have to ask him when he saw him again.

When was he going to see them again? More importantly, when was he going to see Moire?

The sudden flash of intense desire made him clench his jaw. He had been so careful not to include any vid of her, any message, anything that could be found and raise questions, no matter how desperately he wanted it. He had to help her, and the only way to do that was to seem uninvolved. The only things he had to remember her by–the NASA pin, Harrington's sketch–Umbra already knew about. They would think they were only items related to his search.

He had to be very careful.

The days passed, and still the scanner remained dark. Ennis dutifully made a manifest of all the gear in the shelter, ate all the remaining cookies, and wrote several very carefully crafted reports concerning Toren, its apparent infiltration of a Fleet base, their unprovoked attack on the defenseless Bone settlement of Waylands just to get Moire, and speculation concerning Radersent, his ship, and why the crabs had apparently deliberately gone to the sargasso instead of getting wrecked there.

Boredom returned. He could not resist returning to the crab ship, but he restricted himself to the big main entry cavern. Simply making a map of it occupied him for several days.

After one such visit, he returned to see a detector pinlight on the scanner lit, indicating something had triggered it. He spent hours searching, but found nothing. He was well away from any systems with possible asteroid debris, but maybe something from *Frankenstein*'s departure had drifted into scanner range.

Then, a few days later, the scanner alarm woke him from a deep sleep. He had just enough time to register one large ship and three much smaller ones before his comm lit up. No voice, no vid, just a datastream. A confirmation code, one of Umbra's. Ennis quickly sent the response code, and waited. The four ships remained where they were, just inside scanner range.

Ennis raised an eyebrow. Somebody was being extremely cautious–this could take a while. He got up and rummaged around for some food. Madele's treats were long gone and he was having to make do with emergency rations, which lasted forever and were found in great quantities by the salvage crews. They were not designed to be tasty.

Eventually, after multiple challenge/response signals, he got a vid signal. The ships fanned out around the crab ship, a scout detached from one of them, and he was instructed to stand outside the shelter with his hands visible and motionless. He complied, and watched with amusement as the ship's marines in armored suits and vacuum rifles quickly and skillfully landed, spread out in the approved mode, and then came to a crashing halt at the door.

"Open it," snapped the marine commander. She hadn't given a name and Ennis hadn't asked for one. The social niceties would have to wait until they were convinced he wasn't a crab agent. "We must search the ship."

He hoped his stifled snort hadn't made it through the comms. "Only the main airlock has been modified for human use," Ennis said, in the calmest voice he could summon. "And for a full search of the ship I recommend–strongly–that you use localized transponders and a command transmitter."

The first door melted away, and he smiled when he saw the startled reactions the marines couldn't entirely suppress. They were hyper-alert and he couldn't blame them. Besides himself and the *Raven* crew, no human had ever been in a crab ship before. And they had only his word the ship was empty.

As soon as the boarding party was inside, he cycled the airlock. The huge cave area, with its corners hidden in murk, really set the marines on edge.

"Is this normal?" the marine commander asked, suspicious.

"I've never seen it any different. Crabs seem to prefer a lower level of light than humans—I know the survivor shows discomfort around bright lights."

That earned him a meaningful stare. "Where is this survivor? Are there others?"

"Nowhere near here, and no."

"Are you trying to tell me you found this large and apparently undamaged ship with only *one* crab in it? Were there bodies?"

Ennis shook his head. "There's a place where wrecked ships...accumulate. Salvagers found the crab, a human survivor off another wreck, and this ship. The human and the crab were together, and had been for some time. You tell me why a crab would want to be in close quarters with a human if there were any of his own kind around. The crab wasn't even living on this ship. He took us to it when we asked, and I didn't see a single body anywhere."

"That sounds rather incredible, don't you think?" she asked dryly.

"Believe me, sergeant, it wouldn't take much effort to come up with a more believable story. Which is one way to tell it is true."

She didn't look convinced, and motioned the marines forward. He could see her mouth move, meaning she was on a separate secure line. The marines split up in groups sufficient to tackle the tunnel entrances on the 'ground' level. They must not have had time to read his message or look at the map he sent.

Knowing he was going to get yelled at regardless of what he did, Ennis sighed and waved his arms at the sergeant. This made the marine with her aim his weapon at him, but it did end up getting her attention.

"What is it now?" she snapped.

Ennis kept his hands up, just in case his news created a bad reaction. "You are aware you have not secured your retreat?" he said, and pointed to some of the upper tunnel entrances.

She glanced up, frowning. "Nobody could get out of that—or are you thinking of snipers?"

"Those entrances are as easy to get to as the ones your men are heading for, and if you promise not to shoot me I'll show you."

Her eyes narrowed for a moment, then she nodded. Ennis walked across the entry cavern floor to what appeared to be the wall, placed a foot on it, and continued to walk up to one of the entrances the sergeant had dismissed as being inaccessible. He turned, and was quite gratified by the expression of shock on her face. He wondered if his face had looked similar when Moire had pulled the same trick on him. The sergeant's training took over quickly, followed by what appeared to be a countermanding order to the marines to return. She stood with her rifle hanging from its harness, hands on her hips, glaring at the multiplicity of openings she would now have to seal or guard to conduct her search.

"It's a very confusing ship, Sergeant," he said sympathetically.

♔

The marines ended up using a box of colored game tokens that Ennis found in his stash of supplies to mark their way. The sergeant, Anita Jain, reinforced by teams from the other ships, bulled her way through the entire crab ship but it still took over a week. No crabs, living or dead, were found.

Ennis wasn't present for any of it. His time was completely occupied in debriefings, first with the command of the *Tongaku* who made it quite clear he was to refrain from chatting any further about his crab-related knowledge with anyone with less than three stripes on their sleeves, and then with the chief engineer, who was both delighted and appalled at the challenge before him.

"So, how the hell did they get it here? It's huge! You'd need a specialized hull-tug if it was one of ours," said Engineer Gervois. He had a face that was usually immobile and hard to read, and the dark skin didn't help. But when he was presented with an interesting problem his stern expression relaxed.

Ennis reached for a text sheet, switched it to line mode, and started to sketch. He didn't have Harrington's skill, but he was good enough to give Gervois the general idea.

"They found a wrecked ore hauler that still had working gravitics and basically ripped one end off," he said, continuing to draw. "Left the structural beams and the gravitic nodes along the keel as much as possible– there was some problem leaving the site that made this necessary, I wasn't quite clear on why." Actually he did know, but the Chief Engineer wasn't cleared for that. He hadn't even mentioned it to the captain of *Tongaku*. He'd brief Pol Namur whenever he saw him, and the head of Umbra could decide how to handle the information that according to the crab Radersent there was a second, possibly hostile, alien race out there.

Gervois sighed. "Why can't we use that ship?"

"They use it for their business," Ennis said, keeping a straight face. "They were very generous as it was, towing the ship here and setting me up." He was not going to mention how the captain of *Raven* was actively avoiding Fleet, and for good reason.

"We couldn't do an internal field scan, obviously," Gervois said dryly, "but I think we have a fairly good external map of their gravitics. If it was one of our ships I'd say the scanner was malfunctioning, but..." he rubbed his chin. "They clearly have a better mastery of gravitics than we do. I could never get that kind of fine variation in the field, even with research-grade nodes." He tapped at the desk screen and brought up a scan image of the crab ship. The gravitic field looked like a sea of stubby fingers sticking out from the hull, all over the surface. "I wish I could see it go into drive," he said, looking wistful.

Ennis never found out how the chief engineer planned to tow the ship, but he did know other equipment was required since he was put on the escort ship sent to bring it back. The trip was even more boring than waiting for Fleet on the crab ship since he wasn't allowed to talk to anyone on board and he didn't have access to his gear.

When they reached the location of FarCom he was somewhat surprised that the escort ship docked directly at the ship depot instead of dropping him off at FarCom itself first. He had to hitch a ride with some ship-fitters going off-shift, and even then it just got him to the general dock instead of the official visitor's entrance.

Still, there was an aide he remembered from his first visit waiting for him. It appeared that according to the ID scan, he'd never left. At least, he wasn't asked for a pass. Apparently, Umbra had its own way of doing things.

Pol Namur's office looked exactly the same as the last time he'd seen it–dimly lit by hundreds of little golden glowballs, scattered everywhere. Namur himself seemed a little thinner, his eyes more hooded, but his greeting was cordial and relaxed.

"You had us quite worried for a while there," Namur observed, his eyes lighting up when Ennis handed him the datatab folder.

"I was quite worried myself," Ennis replied, suppressing a shudder. "I keep thinking I know how ruthless Toren can be, and then they go even further. Did...our mutual acquaintance get everything to you?"

Namur's eyes narrowed, but the corners of his mouth turned up very slightly. "Yesss...you must tell me sometime about how all that came about. He was still quite agitated when we made contact. If you mean your kidnapping from Lambert Station, we did what we could to clean things up without alerting Toren too much."

"Did they find Colonel Garner?"

Namur nodded. "Yes–but I regret to say she died a few days later. Not from any injuries," he hastened to add. "I believe she felt she bore full responsibility for what happened to you, because of her...habits. This may have led her to take drastic steps to atone. The autopsy found no trace of any drug in her system, so she had not taken any for some time. The sudden, unaccustomed shock was too much for her body to bear, especially when she had exhausted herself trying to find you."

Ennis was silent a moment, wishing Garner had been able to pull herself up earlier without dying in the process. "She had the instincts of a good officer," was all he could truthfully say.

"Indeed." Namur bowed his head, clasping his hands together. The bioplastic webbing was just visible at the edge of his cuff on one arm. "We served together once, a long time ago. Some casualties are more mental than physical," he said cryptically. "Speaking of which, the medtechs will want to have a look at you, just in case those drugs Toren used on you were their own special varieties."

That was an adrenaline-spiking possibility that hadn't occurred to him. "Sir, there is some encrypted data that was sent with me. From a Toren facility that Cameron and her people...took care of." There, he'd said her name. Just a name, and with enough of a distraction attached to it Namur would not give it undue attention. "There is also some vid of them doing it."

"Doing what precisely, Commander Ennis?" Namur's expression of polite inquiry told Ennis he'd taken the bait. "Did this involve any violence?"

"From what I saw, quite a bit of violence. The facility was where they were gestating full-size humans. It was a huge production."

Namur's gaze became distant. "Ah. The super-workers."

"You *know* about them?" Ennis said, shocked.

Namur waved a dismissive hand. "Not as such. There was a mention of them...elsewhere. Now I understand what they were referring to. Is it possible Moire Cameron dealt with this place in a permanent fashion?"

"I believe so." It had certainly looked like a station-sized explosion on the final vid clip. "They rescued a number of the—they call them the Created. I don't think the program was designed just to make workers. One of them was clearly trained as a soldier. You'll see him in the vid clips. It appears," he said, being careful to breathe evenly, to show no emotion, "that they used some of Cameron's stored tissue to make him."

"Aaahhhh." Namur rested his chin on his hands, the planes of his face accentuated in the light of his desk screen. He looked, for a moment, dangerous and deadly. It was easy to forget he had been a fighter, with all his careful elegant mannerisms. But it was just hidden, not gone. "Thank you. Another piece of the puzzle." He smiled, and the deadly look vanished. "I am impressed with you, Commander. Even though you never bring back what you were sent to get, you manage to find everything else."

"If Umbra wants to send me to find Cameron again, I'll go," Ennis said, and hoped he sounded suitably calm about it. "She's expecting me to come and collect the crab anyway. In fact, she had a message for you. Something about if you didn't send me back she'd break in to FarCom herself."

For a horrifying second he thought he had overplayed his hand. Pol Namur sat back, a genuine grin spreading over his taut face. "You know, if there wasn't a war–technically, *two* wars–going on, I would be tempted to see how she would do it," he said, after a moment. "But such are the sacrifices we are obliged to make for expediency. She need not worry; we are most interested in her unusual guest. So much so that we are willing to overlook her curious reluctance to enjoy our hospitality. Now, what can you tell me about this crab?"

CHAPTER 2
WAR TAKES AN INTEREST

Tethys was not one of Harrington's favorite planets. Just barely part of the Inner Systems, it tried to make up for this by excessive bureaucracy, as if to prove it wasn't one of those lawless Fringe stations. And of course, you couldn't drink the water that covered the entire surface, or breathe the air. All the tower structures were anchored to the shallows. The joke in the real Inner Systems worlds was the towers could all be moved to one location whenever the locals wanted to impress a visitor.

For whatever reason, there was an ID check whenever you entered a tower. Harrington adopted a bland expression which he changed to innocent astonishment and curiosity if forced to encounter anyone official, starting when he arrived at the shuttle terminal on the planet's surface. Since he was headed for Government Tower, this happened rather frequently. Why his contact was located in the Atmospherics Department was not clear to him, but that was where his instructions told him to go and request clarification of a certain notice allegedly sent to him. It was all very hush-hush.

He'd never intended to get involved with espionage. It had started innocuously enough, just investigating a story—the sort of thing that could happen to anyone, really. One thing had led to another, catalyzed by his abominable curiosity, and what *should* have resulted in a deep-background, off-the-record, smuggled-in-for interview with a military source with information about the crabs resulted in his waking up in a certain dimly-lit office. He was offered tea and a job, a job precisely tailored to aforementioned curiosity and interest in the crabs. It would, said the shadowy, gaunt man behind the desk, benefit them both.

Harrington sighed. He couldn't even complain that he had been misled. Pol Namur was most certainly military and knew far more than he let on about the crabs and the war. It would have been nice to know, ahead of time, that Namur also knew about *him*.

He studied the locator display, tastefully framed in floating blue and green holoribbons, found his destination, and followed a spiral corridor up to a large hall with delicate arching ribs and a faint scale pattern on the walls. He wondered if it had ever occurred to the officials of Tethys that everyone there was already quite aware of the aquatic nature of the planet, and would perhaps prefer a little more diversity in the decorating scheme.

18

Upon entering his fictitious reason for needing to enter the sacred confines of Atmospherics–and undergoing the obligatory ID check–he was shunted off to a small room with large windows showing the featureless expanse of Tethys and the other towers of the cluster. A rather nice storm was shaping up on one horizon, and he watched it grow and drift until his contact joined him.

She was a fresh-faced young woman who looked like she had just stepped off a shuttle from the local university with a degree in Ephemeral Cultural Analysis, but he knew better. After the preliminary security sweep and yet another ID check (this time, he agreed it was necessary), he handed off his little problem to Umbra with a certain feeling of satisfaction. Yes, there was the trifling detail that his cover was somewhat tattered in places, and his contact made her displeasure plain over that. He accepted his lecture and handed over the datatab folder with a twinge of regret. There would be better pictures, and story, forthcoming. At least, he certainly hoped so. If Moire Cameron didn't renege on her promise.

He'd better hope his message would get through, then, hadn't he? Of course they would go back for the crab ship. They had to–it was simply too important. Not that Umbra would let him know. All part of security, presumably, and he'd already demonstrated he wasn't entirely to be relied on in that area. Sometime, presuming they all survived this, he was going to have to ask Ennis how he had figured out his secondary avocation. It was to be hoped no-one else had, such as Toren. Especially Toren.

That had been a complication he could do without entirely and it only made his inclination to meet up with Cameron more urgent. Her ship was probably the safest place he could be, since she was even more intent on avoiding Toren than he was.

Harrington left the tower and headed immediately for the shuttle terminal. If Tethys had any tempting tourist delights they were well hidden, and if he experienced any more ID checks he might do something rash. Time to go to Kulvar.

♕

Eyan Zandovar did not have a comfortable office. This was by careful design, the result of years of study and expertise. The walls, floor, and ceiling were plain station-metal, not even painted. The lighting was provided by self-contained units, not networked fixtures. The chair he used appeared to be a common, cheap plastic one, but was actually fitted to him and made of special insulating material. The only visible luxury was the slab of slate he used as a desk, imported from Earth at his specific request.

Sometimes he thought the desk was too much, that a plate of clear plastic would have been more in keeping with the overall plan; other times he told himself the slate served equally well. He needed something that was not artificial there.

He had another office to impress his people and any outsiders that might be granted a visit. That one was much more ostentatious, intended to display his power and wealth. This office, however, was where he worked. The entire structure was a scanner in a sense—it could detect anything, would automatically go to defense mode if anyone except himself were to enter without his permission. That was why his chair had to be specially designed to resist high voltage. There were other defenses and security measures, some that he had installed himself, alone. Working for the previous ceeyo as a surveillance operative had taught him a great deal about how to circumvent security, and what he would need to defend himself against a similar operative.

A tone sounded, and he glanced down at his slim personal datapad, open on the desk. He tapped at a certain symbol, and the screen showed three different vid views of the fancy office. It was empty except for his assistant. Zandovar adjusted his vest so it did not obstruct his weapon and tapped the symbol on his main screen, entering a time. He felt the slight change in pressure when the inner door opened, and shortly after that Ghost himself appeared.

"What is it?" asked Zandovar, after a moment of silence. If it had been an emergency Ghost would have spoken.

"The watch for Cameron. There may be something. You should have others investigate." When Zandovar raised an eyebrow, Ghost continued in his staccato style, "I will be in the medical tank next cycle."

It was an inconvenience, but the benefits Ghost provided outweighed it. He was not a natural albino, despite his alabaster skin and white hair. He had undergone forced genetic engineering under a prior ceeyo and would have died of it if Zandovar hadn't found and saved him. Ghost's memories before the incident were vague at best—he didn't even remember his own name, and Zandovar had never cared enough to find out. Now, however, Ghost possessed an almost eiditic memory. Especially for faces, and he was rarely fooled by disguise—even bodymods. However, he needed regular medical therapy just to stay alive.

Zandovar glanced at his personal datapad. Ghost had uploaded some surveillance vid clips and a text file.

"He's not one of her crew? Then why did you have him shadowed?"

"He came here. Met her. At Double Key. Guard remembered him. Had no weapon."

Zandovar raised an eyebrow at that. As a general rule, anyone using the Double Key's secure and secretive meeting services had at *least* one weapon, and usually three. Strange, but not enough to concern him.

"What else?"

"Went on board *Raven* after meeting. Ship undocked when he left."

Yes, that was important. "And has he been here between now and then?" Ghost shook his head. "Very well. I will make arrangements."

Ghost left as silently as he had entered, and Zandovar stared at his screen thinking furiously. If this Harrington was here, Cameron might show up herself. Moire Cameron had troubled him from the first time she had been brought to his notice. Everything about her was just slightly off. She was clearly a very successful pirate, but none of the others he had asked had ever heard of her. Then there was the murderous ex-Fleet officer, less useful to a pirate than someone like himself—why had she taken Ennis in? The ships Cameron brought in were never new, but all showed the signs of recent, and expert, repair. Ghost had managed to track down one of them—it had last been seen fifteen years ago. If she had been grabbing and storing ships for that long surely someone would know about her, wouldn't they?

Unless she was the kind of person who made long-range, careful plans. Like himself. He had been planning to be ceeyo of Kulvar for many years. He had studied the mistakes of the previous ceeyos, and what had made them finally fail. In every case, they had gotten comfortable. Careless. They didn't care what enemies they made, what resentments were building, only motivated by their own desires and pleasures.

Zandovar was very careful to avoid being trapped by comfort. That was the other purpose to the spartan working office. He was also careful to watch for anyone who might, some day, challenge him as he had challenged Olvey. Cameron might not be thinking of it now, but that could change. He preferred to co-opt dangerous talent, to control it, but if he could not he would feel justified in destroying her.

He intended to remain ceeyo for a very long time.

It was their very first non-cave structure on Sequoyah, and Kostas was as proud as a new father. Compared to what they had been putting up with it was indeed luxurious, and Moire felt that complaining about still-visible cabling and missing door switches would be nitpicking. Besides, the crew that had served on *Ayesha* would feel right at home.

The only problem was they were having a meeting in it. And it wasn't going well.

"But we have plenty to do here," she protested for the eighth time. "We'll need at least four ships minimum to get everyone settled, and *Frankenstein* is the only ship that can grab the big wrecks."

"We gotta go back to Kulvar," Yolanda said, equally stubborn. "We can't get everything we need in the sargasso. Weren't you sayin' we don't have much time before things get hot? I see pads for guns but no guns, yeh?"

"Mr. Harrington will also be expecting us at some point," Kilberton added, apologetically.

Moire slouched until her back rested on the wall, tilting the crate she sat on. "So *you* go get him. And do the shopping. I'll go to the sargasso."

Yolanda Menehune made a sound that was a combination of a sigh and a strangled scream. Kostas sat, unusually silent and looking awkward. They had added him, at her suggestion, to represent the construction workers. Mammachandra had been voted to stand for the Bone contingent, and they were both learning more than they really wanted to about the difficulties in store for the would-be Sequoyah colonists.

Kilberton glanced at her, then at Yolanda who was seated next to him. "Explain," he said quietly. "She doesn't know that world."

"Null dump," Yolanda muttered, and took a deep breath. "You don't wanna go back because of what happened—the kids getting shot an' all, right? Think you stay on the low, Zandovar forget about you? Too late. Was too late first time you saw him, but if you hadn't gone see him you'd be dead. No load no deal, *hancha*. What you and that Fleet guy and the kids tell me, he's got a scope for just your code set up now. He set down at table with you—you know how many heavy movers like to trade places? Don't show up, send someone else in your place, he's gonna take it cold. Ceeyo show an interest like that he expect some return."

Moire rocked forward, the crate slamming to the floor. "Do you know what *return* he's expecting from me? Hey, I don't know much about Kulvar but I can pick up a hint that's as big as a battleship. He wants me to bring him *people*. So he can sell them. He's going to have to get used to disappointment there. We can pretend to be pirates and get away with it, but real slavery is a line I am not willing to cross."

Nobody said anything for a while. Then Kilberton stirred. "The Captain and Yolanda are both correct. We cannot give him what he wants, and he will become angry if we either avoid him or do not comply. Is there anything else that we *could* give him, that would buy us time? This unfortunate but necessary connection will not last forever in any case. When we win our war we will not be constrained to doing business on Kulvar."

Good ole clear-headed Kilberton. Did he ever lose his temper? And bless him for assuming they were going to win.

"If we had some web pilots and ships that have no connection to me or the rest of the crew we wouldn't be forced to stick with Kulvar now," Moire said. "Yolanda, any ideas about what Zandovar would like for a rain check?" Scanning the sea of puzzled faces, she sighed and translated to something less antique, "for a temporary substitute?"

Yolanda was scowling again, but it was a thoughtful scowl this time. "Yeah, mebbe. I got one idea—know you won't like it straight up, but could make it work with some cheats. Remember the morgatane we found? Now don' start yelling!" she said, waving her hands. "You gonna say its used for slaving, just as bad, and the whole bit about getting the combines on our heads too. Heard that. What we do, see, is tell Zandovar we found it on this ship we caught. We tell *him* we don't know nothin' about it, don't want the trouble selling it and so on, but think he can make use of it. Only one thing missing, gotta find a way to make it bad that a scan won't find. I mean, it has to show up as morgatane but not work for real, right?" She shrugged. "I dunno, maybe that's a dumb idea. I'll think some more."

"I think it would work very well," Kilberton said, surprising Moire and Yolanda, knowing his pathological hatred of morgatane. "I know there are ways of tampering with the drug that make it non-lethal, but I do not know the process myself."

"All right. You two can work on that. Kilberton, I assume you have an idea where to start asking around for what we need to do to it?"

He nodded. "Madele may know."

Moire scrubbed her face. "How long do we have before Zandovar gets mad at us?"

"Time we got," Yolanda said. "Goin' back no load for him, that's the rig."

She assumed that meant they simply shouldn't return to Kulvar empty-handed. If Ennis were here, he could translate for her. If Ennis were here, she wouldn't feel so depressed.

"OK, we'll have to go back to the sargasso anyway to get the morgatane. We'll leave *Raven* here and dual on *Frankenstein*, that'll get you some log time on that beast so you can solo later," Moire said to Kilberton. "We'll grab a quarters-shipwreck and scoot home. Hopefully by then we'll know if the morgatane plan will work and we can decide our next step from there." She scanned the room. "Suggestions? Objections?"

Nobody had any, but she didn't know if that was the true state of affairs or if they were all shell-shocked. Moire made a mental note to go around to everyone later to make sure. Damned if she was going to do all the thinking around here.

Everybody filed out, subdued and quiet, and headed up the still-dusty shaft bored into the rock of the big cave of D'Accord. She'd wondered about leaving the entrance to the underground areas in the cave, worried about rockfall blocking it if the cave were attacked, but both Gip Farouz and Kostas had said the cave would be as safe as the shaft itself, and the cave would hide the inevitable thermal signal of the shaft..

Plus, there was the emergency exit still being dug. Moire noted that even while they had been down in the big main room Kostas' people had put in the big metal framing for the blast doors. The main command center was looking better, but she needed to make sure the other locations got dug in as well.

She decided to join Mammachandra on her return trip to the large island the Bone people had taken over. Everyone had readily agreed to her suggestion that they not give their enemies a single target, so the growing population of Sequoyah was spread out a bit. Plus, the entrepreneurial types wanted more useful space than was available on the beautiful but inaccessible D'Accord.

"For now it is not so bad," Mammachandra commented as they watched Lorai's shuttle coming in, "but soon it will be more people needing the shuttle and still only one to take. We have the scooters, yes? But I am told you have said they must not be used."

"Not over deep water. Over land or the shallows of a cluster they are fine," Moire said. "It's hard to get altitude on those things, and not really safe. And if you fly too close to the surface of the deep water those giant water-bat things will try and get you. They can jump several meters, and their wingspan is bigger than the shuttle. A scooter wouldn't have a chance."

The shuttle was down now, and a familiar dark, ragged head was leaning out the shuttle door. Alan's face lit up when he saw them.

"Are you done with talking?"

Moire smiled. "For the moment. Are you helping Lorai?"

"We were helping Jens at the new place but she said you were here so I wanted to come too."

"I'm going back over there now, but I shouldn't be too long."

Alan just shrugged and went back into the shuttle. He always preferred to be with her if possible. Lorai waved from the open cockpit partition as they came in.

"Hey, there ya are! Haven't seen you for a while."

"People think I'm in charge or something. I keep trying to instigate a coup but no takers."

Lorai grinned. "Nobody here that stupid, 'cept the prisoners, maybe." The hatch door closed and Lorai executed one of her trademark scram launches. "Sure is nice not having to check for frozen gunk every time I take off," she yelled over the engine. "I could get used to this—only thing left to wish for is another pilot!"

Moire glanced at Mammachandra, who shrugged. Another thing to put on the list. They needed more of everything. Everyone was doing three different jobs, and the kids ran errands and messages until they dropped. On the plus side, that kept them mostly out of trouble, but it was a hell of a way to run a war.

"Say, when you gonna get me those guns for my shuttles?" Lorai yelled again, as if she had read her mind.

She *had* promised her guns. "Soon as we can get to Kulvar safely. Or we get insanely lucky at the sargasso."

"What's the crimp in the pipe? Thought they don't ask questions there."

"Boss-man thinks I should be helping him with his slavery business."

Lorai slewed around in her seat, making the shuttle rock. "You ain't gonna, are you?"

"Hell no! But Menehune thinks I shouldn't go back unless I have something nice to give him as a consolation prize."

Lorai frowned in deep thought. "Yeah, she's probably right. Damn. Guess we'd better not plan on going there much longer though." She banked sharply, then tilted the nose up. Moire heard the engines change their frequency as they lowered the shuttle to the ground.

The hatch popped open and Alan bounded out, followed by Mammachandra and Moire. Lorai emerged from the cockpit scratching her head.

"OK, so maybe I missed some of the here-we-are vids, but why can't we go somewhere other than Kulvar?"

"*You* can, but I can't, or any of my crew. Too many people with long memories wanting to have a chemically aided conversation with me."

Her eyes widened. "Right, that's why you guys sent me to find that Harrington fellow."

"You could perhaps send her again," suggested Mammachandra. "Or one of us would be better, so we still may have shuttles." She smiled.

"We still have to *get* someone there first. Same problem," Moire said, admiring the jury-rigged hangar. It looked like Lorai had persuaded the construction crew to dump two long piles of boulders on the broad rock plateau, and then she had fastened a large tarp over the top. Inelegant, but functional. "We need a safe place to go."

Still looking thoughtful, Lorai hooked up a large power cable to the shuttle. "So, what you need is a web ship nobody knows you know about, like–naah, you'd still have to go somewhere to meet 'em. Never mind."

Moire stopped. "Why, do you know someone?"

She shrugged. "The guy who got me to Criminy, remember? Web pilot, got his own ship, not doin' so hot in the salvage business with the crabs and all. Bet you could hire him, easy, but you'd have to find a way to meet up. Dunno if I'd trust him with this," she said, waving her arm at the rest of the island, "and from what Kilberton told me about the route here I dunno if he could get here on his own anyway."

That was an idea she hadn't considered. An outside contact with his own ship. They wouldn't need a station; they could just rendezvous at a prearranged location. Just like they did with the crab ship and Ennis.

She could send him to get Ennis, too.

"I think we can use this guy. Know how to find him?"

"Send a spew to the station constabularies. He gets in fights a lot, I hear," Lorai said, grunting as she forced the power connector in. "I got some other ideas."

Yes, it could work. They'd still need to get to Kulvar to send any messages, though, and before that, they needed to get the Bone folk some kind of shelter other than the bolted-together cargo containers they were using.

Moire followed Mammachandra up a sandy slope peppered with tanglegrass, and surveyed the view from the top. Most of the container-houses were tucked in amongst the boulders. The hillside went down from the rocky plateau where the shuttle hangar was, large green-grey bushes increasing in size as they got closer to what looked like a freshwater lake. She hadn't seen any of the flying mop creatures here–maybe that was just on D'Accord, which had bigger trees and more underbrush.

"How many people here?"

"In this place? I am thinking not quite one hundred. Others are still at the cave until space is made."

"Can you get me a final count of how many *want* to live here by tonight? I need to know what size shipwreck to get you guys."

"They are also asking for places to work in," Mammachandra reminded her.

"Yeah, and I'll want that wish list too, but first priority is shelter. They can use the containers for work space when they aren't living in them, right? We can probably bring some power taps up from the main core, instead of using Lorai's generator."

Mammachandra nodded. They had reached one of the containers nearest the lake. Jens, her husband, was propped up on some bales of sound baffle. Ash, George, and Hideo were involved in some kind of project at the water's edge, frequently running to Jens to show him things, ask him questions, or for no reason at all.

"I've come to rescue you," Moire said, grinning.

Jens grinned back. He was paler than he should be, and the burn marks were still visible on his face, but his beard was beginning to grow back and his strength was improving. "You mistake. I have been many times told they are assisting me."

"Ah! Well then, carry on."

His eyes widened in mock alarm. "*Bitte, nicht.* I should then keep it for myself when you are needing? Besides, I begin to sleep and then no-one watches them."

Moire gave him a critical look. "Has Madele Fortin been out to take a look at you? If there's any medical supplies you need make sure they get on the list."

Jens made a dismissive gesture, then winced. "I go to her, in fact. It is easier for everyone."

"Think you could persuade your daughter to join us?" Moire asked hopefully. Jens and Mammachandra's daughter was studying to be a medtech. The time to get more medical staff would be *before* the shooting started.

"For us it would be a great relief. We worry when she travels so much around the Fringe. I am thinking–"

What Jens thought was suddenly interrupted by shouting from the group of Created.

"They got out again! Jens, they are out!" George sounded agitated.

"Catch them! *Schnell!*" Jens caught her glance, and gave a weak smile. "We were soon planning to tell you."

"Tell me what?" The kids were racing around, chasing something she couldn't see that was apparently on the ground. Hideo pounced and held up a small squirming green ball.

"Got one!" The green blob indicated its displeasure by emitting a sonic shriek. Hideo ran up and dropped it in an open-ended drum. Moire looked in. At the bottom was a noticeably more slender Munchausen and the green furball.

"Is that what I think it is?" Moire asked, filled with foreboding.

Jens nodded. "Our Munchausen is a parent. Only five survived–they were born too early, after it was injured in the attack on Waylands."

The little nerya was making high-pitched whistles now, resigned to its fate. The others appeared to be energized by the capture of their sibling. George and Alan were racing in pursuit, while Ash was hunting through the bushes. She looked up as the boys went by, yelling, "Go to the water! They hate water!"

The chase swerved towards the lake, and before Moire could move the escaped neryas darted away from the water–and towards her. Three green blurs swarmed up her legs and tried to burrow into the pockets of her jacket, until the Created showed up and grabbed at them. Then they raced around her as if she were a stump.

"Er, do they bite?" she asked, trying to remain still. George had captured one, and Ash was coming up with another squirming in her hands.

"The teeth now are only small," Mammachandra said soothingly, hiding a smile behind her hand.

"That's nice," Moire said, making a grab for one diving under her collar. It shrieked and scrabbled up her face to sit on her head. They might not have teeth but they had something like claws. "Ow! Hey, get this thing off me!"

The little nerya shrieked again, dodging her attempts to grab it. When she succeeded, she discovered it had an extremely firm grip on her hair.

She pulled it up as far as she could without losing a chunk of her scalp, and glared at it. Three little eyes in a puff of green fur glared back at her.

"Leggo, dammit!"

The nerya shrilled in a very similar tone.

A muffled sound made her glance down. At first she thought Alan was choking, but then she realized—he was laughing. She was so surprised she let go of the baby nerya, who promptly got an even better grip on her hair.

"It wants to stay on you!" he managed to say after controlling his giggles. The other Created were staring at him in astonishment. The nerya Ash had captured tried to take advantage of her lax grip and escape, and in trying to catch it again first George, then Hideo also succumbed to laughter. Ash just looked bewildered.

"You should keep this one," Jens said, eyes twinkling. "We have too many."

"I'm not letting it stay on my head," Moire snapped. "It can go in the barrel with its friends."

"When it is not frightened it can be moved easily," Mammachandra said. "Do not be shaking your head sharply or speaking so loud."

Moire sighed, trying to think calm, non-nerya thoughts. "We'll be leaving Sequoyah as soon as we know what to look for. We'll get your shelter first—the construction people brought their own and when we're at the sargasso the cave will be plenty of room for anyone remaining."

Mammachandra nodded. "We should anyhow meet so I may tell them of your plan. I will tell you when I know how many are wanting space here."

The little nerya apparently felt safe enough to release its death-grip on her hair, but only for as long as it took to wiggle down between her collar and her neck. Its fur felt rough, but not unpleasant.

"So, it is better now, yes? Already it feels at home with you." Mammachandra beamed. "So clever, neryas. It knows it is safe."

It wasn't that clever then, because she still wanted to grab it and throw it away. The last of the escapees had been captured and returned to the barrel, and why not complete the set?

"Can we really keep it?" Alan asked, awed, and she winced.

"But of course!" Jens said, completely ignoring her frantic handwaving. "It is time for them to find their own homes, and so they try to leave on their own as you see."

Moire carefully reached for the little nerya. OK, they were keeping it but Alan could be the one to take care of it. That was traditional for kids and pets, right?

Her fingers found it. It cheeped but didn't move—until she tried to lift it up. Then the little fingerlets found a grip on her collar and wouldn't come loose.

She sighed, and accepted the inevitable. "Yeah, we're keeping it. Come on, kid, let's go home before he tries to give us the rest of them."

♔

"So you're really going to Kulvar?" The station police officer shook his head and took a big swig of the erzatz beer Harrington had bought him. "I thought you were making that up."

"I have already been to Kulvar, and recently," Harrington said. "That was why I was equally interested in a weapon and in weapons instruction." He took a more cautious sip of raku. Perhaps someday, if he ever was able to publish the story of Cameron and her crab friend, he would be able to afford the scandalously high price of real imported Earth beer. For now, however, it was impossible—especially when he had work-related expenses such as a self-targeting needle gun and a hundred ceramic needles to go in it. The gun wasn't cheap, but the policeman selling it was so happy to get his asking price he threw in two hours of training in the police range for free.

"That's not enough and don't think it even comes close," the policeman warned. "Look, you remember what I told you about station law and self-defense? Soon as you get past the door seal of your ship there forget you ever heard it. For one thing everybody's part of some gang, even the maintenance guys. Perforate one and you're gonna have the rest land on your neck if you don't kill them all, disappear—or belong to a bigger gang. You're going in alone, so you're lower than sewage sediment in that world. What the hell is so important you have to go to Kulvar?"

"I'm meeting someone there. It would be preferable to stay in safer locations, but strangely enough newsworthy stories always seem to happen somewhere else."

The policeman grinned, and ruefully shook his head. "Yeah, so I hear. Wish I could tell you something more useful, but we don't hear much. Got a wave of criminal refugees when the new guy took over—*that* kept us busy for a while, but he hasn't tried to expand his operations here. And I don't want him hearing about me telling you what he doesn't want known, so he won't decide he *should* expand, know what I mean?"

"You'll always be an anonymous station source to me," Harrington said solemnly. "I don't even know your name, and you could have stolen the uniform for all I know."

The policeman chuckled. "And the reason Dola waved us in to use the range is she's on the take and I'm a habitual visitor, in cuffs. Yeah, I like that story. Remember it if the boss-man takes an interest in you." He scratched his chin. "Look, I really don't know anything, but here's some general advice. Stay low. Don't go out unless you have to, but if you do, think up some reason to do business with one of the mid-to-high-end movers there. They won't want someone doing decomp on you if they think they can make money, so the scavengers will stay away." He shrugged, and drained the rest of his beer. "Hey, thanks. And good luck. You want to file a trip plan with us? We do that for some of the long-haulers; I say you count. That way if you don't get back when you expect, we send out notices to the other stations and next-of-kin."

"Thank you," Harrington said, "but even if I am successful I doubt I will be able to tell you when I will return."

"Ah, one of those kind of stories. Hope it's worth it!" He waved and left.

Harrington considered the advice he had been given during the trip back to Kulvar and found it good. He had left Kulvar earlier because he had felt too conspicuous, waiting around with no apparent reason to be there. He'd left a message for Cameron if she showed up in the meantime and hoped she would wait, and then went to Cullen where he did a report on the strange death of a local Toren office manager who had evidently tried to go for a walk outside the station without his suit helmet. It was always nice to keep up the day job, which helped pay his exorbitant bills, and he had met up with the station policeman with a gun he no longer needed.

As soon as he arrived at Kulvar he found a half-room on the third level and started his research. Naturally there wasn't a criminal services directory—yet—but there were ways. What he needed was something big enough to afford him the protection he needed, but that he could afford if it got that far. He strongly suspected they would be unhappy with a customer who wasted their time and couldn't pay. Unhappy in a leaking-bodily-fluids kind of way.

When he heard about the signal decoders he knew he had found what he was looking for. The Kulvar locals used them for all manner of criminal activities, up to and including intercepting, decoding, and overriding device comms. Quite handy if you felt an urgent need to circumvent your criminal rival's security system to add some explosive devices to his decor. Harrington suspected that such a device would prove useful in the field of crab-human communication. From the sounds of things he could afford a small personal system without having to break into the emergency credit line, and it would make a thoughtful gift when Cameron showed up. She was, he hoped, going to a lot of bother to accommodate him, after all.

He self-consciously loaded his needle gun and stowed it as the station policeman had shown him. It would be much, much better if he could avoid the need to use it, but he'd already seen two shootings since his arrival.

Pulling himself out of his half-room, Harrington quickly scanned the corridor and headed out. The locals gave him the occasional curious glance, and he cursed mentally. What was giving him away? It wasn't what he was wearing—half the station dressed the same way. It must simply be that he was a stranger. *I really should have insisted on the beginner spy kit when I was recruited.*

He threaded his way through the crowded main corridor of the fourth level, being careful not to trip on unconscious bodies, uneven deck plates, or the trash that was everywhere. He also made sure he did not jostle anyone in the crowd. By the time he reached the nover-shop he was perspiring, his muscles tense. It was fortunate the shop wasn't on the lower levels that required a purchased pass for entry. In addition to the added expense, it was much more dangerous for him, at least before he arranged his erzatz insurance policy.

There were two people in the shop, a man and a woman. Their faces were politely non-committal, and as he explained what he was looking for he puzzled over why they seemed strange to him until he realized they had only token bodymods–rather sedate for Kulvar. They were quite knowledgeable about the various units that they produced to show him, and he struggled to ask the right questions. He had to seem like an ordinary customer; that is, one with criminal intent.

"Is there any signal degradation in intercept mode?"

The male assistant raised a lavender-frosted eyebrow. "The signal is copied and monitored to ensure there is no measurable change in signal quality. There is always the possibility, of course, that the initial connection could be detected but that is unavoidable for a personal unit. We do offer systems that correct for this, if the capability is desired?"

Harrington noticed the increased interest in both faces, and quickly decided to drop encouraging hints. It would help continue their motivation to see that he stayed alive, for one thing.

"Perhaps later. We must first make sure this unit will be suitable for our purposes...do you have the specifications for the larger systems available?"

The woman shook her head. "That's in the Downunder shop. We don't even keep the sellsheets here to keep their capabilities confidential." She took the personal unit, which was much the same size as an unprocessed protein brick, and wrapped it up with a packet of probes and cables. The wrapping was hard to focus on, and it didn't seem to have any color of its own; the unit was completely obscured. Despite himself, Harrington was impressed. It wasn't the best chameleon wrap but even that would not be cheap. He wondered if they were always this generous to first-time customers.

"I have included a visit-chit that will be accepted at the Fourth level entrance," she said. "If you don't want your purpose known."

He thanked her gravely, handed over the requisite large number of credit chips, and accepted his chameleon-wrapped package. It immediately matched the black of his vest. It wasn't completely invisible, but people would be much less likely to even notice he was carrying something.

He made sure to take careful note of his surroundings as he left, but he could not help feeling he had done rather well for his first time. Neither of the two shop people appeared at all suspicious that he was not a Kulvar regular, and the delicate hints he had dropped appeared to have taken root exactly as he had hoped. It would not do to let his self-congratulatory mood appear visible, however. Harrington adopted a hard expression and scanned the crowd again. Perhaps he should find something to eat and then retire to his half-room to study his purchase.

He considered his options as he walked back purposefully ("Always look like you know exactly where you're going, even if you don't," the station policeman had warned). It was much easier to move around people this time. Perhaps he was getting the hang of Kulvar; starting to fit in. Then he frowned. Had there always been this much space? The crowd hadn't thinned appreciably, but in front of him—in front of him were a handful of what were locally referred to as "hardbodies", all armed. They were looking at him.

His first panicked instinct was to reach for his weapon, retracted so quickly a muscle cramped in his arm. Harrington forced himself to breathe, to think. This was precisely what he had been warned about, hadn't he? There was no conceivable way he could shoot them all, and he suspected that they were far more skilled in the use of their weapons than he was.

Odd. They weren't pointing their weapons at him. Perhaps the issue in question was a minor one. The important thing was to not show fear. He raised an inquisitive eyebrow and hoped he wasn't shaking visibly.

"Loda wants seeya," said one of the hardbodies.

It was very important to remember he hadn't been shot at yet. Ergo, he might have some small value alive.

"Loda?" Harrington asked. "I'm afraid I don't recall the name."

The hardbody was silent, then glanced at one of his compatriots who whispered something in his ear. "She's under Zandovar," the other one said, more coherently.

Zandovar he *had* heard of. Harrington nodded sharply and forced himself to step forward. The hardbodies fanned out around him in a pattern he could almost imagine was protective. They certainly weren't paying much attention to him, but rather to everyone else. Harrington noted with some alarm that everyone else was finding something other than him to look at.

His alarm grew as he was escorted to the Fourth level and past the guarded entrance. Loda was found in a section that was noticeably cleaner than the rest of the level. Now that he thought about it, the nover-shop had been rather tidy too. Loda herself was tall, gangly, and gaunt of face. She spoke very softly and had a general air of weariness, but Harrington noticed how the hardbodies responded immediately to her commands and concluded appearances were deceiving.

She was looking him over as if she found him puzzling too. "Find whatcha want at th' novers?"

Whatever he had been expecting, it wasn't this. "I believe so. It is difficult to know precisely without using it," he said, and quickly scrambled to explain a possible source of concern. "Not on Kulvar, of course."

"'Course not." Loda nodded, without a trace of sarcasm. "You guys don't work here."

You guys? Harrington drew in a breath, feeling a stab of fear. Did she mean the wireservices? Or, even worse, Umbra?

Then he knew. Cameron. They had found out he was connected to her somehow. Damn and blast.

"Sounds like youse got plans for something bigger'n that," Loda continued, jerking a thumb at the package. He clutched it a little tighter reflexively. "They's good, but not the best. You tell us what youse want, maybe I find it, eh?"

"Thank you. I shall keep that in mind," Harrington said. He hesitated. "No offense, but I don't quite see why you wanted to talk to me. Is there some problem I should know about?"

"Nah, no problem," Loda said, and grinned in what was probably intended to be a friendly manner. It looked more like a rictus. "Just wanna help, 's all. Zandovar's big on that, see? We help you, you help us, everybody wins. Don't have to be them snoop-boxes, beb. Got som'at on ya mind, say out. Read?"

"Er, quite. Read."

Harrington wasn't quite sure how he got out of Fourth level and back to his half-room—he moved in a sort of numb fog. All he could conclude was for some mysterious reason Zandovar, through his minion, was interested in what he was doing. Thus, by extension, what Cameron was doing. Maybe he should leave again—but that might make Zandovar suspicious.

He sat up suddenly on his bedpad, smacking the lamp with his head. Zandovar already *was* suspicious—of what, he had no idea. That wasn't important, not now. He had no way to warn Cameron. And she was coming here to find him.

CHAPTER 3
OTHER DUTIES AS ASSIGNED

Alan ran up and down the cliff trail three times, jumping over the rocks like he wasn't supposed to. He threw small rocks at splatter plants and big rocks into the water of the cove, getting himself and Ash completely soaked. Alan was still at a loss. None of the forbidden fun things were fun now for some reason. Maybe it was because there was hardly anyone on the island to yell at him for doing them.

Alan stomped in a puddle. "It's just moving a ship like we always do. What's so special about this one?"

"We could have *helped*," agreed George. "They *said* they needed everybody, didn't they?"

Hideo looked up from his close examination of a tide pool. "And they won't even let us go there to watch them put the ship in the hole. It's big! Mammachandra said they are going to put it all the way in and cover it up so Toren won't see it."

They all contemplated this and found it good. Hiding from Toren needed no explanation.

"How will they get in the ship to hide?" Ash wanted to know.

"The construction people will dig tunnels to the hatches," Alan said. "I saw the pictures. They are going to do more after this one." He looked up, frowning. Someone else was on the beach, near the end of the left side of the cove, and he didn't recognize them. "Who's that?"

The others gathered near him, suddenly silent. There were a lot of people they didn't know now, and strangers always worried the Created.

They had been seen too. Now the stranger was coming towards them.

"Why are you so small?" blurted Ash, voicing their universal astonishment. Hideo was staring with wide eyes, ready to run if this strange person turned out to be dangerous.

"I'm pretty tall for my age," the stranger said with a scowl. "I'm only nine years old."

Alan started. "I'm nine years old too."

"You are not! You're too big!"

"*You're* too small," George said. "How can you use a spacesuit? They are all the same size."

"I'm going to grow bigger! You weren't always that size, were you?"

"I don't ... remember," Alan said, reaching back to the foggy recesses of his memory. "I think I was always like this. All of us were."

Ash, George, and Hideo nodded.

The stranger's eyes widened. "Oh. You're the ones who were grown or something, right? I heard my Dad talk about that. He was real mad at the people who did it. If he ever finds them he'll rip 'em in half! My name's Marika; what's yours?"

"He's not going to rip us in half, is he?" George asked, his face doubtful.

"No, why would he do that? He's not mad at *you*," she said. "You're really only nine years old?"

"I am. I escaped before them," Alan said. "Mor–the Captain said your escape day is your birthday."

"You escaped? How?" Marika's eyes were wide again. They were dark, so dark you couldn't see the black center. Her hair was the same color, heavy and straight.

"I got on a ship without anyone seeing me. I didn't know it was a ship. When it left the Place I couldn't go back the same way." Alan hugged himself, remembering. The terror, the hunger, the loneliness. Everything had been so strange and confusing. "The ship went to another station and I found her. The Captain," he explained, seeing her start to ask another question.

"And then he told her about the Place and she came and rescued us!" added George. "When they put us in the box we didn't know. We were scared. When they take you away in the box you don't come back again."

Marika looked horrified. She came closer and looked up at George. "Did it hurt?" she asked in a quiet voice.

Nobody said anything for a moment. They didn't like remembering the Place, or what it was like. "Sometimes," mumbled George.

Marika patted him on the arm, startling him. "If Dad ever finds those guys I'll beat 'em up too. I probably won't be able to rip them in half, though, unless they are really small."

Alan was starting to like Marika. "Why not shoot them?"

"I'm not allowed," she said, scowling again. "I can't do *anything*. Well, I can use the surface digger if a grownup is watching me, but that doesn't really count. And I can't even do *that* with this ship they are bringing in. Dad said I wasn't even allowed to be at the site! And Mom forgot to give me the vidlink she promised so I can't even watch!" She sighed. "I thought getting bigger meant you could do what you want, but you're bigger and you can't. It's not fair."

"They won't let us help either, or anything," George said sympathetically. "I wish we could watch, though."

"There's a big vid setup in the cave," Ash said. "I think you have to put in the channel and mod-code and stuff to get anything but the main signal."

Marika brightened. "Really? I don't know the channel but you can do scans, and there can't be that many here. Let's try it!"

They hadn't been forbidden to use the vid setup–yet–but the Created sneaked up to the cave anyway, on principle. Besides, it was fun. They showed Marika the finer points of stealthy movement, which she picked up quickly and with great enjoyment. There were only a handful of people in the cave–Alan saw Madele Fortin, and the old man who studied rocks from Bone. Everyone was busy and wouldn't pay attention to them if they kept quiet.

"Oh yeah, I know this kind," whispered Marika when they got to the vid station. Hideo glanced over his shoulder while he watched the rest of the cave, but the rest huddled around the screen. "See, this is how you get a list of all the channels it can pick up. That's funny, there's a restricted one–hey, there's a bunch!" Her voice rose with excitement, forgetting. She quickly put a hand over her mouth and ducked behind the console, and the others followed. Nobody seemed to have noticed, and they slowly crawled out again.

"Sorry," she whispered. "I've never seen that many before. Even stations usually only have one or two. I wonder what they are for?"

Alan wasn't entirely sure what a restricted channel was, or why it was important. He would have to ask Moire when he saw her again.

"Oh, here it is. That's my Dad's transmitter ID there." The screen flickered and then flared with light.

There was sound but it was only from the construction tug people, not the people they were talking to. Alan could almost figure out what the rest of the conversation was sometimes. They sounded worried, and a few times they yelled. The Created watched silently, the sound turned low, as the ship slowly descended from orbit. It looked funny with extra gravitic nodes on top, like a hat. All the other ships, even the scout, looked tiny next to it. He found himself holding his breath as it finally was lowered with painful care into the giant hole in the ground which now looked barely large enough. The people in the construction tug cheered suddenly, and after a moment the signal cut off.

"They're just going to move dirt over it now," said Marika. "Boring." She fiddled with the console again.

"What are you doing?" George asked.

Her eyes narrowed. "I don't think all those channels can really be restricted, that would be dumb. Nobody could call them. I just want to check..." Her shoulders sagged. "No, they really are. I guess you need a key or something. Somebody ought to be looking at it, though."

Ash glanced at her. "Why?"

"Because one of them is signaling it wants to talk."

⚜

Moire finally had to order Gren to get some sleep. Even then it took a threat to have Madele Fortin medicate him to get him to leave the ship, now safely and permanently grounded. Always one more thing to check, one more thing to try. She was dead tired herself and wanting some privacy so she could give herself a good kick for ever thinking this had been a good idea. It wouldn't seem so bad in the morning, she knew. She also knew they would do it again. They didn't have a lot of choice.

"You should also be resting," Kilberton chided. "How can you expect your crew to be wise when you do not set a good example?"

She flopped a hand at him. "Yeah, yeah. I'm going already." The chair was too comfortable, though. It felt like the gravitics were still on in addition to the planetary gravity—or maybe she was just tired. Moire gritted her teeth and pushed her way upright with both arms and legs. Then the comm lit up with a direct code, and she opened the link, pretending not to notice Kilberton's rolling eyes and audible sigh.

It was Lorai, and she sounded...strange. "I got somethin' I gotta talk to you about." No details, no hey-howya-doin' like usual.

"I can barely stay vertical, Grimaldi. Can't it wait?"

"No, not as such. Sorry." Constraint in her voice, and she wasn't offering to come down to the ship bridge. "I'm putting down just outside the crater."

Moire sighed. "All right, but if I fall asleep you get to carry me back."

A small chuckle, which relieved her greatly. Something was wrong but not dangerously so. Kilberton raised a suspicious eyebrow at her when she closed the link.

"Something is not right there. I will go with you."

"You can follow if you want, but that's it. She's got something she needs to tell me without anybody else hearing, that's clear. If someone got into her shuttle during the last ten hours and is holding a gun to her head, they'd have to be pretty clever to do it without anybody noticing."

He permitted himself a smile. "She would also tell them to shoot her, and to go to hell. My apologies, Captain. I know she is trustworthy."

The night was crisp and clear, with just enough of a sea-scented breeze to wake her up a little. Moire scrambled up the jury-rigged ladders and platforms that led out of the one remaining opening to the buried ship, pausing now and then to rest and admire the night sky. Someday, when all this mess was over, she and Alan could have fun coming up with constellations.

One last ladder, and she was on the soft, loose dirt that ringed the ship. The shuttle was not far away, and Lorai had the bay door open and was pacing back and forth in front of it. When she saw Moire she jumped back inside and motioned her impatiently to join her before glancing around and shutting the bay door.

"All right, who did you shoot?" Moire asked, tiring of mystery.

Lorai gave an explosive snort. "I just might, make things easier if you ask me. But I'm just a dumb shuttle pilot. This is too damn complicated." She stopped, fiddled with a loose cargo fastener in the hold. She hadn't yet looked Moire in the eye.

"Come on, Grimaldi. 'Fess up. You forgot where you dumped the xenobiologist, didn't you?"

"Naw!" Lorai looked up, startled. "I wrote it down this time, two different places. Um, look. You remember telling us before you left, about that gang boss that was expecting you to deliver? You had some kinda plan–did that work out?" She looked desperate.

Moire shook her head. "Turns out when Yolanda opened that container it damaged the contents. Packets weren't sealed right or something. When we got back there it was sludge. Why do you ask?"

Lorai gave a deep sigh, and her shoulders slumped. "Guess I gotta tell you, then. I was checking the restricted prisoner frequencies, making sure none of them had broken a leg or anything just like you said to. So there was a message from that Mengai, the other pilot from the Toren ship you took over. Looked like hell and a biscuit on the vid, just said she had to talk to you 'cause she'd heard Toren was coming here."

Moire frowned. "How did she hear that?"

"Eh, some of the crew like to write little messages on the crates I drop off. You know, crabs gonna eat you, this is the last one so eat slow you damn gene-thief, death to slavers–the usual. I check but I don't always get 'em all. So, I call back. She's desperate scared, Roberts. Damn if she didn't offer to do anything if I'd just get her off planet, and that was just her opening bid. Now, I'm getting pretty core-hot thinking about how she used ta ship those poor kids into slavery or worse without a second thought, so I says really? Wouldya volunteer for slave duty? And she says she would. Didn't even have to think about it. So then I remember you got this problem with whozis back on Kulvar. I don't say nothin', but I tell her you're the one who decides and cut comms. I knew you wouldn't like it. Hell, I don't like it! But if your other plan didn't work out," she shrugged, "thought I should tell you, anyways."

Lorai looked disgusted at the whole situation and Moire was feeling the same way for even considering it. Trouble was, she didn't have any good options now. Either stiff Zandovar, or give him what he wanted.

"Is her island in daylight now?" Moire asked after a struggle with her conscience. "I don't think she really understands what she'd be getting into."

The vids on prisoner islands were set to automatic pickup and display, so they could see it was morning on Mengai's island. There was no response to the call signal at first and Moire was just about to tell Lorai to try again later when a disheveled and frantic face came in to view.

"I'm here. I'm here! Please!"

Moire stared at her grimy, sunburned face, wondering if she should just cut the connection now.

"So. I hear you don't like your accommodations. Funny, I wasn't thinking of making you happy when I chose them."

"If Toren finds me it won't matter where the hell I am. Is it true? Are they coming?" Her eyes were wide and desperate. "Have you told them I'm here?"

Now that was a surprise. Why would she be telling Toren anything? But then, the pilot wouldn't know that. "What's the problem? Used to work for them, didn't you? Think they'd pay a ransom to get you back?."

Mengai shook her head sharply. "After I got caught with the cargo? They're just looking to slag me now. You told her what I said, right? I'll do whatever you want, just get me away from them."

"And what's to prevent you from going to the police and telling them all about me? Or trying to buy your life back from Toren by telling them about this place?"

She snorted. "Yeah, and where the hell am I? Could be the galactic Core for all I know. You don't want me talking about you, and I won't because I don't want *you* talking about *me*. Sell me. You get some money, and I stay alive. Best I can hope for now."

She wasn't repentant, but she wasn't claiming innocence either. Moire considered that a very small point in her favor.

"If we do this, you know where you would be going? Kulvar. The Downunder. They probably won't kill you just for the fun of it, being a pilot and all, but I can't promise anything else. *Anything.* Do you understand that?"

Mengai looked away from the screen for a moment, then back. Her gaze was steady. "I've had plenty of time to think here. Guess I'm not as scared of them as I am of Toren. Maybe I'm wrong, but I won't have lost much if I am."

Moire shrugged. "All right, I'll consider it." She cut the connection before Mengai could object, and sank down until her head was resting on her folded arms.

"You gonna do it?" Lorai said after a while, in a hushed voice.

"I'm sick and tired of being the only one who makes the hard decisions around here," Moire said, snapping her head back up. "Especially for something dirty like this. Either we all accept it or we find something else to try."

She wasn't expecting the debate to be easy, or enjoyable, and it wasn't. But when her informal officer's council eventually agreed to Mengai's plan, she discovered she had secretly been hoping they would refuse.

"I guess we are that desperate," she said to Gren, opposite her at the rough table the meeting room had recently acquired.

"Not just that," he said with a scowl. "She's right–Toren's going to show up sooner or later. Might as well get the prisoners out of the way before they do. Just get in the way, needing supplies, and if Toren gets 'em they could be used against us. Not saying we sell them, or even ask if they would," he added hastily, "but we should think of a plan."

"Yeah," Moire said, tipping her chair back and rubbing her chin thoughtfully. "Something that causes trouble for Toren, I'm thinking. Something public and messy and embarrassing they can't cover up."

Gren grunted. "Sounds like you got a plan already."

"I have an idea. We'll need Mr. Harrington's assistance to make it work," she said, "and now that we have Zandovar's little present arranged, we can go get him."

Another trid graphic floated up on the display, and Ennis leaned closer to get a better look. An exterior view of the crab ship, underneath, showing a series of large hollows. One rounded shape was nested in the second-to-last berth; the rest were empty.

"Each one has their usual interface cluster and what appear to be smaller versions of the main airlock door. They won't open, presumably because they aren't mated to a similar airlock. That ship there is the only one left, and it is badly damaged. Presumably they took all the others when they left the ship. You didn't see any other ships like that in the area, did you?" Namur raised an inquisitive eyebrow.

"No sir. We were looking for anything crablike at that point so I am sure we would have noticed it if they had been there." Ennis thought for a moment. "I don't think they left that ship behind, sir. I think that was the only one that returned. The crab–Radersent–appears to have been significantly injured. He couldn't use one forelimb"

"Interesting." Namur rested his head on his clasped hands. "I wonder what it was they were trying to do at the sargasso. Could it have been connected to this Breaker-relic you mentioned?"

They were alone in Namur's office, or he would not have mentioned it. Ennis wasn't sure how much Umbra had told Fleet about this latest worry, or if Fleet would care if they did know. The only confirmation they had was pilot-reported artificial gravitational anomaly and the very crudely translated testimony of a crab that there was a third alien space-faring race.

"Radersent seemed quite agitated about the Breakers–terrified of them. But besides the one crab ship there's nothing else out there that isn't human, and there's no evidence the crabs went near the human ships. Maybe they were trying to get the device to use against us."

"A desperate measure, it would seem," Namur commented.

"They may be desperate, sir. I don't know what rank or status Radersent had on that ship, but he knew about us destroying that first crab carrier and he even seemed to know a single fighter had done it."

That earned him a glance from hooded eyes. "And how did that topic come up in conversation?"

Careful. He had to be so very careful. He couldn't avoid mentioning Moire—that would be noticeable too—but he had to make sure it was only when necessary, and that he didn't appear to care. In short, he had to lie.

"The salvagers were concerned about having a crab on board. I mentioned Cameron had dealt with them before quite successfully, and this was communicated to the crab."

"Ah." Namur nodded. "And this did not disturb him?"

Ennis frowned, reliving the incident in his mind. "Yes, but...not as much as the thought that we would leave him there. Alone. He was quite insistent on coming with us. In fact, that's how we first found out he was even there. Perwaty tried to protect him by hiding him, but he started pounding on the walls when he figured out Perwaty was leaving for good."

"Yes. Very curious, and serves to point out how little we know of how they think. We need that crab and the translator as soon as we can get them, Commander Ennis," Namur said, giving him a direct look. "You have some arrangement in place to facilitate this, I hope."

"An indirect one, sir. Cameron is very suspicious of any attempts by Fleet to contact her." Except him. Because when he was with her, he wasn't really Fleet any more. "I sent a message to your independent contractor, Neville Harrington, to contact me by code burst when he had news. He already knows we want to get the crab in our custody. I haven't heard anything since."

All they could do was wait, and he had never been particularly good at that. Not when he knew what could go wrong. Moire Cameron took dangerous risks, and she hadn't told him all her plans. He wasn't the only one with secrets. He just hoped hers wouldn't get her killed before he could save her.

♔

Moire rummaged in her cabin locker for what she privately thought of as her Professional Criminal clothes. A headache had been building ever since *Raven* had docked to Kulvar station. "So how does this work? I suppose I don't just wander down there without calling first."

Yolanda shook her head. "He knows we're here. All you gotta do is let his people know you got something for him; they'll tell you how he wants it done."

"He's not going to want to come on this ship, is he?" Moire asked, fighting a sudden stab of fear.

"Nah. He don' go anywhere not his, read? Nothin' personal. Word goes he don't trust nobody." Yolanda leaned against the edge of the bunk and tickled the baby nerya asleep on the blankets. It twitched and made little chk-chk noises before settling down again. "Want me to take care of callin' in?"

"Yeah. Get this over with." She snugged up the sheetleather jacket fastenings, then sighed and loosened them again. "Got to leave room for the gun, I suppose."

"Don't have to ifn' ya don't want to, Captain. Heavy movers got they own muscle, shows load if ya don't carry yerself, see? We got the toolkit. Good idea to have somethin' for emergencies, but it don't have to be big. Knife, mebbe."

That was a relief. If she wasn't carrying a gun nobody would expect her to use it.

Moire dumped her old shirt on the bed. The little nerya woke up, sniffed it, and all three eyes opened wide. Before she knew what had happened it had jumped on her arm and scrambled to its usual position, snugged down between her collar and her neck.

She didn't even try to remove it. She had learned that would just make it more determined to stay. If she pretended she didn't care she might be able to remove the critter before they left the ship. And if she didn't, maybe the baby nerya would get lost on the station and she'd never have to deal with it again. Alan would be upset, though.

"Let's get the shopping taken care of too, unless that will be a problem. Who knows how long it will take Zandovar to find time on his busy schedule."

It didn't take him long at all. Two hours after their message was sent a reply arrived.

Moire read it, then looked at Yolanda who was one of many hanging over her shoulder. "So what's that mean? 'Will see me'? Not very specific, is it?"

"Sure it is. Means 'now'." Yolanda had a sour expression on her face. "A' course we got half the ship out. Not many left if ya want to have a guard on the ship, and you'll need people."

After much discussion they settled on two of the crew besides her and Yolanda. "And Alan," she added.

"What? No. Bad idea."

Yolanda just gave her a tired look. "He gonna notice who shows up. Rest of the kids out with the others, yer sweet man not here. Gotta be someone else he recognizes in the group. Alan can handle it."

"*Alan* can handle it? You do remember what we are doing, right?" She did not want Alan mixed up in their prisoner handover, and she *really* didn't want to know Yolanda—and presumably the rest of the crew—knew that her interest in Ennis was so personal.

The little nerya squirmed and burrowed deeper. Moire winced, and tried to gently remove it, but it refused to budge. It picked up on her moods more than she liked, and if she was angry it seemed to think the world was too dangerous to be alone in its nesting box. If Zandovar noticed it maybe she could sell it to him.

The erstwhile prisoner was waiting for them at the airlock, arms bound behind her and flanked by the two armed crew that would be escorting them.

"Still think this was a good idea?" Moire asked, seeing her pale, strained expression.

"You promised..." Mengai whispered.

"Yes, I did. More to the point now, I just promised Zandovar so you don't get a choice any more. And if you have a sudden urge to get funny," Moire said, leaning closer, "everybody here would just as soon see you dead anyway. Got that?"

She nodded, swallowing hard. Moire jerked her head at the guards and they moved out.

Moire didn't have Yolanda Menehune's ability to scan the crowds and pick up the mental pulse of the Kulvar criminal underworld, but she did notice that their berth was not attracting any hangabouts or toughs. Instead, there were a handful of the quickie stands set up by the poorer inhabitants of Kulvar. That usually meant the area was considered safe from random personal violence, and it was puzzling since there was no reason for them to think her ship was any guarantee of protection.

She kept scanning the faces of people she passed, trying to keep alert, hoping she would recognize the danger signs before it was too late.

Instead, she saw Harrington. She shook her head at him minutely, hoping he would pick up the hint, but he didn't stop. Moire moved so he would be less likely to see that one of the group was wearing cuffs, and kept walking.

"I can't stop now. Get to the ship and I'll see you when I get back," she snapped.

Harrington shook his head. "I have to warn you," he said, speaking so low she could barely hear him. "He knows we are connected."

Moire stared at him. *Zandovar?* she mouthed, and he nodded.

"I tried to stay out of sight–he came looking for me. Or more precisely, his people. They seemed to want to help me," he said, shrugging, " but I don't know why. You needed to know."

She thought about it, glancing at Yolanda who just made a balancing-hands gesture. Could be bad, could be good, no way to tell. It didn't change what they were doing.

"All right, I'm warned. I'll be back."

"But–"

"Get back to the ship!" Moire snarled. This was something she did not need. Harrington was too damn observant.

He backed up, and turned away towards the berth hatch.

There was more strangeness on their way to the fourth level entrance. Nobody seemed to want to get in their way. Even the guards refrained from their usual challenging banter, simply verifying the passkey and waving them in. Moire sneaked a glance at Yolanda, and she seemed to be puzzled too.

Zandovar was in a guarded facility below the fifth level. Moire had never gone that deep before, and everything she saw made her determined never to go back there again. He must have anticipated what she was bringing him, or had found out after she left the ship, because the guarded facility was where the slaves were kept.

Alan was looking a little wide-eyed but was wisely keeping his attention on the prisoner and ignoring everything else. Mengai was breathing rapidly and sweating, but her jaw was clenched and her face determined.

Zandovar was standing before what looked like a ship console. There were controls, and vidscreens, and a single large window that currently showed what looked like a track with gears. Assorted thugs and hardbodies lounged in the background, and the strange white-haired androgyne Moire recalled from their last encounter was holding a datapad as if showing it to the ceeyo for his approval.

Moire stepped inside the room, making sure her hands were visible. "Zandovar. I have something you might be interested in." Yolanda had assured her the protocol was she spoke first. If Zandovar didn't want to hear her, she wouldn't have gotten this far.

He turned his head slightly, a dark eye coolly appraising her. Moire jerked her head at the prisoner and she stepped forward, lips twitching.

"Is this all?"

Forcing herself to sound equally cool and unconcerned, Moire replied, "She's a web pilot."

Gasps of surprise from everyone in the room except Zandovar and the white androgyne at that. They weren't dead yet.

Moire went a little closer, pushing Mengai ahead. "You said you could use anything I could find."

Zandovar stirred from his stillness. "That is correct. I can certainly make use of a web pilot, ah, suitably controlled. Now we should discuss the few remaining business details—perhaps establish rates for future deliveries."

"For her? Consider her a free sample." Now his eyebrows were visibly elevated. They had discussed this at length on Sequoyah, and they had all agreed no money would be exchanged for the prisoner. Of course, they also had to come up with a really good reason why or Zandovar would get suspicious all over again. "My methods don't make it easy to collect crew. It's only worth it to me if I can get a high-value skill, like web piloting, to take the extra time required. So, I might not have another to offer you for a while. I wanted to make sure that was...acceptable to you."

They would have to come back again to Kulvar. It would be very difficult to find another volunteer, and she wasn't sure even if she did that her crew would let her pull this stunt again..

Zandovar looked the pilot over carefully, staring her in the eyes until she started to shake. "Yes. I can see your point–after all, your main business is ships. I see I can rely on you for a quality product when you have the opportunity. But this is much too generous a gesture to accept, although I do appreciate it."

Oh crap. They hadn't considered the possibility he'd refuse. Zandovar was looking over her shoulder, and she turned to see what had caught his attention. Alan was staring at the console vid screens. They each showed a person, naked, in a cramped compartment. One of them appeared to be sobbing, the rest were slumped against the wall either asleep or hopeless.

"Perhaps you would accept one of these, much less valuable, in exchange," Zandovar said. His face revealed nothing; Moire couldn't tell if this was a trap or a test. She went over to the vid displays hoping she could catch a hint from Yolanda without being obvious, but her face was impassive. She was on her own. Well, they could use a little good karma and getting some poor sap out of here would help.

The sobbing slave was female, and not unattractive. She doubted that was what had caught Alan's notice, but it would make a convenient excuse. Moire clasped Alan's elbow and indicated the screen. "You like that one?" she asked, and gave a quick, hidden squeeze. He glanced at her, surprised, but he knew enough to nod and not ask questions.

Zandovar seemed amused, and he gestured to some of the toughs before manipulating the console controls. With a grinding noise a metal container rotated out of the wall behind the large window and moved along the track. It came to a stop with a clang, and the toughs opened an outer, then inner door and pulled out the woman they'd seen on the screen into the room. Another tough tossed something at her, which she first clutched to herself, choking as she tried to stifle her sobs, then scrambled to put on. Once she was clothed, the toughs fastened cuffs on her hands.

"It was originally intended as a secure vault for the storage of valuable merchandise," Zandovar said, nodding toward the window and the geared tracks. "It serves equally well for keeping valuable merchandise that is alive."

Judging from the smell personal hygiene wasn't considered important for slaves. Moire was desperate to leave anyway.

"Is there anything else?" she asked.

Zandovar considered the pilot again. "Her credentials?"

"In her pocket." Moire saw Mengai bite her lip, and hastened to add, "I would not advise using them. If she's on a missing persons sweep it will be noticed. I'd keep her away from any bioscans too. She used to be Inner Systems."

"I will keep that in mind." Zandovar gestured, clearly dismissing them. Moire had just enough time to see the pilot sag a little, eyes closing in relief. Moire had promised to do what she could to keep her hidden, and telling Zandovar to keep her away from ID checks and bioscans was probably the best way to do it.

Now she just had to get her new acquisition back to the ship before Alan tried to reassure her where someone could hear, or the woman succumbed to the sheer panic she was visibly on the edge of. Why did everyone conspire to give her more problems? Getting rid of the pilot was supposed to *help* them.

By setting a ruthless pace and ignoring all questions from her people they got back to the ship in record time. Unfortunately, it couldn't last.

"What the hell we gonna do with her?" Yolanda demanded as soon as the hatch closed. The woman cringed and started to whimper in terror.

"Clean her up and send her home, of course," Moire said. "Why?"

Yolanda shook her head. "Can't do it here. Zandovar would hear about it."

"Damn. I suppose that would not be taken well, now that you mention it. All right, you. Got a name?"

The woman just gaped at her, her breath catching on sobs. "Inathka," she managed eventually.

"Inathka, the good news is we're setting you free as soon as we can. The bad news is we can't do it right now. Who have we got on medical?" Moire asked the crew standing around, watching the scene with interest.

"Nobody. We got the scanner and the manual," said one.

Moire sighed, and wished they hadn't needed to leave Fortin on Sequoyah. Or that they had just one more medtech to go around. "Okaaay then. Somebody do a scan and make sure she doesn't have any unnecessary gizmos stuck in her. And get her some clothes and a shower. Shower's mandatory, by the way. Where's Harrington?"

"Right here," he said, standing just behind her in a doorway. "Handcuffs seem to be in fashion lately. And perhaps some quick face-mods? This young lady doesn't look anything like the one I saw you with earlier," he added, his expression bland.

"This is the Fringe. Sometimes things get rough around here," Moire snapped. "You don't like it, feel free to leave."

"Hardly. I want to talk to the—"

Moire's glare, and quick glance at Inathka, shut him up.

"Looks like Gren isn't back yet. Yolanda, if you have stuff to do go ahead. I'll be up top. Oh, and folks, Inathka isn't staying, so please make sure she keeps to the public areas and her quarters."

Before Moire got two steps away she heard Alan say, "But we rescued her! Why can't she stay?"

Inathka glanced at him and edged away.

"She doesn't want to stay, Alan. She already has a home." This earned her a puzzled look from both Alan and Inathka.

"There were others in boxes there. Are we going to rescue them too?" was Alan's inevitable question.

"I'm afraid we can't right now. It would be too dangerous for them," Moire said, desperately trying to think of how to derail Alan's train of thought. Of course he would expect her to rescue the rest of the slaves; she'd done the same for the Created, after all. "I'll, er, think about it."

Harrington wasn't as easy to shake off. He followed her to the bridge, looking thoughtful, but he didn't ask any more awkward questions about personnel changes. "My apologies for the breach of security. I am told I am too prone to them."

Moire grinned. "Got a reaming, did you?"

An eyebrow was raised. "I'm not sure how to answer that question, given my unfamiliarity with the term. However, now that we seem to be in the clear?" Moire nodded, and he continued, "I do want to talk to...our mutual acquaintance as soon as can be arranged."

"He's not here. Too dangerous. He wasn't happy about that, as far as we can tell. Perwaty is still working on increasing our vocabulary."

"Speaking of which—it has evidently become a matter of some urgency to get him to my *other* employer."

"Oh yes?"

Harrington sighed. "I've gotten more than one frantic message on the subject. And since I am, I hope, shortly going to be leaving scenic Kulvar it would be desirable to send some kind of reply. Do you have anything I can tell them?"

"I'm working on it. We've got a plan, we just have to find some of the necessary ingredients." Which, hopefully, Yolanda was even now taking steps to find. Assuming that Lorai's pilot buddy could be found and was interested in the job. "Won't know for a while if it's done. We can set up some codes now, though."

Moire sat down at the comms station to do that, wishing there were some way she could include a message to Ennis. She'd just have to hope the plan came through quickly, because it was too dangerous to do anything but tell him in person. It had been too long since she'd heard his voice, or seen the little crooked smile when he looked at her, or any of the things that ached to remember. Much too long.

She heard a cheep, a rustle, and then felt the small, soft impact of the little nerya. It must have been startled by Harrington, a stranger, because it burrowed deep and didn't move or make another sound.

"Was that what I think it was?" Harrington asked, sounding amused.

"Hey, I have to keep up my image. And they were out of parrots," Moire said.

"You don't seem the type for pets, if you don't mind my saying so. Why do you keep it?"

Moire sighed, and leaned back in her chair. "It's Alan's. I only keep it for him." She closed her eyes, trying to speak around the sudden tightness in her throat. "It made him laugh," she managed finally. "I never saw him laugh before."

♛

"Nice work." The chief medical officer tabbed through the rest of the medsheet, signed it, and handed it back to Peter. "In future, though, check with me or the board before proceeding with sensory prosthetics. We could get in trouble if that work gets done before all patients are out of triage."

Peter nodded and took the medsheet in silence. Inside, he seethed. It was a miracle he'd been able to save the patient at all—and since he was already working inside the body it made perfect sense to put the senprods in at the same time. Less trauma to the patient, and more efficient use of his time. But they didn't care about that.

Well, he was going to show them again. They hadn't thought they could save this man—they had done the DNA test, it was a man—found in the wreckage of the outpost. Physical trauma was severe, blood loss at nearly 70%. He'd been found in a cold and oxygen-poor environment too. That had been what saved him, plus an extremely fortunate circumstance. He had fallen near a burning contaminant filter for the oxygen condenser system, and it had produced just enough hydrogen sulfide to put him in a suspended medevac state. The loss of blood, the low oxygen level, had not even damaged his brain.

They might even be able to instigate regrowth of his limbs. That would take funding, though, and nobody knew who the man was. The miners had accounted for all of their people. Strangely, there had been several unidentified bodies at the site that no-one had claimed. Peter shrugged. The best thing to do was to ask the man himself, and thanks to his unappreciated work, they could do that.

He started to activate the senprods, sending tiny test signals at first to make sure they were active. There were a few that were not responding; that was to be expected a patient with such extensive damage. There were still enough to do the job.

"You are on Medical Ship Ben-Zachurian, in the intensive care section. You were found badly injured after the explosion of Waylands, on the planet Bone. Please do not feel anxious if you do not remember this, or anything else. You are recovering from trauma that required the insertion of

48

sensory augmentation systems. If you can hear me, please attempt to reply. The detectors will be able to adapt more quickly if you keep trying."

Peter set the message to repeat, and watched the readouts. It could take days for patients to comprehend and then comply with the implant stimuli. Sometimes it was necessary to adjust the signal profile, or even in rare cases go back and re-situate the implants.

Not in this case. There was a stimulus response the third time the message was transmitted. Three hours later there was a definite attempt to communicate. Peter brought in a gurney pad and slept fitfully next to the biotank containing his patient, waiting for recognizable words to begin to form.

When they did, he started to worry that there had been brain damage after all. In all his experience as a med tech, he had never heard a patient say, after regaining consciousness, "What do you want?"

Surprise held him motionless for a moment. He turned off the automessage and put on the audiopickup that connected to the signal transmitter. "This is Medtech Peter Vadnov. Do you remember who you are?"

"Yes. What do you want. Answer please."

Peter blinked. Perhaps he should humor the patient, establish a rapport. It must be pretty unsettling to wake up in a biotank. "Well, I'd like to have a good salary review next time," he joked.

"Authorization code, Pjk23947278 rota 129899-02900-4328, financial institution, Luda Security Trust, non-colony transactions branch. Answer only second question, enter current date in Tethys format."

"Do you want me to verify this?" Peter asked, completely bewildered. The patient certainly didn't sound disoriented.

"Yes."

The medical ship, of course, had its own financial systems network. It was crosschecked, validated, and ported for comparison at every stop. Peter pulled it up on his datapad and, reviewing the message which had been recorded, entered the specified code.

It brought up a secured, key-only account with ten thousand ED. Peter stared at the display. He had complete access to it. He could transfer funds and nobody would be able to tell the owner hadn't done it.

"I...ah, I have verified the account."

"Is yours. More if you help me."

Peter took a deep breath. "Sir, I will help you anyway. You are on a medship; I am obligated to give you treatment."

"Not treatment. Must leave ship. Require assistance. Do what I say and you will be paid more."

Even more than ten thousand ED? He could leave the Medical Association, leave the damn ship and the heavy-handed board. Set up his

49

own medical ship, under his own rules. And he could always back out if he wanted to. The patient was in a biotank, completely helpless without him. Even his communications could be stopped if Peter wanted to do it. He had ten thousand right now. How much more was this guy worth?

"All right. I'll do it. But leaving the ship now would interfere with your treatment. We might be able to restore your arms and legs, and maybe even sight, if–"

"No. Leave now. Remove all biodata from files. Conceal traces when leaving."

That could be made to work in his favor. It would be hard to smuggle an entire working biotank out, but he had some ideas already.

"Why do you want to do this?" Peter asked.

The sensors were not designed to convey tone, or even volume, but somehow the synthetic voice sounded angry. "Toren betrayed me. Must finish job. Promised full information. Lied to me. Must find Moire Cameron. I am Kolpe Anders. I always finish the job."

CHAPTER 4
THE ROAD LESS TAKEN IS MINED

"How many moons again?"

Harrington's voice was barely audible over the echoing din in the cavern. Moire looked up from her plate. Being in the same location as Madele Fortin meant good food that demanded your full attention. "Three. But Coyote likes to hide, hence the name."

She suppressed a grin at Harrington's visible dilemma; ask her about Coyote, or the moons? As she expected, he set the name aside as something to be researched later. "And the other two?"

"Spider and Rabbit. Spider is the smaller one with the big rayed crater."

"This planet is absolutely incredible," Harrington murmured, scribbling impatiently on his datapad. "I don't blame you for trying to fight for it. Oh yes, I've been all over the island and I do know what a weapons pad looks like. And blast doors, like the ones you have in the back of the cavern. You do have the weapons, yes?" he asked. Moire just stared at him until he sighed. "Quite. I suppose I will find out when the fighting starts, then. It would be dreadfully dull if life held no surprises."

It was hopeless to try and make the reporter feel embarrassed; he had all the delicate sensibility of a rhinoceros when he was on the trail of a good story.

"Finish up with your snooping here—we'll be heading out to the sargasso as soon as the cargo's unloaded. You did want to talk to the crab, remember?"

"Of course. I'd also like to know why I don't see the young lady you brought on board wearing the linked bracelets, and what a xenobiologist would think about those giant trees growing in the bay," Harrington glanced at Lorai Grimaldi, who had apparently choked on her drink, before continuing, "and who discovered this planet. Among other questions."

"Does it matter who found it? We got it now," Lorai said, her coughing fit over.

"There are precedents in the matter of discovery." Gip Farouz's gentle voice came from behind her. Moire turned in her seat. The little geologist was holding a plate of food, and she gestured for him to join them at the table. "Fortunately for us the Captain can make that claim, if I am not mistaken."

"Claim's not proof," Moire said around a mouthful of food. "Been doing some research, huh?" She gave him a meaningful look.

Gip inclined his head. "Some things I have heard, that you were once caught in webspace and time. Also I recalled your face, when I showed you the pin left by the discoverer of Bone. When you heard his name you wept. I looked in the information I have to see if there were any ships missing with crew that would have known this man."

"Mr. Farouz has an interest in the history of exploration," Moire explained, seeing Harrington's expression of puzzlement. "Yes, I knew him." She hesitated for a moment, remembering. Remembering how angry she had been that Cisco hadn't lived just a few years longer. "I'm not claiming the planet for myself. It really belongs to the Created–the children like Alan. Toren took the stored tissue from the explorers to make them, you see. Cisco could have a kid he never knew about, just like I did."

Gip's face froze, then slowly melted to sorrow. "It is an offense against God," he whispered. "Why was such a terrible thing done?"

"Toren needed lots of strong, docile workers without inconvenient complications like families," Moire said. The food didn't taste so good now. "We...took care of it. Rescued as many as we could."

When it looked like Gip was about to ask more questions, Moire surreptitiously indicated Harrington and shook her head. She was planning to send Harrington back out, and she didn't want the news spread off-planet that she had been involved in blowing up the complex that manufactured the Created.

"I must help them. Somehow...it is an obligation. They should know they are the children of heroes."

"Spend as much time with them as you can, then. They like you, and you can teach them how to be human. Anything else that comes to mind, too. That would be a big help." They had tried to set up a school, but they just hadn't had enough people to do anything more than haphazard sessions. This was something the elderly Gip could do that was useful and would make everyone else's lives easier; he could keep the Created from wandering around getting into trouble.

"Grimaldi's going up for the last load, Captain," said one of her crew, jogging in from the front of the cavern. "Anything else we need to send up with her?"

Moire finished the last few bites of her meal and stood up. "I'll talk to Kilberton. We're off to get another wreck for quarters, so we won't need the salvage gear."

Mostly what she and Kilberton had to figure out was what to do with Inathka. Flying *Frankenstein* with a ship in tow, they had both agreed, was a two-pilot job. Kilberton was good enough to take a regular ship in to Sequoyah by himself now, but not to do this. That meant she couldn't send him to dump off their unwilling guest, and she didn't want to risk leaving Inathka alone in an uncrewed, orbiting ship until they got back. The only other options were to bring her down to the surface and keep her in a box, or take her along. According to Madele Fortin the former slave now appeared to believe she'd been rescued, but was both bored and starting to ask awkward questions. Since they'd found out Inathka had some electronics skills, Moire had set her to work trying to adapt the gizmo Harrington had given her to use the data in their one and only crab translator. She hadn't told her what it was, of course.

As soon as the shuttle was unloaded Moire had Lorai take her back up to *Frankenstein*. Even on approach she could tell the repair crew had been busy.

"Nice work," Moire told Gren when she got inside. "Doesn't look so skeletal any more, at least in the interior."

Gren shrugged. "I did what I could, but cargo is still a mess. Just can't get it to connect and leave the struts bare like we need 'em. But you can get to Radersent's bin without a suit now, and there should be shielding enough to even do it in drive. Still want him to go?"

"Yeah, just in case his friends-and-relations show up at the sargasso wondering where their ship got to. That's good you've got his quarters connected. Perwaty said he really got agitated being alone last time."

"We put in a vid display," Gren said grumpily. "What more does he want?"

Moire shook her head. "I don't think he can see our vids very well. The kids noticed that too; simple black-and-white graphics work OK but nothing detailed."

Gren sighed. "By the time we figure him out we'll have to hand him over. Seems a waste of time."

"We'll tell Fleet what we've learned and then they can keep going. Who knows? Maybe they can understand why the crabs are fighting us—then we'll only have to worry about Toren," Moire said, grinning when Gren rolled his eyes. "Come on, let's go get a nice wreck to live in."

⚜

Inathka had thought nothing could be more terrifying than the pens at Kulvar. She ought to be fair emit to be out of it and scope clear, near as she could tell. New people hadn't even raised a hand to her, and that old medtech had even run the zoom and pulled out a few pain-nodes Zandovar had rammed in for fun. Sure, they had her boxed up and all but she wanted out, just had to yank the squawker and somebody'd come around. Even when they had ship-drills, she found out, somebody always had the duty of getting her out and lined up with the rest.

So, the scare-bits. She'd seen enough of the new ship with the drills to know it was reworked, like it had been ripped up and put back together only they didn't have the plans 'n all. Inathka knew signal. Knew what size ship should have that size cable rig, and most of that space was just *gone*.

Not behind a jiggered door or even hid, she knew those tricks too. Bulkhead where there should be hunnerts meter more foot-track, same every level she got to see.

People, too. Everybody so damn *mannered*, made her jumpy. First ship, after Kulvar, just left her lone, 'cept for the medtech. Books, trid, food, sleep; that was her sked. Captain said she'd be let free when they got to a safe port. Inathka hadn't believed her, but now she was starting to wonder. She'd finally gotten struct enough to *ask* for something to do, and they hadn't even bothered to scan the skill-scrip Zandovar gave them! And she sure wasn't being kept as bed gear, either. She'd thought the hardbody be the one, way he stared. Then she picked up he never stared lower, not once, even when she was getting the papercover on out of the pens. Bit of this and that and dice ears, figured out he was the Captain's son. Even he told no dock, coulda *looked*. Nothing. She didn't think he was fem-free, either, she could suss that. Was like...no signal no scan, was closest she could tag it.

They were hiding something and she couldn't scan damall. That's what scared her most. Wasn't one bit of signal matched any of the others from her scope. She knew it would be highscore to just stay down, keep the fingers out, but she couldn't. Was what got her that permanent invite from Zandovar, still couldn't learn. Haddaknow was in the blood, gonna get her dead someday.

Captain had tossed her a nice little signalgrab unit, wanted some randomest data in. Inathka could do it, but it sure didn't help not having a goodinfo lookup or anything to see if she was going right. So she added a watcher. Took some core-jumping, get it to make nice with the datapad they gave her. But now when they used the grabber, she'd see what they saw, hear what they heard. Maybe then she'd know what their rig was.

☙

Harrington hadn't been so happy in weeks. No-one was even thinking about shooting him, he had virtually constant access to a living, breathing (he assumed), *communicating* crab, and he'd gotten to see the mysterious sargasso of dead ships that Cameron and her crew salvaged. It was a pity that none of this could be reported just yet, but the day would come, he had no doubt.

He'd been helpful around the ship, too. The transit did not require much of the crew, and in the spirit of fun they had decided their rather...fragmentary ship deserved a full formal nameplate in the main airlock entry. They had done a splendid job with the design, honoring the spirit of *Frankenstein,* and Harrington had provided the ship's motto: *E pur se muove.* The crew, once a translation and brief historical extract had been provided, thought it was hilarious. Moire Cameron just read it and sighed.

Now, however, they had retrieved their ship from the sargasso and were nearly halfway to Sequoyah again. Running the ship in tow was not nearly as carefree as the outbound journey and Harrington did his best to stay out from underfoot. Since he spent most of his waking hours with the crab anyway this was not difficult.

He grabbed his datapad from his bunk locker and headed for the galley for a quick bite. Moire and Gren were already there when he entered, having an argument. Perhaps that was not quite fair–"heated discussion" conveyed the tone without implying any animosity between the captain and her chief engineer.

"Look, it can't be an anomaly, OK? We've only gone this route over twenty times, and one thing gravitational anomalies *don't* do is move around. Even the one that messes up the route from Fringe to Sequoyah is weak from this direction." Moire took a deep gulp from her mug and glared.

"I'm seeing something in the main drive transients," Gren insisted stubbornly, poking stubby fingers on the tabletop for emphasis. "Yeah, it is faint now but it's getting stronger. Didn't happen coming out, you're right about that," he said grudgingly. "Maybe the field isn't trimmed right for this ship. I haven't done a major scan since the crab ship–but the wreck we towed worked OK. Maybe we just got lucky that time."

Harrington quietly got a processed sandwich from the readybox and ate it, wishing he could see *Frankenstein* and its cargo from the outside. It would make a good sketch.

Moire drained her mug, winced, and put it back down on the table. "Just great. Like we don't have enough to worry about. How bad before it affects the drive?" She got up to leave.

Gren followed her out of the galley. "If it gets to 20% I'll have to do manual adjustments."

Harrington could just hear Cameron say, "Call me when it gets there and we'll drop out for a check."

Gren grunted something he couldn't hear, and then there was silence. Harrington found a drybar for a snack, put it in his vest pocket, and headed out for the crab quarters. To reach them he had to go down three levels, through a door still charmingly labeled 'Utility', down the one-level ladder inside, through a newly installed pressure door, and then descend a long flight of stairs that had been added to the inside of the former cargo hold. On the deck were two large shipping containers, dogged in place just like cargo would be, with a big window connecting them. One was the sealed quarters of Radersent, the other where the humans had their communication equipment.

Harrington opened the inspection hatch that served as a door and went in. Jim Perwaty was sitting at the communication console. His brown face had filled out since his rescue from the sargasso, but it was still lean. The Created, of course, were there too and busy with the vid screen gear.

"Hey, there you are," Perwaty greeted the reporter. "Had a vocabulary breakthrough while you were gone! Got the 'child' versus 'child of' thing hammered out, I think anyway. What we were usin' for that before? Seems to mean 'belong to', like bein' in a crew or somethin'.'"

Harrington nodded slowly. "So when he would ask everyone if they were a 'child of Cameron' he really just wanted to know if they were part of her group?"

"Seems so," Perwaty grinned. "Say, since you're here think I'll take a break, go get some grub." He stretched, yawned, rubbed his bristly hair, then pushed up out of his seat.

Alan looked up from what he was doing, mildly curious, then returned his attention to the vid controls. Radersent, on the other hand, seemed concerned—if Harrington was interpreting his slower tendril motion correctly. The long bony head of the crab didn't seem to reveal much emotion, at least not to a human, but the tendrils that hung below it, at the neck, were a general indicator. A gentle flowing motion was good. Slow motion was less good, but frozen in place was *bad.*

"Query, Jim not watch children?" came the synthetic voice from the translator. Once a mere device tag reader, it had been mightily repurposed, rewired, and mangled into the only human/crab translation device in existence. This was easier to ignore now it was embedded in a console with much less of an ad-hoc appearance.

"Jim told him children get looked at," Hideo said helpfully.

"Looked *after*," Ash frowned. "It came out 'watched' because that was already in."

Harrington slid into the communication console seat and brought up the wordlists on the display. He put together the message, "Harrington and Radersent now watch children."

He'd intended to be reassuring, but the crab went motionless. Harrington had just enough time to wonder what horrible diplomatic blunder he'd committed when Radersent started moving again, his whole strange, angular body gently swaying. He was *happy.*

"Query, Radersent name equals watch children yes?"

Unusually incoherent even for him, but Harrington felt reasonably certain of his meaning, at least enough to answer in the affirmative.

"Wow. I've never seen him do that before," George said, awed.

Ash stood behind Harrington at the console, her mouth hanging open. "What is he saying? I don't understand."

When Radersent could calm down long enough to use the translator, it was all variations on *belonging.* And he hadn't stopped swaying like a willow in a strong breeze.

"Oh, I do hope I haven't made a mess of it," sighed Harrington.

Moire stretched in the pilot's chair, still keeping a weather eye on the readouts. It was near the end of her shift, and no sooner had she noted the time than Kilberton entered the bridge with a drink bulb in his hand.

"Anything happening?" he asked.

She shook her head. "Nice and boring, just the way I like it. Oh, Gren was seeing some bobbles in the drive transients but looks like it went away."

Kilberton raised an eyebrow, his dark face suspiciously bland. "The drive isn't behaving in a completely normal fashion? On this ship? I am shocked."

"Gren likes his engines to behave properly at all times," Moire said, grinning. "His paranoia has kept us alive, so I'm not complaining. You weren't on *Ayesha*, so you don't understand what he's been through." She tapped the log, entered ship's status and got out of the chair.

"Yolanda told me stories," Kilberton replied, going down into the pilot's pit after Moire had left. "Just hearing them gave me nightmares."

"I should probably check in with him before I leave, just to be on the safe side," Moire said, and went to the comm. Gren answered, sounding perturbed. "What's the drive doing now?" she asked.

"Damn thing can't make up its mind," Gren grumbled. "Oh, it hasn't reached 20% yet but I was just gonna call you anyway. Stayed steady for a bit, low, then it came and went, but now it's climbing fast and...hold on, it's starting to spike. Holy shit! It's over 30! Drop out *now!*"

Moire gestured frantically at Kilberton, who had heard the exchange with wide eyes. He executed a prompt and correct dropout from webspace while she made a brief shipwide announcement.

"Not a bad place to do it, actually, since we were going to have to do a course change anyway," she commented. Kilberton nodded, his attention fully on his board. Moire felt the dragging pull of the collapsing gravity bubble scratch along her bones, and resisted the urge to scratch. "Hey Gren, we're out. How long do you—"

A proximity alert screamed. Kilberton and Moire stared at each other in shock, and then Moire sprinted to the scan console.

"We're in the middle of freaking nowhere! What could we possibly be crashing into?" Moire complained as she fired up the scanner. First data up was the long-range, simple and fast. "Three objects in near proximity! Moving fast...oh dammit." Where was the visual? Did this crate have anything in its system for identification?

"What?" yelled Kilberton.

"Objects maneuvering at speed! We got ships here! Aaaand..." Oh yes, there was the visual. Her worst fears confirmed. "Crabs! Get us the hell out of here *now!*"

Moire frowned at the screen. The three crab ships hadn't reacted to their sudden appearance yet, and weren't heading in their direction either. In fact, they were moving away. A smaller blip ahead of two larger ones. The smaller blip jinked, and the larger ones matched course–and were closing.

"Hey, I think we got a crab fight going on here," Moire said slowly. "Got a lineup yet?" She glanced over. Kilberton was sweating, hands flying over the controls.

"It's weak, I'll need a good runup to get the lineup right..."

Moire turned back to the scanner. One of the big blips had changed course and was heading for them. "Crap, they've seen us! I'm going to realspace deck!" She slapped the main ship alarm and toggled the wrist control bracelet for the captain's earring as she ran. "All hands, all hands! Ship is under attack! Shipsuits at ready and go to emergency positions! This is not a drill!"

The realspace deck had its own displays, of course, but they took precious time to come on line. They had gotten sloppy, thinking because nothing *had* happened nothing would. Why were crabs out here anyway?

Moire fired up the realspace engines and put them at max speed away from the last known position of the pursuer. Maybe she could get Kilberton enough time for a lineup. The screens blinked on, and she cursed. The crab ship was almost on them already. *Frankenstein* was towing a ship nearly as big as it was, of course they couldn't outrun a crab raider. Close enough already for....

The ship shuddered, and alarms started to sound. "We've been hit!" she yelled. Time to get the guns going.

⚜

"Right, then–time to go," Harrington said bracingly to the Created, all looking at him fearfully for an explanation. "Get your suits ready to use. You will want to be able to seal up in an instant, believe me." He tapped out a brief message to the crab: Attack on ship, suit up. There wasn't much else they could do for him. He'd be safer in his own sealed quarters, which had two layers of pressurized walls, than anywhere else on the ship–and the crew were not entirely happy with his presence anyway.

He fumbled at the collar of his own suit, breathing deeply to try and calm his hammering heartbeat. Harrington knew how very fragile the protection of a shipsuit really was, from personal experience, and he resented being reminded of it.

"Everyone ready? Right then, stay close, and–"

WHAM.

The container they were in rocked hard, knocking them off their feet. Harrington's ears were ringing. A quick look around confirmed the walls were intact. He had a bad feeling that the same was not true in the cargo hold itself.

"Right. Not a drill. Anyone hurt? I suggest we leave now, before that

58

changes. And let's get ready to seal up, just in case."

He removed the safety cover from the oxygen capsule and dragged the crinkled clear material of the shipsuit hood over his face, but didn't seal it completely. The Created silently followed his example. They didn't appear panicked but it was hard to tell with them. When they were frightened, they tended to hide any outward expression of their feelings. A legacy of their experience with Toren, he had no doubt.

He grabbed the handle to the inspection door, swung it, and pushed. The door didn't budge. Harrington's stomach tightened. Even with the Created helping him, the door remained shut. So. Something was blocking the door. Not good.

Harrington cast around desperately, hoping his face didn't reveal how much danger they were in. There it was...the commlink usually left inside since the cargo hold didn't have wired-in comms for the containers. The ship shook again, but he didn't hear anything. A hit somewhere else?

"Bridge, this is Harrington. The children and I are trapped down in Radersent's hold. It appears we've got a hole and I can't open the container door."

A string of curses answered him. "I got two crab ships chasing us and trying to make more holes," yelled Cameron. "You got air?"

"For now. I will remind you that containers are not designed to be used as sealed environments."

More shudders, and shout from the comm. "Tagged him! Damn, if we just had something more than these pea-shooters on the keel..."

Something beeped, and Harrington looked up. Containers like this *were* designed to detect if their contents had been exposed to low pressures, and the vacuum sensor was blinking.

"Captain, the situation is becoming urgent."

The commlink pinged, the intercom pinlight glowing. "All hands, crab hold has lost pressure! Anyone not on emergency duty, suit up and get those people out of there." There was a pause after the intercom shut off, and then Cameron said, "Hey, doesn't Radersent's quarters have an airlock?"

"Yes, but there's a security lock on the outside he can't open."

"I can from here. Tell him. I don't think I can get anyone else to you fast enough, and he's strong."

Harrington felt himself starting to pant, darkness crowding the edges of his vision. "Oxygen! Now!" he croaked, sealing his hood and starting the first capsule. Everyone had three. The Created didn't hesitate. Looking through the window he saw Radersent was already suited up, in his strange baggy suit. Quickly he composed the message. "Radersent go out. Open human door." He pointed, to make sure the crab understood. "Danger humans."

When Radersent seemed to hesitate, he added "Danger children. Open human door now ouch." He wasn't sure why that word was in the list, but he decided it couldn't hurt.

Radersent moved. Harrington hoped the outer door had been unlocked successfully. A minute ticked by, and then he was startled by scraping and banging noises coming from their door. Radersent had gotten out and was removing the obstruction. Harrington motioned to the Created, and as they touched hoods he yelled, "Let's get this door open!"

"Any luck?" Moire shouted.

"No! I need at least three minutes static!"

She swore under her breath. Kilberton wasn't going to get anything near that with things the way they were. Since she'd gotten the guns going at least the crab ships were staying at a respectful distance, but they were getting a few shots in anyway since a freighter doing evasive maneuvers was pure comedy. She had to think of something else.

Moire fired again at one ship that was getting too close, looked at the gun readouts, and swore again, even louder. They had more ammo than that, didn't they? Maybe one of the hits had damaged the feed, because she was showing only five more shells for that gun.

Think. What did she have to work with? She had to get more distance or they were all going to die. If only they weren't towing that huge wreck, she could get more speed...

A slow smile spread across her face. Dropping the wreck would get them speed, and it would give her the biggest damn shell anybody had ever seen. Trouble was, she only had one and it would be the devil to aim.

She opened the comm to Engineering. "Gren! What happens if you shut off the rear nodes?"

A sucking sound, like he'd taken a really deep breath. "You want to get rid of the wreck?"

"I want to drop it on them."

"Can't just shut the nodes off, it'll still be moving with our velocity. Need to reverse 'em."

Just like spitting out a watermelon seed. "Can you do it?"

"Can do, just say the word. Hang on to something though; could be a backflow pulse with our gravitics."

Moire eyed the scanner screens. Just a little too far apart...she dodged, slowed, turned sharply, then sped up. The crab ships followed on the turn, getting closer to one another. Good as it was going to get. "Drop it, Gren!" she screamed.

The door was finally open with Radersent's assistance, but the effort meant they were on their second capsule and still hadn't left the hold. Even all the time spent conversing with the crab didn't prevent the hairs on the back of Harrington's neck from standing up when he saw Radersent standing outside, without a barrier of any kind between them. He seemed...more real. More dangerous.

The hold was a mess. Harrington could see where the enemy weapon had hit, going through both sides. No wonder they had lost pressure so quickly. He gestured to the Created to follow him, moving carefully through the debris. All of it sharp. He looked back and saw Radersent bringing up the rear. Did the crab think he was supposed to come with them?

Then he saw the stairs. A falling beam had hit them, in the upper section, and some of the steps were missing. The ones below looked damaged too. How were they going to get past that?

Harrington saw some cable, but one end was trapped and he had nothing to cut it with. Alan tapped him on the shoulder, and pantomimed throwing something. Seeing Harrington's puzzlement, he tapped himself, then Harrington, and again mimicked throwing something, and then bending down and pulling. Harrington blinked. They were *that* strong? Well, it wasn't as if they had much choice in the time remaining to them.

He led the way up the stairs, making them keep to the wall edge where the stairs were strongest. Radersent still followed, the Created other than Alan huddling close to him. His one good forelimb extended around them, as if for protection.

Alan was indeed strong enough to throw him the needed distance, although Harrington had a bad moment, barely managing to break his fall before landing and possibly rupturing his suit hood. Then it was easier, one Created lifting and Harrington pulling. With Alan the last, Radersent stepped cautiously up the stairs. Harrington could see the metal treads bending under the crab's weight, but they held. Alan glanced at the crab and allowed Radersent's forelimb to extend around his waist. The crab didn't throw him so much as crouch and allow his powerful hindlegs to suddenly extend, but it was enough for the rest of them to grab Alan and pull him to safety.

Radersent turned to go. Ash wailed silently in her hood, her arms reaching out to him as the others held her back. Radersent turned his long head, and one tendril rotated to one side, then the other. *No.* It was a human gesture; eerie to see it being done by a crab.

Harrington tapped Ash on the shoulder and tilted his head toward the exit. They still had to get to the pressure door on this level.

The ship rocked. Gravity changed direction, slamming them into the wall and then nearly tossing them over the railing. Harrington held on grimly.

Radersent was not so lucky. The stairs that had barely held him buckled and collapsed, throwing him against a broken metal beam. The long, narrow head jerked up suddenly and the crab writhed. Something dark was visible on the loose, rubbery surface of the crab's suit where the beam had hit him–then something different, like ocher bubbles erupted and collapsed, forming a dark red blob over the hole. Radersent moved then, slowly, from the wrecked stairs to the roof of his quarters. He twitched, tried to continue, and stopped.

Harrington pushed the Created out ahead. Third capsule now, they had no time. They found the pressure door and opened it, and to his profound relief there was a full-suited crewmember on the other side. As soon as atmosphere was restored Harrington ripped off his shipsuit hood and tapped the helmet impatiently.

"Get that off and give it to me! I have to go back!"

CHAPTER 5
STRANGERS WITH CANDY

Moire felt the itchy shudder in her bones and slammed the realspace engines as fast as they could go, swearing and feverishly trying to keep her eye on three displays at once. If they missed—the sudden flare of light on the screen made her smile grimly and shake her head. She'd done *something*, and as soon as she made sure they were out of the debris field she'd find out how lucky they'd been.

There was no way to aim the wreck and she hadn't tried. It was more a matter of making sure the crabs would run into it when it suddenly appeared in their flight path. She'd guessed right; the crabs hadn't been able to dodge in time. From what she could see on the long-range it hadn't been a direct hit but the next best thing—a glancing blow that ripped the entire side of the enemy ship open. As she watched, the second crab ship pursuing *Frankenstein* shuddered, struck by a large chunk of wreckage. It slowed and moved erratically for a moment, spikes of energy showing up on the radiation meter. Moire turned her ship head-on, to minimize their target area and bring the one remaining gun with ammunition to bear, but then the second ship suddenly blew up.

"Damn, but yer quick, Captain!" Yolanda said breathlessly on the comm.

"Not me. Self-detonation," Moire snapped, scanning for more unfriendly ships. "They do that if they can't get away after a fight." The screen was clean except for the little crab ship that the other two had been attacking before *Frankenstein* showed up. It wasn't moving at all.

"If we can hold position just a bit longer I think I've got the lineup," Kilberton said.

"Status! Everybody report in!" yelled Moire on the shipwide channel. "Are the kids safe?"

"We got 'em out, sure," said a voice over the crackling comm. "But that nutty reporter took my suit and went back in."

Moire could hear loud noises in the background, like someone was wailing. Why had Harrington gone back into the damaged hold? Unless ...

"Any injuries?"

"No."

"*Yes!*" This time she recognized the wailing voice. It was Ash. "Radersent is hurt! He was helping us get out and he fell and his suit got a hole and stuff came out of it!"

That explained Harrington, then. More reports came in. The drills had paid off–injuries, a few serious, but nobody had died. The ship had taken damage but mostly in the open, unpressurized towing section, which made sense since that was the biggest part of the ship. Engines needed some care in use but were quite capable of getting them out. They could work around the hull breaches while they got things re-sealed.

Satisfied she still had a working ship, Moire tried contacting Harrington. "How bad is it?" she asked.

There was only muffled swearing and grunting for a moment, and she started to worry. "Bad. I thought I saw one of his tendrils move, but that's it. I'm trying to get him back in his quarters."

Damn. Crabs attack her ship and the only serious casualty was a crab. A crab they couldn't afford to lose, since he was their only means of communicating with them. Ennis and Fleet wouldn't be happy either.

Moire checked the scanner again. The damaged crab ship still had not moved. She wondered if it could. Why hadn't it destructed already? Was it so badly damaged it couldn't even do that? And what had they interrupted, some crab-on-crab violence?

They needed a crab medic. The crabs on that ship probably needed help to survive. What if they could trade? Trouble was, their translator wasn't available. Even if he was, they hadn't worked out long-distance communications and she didn't want to get close enough to get shot at until they had established a truce. Assuming her crew would even let her.

"Captain, I have a lineup. Do I engage the drive?" Kilberton said urgently.

She thought for a moment, conflicted. "Hang tight. Nobody is shooting at us–the remaining ship is damaged and out of range. Let's see if Gren wants to make any repairs before we go into drive." She called Yolanda to the gunner's chair and dropped down to the bridge level, bringing up Gren's code on the captain's earring controls as she went to her tiny office.

"Yeah?" Gren grunted. He didn't sound too worried. "Ship took a beating. Be a good idea to look at the cooling systems and anything large before we go into drive," he said when she asked. "If you think we're not gonna get any more surprises, I want to give 'em a once-over."

Moire took a deep breath. "OK, one more thing. Radersent is badly hurt. We don't know how to fix him. There's a ship full of crabs that owe us a favor for getting rid of their enemies, and–" She winced and yanked the earring from her ear. Gren's yelling could still be heard from the earpiece in her hand. When it died down a bit she put it back on.

"...how can you even *think* about doing that! Of all the stupid, suicidal.... What makes you think they aren't just trying to lure us in closer?"

"Gren, have you ever tried to set up a fake ambush in mid-space just *hoping* somebody would happen on that exact spot? The little crab ship took damage from the other two; I saw it before they even noticed we were there. Baby never once moved aggressively toward us, it was trying to get away. Plus, in all the time I've faced crabs in battle I've never heard once of them sitting around admiring the view if human ships were anywhere in the vicinity. They fought, ran, or blew themselves up if they couldn't do anything else. I think they're hurt bad, Gren."

He muttered something corrosively profane. "So? I'm not saying we kill 'em or anything, but why risk the ship? We got lucky. Don't push it."

Moire sighed, and slumped in her chair. "How about using the runabout? We could send it remote with some kind of signal device. See if we can get close without getting shot. The kids mentioned something about a screen, or maybe we could use that new gizmo Harrington gave us."

Gren didn't say anything for a moment, which was encouraging. Better than the yelling, anyway.

"Why's this so important?" he asked finally. "You don't usually take risks like this, not with your ship and crew anyway."

"Radersent got hurt rescuing the kids. They would have died if he hadn't opened that shelter before their air gave out. He acted like crew back there. I take risks for my crew."

He sighed heavily. "I don't think your *real* crew is going to like this. If you do it remote and don't take stupid risks, though, I can live with it. But let's not hang around trying to make it work. Something brought all these ships here; there could be more coming."

That was Gren, always trying to cheer her up.

"We're going to wait for Gren to run some system checks," Moire said, seeing Kilberton's head swivel her direction when she left her office. "Are you lined up?"

"Yes. Is there anything wrong?"

"Nah, but he wants to make sure nothing is loose. I'm going to do some checking too. Keep my comm line keyed on. You too, Yolanda," Moire called up to the gun position. "Watch that ship and let me know if they so much as twitch. I'll see if we can't get the shell feed fixed too so we've got more than one gun."

She jogged down the corridors, noting damage and eyeballing crew. So far everyone looked shook up but not panicky. Gren would need someone to configure the runabout, and she had to find the communication device and figure out what to get it to say.

She found the walking wounded and people without an immediate task in the galley, as she'd expected. George and Hideo were bickering and cleaning up some supplies that had launched themselves from a locker with a defective catch. Ash was mopping up a pool of sticky liquid and describing with wide eyes and expansive gestures her escape from the hold to some sober-faced crew. She saw Moire and scrambled to her feet. "We have to get Radersent and put him in the med scanner so he will get better!"

Moire wrapped an arm around her. "Where's Alan?"

"He went to help with fixing," said Hideo. "We're cleaning messes even though we didn't make them this time."

"Can you help Radersent?" said Ash, tugging at her and looking worried.

"Harrington is with him," Moire said soothingly.

"But—"

"Even if we brought him here, we can't fix him. Our med scanner only works with humans."

"But the med scanner can fix *everything!* And he's hurt!"

"Is there really nothing we can do for him?" asked Kwife Ivers, the assistant engineer. He had some nasty gashes on his head and one leg stretched out stiffly in front of him.

Moire took a deep breath. "Maybe. I'm working on it. Where's Inathka?"

"In quarters. You want her?"

"I want that comm device she was working on."

Hideo looked up from his cleaning. "It's in the repair place. I saw it there."

Even better, no awkward questions from the ship's outsider. "OK, kids, you can leave the cleaning for later. I need you to help me. Hideo, go get that device and meet us at the maintenance bay."

"What are you going to do?" Ash asked.

"I'm going to see if we can do something to fix Radersent."

⚜

It was no-one's fault but his own, really. But what else could he have done? The Created were only in shipsuits on their last oxygen capsules. The heavy-duty working suits like the one he was wearing were in limited supply, and more importantly, in use elsewhere getting their damaged ship put back together. It was fortunate they had not needed to take this one back.

On the other hand, if they had come to get him he could have persuaded them to help get Radersent back to his quarters. The crab was extremely heavy and awkward to get a grip on. Harrington had been forced to use a length of cable tied underneath Radersent's forelimbs. He fervently hoped he wasn't doing any more damage to the already wounded crab.

At least he was still alive, and appeared to understand what Harrington was doing. As much as he could, he was helping. He couldn't stand or walk, though.

Harrington took a look around, panting with exertion. There was just enough room in the worksuit for him to pull one arm back into the center and wipe his face, and he did. He had managed, somehow, to get Radersent to the edge of the cargo container with his quarters. Now he had to get the crab down to the entrance–again, without causing more damage–and inside. The security door, fortunately, was already open. The crab airlock could be more of an issue.

First things first. What he needed was something like a ramp, Radersent twitched, spasming, and Harrington knelt beside him feeling helpless. He lightly touched the head-tendrils on one side, hoping that would be understood as a comforting gesture.

"Not to worry; we'll soon have you out of this," he said bracingly, forcing all of the worst-case scenarios firmly from his imagination. One tendril tightened around his wrist, then loosened. Enough blather–if Radersent was going to survive he had to *do* something.

The main lights had died or had been turned off and the remaining emergency lights were faint, which meant he had to search the wreckage up close, within range of his suit light. Harrington examined a bulkhead beam with fragments of hull still attached. It would make a nice ramp, but was far too heavy for him to move. Nearby, however, was a smaller cross-beam under some debris. It wasn't very wide, but perhaps he could find another.

He wrapped his arms around the protruding metal and heaved. It shifted, a little, and he rearranged his grip and lifted with all of his strength. Suddenly the entire thing came free and he slipped and fell hard. Something smashed into his legs, making him gasp with pain, and as he struggled to get up he nearly impaled his hand on a sharp spike of metal nearby. Harrington broke out in a cold sweat, suddenly realizing he could have landed on it. The last thing they needed was another wounded person.

Working carefully, he pried up the wreckage trapping his feet. No suit tears, fortunately–it appeared Moire Cameron provided her crew with sturdy equipment. It made him wonder what else they did in their spare time. He dragged the small beam to the crab container, limping all the way, and put it in place. It wasn't enough, he could tell, and where was he going to get more?

Harrington sagged against the container wall, pain and despair overwhelming him.

"I don't have *time* to give up," he whispered to himself. No more beams. Lots of debris, however, including the piece he'd nearly killed himself on. He could pile that up, perhaps. There wasn't time for that either, but he wouldn't think of that now.

As he was moving his third chunk of wreckage, a gleam of light at the top of the stairs caught his eye. A suited figure–he couldn't tell who–was descending, barely hesitating to deploy a wireframe ladder over the missing section. They had a carrybox on their back. Harrington stared, bemused. His first thought was someone had been sent to bring him back. The next was to wonder if his suit comm was broken, since he hadn't heard anything from the crew since the captain had contacted him.

As they got closer, he saw it was the chief engineer, Gren. Gren tapped his wrist and held up three fingers. Harrington stared at him, puzzled, then enlightenment dawned. Channel three. Now, how did one change the comm channel in this thing?

There, he had it. Gren was unlatching the carrybox fastenings from his suit and swinging it down, grumbling all the while.

"...and she wants it kept quiet for now, no point in getting everyone upset until we get them talking to us. So where is he?"

Harrington just pointed, too tired and confused to talk. 'She' obviously meant the captain, but the rest was a mystery.

"Radersent is too heavy for me to lift," he finally gasped. "He can't walk. I'm trying to get him down...."

Gren jumped up on the one narrow beam that was leaning against the crab shelter, glanced around and then up at the curving hull above, and grunted. He then went to the carrybox, rummaged inside, and took out a handful of components that he assembled and clamped to an intact bulkhead.

"Good you've got that rail there," Gren said, threading cable through the device. "Take some of the weight. He doesn't have anything like a latch point on his suit, does he?" Harrington shook his head. Radersent's suit was a loose, leathery thing. "Guess we have to load him on something."

Harrington had already scouted out a piece of loose sheet metal for precisely that purpose. "It might be a trifle small, I'm afraid," he said, once he got it up to the container roof and saw how big Radersent really was.

Gren glanced up, looked at the crab and the sheet of metal, and shook his head. "Should be fine. Just need center of mass and something for us to grab on to." He made an adjustment to the tool he held and quickly drilled some holes in the metal sheet, then threaded one end of the cable through and fastened it off. "Let's get him loaded."

"You are quite efficient at this," Harrington wheezed as they both tried to get a grip on the crab and shift him on to the improvised sled. He felt the crab shudder as they lifted, and hoped they hadn't hurt him.

"What we do most of the time," Gren said curtly. "Move around damaged ships. First time it was our own, though."

The cable device acted as both a tug and a brake, and with both of them to guide it, the sled descended the rail without mishap. Gren shifted the device to move Radersent to the entrance to his quarters, and they faced their next difficulty. Neither of them had ever seen the crab airlock in action.

As they stood there, studying it, Harrington felt a tap on his leg. Radersent was conscious.

"Think he can do it?" Gren asked dubiously.

"I rather think we don't have a choice," Harrington said. "We could ask

68

him if we had the translator—but that's inside too."

Gren was very strong, fortunately, because Harrington was exhausted. Reporting was not supposed to be so physically demanding; he distinctly remembered thinking that was an advantage. Somehow he never ended up with the easy kind of assignments. He would have to think about why.

He concentrated on watching what Radersent was doing, held up by two straining humans. They would have to get out again at some point, after all. This airlock was not as sophisticated as the one he'd heard about on the crab ship, but it did rotate and shrink in on itself before sliding away. With some awkward shuffling and stumbling, they managed to fit in the suddenly crowded lock chamber and then position Radersent to cycle.

Harrington had only seen the crab's quarters from the human side of the window. It seemed different in the slightly thick, foggy atmosphere and dim light. Radersent feebly indicated a surface with curved indentations and branchlike structures that must serve him as a bed, and they dragged him the last few meters. The crab twisted and sank down on the bed, forelimbs dangling.

"What now? Is he still awake?" Gren tilted his head, looking at Radersent.

"I wonder how he removes his suit, or if we—" Harrington stopped, seeing the slow, twisty motion of the head tendrils. The top surface of the crab's suit split and folded down, revealing his head. Harrington wasn't sure if there was any damage, but he was quite sure the dark, thick fluid near the throat slit should not be there. "Hell and damnation. We don't even know how to put a bandage on him."

"Maybe we can ask, now," Gren grunted. "You stay here. I've got to modify the communication console anyway."

"Why?"

Gren gave him a humorless grin. "Captain wants to talk to the *other* crabs. The ones in the dead ship right out there." He pointed towards the hull.

Harrington was so stunned he didn't even protest as the engineer cycled through the crab airlock. The controls were simple enough, fortunately, but it was still a relief to see Gren on the other side of the window. Harrington puzzled out what the crab side of the device looked like and tried to shift it closer to the wounded Radersent. It took a few attempts until he figured out a steady pressure released it from whatever was holding it in place.

Gren, meanwhile, had performed whatever modifications were needed to the system. "All right, how do you use this thing?"

"The display has a list of terms we know—or think we know. You string together what you want to say, and send it."

"Huh." Gren peered at the console, tapped at it for a minute, and looked up. "Got anything on your end?"

Something had definitely happened to the device Harrington was holding. What he had thought was just more of the grainy material the crabs used for everything had faint glowing markings that changed, fluctuating and gradually fading. Radersent twitched, his tendrils limp but straining to reach the device. He touched it, seemed to lightly caress it, then the tendrils fell loose.

"Did he say anything?"

"Acknowledged the message, I think."

Harrington looked at the engineer carefully. "What message?"

"That we're going to try and get those crabs outside to patch him up."

"OK, we're getting the visual feed," Moire said. The others gathered around the communications console or craned their necks from their positions.

"Whaddya see?" Yolanda Menehune shouted down from the gun turret.

Gren pointed to the display. "Think they got holed like we did. See that? Only whatever hit us went right through. Theirs detonated inside their ship."

It was hard to tell with only dim starlight for illumination, but one section of the dark crab ship was even darker, and reflected nothing. Moire narrowed her eyes. Had there been motion in the darkness? The scanner magnification was already at max. "I'm going in closer."

"Are you recording this?" asked Harrington.

Moire sighed. "All right, we'll record it. It's not going to be cleared for publication anytime soon, though." She flicked the switch.

"I'm sure Fleet would be interested," he said, deadpan.

"Do tell," she answered, refusing to look at him. The little runabout scooted closer. She wondered if the crabs had detected it yet, or if their sensors were down too.

There. Definite movement. The vague outline of one...two crabs. Possibly a third. The one in front was wearing a spacesuit very similar to Radersent's, and held something against its narrow chest–something with a star-shaped base, and a long, deep cup on the front. Moire stopped the runabout.

"I think their detectors work," she said, keeping her tone even. "Looks like the guy on point has a weapon." Or it was a crab vid-camera and that was the local reporter, recording for posterity. "On the bright side, they are still alive."

"How is that the bright side?" Gren grumbled.

"Well, we could go through the ship and hope we find the first aid supplies but without a translator we'd end up using Soup of the Day instead of bloodglue. We need *live* crabs, Gren. And I'll point out Hotshot there hasn't fired yet."

"Probably out of range," Gren muttered, but without heat. "Close enough for the screen?"

Moire shook her head. "I don't think so. I'm going to try the lights first anyway."

Just to make sure, she nudged the runabout sideways. The armed crab followed with his weapon. That was impressive; she doubted she could have seen it at that distance. Time for the light show.

One. One two. One two three.

One. One two. One two three.

"How long are you going to keep that up?" Gren wanted to know.

"I don't want to risk the gear unnecessarily, and they've got every right to be paranoid. We're not desperate yet. I think. Hey Harrington—what's the word from Perwaty? Radersent still with us?"

Harrington shook his head, lips compressed thinly. "No change. He seems to fade in and out of consciousness, and doesn't move much."

On the other hand, they had a ways to go to get from Fundamentals of Counting to "take me to your medic," and Radersent could take a turn for the worse any minute.

Nothing from the gaping hole in the crab ship. The figures there weren't moving.

"Captain, I'm seeing something from...I guess it's the front. Flashing light." Yolanda called down to the bridge.

Moire stopped the runabout display. "Did you see how many?"

"Not sure. There's a bit of stuff sticking out that blocks it from my position."

Moire glanced at Gren, who started punching through available vid pickups. "That should be it. Give it a try," he said, without turning his head from the display. Moire hid a smile. Despite his gloomy predictions, Gren was as excited as the rest of them now.

She started the display run again, just once.

"Lights! And there's...four flashes. Just four."

Yolanda gave a whoop, and Moire let out a breath. The release of tension on the bridge was palpable. Maybe this would work after all. It seemed reasonable to conclude the crabs were willing to talk, or at least able to understand that's what the humans wanted to do. Of course, they might be trying to lure them in for a suicidal attack, but that didn't seem to be the crab way.

"Time for Phase Two, Captain?" Harrington asked.

"Yeah. Let's get in a little closer. You know," she said, shaking her head, "I really didn't think we'd end up conducting negotiations with an alien race using cartoons."

"Given the mind-numbing tedium of the vast majority of diplomatic negotiations I have suffered through, it could start a delightful trend. Shall I bring up the first of the series?"

Moire nodded. The runabout was drifting closer, and she kept a careful eye on the armed crab to see if there was any hostile reaction. The screen output was also being displayed on another, smaller screen on the comm console. George had really done a good job on short notice. Simple black-and-white images like they had used with Radersent. They already had stylized human and crab outlines in use, so only a few more graphics were needed.

The first sequence showed two humans on one side of a thick line, and two crabs on the other. Letters drifted from one human to the other and back again, and squiggly symbols between the crabs. Then there was just a crab, a human, and a little console. Letters flowed from the human to the console, and came out as the same symbols used between the cartoon crabs, and their symbols changed to letters.

She let that run repeatedly until the runabout was barely five meters away from the watching crabs, and stopped the runabout. The one with the weapon seemed transfixed, and she could see the head tendrils now, only loosely touching the device it held. There were more crabs too, she could see them in the darkness. One, in fact, that was huge, a third again as big as the others.

"I think we have their attention," she murmured. "What do you say, Gren? Looks like we have at least five there, including the giant." Gren just grunted, focused on the screen. "OK, let's hope they understand we have a translator. Next set."

This was the tricky part. She was counting on them being completely desperate, or it wouldn't work. Now the cartoon showed a simplified *Frankenstein*, an outline of the crab ship, and the runabout going from one to the other. In an inspired bit of design, George had even added the blinking count-sequence to the runabout. The runabout left the human ship, a cartoon crab got on, and both returned to the human ship where a human stood next to the translator.

Gren pursed his lips. "They aren't gonna go for it."

"None of their options are ideal," Harrington said. "And we have no information one way or the other on which they would consider preferable."

As far as Moire could tell, there was definite death from starvation, freezing, or atmosphere loss, definite death if their enemies found them again, or slightly less-than-definite death chatting with rampaging humans that had not yet shot at them personally.

The minutes stretched on. They had another set of cartoons, reassuringly showing the brave volunteer crab being returned to its ship, but she wanted to keep it simple. Of course the crabs were going to discuss their choices. It would take time.

A few minutes later, there was movement again. She wasn't sure, but it looked like the giant crab had raised one forelimb, and then the armed crab stepped forward to the edge of the ragged hole in the hull.

"Nuh-uh. No crab marines on my ship." Moire scooted the runabout back, to make it clear.

"Wait—what's it doing?" Gren pointed to the screen. The armed crab was removing the device hanging from its neck and offering it to another crab.

"Of course, for all we know they've got thermal grenades in their trousers," Harrington murmured in a voice low enough only she could hear.

"Stop trying to cheer me up," Moire muttered, and gently moved the runabout back to the crab ship, turning it to allow the crab to board. "Looks like we've got a passenger. Anybody see if that crab's holding on?"

"Practically wrapped around the controls, Captain," Yolanda called down.

"Right. Diplomacy time. Yolanda, Kilberton, stay at your positions, same orders. Interrupt any time you feel like it, your comms have priority override. Gren, get back to the engines and lock down. Everybody, be ready to go the instant I say the word. Any questions?"

Gren looked like he had a lot of complaints, but he just sighed, shook his head, and clomped out. Kilberton hesitated, then said "I would feel better if you were armed."

"I've already got two people with rifles in the cargo area, and more in the corridor," Moire said. "We don't have a lot of vacuum-capable guns and they're pretty noticeable."

"Take a knife," Yolanda called down. "Crab's in a suit, all you'd have to do is cut it." Something tumbled down and hit the deck—a knife in an arm sheath. Moire took it out. It was a dark, oily-looking blade. Ferro-ceramic.

Well, she could handle that better than a gun, and it would make her crew happier. "Thanks. Wish me luck."

Moire trotted down the corridors to where the armed crew were gathered. Her suit was waiting, and she hastily put it on, remembering to strap on the knife. It barely fit over the suit. She toggled the comm. "Kilberton, where's the crab?"

"Just now coming up. I am about to turn it around the ship."

"Can you get it through the hole in the hold?"

"Perwaty has the vid set up; it shouldn't be a problem."

Moire negotiated the pressure doors between the corridors and the still-ventilated cargo hold, and started down the damaged stairs. She could see two suited figures shifting debris away from the hole in the hull—that was good. Not very polite to damage their visitor before they'd even had a chance to talk, after all.

There it was. A little silver dot, getting closer. A darker, irregular shape visible on top, partly obscured by the display screen attached to the runabout. She checked to make sure the knife was secure.

"OK, everyone, let's keep it tight. Rifles, get in position and check your field of fire. Mr. Harrington has volunteered to be Ship's Greeter; please do not shoot him." She'd argued that since it was her idea, she should be the one to take point but there had been a minor insurrection and she'd had to back down. Moire wondered where all the unfettered power of command was and when she would get it. Everyone agreed, however, that the Created were to stay in their rooms with the doors locked from the outside, no matter how "unfair" it was.

The runabout slowly drifted through the hole in the hull. They'd launched it from there so they knew it would fit, but now it had a fairly bulky passenger and limited visibility to guide it.

"Harrington—get on the command channel and help Kilberton guide it in. Is there enough room, or should we run out a gangplank?"

"I don't believe that will be necessary, Captain. Although appropriate and in keeping with your piratical cover, the allusion would, I believe, be lost on our guest." Harrington broke off and started giving directions to avoid a collision with a twisted beam before she could respond in kind.

She could see the crab distinctly now, hunkered down and holding on with every available appendage. She wondered what it was thinking. Incoherent desperation?

"Right, that's a good spot—set it down," Harrington said. The crab didn't move when the runabout rested on the deck. Harrington moved closer, and Moire thought she saw the crab twitch.

"Hang on a second. I think our crab is a bit nervous."

He stopped. "We don't have an infinite amount of time, Captain," he said, turning to look at her.

"I am aware. Try waving and pointing, or something."

That at least got the crab's attention, and when Harrington started walking towards Radersent's quarters, then stopping and looking back at the crab, eventually the message got through. The crab moved slowly and stiffly, head turning with every step. Moire followed at a distance, which had the effect of hurrying the crab. She could tell when the crab airlock came into view—the crab's tendrils fluttered, and then, strangely, the crab seemed more relaxed. At least, the crab only balked a little at entering the airlock with Harrington.

"That's a brave crab, all right," Moire commented, moving for the human side of the setup. "From what Radersent told us, these guys still have us confused with their long-lost enemy."

"Oh yeah, those Breakers or whatever," Yolanda chimed in. "Still no movement from that ship, Captain. Ran a scan just now. Their IR profile is degrading, and the rest too. I think that ship is dead. No kinda power anywhere."

Well. Interesting, and provided a possible reason for their cooperation. Gradual heat-loss in a suit was a very slow and unpleasant way to die.

Through the window was an interesting scene—two humans, two crabs. Perwaty was kneeling by Radersent. The other crab was standing nearby, and Moire could tell they were talking. Tendrils rustled; in Radersent's case, weakly, but he was still moving. The other crab had deflated its suit helmet.

It was very strange how much her idea of a crab was based on Radersent. This crab had a narrower head that seemed lean and hollowed out, comparatively. The skin was grey, shaded in places, but with none of the dark marks Radersent had.

"Visitor's in the crab quarters," Moire said for the benefit of those outside. "Radersent's having a chat. So far so good."

Something going on. More crab talking, Radersent trying to move his one working forelimb. His tendrils extending, holding still. Pointing to the console.

The strange crab moved. It saw her in the window and cringed, almost collapsing to the ground. Had she startled it? No, it was holding the same position. Then its tendrils went out, fully, in a fan shape. It was almost exactly what Radersent did when he saw her, except this crab did not show its throat.

Still staying low, it shifted closer to the console. Even with Radersent providing help, the device seemed to puzzle it. After few minutes it managed to send a message.

THIS HE BELONG SHE SHIP COMPONENT LEFT RIGHT UP DOWN YES GO.

Moire raised an eyebrow. This could take a while. Radersent had clearly adapted to human speech modes, and they didn't have two years to train this one. Well, first things first.

QUERY NAME, she sent.

THIS HE ENGINE FOUR WATCH was the reply. Good enough. Engine Four Watch appeared to be watching her with apprehension, judging from the taut tendrils.

Moire sent HUMAN NOT BREAK CRAB SMALL SHIP. QUERY CRAB SMALL SHIP BREAK HUMAN.

Some discussion with Radersent, then careful manipulation of the console. CRAB SMALL SHIP BROKEN NOT BREAK HUMAN BROKEN BROKEN NO FIGHT HELP.

That seemed to be OK too. The last bit was a trifle obscure, but the message confirmed her suspicions and gave her hope. Now for the big one.

RADERSENT NEED FIX. QUERY CRAB SMALL SHIP FIX RADERSENT YES.

"Captain, I'm seeing some strange signals on the scan," Kilberton broke in. "Coming from our position."

"Yeah, not really surprising. Probably Engine Four Watch here calling back for instructions. He's got to have some kind of commlink; I wouldn't send one of my people out without one. Keep an eye on it and record if you can."

Engine Four Watch appeared to have received instructions, and was now eagerly sending a message. QUERY HUMAN MOVE CRAB STAR STAR SMALL SHIP YES HELP.

"Huh. That I was not expecting. Radersent must have told them about *Frankenstein*," Moire said.

"Move the ship in webspace?" Kilberton asked. "That is what came over the link here; is that really what he said?"

"Apparently. I agree this isn't a healthy neighborhood, but I would have thought they would want help getting their ship working again."

"We can't fix their tech, but we can take 'em where someone can—and that would be crabs with *working* ships. And guns. I don't like it," Gren said pointedly.

"Yeah, and we have working guns too, or will as soon as you get the ammo feed fixed," Moire replied. "Look at it from their perspective. They'd be introducing armed, dangerous aliens somewhere they call home. If we take them via webspace they can't call ahead and set up an ambush either. We can work something out where we just go, dump 'em, and leave. Straight reversal, don't even need to change lineup."

"Huh." Gren was silent, thinking.

"It is true," Kilberton said. "If we know we will do no changes, a simple dropout to normal space and back again is very quick. We would only need to know how long to drop out to safely release their ship."

Yeah, wouldn't want to smash these guys up like the wreck they had been towing. That would be rude. Moire thought for a few minutes, reviewing the options, the dangers. They needed more information, such as where the crabs wanted to be dropped off, and how bad their life support situation was, and the prognosis on getting Radersent back on his pseudopods.

"Harrington and Perwaty, you guys take over the questions. See if you can get coordinates worked out, but don't show them any starmaps with station names, OK? Everybody else, Officer's meeting on the bridge. You too, Gren. Get Ivers to lock down again after you leave."

The mood was serious but not somber on the bridge, which Moire considered a good sign.

"Comms off? OK, people, tell me what you think. Is this too much of a risk for you?"

After an initial hesitation, Yolanda Menehune said "How sure are we they aren't gonna lead us into a trap?"

"They can try, but I don't see how they can get us in time without shooting their guys. And I think we can agree these crabs are in fact stuck in a dying ship and desperate to stay alive. So, they will want to get to someplace they regard as safe. Hence, no withering cross-fire. Not until the ship is free anyway and by then we'll be gone."

Gren sighed. "Still a risk. Is it worth it?"

"We can learn more about the crabs, which might help Fleet," Kilberton pointed out. "Besides, Radersent will die if he does not receive medical attention. They have agreed to help him if we help them, and we should keep our word."

"I'm worried about their ship," Gren said, surprisingly. "How are they gonna stay alive long enough to get where they want to go?"

"If there are problems they must have some way to deal with it," said Moire. "All Engine Four Watch asked about was a tow. Any other questions?" Nobody said anything. "Right. Vote. In favor of crab rescue?"

The only vote against was Gren. "I don't want Radersent to die, but I just don't trust 'em!" he said. "We got the whole ship to think about."

"You're right. I'm worried about that too, so I want you to come up with countermeasures. They can't get up to much when they are in tow, but let's make sure it can't happen at all." Moire switched on the bridge connection to the crab communication console and enabled the general comm link to Perwaty and Harrington. "Hey, how's the interrogation going? Got the location?"

"Er, yes. We think so." The note of constraint in Harrington's voice was noticeable. "Captain, there may be a disturbing development. Perwaty thought to ask what they were doing in the middle of nowhere."

"And?"

"Well, if I understand this correctly—'star-star' is the way to say webspace, correct? They were on their way somewhere else, the location they gave us, in fact, and they were forced out."

Moire frowned, not understanding, then drew a deep breath. "Forced out of *webspace*? By those two enemy ships?" That was impossible. Webspace was safe; nobody could detect a ship in drive until it dropped out of the gravity bubble. And yet....

"Gren. What would have happened if we had kept going with the anomaly building like it was?"

He stared at her. "The instability would collapse the—oh. They did that to *us*? But...I've never heard of this before."

"Probably because it worked," Yolanda said sourly.

Moire shook her head. It was starting to make sense, finally. "No. It happened to us because we had a section of ship that looked, gravitics-wise, like a crab ship! Remember? We tuned it that way to tow the one Radersent came from and never changed it. That's why we landed in the middle of that fight! The bad guys were after that little ship but got us too."

"Then it could work for human ships." Kilberton's normally dark face was an unhealthy grey. "It's just tuning. They could do it to us. They have a way of scanning webspace. Fleet," he said carefully, "needs to know this."

CHAPTER 6
BASE CANARDS

"Hey, there he is!"

Ennis looked up from his datapad and stifled a grin. His contact, the guy he'd been waiting for in the commons for the last hour, was standing in the doorway with a stunned what-did-I-do expression.

"Don't worry, Max. I'm the one who's in trouble. Or would be, if I was guilty as accused. Go ahead, show 'em what you brought me."

Max gave him a dubious look, shrugged, and pulled out a handful of textsheets from his jacket pocket. Svena pounced on them and started scrolling with an eager expression while the rest of the group tried to look over her shoulders.

"Awww. It's just stupid circulars," Svena announced with great disappointment.

Ennis nodded. "Just like I said. Now pay up."

"What did they think they were?" Max asked, now completely confused.

"Love letters, blackmail demands, pornography, illicit copies of *Cosmographica*, compromising vid of the entire Fleet Supply Home Division wearing nothing but chocolate and having an orgy, or fashion magazines. And those are just the ones I heard about," Ennis added, pointing to the little plastifiber box taped to the wall of the commons labeled "Party Fund". The bet losers cheered up marginally and deposited their chips inside. Ennis knew the fine line between an officer acting friendly to enlisted (willing to make bets) and taking advantage of them (taking their money). This way, everyone stayed happy.

Max scratched his chin. "Waaal, if there's a market for that, maybe I can ... but I won't do fashion mags. Man's gotta have *some* standards."

"You should have thought of that before you agreed to smuggle circulars into FarCom," Ennis said, gathering up the textsheets and placing them next to his datapad. "Everything quiet out there?"

He pretended to work while Max described the latest courier run and relayed gossip and rumor from some of the outposts. When enough time had passed that most of the original group had wandered off or focused on some other source of entertainment, he gathered up his gear, got a leisurely refill of his mug, and left the commons. That little scene should handle any overactive imaginations. Now they knew Commander Ennis had some unusually lowbrow tastes, like reading circulars. The others knew he'd been enlisted once, like them, and still had friends in the ranks, and that would account for him occasionally being seen in the commons.

As soon as he could get to his workspace in the secure area Ennis sat down and quickly scanned through the relevant circulars. He'd been bitterly disappointed so many times before that it took him a moment to realize the message he had been waiting for was real. There it was, in the Warning/Bad Hire section. Even devout circular readers didn't place much reliance on those entries; too prone to vindictive and false accusation. Supposedly ship captains could put in warnings about bad former crew, but he'd never heard of any of them actually *reading* them. Which made that section perfect for coded messages that would never be discovered as fake.

Michael Ivan Sanchez, cargo joey, claimed employment on Yonjin Star Line IV, *Cullen Station,* Lady of Leisure, Fred's Folly, *actually employed Core Ore Freight,* Labrador Star, *dismissed for assault, theft, malingering, and breach of promise. Sworn by Captain Alan of Munchausen.*

Mentally reviewing the simple code they'd agreed on, he raised an eyebrow. *Lady of Leisure?* Why was that name familiar?

He went to see Namur, racking his brains without success. It was technically still downtime on Namur's schedule, but Ennis checked Namur's access status and it was green. Namur would want to know about this even if he was just waking up.

"Contact, sir," Ennis said as he entered. Namur regarded him from behind the desk, eyes gleaming in the shadows.

"You are quite sure? This method of communication you had set up would seem a trifle prone to false positives, would it not?"

Ennis handed over the textsheets. "That's why there are multiple messages. Two in the three datasheets I just got, both with the same information. You can't tell what will get dropped off with each stop when they add new content, so redundancy is built in. Cameron called it packets and bit-checks. Some kind of antique comp term," he added offhand. "Look, see the reference to 'Captain Alan of Munchausen'? All the fake messages have something like that."

Namur sat up, or the support structure of his chair sat up. Working with Namur for so long, Ennis had learned why the head of Umbra was never seen anywhere but in his office and behind his desk. The "desk" was his life-support system. Ennis had not asked, but any injuries so severe that they could not be handled by regrows or support webbing or neuro-prosthetics implied that most of Namur's bodily functions had been replaced in some way.

"Ah. What manner of transport has been arranged? Where do you go to meet it?"

"Ship called *Lady of Leisure,* and port of call is Cullen. Never been there, but the poop sheet says it's a pretty law-abiding place for the Fringe. What's the status on the reward?"

Namur gave a thin-lipped smile. "I admired Toren's technique so much I decided to borrow it. We carefully leaked information that you were already apprehended and the reward paid out, and also started rumors that the reward scheme was a slaver lure, and just to make absolutely sure we rerouted the contact address to us and sent spurious messages on in their place. You will want to be cautious in any event, but I believe you can survive a brief visit to Cullen. The messages we have intercepted have died down considerably, in any event."

"And what have you intercepted from Toren?" asked Ennis, feeling skeptical. Umbra's tricks probably had fooled the eager volunteers, but Toren itself would not be fooled.

Namur was silent for a moment, apparently absorbed in studying the simple ceramic tea cup in his hands. "Something strange. We have heard from...sources that they are quite perturbed at what happened at Bone. More than a simple mission gone wrong would imply. For one thing, they don't really know what happened and are trying desperately to investigate without drawing attention."

"Which is next to impossible to do on Bone, as I found out."

"Precisely. Some of the more eager elements in Umbra wanted take advantage of the situation to either infiltrate or spread disinformation," Namur said, looking regretful, "but the risk was too great. Anything connected with this project, whatever it is, receives the highest level of scrutiny. Which brings me to your briefing before you depart. There are...we have been able to confirm some suspicions recently, thanks to that highly informative data drum Cameron managed to obtain. Someday I would like to know how the thermal bomb chemicals got on the casing—but I digress. Encryption was light, possibly because the data drum was in a place considered sufficiently remote and secure.

"We found personnel lists, and after some research patterns emerged. A small subset of people were officially dead. These generally had no close family or were estranged from them. Others, if they had family, those family members were employed in highly classified Toren projects and usually on remote Toren-controlled stations."

Ennis frowned. "Hostages?"

"Say perhaps an insurance policy against sudden pangs of conscience. None of them appear to have been coerced. Quite a number of medical specialists of various types, bioengineers, et cetera that would be useful to the super-worker production facility. However, there were others on a separate list that were completely different. Ship builders, mechanics, even gravitics engineers. We've checked them as well. Every single one was once employed in Toren's military shipyards."

Ennis felt a growing chill as he thought about this. "What, they want their own Fleet? With their own grown-to-spec soldiers. Sir, what the hell are they planning?"

"Add in their penchant for corporate colonies, majority control of civilian space travel, and a strange reluctance to tell us what they have learned from all their investigations of the crabs, and suspicious minds, mine among them, think they have very grand plans in play," Namur said dryly. "Plans that appear to have no need of a strong or victorious Fleet. They were rather upset when your Captain Cameron took out that crab carrier."

Hoping his startled reaction hadn't been noticed, Ennis hastily said, "But wouldn't they be worried about the crabs? It would take them years to build up a fleet big enough to handle them on their own, and they couldn't hope to keep it hidden from us."

Namur lifted an eyebrow. "They wouldn't need a big fleet if we had already weakened the crabs for them. You understand that at this point we can only speculate that is their intention. We need more information, hard information, and you will be in a position to get it for us."

"Sir?"

"Cameron knew where to find this super-worker facility. We didn't even know it existed. She managed to get a large amount of extremely sensitive data out of it and I very much doubt she did it alone. I'm ordering you to find out as much as you can about how it was done and if she knows of any other such facilities."

"I'm tolerated there, sir, but not confided in. Cameron's setup is our only uncompromised source of information on the crabs. Is it worth risking that to pursue the Toren lead? If they think I'm being too nosy they could kick me out and refuse to have anything more to do with Fleet." It was wise, Ennis thought, to protest at this point.

That earned him a narrowed glance. "Toren is just as much a threat as the crabs–more so, since they hide among us. The crabs attack openly. Either one can destroy us. We need information on *both*." He paused. Ennis realized that Namur had been uncharacteristically hesitant throughout the conversation, which was not reassuring. Had Namur figured out his primary motivation for returning? Did he doubt his loyalty?

"There is one other thing you should know," the head of Umbra said slowly. "There are only two others besides myself who do, and I would not tell you if you were not heading where you might discover...we received a transmission three days ago, from Kulvar. It was sent to an older Umbra commcode, but one that no-one outside of Umbra should have known."

"Did it use Umbra encryption schemes?" Ennis asked.

Namur smiled. "It was *un*-encrypted. Plain data. All about Toren, most of which we already knew...but it was completely accurate. The rest we are checking on. What we want to know is, who sent that message, in the clear? None of our people would have done it. But who else would have sent it to that code? And who else knows so much about Toren and wants us to know as well?"

Harrington stepped aside to allow one of the crab crew to go past him. The corridors were rough and rounded, like most surfaces in the ship, and had the occasional alcove in the wall which was quite handy for the smaller humans to take refuge in to avoid being trampled by accident. They'd managed to repressurize most of the remaining ship, which was also rather useful. Even if he couldn't breathe the stuff, atmosphere permitted sounds to be heard. Fortunately his helmet dampened the volume. Crab voices had some low, almost subsonic components that caused eventual headaches if he listened to it too long.

Strange how his suit now seemed like a second skin since he spent all his waking hours in it. Doubtless it *smelled* like his skin at this point and none too pleasant, but how many chances would he have to experience this? Hygiene could wait.

Sometimes it was too much. He found himself almost frantic for a handlight to cut through the gloom, to see the huge, lurching figures before they were less than a meter away. Each time he had to remind himself crabs found human levels of light painful, and the humans were guests here.

Helpful guests, he hoped. The emergency capsule he and Perwaty were using as their quarters had solved a problem for the crabs, namely a huge hole nobody had additional material to patch. By cementing the capsule in place as part of the hull the crabs had recovered some of their ship. It couldn't be any fun for them to spend all their time in suits either.

Suddenly a section of the wall moved towards him and he cried out, terrified. When he realized it was just the giant crab who appeared to be in charge, not a hull breach, Harrington was slightly relieved. His knees were still weak and his heart was hammering in his chest. Then he noticed she wasn't moving, even though he was plastered against the wall and there was plenty of space for her to go by.

She appeared to be looking at him. He shook himself mentally and made the deep head-nod that they had adapted as the human version of the crab salute.

One massive forelimb lifted, and pointed at him. "HOOOMIN," the crab boomed, and Harrington tried not to wince as the sound bounced through his head. Now what was this all about? Then the crab bent the joint at the end of the forelimb and indicated herself. "HSSSSURRRWYYNN."

He blinked, suddenly understanding. Earlier, during his shift attending Radersent, he had attempted to discover what the crabs called themselves. The giant crab had been present. No one had answered him and he had thought his question had not made any sense to the crabs. He nodded to her again.

"Hsurwyn. Thank you, I'll make a note of it," he said shakily, even though she couldn't hear him. She moved off, and he let out a sigh of relief. It was *never* comfortable talking to something the size of a rhinoceros in close quarters.

The anomalous human walls of the emergency capsule were now visible in the murk and he hurried towards them and the sanity they represented. Harrington struggled with the awkward and highly annoying airlock, which was really little better than a thick door and not for the claustrophobic.

"Oh, there you are," mumbled a drowsy Perwaty from the one and only berth. "S'pose I'd better get up then."

"He's doing much better," Harrington said. "Talking more like he used to, anyway. Do you know what they are doing with that device over his wound?"

Perwaty scrubbed his bristly hair with both hands, yawned, and blinked. "Not a clue. Looks like it's doin' something good—hope they finish with it soon though. Got a message. They gonna drop out in ten hours an' get everybody switched over."

"Ah. And does our little home away from home remain?" Harrington asked, switching places with Perwaty and compacting himself as best he could while Perwaty wrestled his suit free.

"Guess so," Perwaty grunted. "They didn't say."

Harrington fiddled with his vid camera, shaking his head when he saw the results. "Blast. I still can't get anything decent with their light levels, and this unit doesn't have built-in gain. Over a week *living* with bloody crabs and not a scrap of vid to show for it!"

"That communications thingy's got a vid setting, don't it?" Perwaty said, shrugging his suit into place. "Want me to turn it on for ya?"

"Worth a try, anyway. Thanks. Oh, and according to the big one, crabs are called Hsurwyn."

Perwaty grinned. "The She?"

"Sorry?"

"That seems to be what the others call her, anyway. Ever get the feelin' we aren't really usin' the same words?"

Harrington sighed. "Altogether too frequently, I'm afraid. *The* She? Are there no other female crabs on board? There aren't that many crabs total, true, but I would have thought...." he trailed off, realizing he had no data to base any speculation on.

"Dunno. Maybe the others died in the fight." Perwaty shrugged. "I'm off. Anything you want me to do 'sides the vid?"

"You might try asking them how we take care of Radersent once they've gone," Harrington suggested.

Perwaty nodded, sealed his helmet, and wedged himself into the airlock.

Once he was gone and there was room, Harrington struggled out of his own suit and left it hanging to air out while he wrote up the notes for the day. As tiny and annoying as the shelter was, he wondered how he would have survived this long without it–something that *wasn't* alien. Would Radersent have survived so long in a human ship without his place of refuge?

Even so, the only reason he and Perwaty were there was Radersent's plea that he not be 'alone.' It still didn't make sense. The crab wanted humans there, even though he would at last be with his own kind? How much did Radersent think of himself as a crab now, or was there something they were missing?

He slept fitfully, dreaming of full, fluent conversations with the crabs he had gotten to know during his stay, his mouth somehow uttering the deep, loud sounds of the crabs and they speaking the human tongue with, strangely, a Chinese accent. Clearly his subconscious needed a bit of cleaning out.

The communications buzzer woke him and dissolved all memory of what they had actually *said* in this flight of fancy.

"Harrington here."

"Menehune. Captain says take all the comm gear out of the shelter but don't worry about the rest. We gonna do this quick, gottit?"

"Right, then. When do we drop out?"

"'Bout an hour. Don't tell them, but we're maybe three hours from where they said. Just say somethin' like 'soon', read?"

"Very well." Harrington looked at his dangling suit wearily. It would be much more comfortable back on board, he had to admit.

He gathered as much of their personal gear and the communication equipment as he could before leaving. The ship link he left for later, just in case something came up.

Perwaty was in what he privately thought of as Crab Medical, though for all they knew it had been an equipment bay before. That was where Radersent was, and whoever was treating him.

"We've got less than an hour before dropout. Is he ready?"

Perwaty nodded. "Guess so. They know, anyway. Far as I can make out only thing is he's not supposed to walk by himself yet. Got a clever rig all made up ta carry him with," he said, pointing to a strange jumble of gear.

There were two crabs present, one Harrington had seen frequently called Star Watch Mover. The other had never given his name or even gotten near the communication device; he seemed to think it was radioactive, as were the humans. Star Watch Mover was more friendly, but was not communicative now, apparently busy with last minute medical tasks. Harrington occupied himself with his datapad, sketching the crabs. He *would* have some visual record of all this!

The crabs all had what looked strangely like an ascot around their necks. Radersent had never worn anything like that before, and Harrington wondered what it meant now that he was. At first he had trouble telling them all apart, but now he could see the differences in the bony head structures and subtle grey shadings. None of them had the black marks Radersent did, and when the strange device was removed from his injury and Harrington saw a fresh black mark on his skin he understood—those were scars. Radersent had been badly injured before, then, but was it before he was wrecked in the sargasso? Or had he survived some accident while there?

His first indication that the ship had stopped was Cameron's voice over his commlink. The gravitics and other modifications needed to carry the crab ship had required a physical connection for any communication signals when in drive, hence the setup in the shelter.

"Harrington, are you ready to go?"

"Yes, Captain. They are just now getting Radersent back in his suit." It looked like the crabs had repaired that, too.

"Good. Meet us outside."

Harrington stood up, and the crabs big heads swung around to look at him. "It's time," he said to Perwaty. They worked out a message on the translator for the crabs, which seemed to work since they arranged Radersent in the jury-rigged crab stretcher and hoisted him up.

The interior of *Frankenstein* hadn't changed, and he saw with relief the familiar—but now surprisingly tiny—suited human shapes. He grappled with his share of the communication equipment, carefully not glancing at the figure removing some devices from the exterior of the crab ship near the supports. Gren and his little doomsday devices, and how fortunate they had not needed to use them. Cameron had been very blunt about the whole thing, but it was still a shock to see them in the flesh, as it were.

Harrington was quite surprised to see the giant crab leaving the ship with them. She moved with some awkwardness to the opening in the cargo bay leading to Radersent's quarters, followed by the stretcher crew. The massive head turned around, seeking, and then she pointed at him. He swallowed, then realized he was carrying the translator setup. He hurried up to where the giant crab was waiting. Facing her was Cameron.

"I'm not sure what she wants, Captain."

She gave him an amused look. "Well, I want to tell her how we're going to do the handoff. The operative word is 'quickly', and they probably want to stay suited up just in case."

The screen was in place and displaying another set of cycling graphics. Harrington was madly using his vid camera as much as he could, while there was light. The crabs were paying attention to the messages being sent through the translator, occasionally staring at the graphics on the screen.

Harrington got closer, and saw Cameron sending the message CRABS FIX RADERSENT YES. HUMANS MOVE CRAB SHIP YES.

The giant crab leaned forward. Unlike the other crabs, she had only three tendrils on either side of her long head, and they were longer and thicker. She trailed them over the crab side of the interface, apparently conferring with her crew on how it was used, and sent her own message. YES YES. FIX YES. MORE FIX.

Her head lifted, and the giant crab and Cameron stared at each other for a moment. Then the crab turned ponderously and returned to her ship, the rest of her crew following. Radersent was safely ensconced in his shelter again, and the humans were working on the framework that had been holding the crab ship in place.

"What the hell was that all about?" Harrington asked when they were all back inside. "More fix what? Their ship?"

"I have no idea," Cameron said absently. "Not our problem anymore, once we drop them off."

"I want to watch," Harrington stated.

"Of course," she grinned. "And record, but if you keep this up you owe me some high-capacity datacubes."

He scrambled to drop off his suit and finally change into some fresh clothes, then ran for the bridge. He did his best to stay out from underfoot once he had set up the exterior vid—everyone was tense and alert.

At last the readout hit the setpoint. Cameron slapped the dropout and the ship alarm within an instant of each other, and Harrington felt a slight shudder in the deck.

"They're clear!" Kilberton yelled from the scanner, and Cameron lunged at the controls.

Then she sat back with a sigh. "Back in the web. See anybody waiting, Kilberton?"

"Not that I could tell, but...there was something big out there. Not moving."

Harrington turned to the vid display. Barely ten seconds of recording. He switched it to replay.

"My God. What is *that*?" he finally managed to say.

Whatever it was, it was bigger than the biggest human station he had ever seen, and not a natural formation. It also didn't look like the construction of a crab ship.

"I think they got where they wanted to be," Cameron said dryly, staring at the screen. "What kind of signal intercepts, Yolanda?"

"Not," Menehune said with a sour expression. "Nothin'. Dead. Nobody home."

"Nothing? Look at that! That's *got* to be a base of some kind!"

"Perhaps it is no longer in use," said Kilberton, who had joined the group crammed around the screen. "Look, there. That is an impact crater. This is very old. And more debris damage near that structure at the end. I do not think they would leave that if they could fix it."

It made sense. The whole thing had a worn appearance, and now Harrington could see more craters, and other scrapes. And then, just at the end of the clip....

"Look. Something moving. Just under that immense cube that sticks out from the main wall."

Yolanda pushed forward and fiddled with the controls, increasing the magnification. It was indistinct, but clear enough to see it was a crab ship, moving from behind the giant structure.

"Well, that's a relief. Somebody will get to them before they freeze there," Cameron said. "Now, where were we before all this hit the fan?"

"Where do we go now, Captain?" Harrington asked, mentally noting the strange phrase for later research.

"Back to the sargasso. All the ship repair equipment is there, and if those damn crabs know how to trace us already I don't want them following us to Sequoyah," she said grimly. "Now did we have another ship picked out for—"

Harrington heard angry voices approaching the entrance to the bridge. Two of the crew were hauling the woman he had first seen on the docks of Kulvar wearing cuffs. She was struggling and terrified.

"No. No, please! Don't hand me over to those things!"

Cameron gave them all a frosty look. "What's happening, and why did you bring her up here where she has no business being?"

"She's already seen it," said the redheaded, bearded crewmember. "Heard her scream, see? Went in to see what's up. She got a snoop-loop somewhere, and she saw the whole thing. Visitors," he said, shifting his glance. "Here."

He handed her what looked like a thin datapad. With unashamed curiosity, Harrington peered over Cameron's shoulder. The screen was showing a still view of the scene that had recently taken place in the hold, with the giant crab, but at a strange, low angle. He frowned, trying to remember what had been located at the proper place to take that shot.

"It's the comm unit. She got into the vid of the comm unit," he gasped. "I didn't know you could do that. It's my fault—I should have left the vid off. I'm sorry."

Cameron went up to the woman. Her face was tired and sad. "Mr. Harrington, you are not at fault. She's the one who hacked into the unit. That offer I made to set you free, Inathka? I'm afraid it's on hold for a while."

CHAPTER 7
TO SEEK NEW FRIENDS AND STRANGER COMPANIES

Peter Vadnov fumbled with the keytab, glancing nervously over his shoulder until the door clicked open. He scrambled in and slapped the door closed, activating the security lock. Even someone with a keytab couldn't enter now.

"Vadnov. You are late," said the mechanical voice of Kolpe Anders. Vadnov slumped against the wall and slid down, his knees suddenly weak. Adrenaline reaction, the calm remnant of his mind diagnosed. "What is wrong? Did you succeed?"

He had to swallow before he could speak, his mouth was so dry. "I succeeded," he whispered. "They had the compounds you need." The thought was enough to move him shakily to his feet. His patient needed care. Of course this hellhole wouldn't have the drugs in the correct port-lock packaging for a containerized patient, but he'd anticipated that. Vadnov went to the storage trunk and rummaged around for the box of converters.

As he pulled one out, he saw the splash of blood on the back of his hand and had to fight back a surge of bile. Dropping the converter he dashed to the tiny bathroom and scrubbed frantically at his hand. When he looked up at the mirror and saw more blood streaked across his face, he vomited.

Finally he was able to clean himself up and return to his task, but his hands were shaking so badly he tried twice before getting a good connection to the drug port. Vadnov carefully checked the dosage readout and the secondary residuals in the container fluid. He didn't want to lose the patient now, after all he'd been through.

Medtech Peter Vadnov was not having a good day. He hadn't had a good day since leaving *Ben-Zachurian* in the medical waste pod with his strange container patient. He'd think about it sometimes when he couldn't sleep–which was more and more frequently–wondering where it had all gone wrong. He wasn't sorry for helping Kolpe escape, or even for erasing all the records. Kolpe had known how to get at the copies the medical board had, so now there really was no trace of him on the medship. He wondered how Kolpe had known how to do that.

They had gone to Kulvar. Vadnov had heard of the place as dangerous and full of criminals, but Kolpe had insisted....

"I...I think we should leave Kulvar," Vadnov said, hesitantly. "We can find a way to conduct your...business from another place."

89

"No. I must be here," Kolpe said immediately, just as Vadnov had known he would.

"What I mean is...it is too dangerous for me. And you. I don't know how to live in this place, and if anything happened to me...well, I don't think they have many medtechs here that can care for a containerized patient. If they have any."

Silence for a moment, then the mechanical voice spoke again. "What danger?"

Vadnov had learned this was how Kolpe thought. Facts, and only facts, interested him. "Someone was just killed right in front of me," he said, swallowing hard. Fighting not to see the severed veins, the open trachea, the brief white glint of bone all swallowed up in gouts of scarlet blood.

He'd worked on patients with massive trauma many times but it was different, so different, *seeing it happen* and knowing there was nothing he could do. Not when the killers were right there, weapons in their hands, dragging the body away. They'd seen him, of course. They didn't care. Just made some cryptic comment in their thieves' argot–something about a "blue-noser"–and left.

Vadnov shook himself. "That wasn't the first time, either. Two people were shot just outside the hostel the second day we were here. This is supposed to be the safe level! And you want to go where the *real* criminals hang out.... I don't even understand what they are saying half the time. What if they get annoyed with me asking for translations and kill me?"

More silence, and Vadnov noticed with bitterness that Kolpe hadn't disagreed with him. "Hire help," Kolpe said finally. "Guards, and guide. Get access to Zandovar."

Vadnov struggled with himself. It would be much better to have people who knew how to operate in Kulvar working for Anders, but they would have to be criminals themselves. Besides, if Anders had other people available he wouldn't need Vadnov as much. No, he still needed his medical skills. They had left the ship before Anders had fully stabilized.

The real danger would have been if Kolpe had insisted on getting the comp mods added to his interface that would allow him to access networks. Fortunately he had been in a hurry to leave, and Kulvar didn't have the facilities. Vadnov's job was safe, for now.

"No reply?"

He knew what Kolpe was asking about. Vadnov had been carefully instructed in transmitting a data packet to the semi-public address of the main crimelord, Zandovar. Kolpe seemed to think this would get him access.

"Nothing yet. It might not have been...useful to him."

"I have more information. Much more. I will find what he wants, and then he will give me what I want. He can find her! He will do it! I have information!'"

Vadnov said nothing, using the room's tiny comp to search for likely bodyguards. Sometimes he wondered what Kolpe Anders was planning. He didn't have enough for his medship yet, or he would be thinking of leaving. He should leave. This was dangerous, too dangerous for him. But first he needed the funds for his medship.

Ennis glanced around the corridor for clues. The commercial sector of the docks was not as well laid out for confused visitors as the passenger areas, but there had to be *some* signage. Finally he caught a glimpse of a fragment of the more usual sign; where the rest had been he saw a faded paint-pen scribble: "Bths 1045-1087" and an arrow.

He took out his datapad, both to check the berth number and to use the reflective screen surface as a mirror. This had been a quiet trip so far and he wanted it to stay that way. Nobody following now, either. He'd made sure to remove anything that would give him away as Fleet; even the datapad he was using was a civilian model instead of his usual military one. At each stop he had switched out clothing via the trade-up shops.

Arriving at the correct berth, Ennis pressed the annunciator next to the door. Nothing happened, so he pressed it again.

"Mmmm?"

"This *Lady of Leisure?* Cargo delivery."

"Whaa? I already got all the—Oh! Gottit! I was wonderin' when...comin' right down."

Ennis raised an eyebrow, wondering if the rest of the crew was like that. Still, this was the ship Moire had sent him so she must have checked it out somehow. Right?

He heard a series of muffled thuds through the door that could have been hurried footsteps or someone falling down stairs, and then the hatch flew open. The man opening it was short, stocky, and looked like he made a habit of falling down stairs. His nose had been broken at some point and still deviated from its original heading; there was an extensive patch of new, pink repair work under his jaw; and he currently sported a pair of fresh, colorful bruises. He grinned at Ennis.

"Hey, now yer here I can get *paid!* Name's Palmer. Welcome aboard! Um, you got gear?" Palmer asked, suddenly noticing Ennis wasn't carrying anything.

"Storage locker. I'm hoping you have a float cart or something. It was too heavy walking around the station." Ennis also wanted to be able to run in an emergency, especially if his "contact" was a setup.

"Oh yeah, I gotcha covered. So, you a big pal of Grimaldi's, eh? She sayin' she'd do anything ta help you, and what'm I doin' for work these days?"

Ennis stared at him. "Are you serious? Lorai Grimaldi? I admit she hasn't actually shot me, but I could see her thinking about it more than once."

The manic cheerfulness in Palmer's eyes calmed down. He grinned, but it was a slow, real grin. "Yeah, pretty much what she said. Sorry, tov. Hadda check you out. She said you got some nasties on yer list and don't listen ta any fairy tales 'cos they might have switched places with ya, read?"

Looked like he wasn't the only one with suspicions. "And what is your connection with Grimaldi, if I may ask?"

"She crewed on the last run to Criminy, 'fore it blew up. She was lookin' for someone. Found him, too, and dragged him back inna airbag." Palmer shook his head, briefly somber. "Glad she was there. Ship full of wounded, had my hands full gettin' in and out. So she sends a spew ta get my attention–I ain't gonna ignore that. Plus I was needin' work. Pick up this dope for my friend, she says, and the pay's good."

"OK, but what prevents you from grabbing the money and leaving me here?" Ennis asked.

"You *nuts!?* She'd *hurt* me!" Palmer protested, eyes wide. "You don't know what she's like when her core overloads. Damn near chews through bulkhead and spits out rivets. Not crossin' her no matter how much I'm paid. Pure compressed foolishness, as Mamma would say."

"Not good for your health, I agree. I'd better get my gear so we can leave as soon as possible."

Palmer rubbed his chin. "Seems 'ta me, less you go out the better. An' it's just me on the ship an' I don't care ta leave her in this kinda game, you got me?"

"But I need it!" protested Ennis.

"Nah, nah, 'sall good. See, I crew this ship solo most times. Gets old runnin' yer own errands. Got some good salvage, and a bit of downtime, made me up some helpers, guess you could say. Gonna send Mehitabel for yer gedunk, an' we can stay in-ship an' safe."

Mehitabel proved to be a medium-sized float pallet modified with a remote manipulator and a humanoid-shaped frame on the back that Palmer covered with scruffy clothing and a loose hood. In the shadows it would be sufficiently convincing to not attract attention, but it would not pass any kind of direct scrutiny.

"You've done this before?" Ennis asked, dubious.

"Sure! Now, not in the middle 'a prime cycle or anythin'. See, I got the vid all set up, so if I see there's trouble I just call the blues from right here."

It was not exactly a polished console, but Ennis was impressed. It even had a signal transponder that could pick up or transmit security codes, like the one on the storage locker. A few detours from the direct path kept the float pallet unobserved. The transfer occurred without difficulty and the gear arrived back at *Lady*.

"When can we leave?" Ennis asked, doing one last paranoid search with his pocket security scanner.

"Um, right now," Palmer said, watching him with doubtful fascination. "But ya gotta decode 'em for me. The coordinates, that is."

Ennis stared at him, confused. This hadn't been part of the plan. "Perhaps you should show me the message you got."

Palmer waved him up to the bridge, talking all the way. "Now, she may not look like much but this ship's a real lady n' everythin'. Got 'er in salvage, last owner'd used the hull for bumpers 'n the yard kept her downflow of a refuel depot for years. Looked like she was made outta compressed crud, but I checked her anyway—turns out she was built to be a private ship for some rich guy on Irukyn-Riu so the engines and plant were just prime—an' I just reskinned the hull an' had a nice little ship...here ya go. That's all I got."

Ennis had to read the screen twice before he understood. He was so close—he didn't want to miss this chance and have to wait even longer for a cycle of messages to go through.

It was short. The last line was a garbled string of letters and numbers, and the words "Perwaty's friend has a nice door."

Why was that familiar—yet off? Perwaty's friend meant Radersent. Radersent has a nice door. Yes, that was it! But who had said that? They had been on the crab ship, getting ready to tow it to the pickup spot, and...Alan. Alan had said it, admiring the melting airlock technology of the crabs. An image flashed in his mind. He had a vid still of that moment. Moire had given it to him, when he hadn't dared ask for a reminder of her and she hadn't said anything but she seemed to understand....

It was on his old datapad, and of course he had brought it with him, not wanting to leave it within unsupervised reach of Umbra. What had she done to the still? There were many ways to leave data in the still code itself, but that would require a decent comp and other information he didn't have. She hadn't told him about leaving a secret in the picture so he could be ready for it. She wanted him to be able to find it when he knew it was there, though, so whatever it was had to be accessible with just the gear he had. The datapad.

It took him an hour, with increasing levels of profanity, to figure it out. Moire had changed the actual image, on one corner, so that if he set the right properties to their most extreme level he could make out some faint but clear text. It was a simple algorithm code, and putting the string of nonsense characters in generated a valid and reasonable set of coordinates.

Palmer didn't look convinced when he showed him. "Sure, I can *get* there, but there's nothin' there, if ya know what I mean. It's just...empty. No star, no station, no nothin'."

"Good. Nobody else will be there," Ennis said. He remembered what Moire had told him about the secret Toren site, also located in the middle of nowhere. This was a clever use of the enemy's own methods.

The location was a significant distance from Cullen. The trip took a while. Palmer had been telling the truth about flying solo, but however grungy the bridge was Ennis could see no sloppiness in his care of his ship. They split the watch in half, playing cards during the switchover. Ennis monitored gauges when Palmer slept.

Once they got there, however, boredom set in.

"You sure we're in the right place?" Palmer asked after five days of waiting.

"They aren't going to be able to stop here whenever they want. They might have come earlier and left. They don't know when we will show up either," Ennis pointed out, examining the cards in his hand. He'd never been fond of playing cards but there was not much else to do. "Look on the bright side. Nobody is shooting at us."

Palmer nodded thoughtfully, discarding a card and picking up another. "That a problem for ya?" he asked with a grin. "Don't strike me as the trouble-makin' type."

"I get enough just doing my job; I don't have to look for it. Like you do," Ennis said. "Call." He laid out his hand on the table.

"A good fight is fun, healthy, an' relaxin'," Palmer said, running an appreciative eye over the cards before laying his own down. "A'course, I just use me fists from preference. Gotcha on points. Pay up."

"That's not what you told me about the last one. Remember? Broke off a light fixture and went after the cargo loader?" Ennis looked in his pile of handmade chips for his fine. He'd refused to play with real money so Palmer had made up some plastic chips. As the time wore on they decided to award themselves daily "pay." The denominations got stranger as their boredom increased. "Here, one cheese asteroid and an elephant." He tossed the plastic chips over to Palmer, who caught them midair.

"Hey, she started it! Tried ta take my face off with a snack tray," Palmer said, pointing to the shiny pink patch on his jaw. "All in fun, really. But you got people shootin' at ya—that's not games, that's serious. You been in a lot of them kinda fights?"

Ennis sighed. "Too many. And it never gets any easier."

"Maybe should be thinkin' on another line a work," Palmer said, gathering and shuffling the cards. He stopped, shuffled again, then let the cards fall with a troubled expression on his face. "But you didn't, didja. I wouldn't last at that kinda thing. I'd be afraid after the first shot."

"Who said I wasn't?" Ennis retorted. "Any rational person would be afraid; I just didn't let it stop me."

"How? How do you not let it?" Palmer was looking at him intently.

This was a very different conversation than they usually had. Ennis wasn't sure what was going on. "Mostly by being more afraid of something else happening if I failed. Something more important than me getting hurt or dying."

"Oh." Palmer digested this. "But...what if there wasn't? What if you had to do somethin' that just made yer bones jelly, but nothin' really bad would happen if ya didn't?"

Now he was completely mystified. "Like what? You owe Grimaldi money but she hasn't asked for it yet?"

"Naaah!" Palmer's face was a deep red except for the network of paler scars. "Nothin' like that." He struggle for a moment, then burst out. "I got this spacesuit, see. Top of the line, I checked. But it got so many a them little bits and pinlights and such I can't keep it all straight. I read the manual five times, but soon as I get the damn thing on I forget everythin'. I *hate* vac," he said, his face working with emotion. "Can't stop thinkin' 'bout how much I hate it. No room for nothin' else then."

Ennis blinked, keeping his face carefully neutral. That was a handicap, all right, and he wondered how the hell Palmer had gotten this far running his ship solo in the Fringe when he couldn't even suit up. It explained the clever remote float pallet and the other gadgets Palmer had invented, though.

"OK, so you need to have something else to think about. Something you care about strongly. The other thing is, you need to know your gear and not just from reading about it. Where is this suit of yours?"

"You got some kinda idea? Whatcha gonna do?"

"Yeah." Ennis grinned. "We're going to play cards."

The suit was clearly used, but as Palmer had said, good quality. Ennis would have preferred something simpler and less distracting, but it was the only one on the ship. He tried it on himself, making matter-of-fact comments as he demonstrated the basic features. Then he made Palmer do the same thing, quizzing him on what he had said. Seeing the sheen of perspiration on Palmer's face just from this mild step, he abandoned any airlock drills for the moment.

"Now we play cards. No, put on the helmet and seal it up. Remember where the comm controls are? That's right, on the left sleeve and inside the right wrist."

"What are we gonna play?" came the amplified voice of Palmer from the comm. He held up his hands, looking quizzical. Spacesuit gloves were not designed for card handling.

"Nerts!" Ennis said, and Palmer guffawed. Nerts was fast, furious, and very silly. " I'm going to beat you at that game at last!"

They played Nerts for hours. Ennis knew Palmer was making progress when he absentmindedly tried to scratch his head through the helmet. Then he made Palmer take the suit off and go through the maintenance schedule before racking out. It was more than enough for the first day, and he didn't want fatigue to make him frustrated.

The following days, Ennis came up with more and more things to try. As Palmer became more confident wearing and using the suit, they moved the card game to an airlock. First with the inner door open, then shut but not cycled, and finally, with the airlock evacuated. Ennis made sure proper airlock procedure was part of the game, requiring Palmer to go through the sequence to discard and pick up cards until it was second nature to him.

Opening the outer airlock door was the hardest step. "I just don't feel like that'll ever be easy," Palmer confessed, looking out at the darkness. "There's a whole lotta empty out there."

"If it gets easy you get careless, and that's when you make mistakes," Ennis said. "You gonna play this hand or what?"

With a visible effort, Palmer wrenched his gaze away from the open airlock door and looked at his cards. He'd made a plastifiber holder that was easier than trying to grasp the small cards with gloves. "Um, one discard." He took the card and wedged it in the inner airlock window to indicate it was no longer in play, and Ennis dealt its replacement and wedged it in the window on his side, facing Palmer. Palmer squinted at it, looked at his hand again, furrowed his brow in thought, then looked at Ennis, startled. "Hey! That was from the bottom of the deck! You're *cheating!*"

With lightning precision Palmer shut the airlock and cycled through. Only when he tore his helmet off, breathing hard, did he seem to notice Ennis was grinning.

"You think that's funny?"

Ennis nodded. "I've been cheating the whole time. Mostly to let you win, mind you. But this is the first time you weren't too scared to notice. And that was a nice airlock cycle, too. You didn't forget anything even though you were angry. Good job."

Palmer just stood there, stunned. "You goddamned son-of-a-bitch," he said, awed. "Now I know why you get shot at so much."

Moire reached for the shipwide comm and toggled it. "All hands, dropout in three minutes. Combat positions. Dropout in three, combat."

"Aren't you being a bit paranoid? If they were tracking us they'd have gotten us at the sargasso," Yolanda Menehune said, scowling and flipping on scanners. "Gren hasn't seen nothin' the whole trip."

"Aha, and you call *me* paranoid," Moire said, watching the readouts carefully. It was one thing to overrun a dropout when the safety alarms had something to work with. Here, it would just mean a lot of tedious realspace travel or microhops to get back where they should be. "Everybody ready? I want those scans running the instant the gravity bubble pops, got that?"

Menehune rolled her eyes, but nodded. Kilberton called down from the gun position that he was ready too. She reached for the dropout switch and pulled. "Dropout!"

"Got a ship on the scope, Captain," Menehune reported almost immediately. "Just the one. Gettin' the details now...volume matches, profile...Lorai said there was a big scratch near the front airlock, gonna look for that now. Huh, that's funny."

"What?" Moire's panic levels went up.

"There's somebody outside on the hull. Hail 'em?"

"Yeah. Maybe they just felt like doing a check or something."

Menehune had to repeat the hail a few times before there was a response. When Moire heard Ennis' voice, sounding breathless, she nearly jumped.

"This is *Lady of Leisure*. And if that isn't *Frankenstein*, then there are two of the ugliest ship in the galaxy."

Moire took the comm. "Yeah, yeah, everybody's a critic. Where's the pilot? Or have you been studying web in your off-time?" Ennis laughed, and she couldn't help smiling. Damn, but she had missed him.

"He's...um, on his way. We got a little bored waiting so he decided to check the hull for, ah, damage." Moire and Yolanda exchanged a skeptical look.

"Did he get the cargo?"

"I assume so; the holds are nearly full. Is everything all right?"

Moire rubbed her forehead. "Long story. I don't want to hang around any longer than I have to. There's...some stuff you—or rather your friends back home—need to know."

"Everyone OK?"

"None of my people are dead, so yeah."

"None of *your* people—how do you manage to get in so much trouble so fast? Never mind, here's Palmer."

Moire left Kilberton and Menehune to work out the docking issues, which were always fun for the very non-standard *Frankenstein*. So why did they usually end up using it? *I'm not a very organized pirate*, Moire thought. They never bothered connecting personnel hatches, since they didn't match standard locations, so she went to the main cargo hold instead. Everyone who wasn't already on the bridge or in Engineering was there, ready to move cargo.

The big status lights on the door cycled and it cracked open, slowly. Ennis stepped through as soon as it was wide enough. His eyes searched the room until he saw her standing at the head of the stairs. Moire tilted her head at the passageway she had come through and left, waiting out of sight in the corridor. Soon she could hear his quick footsteps up the metal stairs.

Too many emotions, bottled up over months and suddenly released, made it impossible for her to speak so she didn't even try. Ennis wrapped his arms around her and held her so tightly she could feel the tiny tremors in his body. She'd forgotten how well they fit together—or rather, her brain had. Other parts of her hadn't. He kept kissing her like he was afraid she would disappear.

"I didn't even get shot," Moire whispered after a while.

His arms tightened painfully, then relaxed. "You are not. Allowed. To die," he said through gritted teeth, holding her face in his hands. "Is that clear?"

"Not in your chain of command, love," Moire said with a shaky grin. "Never was, now that I think about it. And the enemy always gets a vote."

Ennis closed his eyes, shuddered, and kissed her hard. "Then, as a favor? For me? You perform the impossible for other people. You don't want me to feel left out, do you?"

"I promise you won't feel left out," Moire said, stealing another kiss. "I want you around as much as possible—so I'm really hoping you have some way of getting excruciatingly sensitive information back to Umbra without taking it yourself."

Ennis enfolded her again. "What have you done now?" he asked in a resigned tone, shifting to rest his head comfortably against hers.

"Dropped out in the middle of a multi-crab fight, got holed by one of them, blew up another, and rescued the ship they were ganging up on so they could repair Radersent after he got injured in the fight. Oh, and the reason we dropped out is the crabs have some way of diddling with ships in webspace. Crab ships only, as far as we know."

She looked up. Ennis had gone white, and his mouth opened as if to speak, then shut again.

"But if only crab ships...how did you...?"

Moire put her arm around his waist for reassurance, and tapped the corridor wall. "*Frankenstein* was tuned up to tow the crab ship for you guys, and we never bothered to change it. Gren noticed something funny with the gravitics but it didn't get really bad until we were almost on top of them. I had him write up a report with everything he saw, and Kilberton too—he was piloting at the time."

"We'd know if they were able to detect and intercept our ships in webspace," Ennis said finally. Moire lightly ran her fingers over his back and felt him start to relax. "Strange, though; if they can do it for their own why wouldn't they be trying to get us? That would be a huge advantage."

"I was wondering about that myself. A lot of this doesn't make sense, like the huge facility where we dropped them off—it looks like it hasn't been used for thousands of years. And—" She felt his muscles go taut.

"What? Facility? Dropped off *who*?"

Moire sighed. She could be breaking this more gently, but maybe it was better to rip the bandaid off all at once. Did they still have bandaids?

"The crab ship that had been under attack was badly damaged and couldn't move. We had Radersent dying from injuries we didn't know how to treat. So we worked out a deal with the survivors. They patched him up, and we towed their ship to a place where they could get rescued. At that place we saw this immense...thing. Super-station or something. But old. Craters and other damage all over it that hadn't been fixed. It didn't look like the crab ships we see now, but crab-like. Harrington has some vid of it. He insisted," she said, rolling her eyes. "Anyway, we didn't hang around to see the welcoming committee. That's it, really. Oh, and I used the ship I was towing to take out the attackers with so we went back to the sargasso and then dropped by on our way home to see if you were here yet."

Ennis shot her a look out of narrowed eyes. "You have got to be leaving something out. You're making interstellar war sound like a shopping trip again. I remember the last time you did that."

"Well, I could do the long version with sound effects and descriptive interludes, but I thought you might want to send a message back with Palmer before he leaves. You understand with all these crabs showing up unannounced I don't like to sit here twiddling my thumbs. This ship doesn't have nearly the guns it should."

"Why the hell not?" Ennis yelled. "There were plenty of ship-mount guns in those wrecks in the sargasso; I saw them!"

"Because I wasn't *planning* to commit interstellar war on my lonesome, it just happened! This was only supposed to be a one-time tow ship so Umbra could add a crab ship to its collection!" Moire glared at him.

Ennis leaned against the wall, rubbing his forehead like it hurt. "Sorry. It's all a bit much at once. I've been away from you too long and I'm out of practice."

Moire hesitated. "Are you going to have to leave again? This is serious. Fleet needs to know." As soon as she said the word "leave" Ennis reached for her again, one hand stroking her hair.

"Yes, they do. But they really need to know more about the crabs, and if you've been communicating with "wild" ones, not just Radersent, I think I should stay here. I will send a coded message back with Palmer though." He loosened his hold and looked at her. "And ... a request for something you may not like. A courier."

"As long as they stay off my ship I can deal with it. You need a secure room to do your spy stuff?"

He smiled. "As long as nobody comes in here, this is fine."

"Right. I'll go check on the loading." She gave him a kiss and a grin, sidestepping his reach.

The cargo loading was almost complete, and half an hour later Ennis joined her in the bay. He had a dull grey datatab in his hand.

"It's encrypted and volatile–any attempt to read it without the correct equipment erases the content," he said, handing it to Palmer who nodded and tucked it in a shirt pocket. "Here's the address and the rest of the instructions. I'm not saying swallow it if captured, but don't show it off at the bar, either."

Palmer looked at the text sheet with the address, shrugged, and added it to the pocket. "I can do that. Mind if I ask a favor of you, same?" He pulled out a different text sheet with a flimsy printout wrapper. "For Grimaldi. Want ta thank her for puttin' me in the way of this job," he said, face reddening.

"Every thirty days, same coordinates," Moire said. "Don't let anybody on your ship for that run unless we tell you ahead of time. Whatever you do outside of that is your own business."

"Gottit." Palmer turned to Ennis and held out his hand, mumbling and his face turning even more red. "Thanks for...thanks for the card games. I'll keep yer chips for ya, ya damn cheater!"

CHAPTER 8
FRIENDS AND RELATIONS

Awareness emerged as unconsciousness slowly drained away. Ennis drowsed for a while, first wondering at his uncharacteristic inertia, and then, as he woke up further, at why he felt not only happy, but secure. It made no sense. He was in a highly-reworked ship traveling through the fringe of the Fringe, possibly being tracked by crabs even now, and yet there was a noticeable absence of the constant nagging need for watchfulness. Even on FarCom he had never entirely allowed himself to let his guard down.

It couldn't entirely be because of Moire, though she certainly helped. He smiled, stretched, and sighed when he touched both ends of the bunk. How fortunate neither of them were large.

There was something he needed to do. Moire had asked him, as she was leaving to start her shift and he was not really awake, just listening to her voice. He racked his brain, trying to remember. No, he was *not* going to use this as an excuse to go to the bridge. He had real work to do, work for Umbra as well as for Moire. Harrington! That was it. She wanted him to help Harrington with the crab translator. He frowned. She'd mentioned Umbra, too, and that didn't make sense. And another name he didn't remember.

He sighed, stretched again, and got his gear together. Shipsuit was definitely not optional, not on this crate. The crew did good work but *Frankenstein* was still, at best, an experimental design. He'd find Harrington who would explain everything. But first, food. Ennis closed his eyes, bringing up a mental map of the ship from the last time he'd been on board. Even when you knew where the galley was, it was equally important to know how to get to it since nothing was laid out in the usual way.

Whistling a tune in a randomly changing key, Ennis headed out. One of the crew was in the galley when he reached it; the assistant engineer, who greeted him by raising his mug.

"Welcome back, Commander."

"It's good to be back–Kwife, right?" Ennis said, scanning the available food options. They were all processed, and he couldn't help a sigh. "Where's Madele Fortin?"

Kwife laughed, and gave him a sympathetic grin. "Dirtside. Sequoyah. You got spoiled, eh? They need her more than we do. Got a lot more people since you were there last. Don't worry, that stuff is pretty good. Just not as good as hers."

Ennis decided the cinnamon protein-bread would do, and sat down with that and a juice bulb. "Any idea where I can find Harrington?"

"Probably down in the tank. Where the crab lives," Kwife explained. He drained his mug. "I can take you there, if you like. We've made some changes since you left, and of course getting hit in the fight didn't help."

Ennis was glad Kwife had offered. The route had two pressure doors now, one with a hand-lettered sign stating shipsuits were mandatory beyond that point.

"Took us a while to get it patched up and sealed," Kwife said, seeing him read the sign. "Captain wants us to be cautious, just in case something breaks loose again."

"Wise," Ennis murmured. They reached the door to the hold stairs. "I know the way from here. Thanks."

Kwife waved goodbye, and Ennis started down the stairs to the two big cargo containers on the floor of the hold. The stairs had been repaired, he noticed, and then he saw the large patch on the hold wall. The hull wall. His cheerful mood abruptly chilled. Exactly how bad had this fight been?

He fingered the collar of his shipsuit, double-checking that the oxygen capsules were in place. The door to the human side of the structure was closed, and he knocked before entering. Harrington looked up as the door opened.

"Ah, there you are! You're looking well–running around the galaxy seems to agree with you. No hair-raising adventures getting to us, I trust?"

"Very dull. I wasn't even shot at," Ennis said dryly. "No kidnap attempts, no explosions. Not at all what I am accustomed to."

"You should have gotten here sooner. There were quite enough explosions for my taste," Harrington said, turning back to the console. It had a number of controls and inputs. The old battered code reader Perwaty had first used to communicate with his shipwrecked companion was plugged in, but so was a sleek, modern device Ennis found familiar. "Yes, we decided that we ought to work on a system that was a trifle more robust," Harrington added, seeing the direction of his gaze. "I had the distinct suspicion that He Who Dwells in Shadow would be in the market for a crab translator that would be more amenable to mass-production. Besides, this lets us do some analysis."

"Namur wants the source," Ennis pointed out. "Not that this isn't helpful."

Harrington sat back. "You know, this may be an awkward question, but what precisely is Radersent's legal status?" He gestured at the large window into the crab quarters. Radersent was visible, but instead of standing as he usually did he was draped over a large branching frame-like structure. "The reason I ask is it has become apparent he regards himself as a member of this crew. More precisely, Moire Cameron's crew. He became rather agitated when he thought we were going to leave him with the other crabs, you know, even though he was quite badly injured at the time. You'd think he would have more pressing issues to concern him. I understand Umbra's interest and only wish to promote it by pointing out that 'handing over the crab' might possibly be...counterproductive."

"Are you saying he wouldn't help us?" Ennis asked, studying the display for a moment before tapping out a greeting. He wasn't sure if the crab could recognize specific humans, and in any case he had been gone for a long time. Radersent responded with a graceful wave of his head-tendrils, but didn't get up. "Is he feeling all right? You said he was badly injured."

"He is *much* better than he was," Harrington said with feeling. "Yes, very bad. We would have lost him without the help of the crabs we rescued. I'm not entirely sure what his motivation would be, in Umbra's custody. We're still piecing this together, mind you, but it appears crab social structure relies heavily on personal loyalty. Almost feudal, in a way. He would have no 'connection' to Umbra, at least nothing like that with the Captain. And I don't believe he understands any connection between her and Umbra. It's very strange."

Ennis stared at him. "Even though we're all human? It isn't clear we're all on one side?"

"It appears all the crabs are not. Bear in mind we interrupted a crab-on-crab battle, so that seems credible to me." Harrington shrugged. "He uses a term we haven't translated yet for the crabs we met. There's definitely the negation-pitch, but Inathka thinks there is also the same base phoneme for family or allegiance, so a tentative meaning might be 'not one of us'. Even though we see them all as crabs."

"Inathka?"

Harrington hesitated. "Right. You haven't met her. Speaking of legal status—we're not quite sure what to do with her." He started working with the advanced comm device, inserting a datatab. "She used to be a, let us say, involuntary worker belonging to the ceeyo of Kulvar. In a series of events a dutiful Fleet officer should probably remain in official ignorance of, she was transferred to the ownership of the Captain. Who, I hasten to add, was fully intending to release her unharmed at a more law-abiding location. However," he said, removing the first datatab and inserting a second one, "we let her help out and this Inathka was observant, curious, and extremely skilled with comm devices. She planted a hidden link in this very device that allowed her to see some of the negotiations with the crabs. I am quite certain Namur doesn't want word reaching Toren that we might have sources of information they don't know about."

Ennis grimaced, rubbing his forehead. "Damn. No, you are right. What a mess. But you said...she's still working on this?"

Harrington took the second datatab out. "Oh yes. She is quite good—

very intuitive about signal analysis. We've made a lot of progress with the translator with her help. Still, given the sensitive nature of the data, the Captain insists on keeping her isolated from direct contact with the main copy of the data and the device. She asked me to vet Inathka's work, given my extracurricular activities, but I pointed out *you* are an official member of Umbra and more likely to spot any funny business than an ad-hoc civilian like myself."

So that was what Moire wanted him to do. Now he just had to figure out how to do it. How had he ended up with Umbra anyway? Where had he gone wrong?

"I've just got a lovely batch of data for her now, and it seems Radersent is getting tired again, so off we go." Harrington gathered up the data tabs, tapped out a brief message to the crab, and got up.

Ennis turned to follow him, and stopped, transfixed by the image on the big display screen. He hadn't noticed it until now. "What the hell is *that?*"

Harrington looked grim. "A structure we found at the location the crabs wanted to be dropped off at. Their ship had no mobility."

"That looks...dangerous," Ennis said, staring at it and feeling very cold.

"Possibly."

"Possibly? Look at it! I've never seen anything like it before! It's bigger than FarCom!"

"I agree, but according to our scans *and* the crabs, it is abandoned. Notice the craters."

Yes, now he could see there was extensive damage. His heart rate slowed a little. "How old is it? Did you ask?"

"Well, that's one of the things we think might not be getting translated correctly," Harrington commented, opening the door. "Because if Radersent understood us, the answer is 'over two thousand years'."

⚜

Moire lounged back in her chair, feet on the console, and cast an eye over the realspace panel. The sargasso remained its inert self. Nobody was talking on the main channel, reserved for communications to the bridge, and the few times she had visited the crew channels it sounded like work was progressing well. They'd developed a rhythm; everyone knew what needed to be done and how to do it efficiently. All she had to do was stay out of the way. Maybe this being-in-charge gig wasn't so bad.

Hearing the sound of approaching feet, she glanced over her shoulder. As she had hoped, it was Ennis.

"Lunchtime," he announced, holding out a plastifiber box. "We have a fine selection of processed starch with protein paste, various flavors; synthetic flavored gooey squares for dessert; and vitamin and whatnot-enhanced beverages. Oh, and I figured out where you hid the coffee so we have that too."

Moire sat up. "Then I forgive you for the vitamins. Thanks for saving me the trip. You didn't want to go out to the wreck today?"

He gave her a wry expression. "You said we're going back to meet Palmer once the wreck is dropped off, which doesn't leave much time. If I'm going to be telling Umbra they can't have Radersent shipped to them in a box it would be a good idea to have something almost as useful to give them instead, agreed?"

"Yeah, suppose so. What have you figured out?" Moire mumbled around her erzatz sandwich.

"Not much." Ennis sighed. "Harrington was right; their system of communication is complex. No hope of us ever being able to speak it directly. The crabs have some way of creating up to three distinct sound frequencies superimposed on each other, and one seems to be their version of grammar. I'm focusing on getting as much raw data assembled and organized as possible and hoping the cryptos on FarCom can figure it out."

"Any chance they'll share if they do?"

Ennis shrugged. "Above my pay grade. I hope so, since it would help us learn more. Of course they might just as easily decide that handing ultra-classified information to an infamous space pirate of the Fringe would be viewed dimly by the command, even if you did give them most of it in the first place." He took a swig of the vitamin drink. "Such is Fleet logic."

"Well, no sense in borrowing trouble. Oh, speaking of trouble. What the hell were you thinking giving Alan a sniper rifle? I mean, you got Ash and George and Hideo books and toys and so on. Why?"

Ennis shifted in his seat. "He won't be shooting anyone unless you give him ammo. Look, you aren't going to make him stop wanting to get his hands on a weapon; it's too late for that. I've just given him a non-lethal outlet. Without ammunition the programming directly reverts to a laser training setup. He can practice and get better, and I can set it up for situational judgment-call scenarios."

"Really." Moire studied his face. Something else was going on, and she suspected she knew what it was. Alan was the only one of the Created that still harbored a grudge against Ennis for shooting her. Maybe this was his way of trying to make amends—but it made *her* life more difficult.

The comm board pinged before she could accuse Ennis, and that was probably a good thing. No point in bringing up bad memories.

"Now what? Who forgot the main channel code?" she groused. Ennis stood up and went to the comm display.

"Interesting. I didn't know anybody was still out scouting," he commented.

"Gren said something about looking around for more guns to add to the ship," Moire said, getting up. "You should approve. What are they saying?"

He shook his head, looking puzzled. "Gibberish. See, it's way out there.

Further than any of the wrecks. Is it perhaps a new wreck, coming in? Have you ever seen that?"

"No. And that's a pretty strong signal for a wreck, anyway. See if you can use the encrypt mode to get something comprehensible. I'll check with Gren."

Moire tapped at the control bracelet for the captain's earring, bringing up Gren's personal channel.

"Gren, you got anybody wandering around the edges of the sargasso? We're picking up a signal."

She heard his breathing, then "No. Everybody is here on the wreck. Where is it coming from?"

Moire glanced over at Ennis. "Location?"

"Other side completely, core-wards. It isn't moving." He headed for the scanner controls.

Moire relayed this information to Gren. "It doesn't seem to be a distress beacon either," she added, watching Ennis. He stiffened suddenly, then lunged back toward the comm panel and frantically started manipulating controls. "What are you doing?"

"Running that signal through the translator," he said grimly. "That's a ship out there."

Moire joined him at the console. They didn't have it set up for the synthetic voice on the bridge, just the display. The translator understood the signal, and it took her a moment to understand the words on the screen.

"Fix Radersent?? Are you sure that's right?"

Ennis' face was pale. "I didn't even run it through a filter–I just plugged it in to our end. That's the signal Radersent's device emits. They know about our translator."

"That's not all they know," Moire snarled. She toggled the all-channel emergency broadcast. "Evacuation! This is not a drill! Drop tools and RUN!" She pointed Ennis to the guns as she ran to the web-pilot's pit. The damn crabs had known exactly where to go to find them, and there was only one person that could have told them. Harrington and Perwaty didn't know the coordinates of the sargasso, even if they had wanted to tell the crabs. It had to have been Radersent.

She frowned. There was plenty of space for her ship to clear the sargasso and get a lineup to escape. Even if the crab ship tried to intercept them before her crew got back, they wouldn't make it unless they had far better realspace engines than she'd ever seen. The crab ship wasn't moving, though, and it was way the hell out. Why were they signaling out there instead of coming closer?

Moire set up a preliminary lineup and locked it in. They still had to get away from that alien web-mine in the center of the sargasso before she engaged, but it would save time if they had to bug out in a hurry.

"You did have these things fixed, right?" Ennis's voice came over the comm.

"Yeah, the one that got damaged and the auto-feed; they all work." Reports were coming in over the captain's earring—one group of crew already back on the ship, another on the way.

"I hope the crabs didn't figure out how to track human ships in webspace," Ennis said.

Moire kept her hands on the controls and her eyes on the scanner. Still no movement. "Thanks for adding to my paranoia," she muttered. "Doesn't feel right, though. That's a pretty quick turnaround, or would be for us. They don't seem to adapt that fast. Plus, if you had that kind of secret weapon would you use it like this? Showing up waving your tentacles to ask for another installment of Human as a Second Language?"

People, running into the bridge. One of them was Kilberton, closely followed by Menehune.

"Take over," Moire said to Kilberton. "Prelim is set. Soon as we've got everyone aboard that's on the wreck we'll go to the safe distance. Yolanda, monitor the signal. Tell me if it has changed."

"What signal?" Menehune said, looking bewildered. Oh yeah. She hadn't mentioned that yet.

"There's a crab ship sitting on the other side of the sargasso and it seems to want to talk to us."

"*Shit!* Why here, why now?" Menehune spun to the comm console.

"That's what I'm going to find out," Moire snapped. She found the code for the commlink in the human side of the crab quarters and entered it in the control bracelet. "Bridge. Who's there?"

"Perwaty, Captain. What's wrong? Are we under attack again?"

"That's what I want to know. So you ask Radersent why he told the crabs we rescued where to find us, because there's someone out there now who is sending us our own translator code," Moire gritted.

"Y-yes Captain!"

She muted the captain's earring, and turned to Yolanda. "Get Harrington up here. Oh, and pipe that signal to Inathka but don't tell her anything. See if she comes up with the same answer we did."

"All crew on board," Kilberton called out.

"Right. I'm moving us out to departure distance," Moire said, swinging down in front of the realspace controls. "Let me know if there's any response from those crabs."

"Uh, Captain?" Perwaty's hesitant voice came over the comm. "Radersent says he didn't tell them."

Moire turned off the mute. "Then how the hell did they know where to show up? They're practically quoting him!"

"I'll ask." Moments ticked by. Moire tried to ease the tension in her muscles. A quick glance at Kilberton got a headshake—no crab movement. There they were, only seconds from escape. But where to? If they could be tracked, she couldn't go back to Sequoyah. She couldn't go anywhere, really. And this ship only had three guns. Perwaty spoke up again. "Um, I *think* I got what he's saying. The ship he came here on, the other crabs—*some* of the crabs knew it was coming here. He told those crabs that fixed him he was on that ship. That's all. Oh, and he's asking why they came here himself. Keeps saying 'bad place crab, crabs go away now' and something about the Breakers."

Moire leaned back in her chair, suddenly thoughtful. Maybe they weren't about to be shot at after all. Maybe Radersent hadn't betrayed them. That didn't change the fact that the crabs could show up at the sargasso some other time with unfriendly intent. They needed access to the wrecks if they were going to defend Sequoyah. So, one way or another, she had to do something about that ship full of crabs hovering just inside scanner range.

Just as she was about to call him, Gren showed up on the bridge, followed by Harrington who was looking even more rumpled and Roman than usual.

"Perhaps I'm not quite awake yet, but I could have sworn Yolanda said something about a crab ship here," Harrington said, blinking. "Didn't you already move it?"

"New one. Not a wreck and stuffed to the bulwarks with crabs," Menehune said, scowling.

"Okay, everyone. Listen up. We've got a nice messy situation on our hands and we need to do it right the first time." Moire outlined what they knew and what she suspected. "Things we don't know—why did they come here, apparently just to talk to us? Who else knows about this place, and are any of these people going to show up later? We may not have answers to any of this but we still need to make some decisions. Suggestions?"

"They haven't made any hostile moves, Captain," Kilberton observed. "In fact, I think they sent that signal before they were even in scanner range."

"Same signal, too," Menehune said. "Got a message from Inathka. She figure it out just like you said. 'Fix Radersent.' They've been sending it for the last forty-odd minutes."

Gren's forehead was corrugated with thought, his arms crossed over his chest. "Ya know, I was remembering what Radersent said back when we found him, when we couldn't move his ship the first time? That gizmo the Breakers made was designed to destroy crab ships. They were scared of it, scared to come here. Hell, it got everybody on his ship but him, didn't it? I'm thinking they only came *here* because they didn't have any choice. They want to talk to us and this is the only place they know we show up. This bunch of humans in particular, that is."

Moire felt her eyebrows go up. This, from her crew's professional pessimist!

"It fits what we know so far," Ennis said, hanging halfway down the gun ladder. "But we're just guessing. We need to get more hard data and the only way to do that is to talk to them."

"Yeah. Would be nice if they had some kind of ID, so we know we're talking to the same bunch and not just somebody that copied a transmission or something." She stood up, an idea suddenly popping into her head. "Hey Yolanda. Send 'em a ping or something, anything. But send it four times, then wait, then send it four times again."

At the comm board, Menehune nodded. Harrington, looking marginally more alert now, had a speculative expression on his face.

"Do you think they might actually be the same ones? Found a new ship and set off again?"

"Or their allies. Somebody was waiting for them at the dropoff, and there could have been others we missed. And then there's—"

Yolanda interrupted. "Got a ping back! Now two, close together...three. Yeah, same pattern. One, two, three."

Moire let herself relax just a bit. Their visitors had been told the whole story, then, and not just the executive summary. Or, if Harrington was right, maybe their former exchange student/hostage Engine Four Watch himself was on board.

She nodded. "Right. This time we don't have all the advantages, but we've been introduced and everyone is being polite. Now what? They want *something*, and I don't think it's just idle chitchat. They know we are armed, so I bet they are too. Let's figure out a way to go see what they want without risking everything."

"Split your forces," Ennis said immediately. "Run if things go bad."

Gren snorted. "Only one working web ship. Yeah, there's plenty of wrecks and we got the skills to fix 'em but we ain't *that* fast."

"The bulk of us could stay on *Frankenstein* while the dropship makes contact," said Kilberton, "but that would leave the dropship vulnerable, without escape."

"The dropship can hide out in the sargasso," Moire pointed out. "The crabs don't dare get too close or that gizmo gets triggered. Sure, it wouldn't be fun, but we could find a wreck and make it livable for a while. *Frankenstein* could pop back in a week or so and make sure the coast is clear. Dropship crew will be volunteers only. Except for you, Kilberton. You're staying here."

This set off a firestorm of argument, the others correctly interpreting this as meaning she was going on the dropship. Moire heard them out, surprised at her own calm, and finally put two fingers to her lips and emitted an ear-piercing whistle.

She glared at their stunned faces. "It's not up for discussion. I'm going. My decision to take this risk, and besides, if Harrington is right I'd end up visiting them anyway."

All eyes turned to Harrington, who held up his hands. "Personal command is quite a popular concept with the crabs, I'm told. Sorry, but there it is."

"Do we have to actually meet them to talk?" Kilberton asked. "They sent us a code that we translated."

"Good point. Let's see if Perwaty and Radersent can come up with something to try."

They tried several different variations of 'what do you want', suitably translated, but all that came back from the crab ship were either repeats of the first transmission or two other short communications that had clearly come from Radersent's medical emergency.

"Damn. They don't have the databank," Ennis said wearily. "All they have is what they captured, whole."

"Just a phrasebook, in effect," Harrington said, leaning against the wall.

"Not even that. The only thing they can really communicate is a willingness to communicate."

Before her crew could get organized enough to thwart her, Moire started issuing orders. It took some more yelling, but in a remarkably short time she found herself piloting the dropship away from the sargasso but parallel to the crab ship. They were transmitting the four-beep code as they went, hoping the crabs would figure out what they were doing.

Ennis was with her. She wasn't sure if that was good or bad, but she agreed he had a right to be there as the only Fleet representative in the sector. Radersent had joined them too. Moire was fairly sure he had volunteered–but he had never refused anything she asked of him. It would certainly make translation easier, and if the crabs had really been referring to him instead of using the first phrase in their list, it would be handy to have him present. Harrington would have glued himself to the dropship in order to go, and she found four more of her crew willing to be backup.

She watched the board; *Frankenstein*, following the plan, was going deeper into the sargasso for safety but still keeping the core between it and the crabs. And the crabs were–yes. They were following the dropship. Nice and slow. She angled the heading so they would meet a hundred klicks away from the edge of the sargasso; that should be far enough away from the gizmo.

Moire glanced back in the cabin. Radersent was hunkered down on the deck, carefully holding the translation device. Gren had rigged some webbing to function as a support and to keep him from being thrown if she had to maneuver hard, but it wasn't much. They really ought to build him a suitable seat, with a harness or something. Wasn't right to keep him rattling around loose like that, especially when he was still recovering.

"Unknown on visual," she announced. "Everybody ready?"

Tense nods, sober faces. She'd issued rifles for the ones staying with the dropship, since it didn't have weapons of its own. Things would have to be pretty bad already for her to allow using them, but it was better than nothing.

Damn, their ships were dark. She drifted the dropship closer, wondering what to do next. If this was going to be a habit they'd better come up with some protocols.

"Captain. Something is flashing underneath," called Joey, one of the rifles.

He was right. She nosed the ship down, slowly and very very non-aggressively. An even darker space on the surface of the ship was opening, the edges folding back on themselves. The flashing light was not very bright and reddish in color.

"Do they want us to dock the ship inside? We are *not* going in there," Moire said. "Wait a minute—are those crabs? I can't see. Searchlight is bright for us and would be blinding for them. Any options?"

"Forward light can't be adjusted...wait, we've got running lights, right?" Ennis asked. "Standard, or Inner Systems?"

Moire shrugged, the question meaning nothing to her. "Hey, Kilberton," she said over the main comm. "This dropship, do you know what kind of running lights it has?"

"Inner Systems, Captain. We found it on that old freighter, remember? It was originally from there."

"What's the big deal with Inner Systems?" Moire asked. "They use different bulbs?"

Ennis stared at her. "What's that? No, Inner Systems ships use colored running lights to stand out from their surroundings—more crowded. Industrial and Fringe ships use bright white. I think we can use these without causing too many problems."

Moire thought about it, and nodded agreement. Ennis hit the switch. The improvement was marginal, but enough for her to see the welcoming committee, some curiously familiar long sinuous shapes, and the fact that this opening was not deep enough for the dropship.

"They've got those damn self-aware tentacle ropes," she muttered. "Dammed if I'll anchor this ship with them; we wouldn't be able to get away. Waitaminit. Kilberton said this dropship came from the freighter—we have a ramp on this tub! For freight! We can extend that, they can grab it, and if we suddenly remember an urgent appointment elsewhere we just leave the ramp behind as a thoughtful farewell gift." She scanned the board. "Huh. Not here. Controls must be at the back hatch. Time to seal it up, folks. Alia, take over. Rotate and just give enough room to extend the ramp," she said, waving her replacement pilot to the chair. "Joey, you stay live with the rifle but don't set foot outside the ship unless I say so, got it? Helmets on, people."

She left the cockpit and sealed the door. Venting the whole ship was a pain, but so was rotating out in twos and threes through the airlock. Not good from a running-away perspective. Watching the tentacle-ropes reach out and grasp the ramp she felt her heart rate accelerate. She glanced at Ennis; he was focused on the group of crabs ahead in the bay.

We can run if we have to. Moire waved Radersent forward. The ramp was too narrow for anyone to go with him, and he'd be least likely to commit a social solecism by mistake. She and Ennis went next, followed by Harrington who was feverishly trying to record everything with his in-helmet vid. She hoped the crabs wouldn't think he had a nervous disorder or was about to explode.

Her hands were sweating, her breathing harsh. This was nothing like the last time. This crab ship was undamaged, functioning. So was the crew. She could feel the gravity change sharply at the end of the ramp, and wondered again at their phenomenal control of gravitics. The crabs were all wearing their own version of spacesuits, baggy elastic things with long narrow panels on the head instead of clear faceplates like the humans had.

"Damn. How big do they get?" Ennis murmured. Two of the crabs were noticeably larger than the rest. The largest was in the center, with a group of smaller ones. The second large crab was off to the side, with two crabs standing nearby. Radersent was smaller than any of them.

"The crabs we rescued had a giant too," Harrington commented. "Recognize anyone?"

"No, but I'm noticing something. None of them are carrying anything. There's just that pile of stuff on the deck, and none of it looks like the weapon we saw. Guess they are trying to be polite too," Moire said. She took a deep breath and tried to relax. Radersent was waiting for her to catch up, his long head turned back to face her.

She nodded at him, slowly. He understood that human gesture. Radersent turned back to the other crabs, extending the translator with his one good forelimb. Since there wasn't anything to rest it on, Harrington came up to hold the human end.

One of the smaller crabs shuffled forward, but instead of going to the translator it picked up a rough oblong from the pile of equipment on the deck and held it out. Something must have been said over the crab frequencies, because Radersent reacted, his chin lifting and his body shifting in a minute version of the happydance. With his tendrils he awkwardly shifted the translator so he could use it.

"Travel crabs make word finder not tied," was what displayed when he was done.

"If they made a translator of their own why didn't they use it?" wondered Harrington.

Moire shook her head, starting to grin. "No, it isn't a translator—not yet, anyway. It needs data. They must have figured out how Radersent jiggered his device, and worked up something that transmits the same way."

"Travel crabs need words," confirmed Radersent.

"Tell query first," Moire sent from the translator. They'd already hammered out a list of questions for Radersent to ask.

Things went much more quickly than the last time; since Radersent could communicate himself, the only bottleneck was explaining it to the humans.

No, these crabs had not followed them. They knew the humans came to this spot, that was all. The crabs they had rescued were alive and well. That was clear enough. When it came to explaining why they were there it got more confusing. Something was not completed, something important.

"Fix Radersent," the biggest crab said, and indicated Radersent's damaged forelimb with its own. "She fix crabs." Pointing to the other large crab and her group.

"They went through all this to bring us an orthopedic surgeon?" Ennis asked incredulously.

"They went to a very dangerous place to meet dangerous aliens and bring them an orthopedic surgeon," Moire said, feeling shaky again, "because they want something. This is getting way out of my league."

By now everyone, human and crab, was crowded around the translator. She'd gotten to know a little of Radersent's body language, just from being around him so long. Assuming the visitors were the same was potentially dangerous, but if she did she would have sworn they were...curious. Any time a human moved their hands, especially tapping out words on the translator, every crab's attention was transfixed. The small crabs would go completely motionless if she moved, but not Harrington or Ennis or Radersent.

There was evidently quite a discussion going on between the crabs, judging from Radersent's reaction but he wasn't translating any of it. She tapped him gently, indicated the translator and he started communicating again.

"Much she fight past. Not fight crab now here. Query?"

Ah. Good question. "Crab here not fight human here. Human here not fight crab here. Past crab fight human. I fight past crab."

Big reaction. Head tendrils moved with great energy and motion. Radersent had hunkered down a little, so she tapped out, "Query Radersent good?" That got her a human-style head-nod. "Query crabs travel here? Query crabs talk humans?"

Radersent spoke. The other crabs stopped moving. The biggest crab moved forward, barely a meter away from her, and Moire could tell the crab was focused on her. She swallowed, not daring to look away.

"He's got something," Harrington said in a tight voice. "Hold on...'More fight she say place. More fight crab she say place no fight. Query more fight human she say no fight. Say words crab human. Query?'"

"Something is not getting translated right," Ennis said. "What the hell does 'more fight she' mean?"

Moire slowly raised her hand toward the giant crab. Their helmets were transparent, unlike the crabs; she knew the movement of her mouth could be seen. "More fight crab she?" she asked, still looking at the crab. "Tell Radersent to ask. Is that her name? What she is?"

Muttered conversation over the comm frequency, then Harrington replied. "To our limited understanding, it seems to be yes."

She didn't have it all, but she had enough. They could figure out the fine details later. It was completely, totally out of her league but there was no one else to do it. Again.

"They want a neutral meeting ground. To talk. Humans and crabs. That's what they want."

CHAPTER 9
UNFINISHED BUSINESS

"Okay, so it looks like that star there would be perfect for the dog-leg," Moire said, pointing at the screen. "Mass and relativistic skew is good, and it gets us in position for a deep straight shot to Sequoyah. We can drop out and make sure we weren't followed." Kilberton studied the diagrams and the hoverdata, did a few calculations, and nodded.

"Shouldn't be much of a time hit either," Gren said. Moire's office off the bridge was not roomy, and with Gren's bulk added there really wasn't much empty space. "Since we had the time, I tuned things up. Fixed the towing gravitics too, so we shouldn't look like a crab ship in webspace. Dunno exactly how much better it will be, since we've bent spec on this ship too far for me to even guess. But it will be better."

"That's good news, Gren. You've worked hard on this. I'd appreciate it if you'd write up what you did, both for the crab tow and the recent changes. I think Fleet would like to know that." Moire stretched, carefully, and yawned. "No rush. Looks like we'll miss the next rendezvous with Palmer. Have to wait for another month."

"When do we leave, Captain?" Kilberton asked, standing up and ducking his head to avoid the ship-status readout on the wall.

"Just waiting for the last of the stowage. Yolanda and her team found a better set of guns on the TripleSun freighter, so we're taking those instead. Plus I want our little friends to be gone for a while before we head home."

Gren grunted agreement. "Big help having that remote for the translator now. Nice of 'em to let us know they were leaving. How's he doing?"

"Radersent? They put some kind of weird goop on his forelimb. Looks like a cast to me but they said it stays on and 'goes in' or something. I didn't get all the details but Harrington thinks he'll be restored to full function for the first time since we met him." Moire glanced at Kilberton. "Anything else? I'm guessing we've still got a few hours before we get going, so rack time would be good. I'll be on deck but I want you to take us out."

Moire did a quick check of the ship status and long-range scanner after they left. Someone was always on guns now; she'd learned the hard way. She should really be heading for rack time herself but she was too tense and wound up to sleep. So they'd survived yet another unscheduled crab encounter. Those weren't getting any easier with practice, since the parameters kept changing. They needed more information–good, solid information.

115

She went to the fourth level and what used to be the substation room for all the powered cargo holds before they'd gutted the ship. It was now the headquarters for the Crab Linguistics and Cultural Studies group, or Ennis, Perwaty, Harrington, and a chastened Inathka. Harrington had persuaded Moire to let Inathka out of cabin arrest, under supervision. Inathka was still terrified by real live crabs but found the cryptographic analysis too fascinating to resist. Any attitude problems were swiftly cured by threatening to keep her away from the data. Ennis had done some scavenging of his own in the sargasso and found some working screens and a datacenter, which was a big help.

Ennis was leaning back in his chair, three textsheets in front of him.

"We need a high-resolution infrared imager!" Harrington burst out as soon as Moire came in the door. He and Ennis were the only ones in the room.

"Why?" She was getting used to single-minded comments from this bunch. Ennis grinned at her resigned expression, and she grinned back.

"They use it for markings. We thought we were seeing all of the writing, but George asked why they couldn't apparently see blue and it got us thinking. Perwaty borrowed a thermal imager from Engineering–it has a bit of recording memory, but not near enough–on the visit where we did the last upload to their translator. Look here," Harrington said, holding up a handgrip device with a small screen. "See the edge of the doorway? That symbol looks nothing like the one we see with a regular vid, as you can see…. Drat. Where did it go?" Harrington pawed through the hardcopy, textsheets, and other junk piled on the table.

"Day 12, file 127 has a good shot," Ennis said, and Harrington tapped at his screen. "It looks like they see a different spectrum than we do. Anything with a shorter wavelength than a green-blue doesn't seem to register, and they definitely can see further beyond red than we do. How far, I don't know."

"Interesting." Moire looked at the vid still on the screen, and then at the handheld. The symbols on the door frame of the crab 'vestibule', where they usually met and talked, looked very different with the infrared. Probably translated as "watch your head" for the gigantic females, who didn't have a lot of clearance through it. "All right, I'll put it on the list. But try and come up with some criminal purpose too, OK? It helps when we go shopping so we know where to look. Not a lot of xeno-sociologists on Kulvar," she added. "What else have you found out?"

"Confirmed the gender ratio. Bouncy was the best one to ask; all the others tucked their chins and didn't seem to even understand the questions. He said it is about 20 males to 1 female, now."

"Now?"

Ennis rubbed his head and sighed. "They say that a lot. As compared to the olden days, I suppose. That's a hell of a ratio, and he implied it was even more skewed earlier. I didn't want to ask too many questions about how they reproduce and such for fear of giving offense. You might be able to do it, but not me."

"That female thing again? How can they even tell human males and females apart, since we're pretty much the same size?"

"They think that's completely strange, but it's not just human females. You in particular. Bouncy said everyone who talks to humans was given a— we think it means 'surface copy'–of you."

"Great. Now I'm on wanted posters for two sentient species. That's got to be a first," Moire said dryly. "Why do you call him Bouncy, anyway?"

"He appears to think talking to humans is quite a treat," Harrington said, "and while Radersent's happy motions have rather a swaying effect, he generally goes up and down. A bit disconcerting at first, but one becomes accustomed."

"It's good to be getting names," Moire said, collapsing into a chair and sitting down to look at some of the hardcopy. "We may need to be diplomatic translating them later. Not like we can pronounce the real ones, though, so something has to give," she said, yawning.

"Your idea about calling the friendlies Hsurwyn is starting to spread in the crew," Ennis noted. "Too early to tell, but I think it may help."

"Yeah, that was standard practice even in my day," Moire said, grinning. "Give the bad guys bad names. Nice polite ones are Hsurwyn, but anybody shooting at us stays a crab." She looked up again. "Speaking of which, did you ask if we will get other visitors at the sargasso, all subtle-like?"

Harrington steepled his fingers and looked smug. "Even better. I idly mentioned that all kinds of human ships sometimes come here, and that they may not be allied with you. I somehow neglected to mention the crews are usually dead by the time they arrive; a shocking oversight on my part. I was assured that they have no intention of coming back–I believe they even thanked me for the warning. The Breaker device terrifies them, so I tend to think they were telling the truth. Does this mean we have our neutral meeting-place settled?"

Moire leaned back in her chair. "Yeah. I discussed it with Kilberton, tossed in the latest crab attack reports, and came up with three stars reasonably remote from any human settlement and told them to pick one. I hope they understood we weren't promising to show up there on a regular schedule. Sounds like they will, though."

"Curious. They do seem quite interested in talking to us," Harrington commented. "Speaking of allies, we were able to confirm the ones we rescued are allied with the recent lot that showed up at the sargasso. We decided to call them the Galactic Health Organization, or GHO for short. By the way, what we thought was the name of the rescued ship? Left-Right-

Up-Down-Yes-Go? More accurately a job description. They are explorers."

The mist of fatigue suddenly burned away from Moire's mind. Everything in the room snapped into knife-sharp focus. "Explorers," she whispered.

"Yes, and it seems some of the other larger groups, or families–similar word clusters, anyway–don't like that. They are a small group, or whatever, and the GHO apparently helps them when they can, and–"

"Moire. What's wrong?" Ennis was staring at her, one hand reaching out then dropping.

She struggled for a moment to speak, to put the emotions into words. The bone-deep knowledge that no one was going to rescue you, no one *could* rescue you. All alone, and dying. The ship that had done so much ripping itself apart. "Sometimes...I wondered if we did the right thing, rescuing them. Not for Radersent, but for...humans. Now I'm sure. They were explorers, just like I was. Nobody rescued us, though. Everyone died except me." The crabs–no, *Hsurwyn*–of the explorer's ship would survive, because of her. She closed her eyes, the faces of the crew of *Bon Accord* flitting through her memory, and for the first time she felt at peace. "I did the right thing."

Zandovar sipped coffee from the plain white bone china cup, contemplating what his next move should be. He was dealing with someone insane, frighteningly intelligent, or more likely, both. This Kolpe had managed to gain his attention in the traditional way–by buying it. The information the man provided had proven accurate and extremely lucrative. Of course Kolpe wanted something, and now Zandovar had to decide whether further business would be worth the hazards.

Ghost had been able to find nothing on the man, even with his DNA. That was disturbing. The information Kolpe had given Zandovar was highly restricted and well-defended. He knew, for he had attempted to access that company's data himself without success. But now he had the schedule and special codes used to indicate valuable cargo, and all he needed to do was decide if he wanted to use it or not.

There was more to this transaction than gain. Kolpe was interested in the same person he was; Ren Roberts, or as he now knew, Moire Cameron. Both Kolpe and Cameron could be valuable assets, but he could only keep one of them. Which would be more useful? Cameron, at least, was sane.

"You say you have only contacted me," Zandovar said at last. "Yet you transmitted a considerable data file to an off-station source shortly after arriving here. How can I be sure others will not want a share of what you promise?"

"Other enemies," the harsh synthetic voice said. "Not involved with the Cameron project."

Zandovar raised a skeptical eyebrow, wondering if the optic sensors on Kolpe's container were good enough to see it. "You have convinced me you have information I can make use of. We can do business on that alone. I am *not* convinced that killing Cameron would be practical. She has proven valuable to me as well. You are asking me to risk a great deal—my people, my station—for your revenge. And I *would* be risking them. She is capable and dangerous, and not alone."

Silence. A light blinked on the container readout panel, and the medtech silently got up and did something to the controls. The medtech was another mystery. According to the guards, who were all Zandovar's people in reality, Peter was really just a medtech, and had no criminal connections or knowledge at all. Usually he sat in silence at these meetings, terror radiating off him like heat, but he never hesitated to attend to his patient when he was needed.

"My analysis shows Cameron has a base of operations," Kolpe said finally. "My prior employers knew she had found a human-compatible planet. It is possible she uses the planet as her base."

Zandovar froze, cup halfway to his lips. That would certainly be a prize worth the effort, if true. Even if he did not want it for himself, there would be others that would pay handsomely for the information. "I require proof, not assertions."

Ghost looked at him intently, and Zandovar nodded permission for him to speak. "She asks for weapons every trip. Heavy shells. Unusual for ships. Used for planetary defense."

"I can get proof," Kolpe rasped. "If you can place an item on board her ship without detection. When does she usually come?"

"She doesn't," Zandovar said dryly. "I cannot predict when she will next arrive. However, when she does, I can arrange for certain items to be available for sale. Weapons. I have not permitted anyone to sell them to her before now, because I am not certain what use she will put them to and if they would be used against me. I am willing to make a small exception for the information, if you are correct. If you are not—why then, you will have put me at risk." He inclined his head at Ghost. "Go with him and find out what he will require for his plan. Send it to me before taking any action."

Ghost silently stood and walked away. The container, after an awkward turn, followed, and so did Peter. "You may wait," Ghost said in his choppy fashion to the medtech.

"I must remain with my patient," Peter said, his voice faint and shaking. "He needs me."

Something changed in Ghost's face, very briefly. It almost looked like an emotion. Zandovar shook his head and finished his coffee. Ghost never had emotions.

119

"Wait! Dammit, what's the rush?" Kostas caught up with Moire, wheezing a bit. "Somethin' you not tellin' me?"

"Of course. I've got so many different secret plots going I can't keep them straight," Moire snapped. "That's why I need to talk to everybody on the council–and not here in the cavern where a mere three hundred people can overhear."

"Oh." Kostas grinned, opened the inner, ordinary door inside the cavern blast door, and waved her through. "Mind I ask about somethin' personal, then?" Moire nodded, heading down the dusty corridor bored into solid rock. "So, that full-grown baby you rescued, the Created? My family's been helpin' out when we get the chance, and my wife started wonderin' what you plan to do for 'em. See, kids need their own family. Doesn't have to be much of one, see, but it has to be *theirs*. Maybe you already got somethin' set up for adopting, I dunno. Promised 'em I'd ask, anyway. We've gotten real fond of her."

Moire stopped and stared at the burly construction chief. Everybody, especially the Created, knew he had a huge soft spot for kids and his daughter had taken the Created as playmates without a second's hesitation. His wife Alice, the electronics and signals specialist, was more of a mystery. She didn't talk much, but around Kostas it was difficult getting a word in edgeways sometimes.

"You really want to adopt her?" Kostas nodded. "Are you sure you can handle her? *You* can, sure, but..."

"Alice rigged up this harness for Aurora–that's what we call her–with tension pulleys and spring gear. Keeps her from goin' too far or falling. Yeah, I think we can manage. They learn real fast."

Moire shrugged. "You're doing a better job than I am so I don't have a problem with making that permanent. Remind me before I leave and I'll write up some kind of formal document, on the odd chance it will have any legal weight off this planet."

Now they were deep underground. Last time she had been here cables were everywhere and rooms were only roughed in. "Hey, it looks civilized. Is everything wired up? How about the worry pit?"

"Yer *command center*, Captain, is almost done," Kostas said, grinning again. "Alice got a wild hair–y'know, since we're stayin' she's really working hard on adding any security tweaks she can think of–anyway, she thought we oughta have some decoy transmitters, maybe fool Toren into attacking the wrong place."

Moire just nodded, since they were now in the meeting room. It held actual–if handcrafted–chairs now, and a table that had never previously served a different function in a cargo bay. By Sequoyah standards, that was pure luxury. Everybody else was already there, since she had broadcast a priority signal as soon as *Frankenstein* dropped out of webspace.

"My apologies for the firedrill, and especially to those I woke up in the middle of sleep cycle," Moire began, taking her seat. "We made record time getting back, thanks to Gren's tweaking the gravitics and the new route has a clearer track. I want to leave in the next twelve hours and make the next rendezvous with Palmer. Ennis has some hot data for Fleet about the crabs–that is, the Hsurwyn. We made contact with some that want to be friendly, or at least prefer talking to shooting. I'm thinking that should be encouraged."

"We can't possibly deorbit the wreck you brought in twelve hours," Kostas protested.

"Not planning to. I'll be taking *Raven* for the trip, and Kilberton will stay and help with the deorbit and can go back for more. The new route is much more stable, and he's familiar with the sargasso and how *Frankenstein* handles. We're offloading some guns we found–I'd like you to take a look and see what we need to adapt them to planet surface operations. Unless Palmer has some surprises for us, next stop would be Kulvar and we can get the equipment there. Anything else we need in a hurry?"

It took time, time she didn't have, because everything kept coming back to the crabs. She finally had Harrington, still in orbit, connect up and transmit some of the vid they'd taken at the sargasso. Then people started calming down. Since these were supposedly secure transmission capabilities, she had Alice check for signal leakage. Damned if this was going to be a complete waste of time.

Moire sighed, and tried to remember the people on Sequoyah hadn't been spending so much quality time with well-behaved crabs. They had a right to worry.

Reminded again about needed equipment, Mammachandra made a good point about medical supplies. There wasn't much Moire could do about finding medtechs on Kulvar, but if they expected shooting in the near future they ought to have the gear to handle it. Maybe she could get an autodoc, at that, or more med-scanners. Anything would help. Madele Fortin was the only medtech they had and she wasn't young.

Kostas, sneaky devil that he was, had long ago figured out how the Cameron Chaos Factory worked and always kept his wish list updated and annotated. She needed more people like him.

Everybody agreed they needed more light transport. And everyone agreed that a station like Kulvar was unlikely to have any. Finally Moire had her shopping list and people started to leave. She also had a pounding headache.

"Captain–if our calculations are correct I would have time for at least two round trips to the sargasso," Kilberton said. He and Kostas had been having a separate discussion for a while now. "If we can find ships with working realspace engines, we can set them up to maintain orbit until we are ready to put them in place."

Moire rubbed her forehead. "Sure, if you feel up to it. You'd better take Gren with you, then, and I'll take Kwife. Gren's better at rough-and-ready ship mods, and you might need more tuning on *Frankenstein*. Oh, hey," she said, sitting up. "Decoys. Just like the transmitters. We could leave some up there and make Toren think we've got a fleet!"

Kostas grinned. "You can put transmitters on ships too, Captain. I'll talk to Alice."

👑

The temperature of the air was perfect—slightly cool. Clean and odorless. Zandovar poured more water from the purifier and regarded the screen again. Everything was prepared. He was forced to admit Kolpe Anders had done well, and even that there were tricks he could learn from him. He could not always have been so...obsessed, so fanatical in his hatred, or he would never have become such a capable operative. Zandovar wondered who had employed the man before this.

They didn't even need direct access to Cameron's ship for this part. Zandovar had managed to procure, from a corrupt Fleet source, a handful of Takamet guided mini-missiles. Cameron had snapped them up. Kolpe provided the knowledge to modify the guidance package of one which, with some added electronics. Put together, this information would provide initial heading from Kulvar, gravitic field readings, duration of webspace flight, and other information. This information would yield the location. Any scans of the missiles would reveal guidance circuitry, as expected. The information gathered would be sent in burst format to dormant, miniaturized data-dots released as dust from the missile packaging. They *would* have to break into her ship to retrieve it, but he had plans for that too.

The old ceeyo had held parties, called midnites, to show off his power and prestige. Security was guaranteed to all who attended. He could use the custom for several other purposes besides as cementing his position. Moire Cameron would receive a very pointed invitation to this midnite, and Zandovar could wait for the data to come back to decide whether or not she survived. Yes, if they had a solid location, he would take the risk. He smiled. Thanks to Moire Cameron, he even had his own web pilot to help him make that decision.

CHAPTER 10
MANDATORY FUN

Meniran shifted in the full-length console seat, glancing impatiently out the viewport at the curve of the planet below. She called up a light mandala on the screen to distract herself, to seek calm. It was so *irritating* to be forced to a physical meeting instead of vir-sim! Security was a paramount concern—the Long Range Plan was so close to completion, and in danger—but acknowledging the necessity of the personal meetings made it no easier.

Her organization had done nothing that could have triggered the meeting. That was not even a possibility. There were disquieting rumors, disturbing snippets of information...no. She had planned very carefully, monitored every project under her responsibility—and a few that were not. Meniran had not reached the top echelon of Toren by trusting her peers without question.

Finally the private shuttle docked to the Hub ship. Meniran strode out, eager to get the meeting over with. She carried nothing; all secure data was already on the Hub and even she was not allowed to download private copies. Her assistants did not follow her past the Core Zone boundary. Security was paramount.

She scanned the room discreetly as she took her place at the table. Faces were tight, hardened against revealing any emotion that could be interpreted as failure—much like her own. Meniran was shocked, and the first icy wave of fear washed over her. Did they all know? No, that wasn't possible. They weren't all looking at her, either. But then...that meant there were other problems she hadn't heard about, which was even more frightening.

The first to report was Security Services, the military wing. She knew about some of those issues, but wasn't involved in any way that would reflect badly on her.

"Equipment and ships are proceeding as scheduled. The loss of the generated worker facility, which was to supply the main forces once the trial program had finished, has put the rest of the schedule at risk. If we do not rebuild the facility, another source must be found."

"The generated soldiers were not part of the active phase of the Long Range Plan," Bren Li, the Intelligence head, commented. "We can work around the loss for now."

Lennox gave a short nod and continued. "There is a possible breach of secrecy related to the operation on Bone." Meniran sat up. "All personnel and equipment involved were scrubbed of identification and data, however several anomalies were discovered. Detailed investigation has been hampered by the need for continued secrecy, so the investigation is not complete. Wreckage was found of the primary vehicle in orbit. However, the surface transport vehicle is missing and no wreckage of any kind has been found that matches it. The entire landing team has been confirmed dead, with the exception of the contractor Kolpe Anders—no body was found. Strangely, a large number of witnesses from the Waylands facility are also missing, and we have been unable to determine where they have gone. Others mentioned a large cargo ship in orbit at the time that might have given them transport."

"Was there any Fleet presence?"

"None."

"Is it possible Anders was captured and taken off-planet? Someone with inside information sent Fleet a message, and it was after the attack on Waylands," Li interjected. "Or perhaps his data store was found."

"We have no proof he survived," Meniran said, keeping her voice calm and slightly disinterested while her pulse raced. "The building was destroyed. The local constabulary don't have the capability or the interest in doing tissue sweeps for proof of death. If there wasn't a body, breathing or otherwise, they don't care. Besides, his mania for security exceeded even ours. Whatever data he had he either encoded and tripwired, or simply memorized. He has never leaked or lost data at any time we have employed him."

"Yet someone accessed one of his accounts," Li shot back. "One we set up for him for a different job, that had a transfer flag. Approximately seven weeks after the attack, the entire amount was transferred to an Inner Systems fee-service crypto account."

Meniran glared. "Kolpe would never do that. He knew about transfer flags, and much better secure encrypted banking options than a fee-service crypto. That's what someone who watches trid shows would think of as secret and secure."

"Then we have a problem, do we not? Whether or not Anders is alive, his information has been compromised. We can't risk discovery. There is another serious development," Li said, and brought up the four-sided trid display in the center of the table. It showed a data plot. "Something has happened to the war. At the same time we are seeing a sudden change in crab attacks over the last few months, Umbra has stepped up operations. What those operations are remains unknown. We have contacts in Fleet and in FarCom itself, but Umbra is closed to us. Note too, the total number of attacks is down and the locations are restricted to the very edge of human space."

"What has caused it?"

Li shook his head. "It could be internal politics on their side. It could

124

also be the result of whatever Umbra is doing. The worst case scenario would be that contact has been made. We have no information. The immediate issue is Fleet has not been degraded to the level the Long Range Plan requires—we know this for certain—and the crabs likewise do not appear to be defeated. With the loss of the generated soldier contingent we have no viable plans to counteract this. Fleet *must* be too weak to oppose us, and the crabs must not be a threat before we can solidify our position."

That was enough to light the fuse. The Long Range Plan, that they had struggled for so long to prepare for, was threatened. Argument erupted at the table, some even losing their carefully maintained composure. They could not afford to fail—and if Fleet found out while it still had strength to take action, Toren could be destroyed. And she, and the others in this room, would be destroyed along with it.

"Are you all blind?" Meniran snapped, interrupting the head of colony development pleading for a wait-and-see attitude. "We are already in the active phase of the Plan. *Someone* is attacking us. Someone who has the capability of annihilating one of our strike force teams *and* the ship they came on, yet not leave a trace behind. Someone who had the ability to break Kolpe Anders' security. Something is making the crabs hold back. It's Fleet—Fleet and Umbra. We have to go to active status ourselves. No, I am not saying we should directly attack," she said, forestalling Li's objections. "They are fighting in the shadows, and so should we. If we can't break Umbra's security, we should track their activity and learn what we can from that. Also, we never intended to stay fixed in any location in the active phase. The core team should stay mobile and so should our necessary assets. We can't risk losing anything more."

"It's too dangerous. If we are all missing at the same time, it will be noticed."

Li sat back, a thoughtful expression on his face. "Not if we do it carefully. This is why none of us show up on the corporate charter, and why this division is under R&D. We will have to ask the Chief for approval, of course," he said, looking at Meniran. "Let's put together the proposal now. One thing I know will be required—a base of operations, unknown to Fleet. Has there been any progress with the Bon Accord project?"

"Kolpe Anders claimed Cameron was going to be on Bone," Meniran said through gritted teeth. "But since that mission was a total failure, no, I have no progress to report. The project was not the highest priority. If the resources I have been requesting for the last year are now available, I can promise results. Ships. I need ships." She fought to contain her anger. How dare he imply it was her fault. "Well? Do I have them?"

Li's eyes narrowed. "Yes. The matter is more urgent now. We need a base, not just a future colony. Do what you need to do."

"You not feeling well?" Ennis asked, deadpan. "I don't see any new craters on your face."

Palmer grinned. "Too busy runnin' yer damn mail service to get in fights," he said, tossing Ennis a long, featureless grey box. "They said that was you, eyes only."

Ennis looked up from his examination of the box, surprised. "They didn't come along?"

"Nope. Sat n' watched the dock until I left, though. Sometimes I really wonder what the hell yer up to, and then I get some sense and think I don' wanna know."

"It's all very dull. Tax forms," Ennis said. "I'll be back."

"Sure, gotta read those tax forms," Palmer nodded, and went back to watching the cargo offloading and offering unneeded advice to the crew.

Ennis ran up the stairs and down the corridor to the storage closet that had been set aside for his use. Some humorist in the crew had labeled the door with "Fleet Personnel Only." The box was biometric secure, plus an inner coded lock, and was much larger than the communications with Umbra usually were.

When he opened it, he discovered why. Besides the usual orange-and-red striped classified datatabs, the box contained two smokey-clear datacubes. One had a gold foil stripe with the words "Diplomatic Communique" impressed in the surface. Ennis felt his eyebrows crawl up. "I am not getting paid anywhere near enough for this," he muttered, quickly reaching for his encoded reader. Perhaps the orders would explain. He hoped the plain datacube had something useful for Moire and her crew, because the other one spelled nothing but trouble.

Ennis scrolled through the orders, the sinking feeling in his stomach only increasing. It was as bad as he had feared. The traditional reward for a job well done was another job, only harder, since clearly the last one was too easy.

He replaced everything except the plain datacube in the box, reset the code, and locked it. Opening the door, he saw Alan sitting in the corridor against the opposite wall, his sniper rifle cradled, as always, in his arms. Alan looked up as the door opened.

"Why do you go in there? There's nothing to even sit on, just shelves."

"I have to look at secret things where nobody else can see," Ennis said, cautiously feeling his way. "Those are the rules."

Alan scrambled to his feet. "Nobody? Not even Mom? Why? She wouldn't tell."

"Not on purpose, no. The best way to keep secrets, though, is to only tell people who really need to know. Remember when you forgot you had a round chambered and dropped that rifle on the crate in the hold? We didn't even tell Ash and George and Hideo about that, and you trust them, right?"

Ennis started walking back to the hold.

"Yeah," Alan muttered, clutching the rifle so tight his knuckles were white. "But we fixed the hole in the floor."

"Yes we did, and I've never been so glad I learned to use a cap-welder," sighed Ennis. "And *you* learned to always clear your weapon, so it was a good lesson—but not one your mother needs to know about right now. Your friends might not mean to tell, but they might by mistake if they knew."

"George talks a lot," agreed Alan. He saw Moire across the hold and walked faster. "He has secrets he doesn't tell you," he said, pointing at Ennis.

Moire grinned at Ennis' expression, and he compressed his lips to keep from grinning back. Her smile always made it difficult for him to concentrate. "Yes, I know."

"You do?" Alan stared at her. "You don't care?"

"It gives me an excuse to interrogate him," she said, her mouth twitching. "It would be boring if I already knew everything. What if you already knew how that new game Palmer brought you ended?"

Alan looked thoughtful. "What does 'interrogate' mean?"

"To ask lots of questions. It's horrible," Ennis said. Alan glanced back and forth at Moire and Ennis, uncertain if he was being teased or not.

"Is that what you do? I hear you both laughing sometimes," Alan said, suspiciously.

"He's very ticklish," Moire said. "Useful interrogation technique. So, what does the puzzlemaster have to say for himself?"

Ennis took a deep breath, happy for the change of topic but still not sure how best to proceed. "He, ah, sent a lot of information," he said, handing her the datacube. "You and Harrington are cleared to see this, and really anybody you deem trustworthy. He'd prefer you not send it to the newswires, though."

"Like I usually do," she said, examining at the cube. "It's almost black. That means it's pretty much full, right? That's a lot of data."

Ennis nodded. "I don't know exactly what's in there myself, but it should be good."

"His face has a secret," Alan interrupted. His voice wasn't accusing, merely observing.

"I know," Moire said gently. "I think he wants to only tell me."

Alan looked at her, then at Ennis, nodded, and without saying anything more wandered away to where the other Created were 'helping' the unloading. Ennis noticed that while he carried his rifle properly, his grip was relaxed.

"What was that all about?" Moire asked.

"A child's garden of OPSEC," Ennis said. "He's figuring it out. And I think he only occasionally wants to shoot me now. Progress."

Moire smiled, a little sadly. "Speaking of secrets...."

"There's another datacube," Ennis said, sighing. "For the crabs."

"*What*?" Several heads turned their way. Moire crossed her arms over her chest and gave him a searching look. "Explain."

"This goes...almost all the way to the top. No, I'm sure they've cleared this with NorStar Council, there's no way a diplomatic—they want to make contact, direct contact, with the crabs. So, the good news is we already did it and they approve. The bad news is they want us to do it again, and give them that cube. Plus figure out a way for them to read it. Namur has some suggestions about that, and—"

"In our copious spare time. Look, I'm all for intergalactic chitchat but I've got more immediate responsibilities. Every day I'm passing notes for FarCom is a day I'm *not* building defenses for Sequoyah. I can't fight two wars and win, not with what I have to work with. If Fleet wants to talk to the crabs, great. I'll introduce them. Give 'em a translator device. Or if they want to send some of their ships to keep Toren away, then I'll go deliver messages. The rendezvous point we set up with the Hsurwyn is a long way away, on purpose, and it takes a long time to get there. I've asked my crew for a lot, but this is pure risk with no gain. I'm sorry," she said, looking away. "I want to help, but I can't. I've done what I can."

Ennis rubbed his forehead. It would be easier to argue if he didn't agree with her. The orders had been very explicit, and speed was stressed. *Use any means at your disposal.* What did he have? No ships, no weapons, and offering to train Alan in ship-boarding techniques would be both insufficient and counterproductive.

He blinked. It didn't have to be Alan, did it?

"I'll fight for you. The way Fleet kept moving me around I picked up a lot. And Umbra, too."

Moire's face twisted in distress. "Don't, please."

He waited until she looked at him. "You know that I want to. That was never in question," he said softly.

"You'll get in trouble with Fleet. I'm not asking that of you. I don't want to make you choose."

"I've already chosen. It's too late for that," Ennis said, taking her by the arms. "I can't promise help from Fleet, but I'll ask. I'll ask for anything you want. I *can* promise my help."

"But—"

"They told me to use any means at my disposal. They forgot to issue me a carrier, so you'll have to make do with just me." Moire chuckled, then shook her head. "I'm serious. They are desperate, Moire. Use it. Use me. Let me help you."

She was silent for a long time—too long, but he forced himself to wait.

"You know, it just wouldn't be the same without you. Promise you will stay until Toren comes. That's my price. Make up whatever story you think Umbra will believe–maybe I don't trust you to leave, or something. That I think you know too much and will tell them my secrets. Can you do that? Without burning your bridges to Fleet?"

"I will stay until Toren is defeated and Sequoyah is safe," Ennis said. It sounded like a formal oath, and he meant it as one. And with the strange sympathy they had developed, he knew her unspoken question and knew she knew his answer. *Even if you are dead.*

They stood and pretended to watch the unloading for a while, leaning against each other and companionably silent. Ennis captured her hand and gently rubbed his thumb against the slightly raised scar tissue on her palm. It was barely visible now, but he always knew it was there.

"I'd better get a response coded up for Palmer to take back," Ennis said finally. "Come with me and help me decide the official story. You can add your wish list, too."

"You know," Moire commented. "It just occurred to me we don't need to be quite so discreet any more–not that any of the crew is really fooled, they just know we don't want it talked about."

Ennis raised an eyebrow. "Why is that?"

"We only did it to keep Fleet from ever finding out and causing you problems. But if they have ordered you to, er, use your initiative, how can they blame you for doing just that?" Moire assumed an innocent look. "Unless you object, of course."

He shook his head, grinning. "It may make writing my final report a little tricky. Official guidelines discourage the use of euphemisms."

♔

Inathka scowled at the data cube. She didn't like it. She didn't like what it meant. She didn't like the job it had given her, and she *especially* didn't like all that juicysweet info just sittin' there, waitin' for her ta crack and snoop.

Well, they said she could. Then again, Herself said the more Inathka knew, the harder gettin' loose would be.

She heaved a huge sigh, and brought up the processor code again. Gotta be somethin' missing somewhere. She still wasn't sure about these people but her skin didn't itch around 'em. The Harrington was all right, even if he did talk funny. Then there was Ennis, and her skin told her he was dangerous, real bad edge, but not to her–and not anybody on the ship.

So if the Harrington and the Bad Boy liked the critters, maybe they were okay too. Hard thinking about it. But gottaknow kept comin' back up. Wonderin' what they were thinking; why they were wanting to talk to Herself.

The screen blinked, and Inathka gave a satisfied grunt. Got the header info, anyway.

"Success?" said the Harrington, looking up from his own workings. Always lookin' so calm, like he was just bein' mannered to ask. Or maybe it was the nose keepin' the distance.

"It ain't chatty yet but maybe allowing as how it might know a commcode that's through," Inathka said.

"There are times when I consider constructing another translator, just for you," he said, going all pain-face. "Not to hurry you or anything, but the goal is to have a working device before we arrive."

"Yeah. That's what I hear said," Inathka snapped. "So's why them core-blisters what give the instructions don't do it themselves? Can't look at the real thing, that's for the critters only, not us ratty protein crusts. Give us a little bitty sample like to play with instead. Gonna work perfect first time when *they* plug in, 'shah! So rad-hot they gotta be all *seeeekret* an' shit, but we ain't gonna know if we translating 'hello-sailor' to 'gimmee da money'? That's dumber than *govmint*, and I din't–" Inathka narrowed her eyes. The Harrington had flashed a funny look just then. "Waitaminit. Is this..." she swallowed, cursing the haddaknow in a language she just invented for the occasion. "Please, Mr. Nev. Don't tell me this govmint stuff. Please?"

"Do you really want me to answer that question?"

"Already did," Inathka said glumly. "Never woulda thought it of her..."

"Oh, come now. It's not as if we are all government employees, we just fell in with bad companions and easy living did the rest. In point of fact, I joined this circus in circumstances very similar to your own–with slightly less forcible slavery, however. Curiosity and desperation; a dangerous mix."

"Workin' for the govmint," Inathka muttered. "I went wrong, surely."

"Look at it this way–their intentions are good, even if the execution is less than stellar. Some of the Hsurwyn apparently don't want to fight humans, and the government wants to talk to them to encourage this behavior. And as you have noticed, the government needs all the help it can get in that regard."

"They just gonna bust it up edgewise; they always do. I'm thinkin' we make real sure the critters unnerstand we just passin' the message for someone, read? Captain don't need govmint stupid all over her."

The Harrington, he had that funny look on his face again. Inathka was starting to worry every time she saw it. "How strange you should mention that. Er, I hope it won't disturb you, but it appears the Hsurwyn think the Captain *is* a government. Ships, er, ship, crew, et cetera under her command."

Inathka thought about this for a moment. "Don't rightly mind. Herself ain't dumb." A sudden, horrified thought made her start. "Hey, does bein' a govmint *make* you dumb?"

"I devoutly hope not," the Harrington said. He looked about the same as she felt.

After that little chat Inathka didn't feel right about taking her sleep hours 'cause they were there. She hadda do the job right now, for Herself. So the critters wouldn't get mad from the govmint stupid they were translating. So she kept goin', long as she could, until the code started blurring.

Then one day Herself in person was standin' in the door.

"We there already?" Inathka asked. "I got it workin', but only just. I mean..."

"We're here, but they aren't," the Captain said. "I'd like you to come to the bridge and take a look at something."

Not like there was goin' to be an argument, and besides, the gottaknow was stirring. Inathka headed for the door.

"Take your datapad," says Herself.

Inathka doubled back and snagged the pad, keeping her mouth shut but her brain yammering. Wasn't supposed to take anything out of the room, that was the rule for her. Datapad had her updated notes, and the stuff the govmint folks had figured out to use with the translator.

"Um, but they aren't there, right?"

The Captain kept on moving, but not running-like so maybe nobody was shooting or yelling. "They left something behind. If I had to guess, it's an answering machine."

Inathka blinked. "A machine with answers?"

The Captain laughed, and shook her head like it was at herself bein' dumb. "Sorry. They probably call them something else now, if they still have them. A machine you can leave messages on. The problem is I don't know for sure the friendlies left it. I'm hoping you can figure that out."

They let her run the scan board up on the bridge, Herself and Ennis watching every little move. Inathka didn't mind. If she'd been trying a sneak, sure, that'd be twitchy for her. Since she was on the same line as the Captain she just ignored them both and focused on the board.

The answer box was a cute little thing. Maybe a little crumbly around the edges, but the critters seemed to make their gear like that. It was broadcasting the 1-2-3 signal loud and clear.

"Anyone could have set that up," Ennis said. "For all we know sending the countersignal triggers a bomb."

Inathka slewed around. "I thought they were friendly!"

Ennis shrugged. "The ones we've talked to seem to be. What we're gathering is there are other groups that don't approve of talking to humans at all."

That added some thrilladanger to the day, didn't it? Inathka chewed her lip and looked at the spectrum scanner readout. There was a pattern that looked familiar. "I wanna send a blip. Two frequency mix, one pulse. Shortest translator code we use. I think they got a scanner going."

Herself nodded. Inathka sent it, then watched the signal detector. It beeped and showed the waveform she was expecting, and she sighed and sat back, feeling smug.

"Might be loaded hot, but they got the translator code exact from our guys. See that edge on the signal scope there? Only on their device, not ours. Plus I'm seein' the trace from their comms. Looks like they made it so a ship without their own translator could talk to us, just in case."

It took a while, but she figured out the rest of the gizmo while Ennis and the Captain argued in the background. Once the four-signal was sent, it transmitted a brief message about 'say more'.

"So whadda we want to say?" she asked.

"We can't wait more than a day, max. We've got that invite," Herself said, looking irritated. "I'll come up with something. I suppose we don't want to leave the love note from your shadowy friend out here unsupervised?"

"No, that would be a bad idea," agreed Ennis.

Inathka kept her face all empty-quiet, like she was just waiting around bored. She just knew govmint would be trouble...but then, the Captain hadn't looked angry talking about them. More annoyed, like it was work she didn't want to do. This other thing, now, the 'invite' that she wanted to blow up but couldn't. Who was doing that to the Captain? And why?

Inathka kept up the bored even after she got the message to send, and she left the bridge when that was done all docile-like. Then she doubled back, going quiet, and did a quick listen at the door with a hollow tool handle at the seal.

Crude, and it didn't work that well. Well enough to hear a few words, two of them 'Kulvar' and 'midnite'. Not a good combination. No wonder Herself was wound up. But why was she going to a Zandovar midnite if she didn't have to? Surely the govmint wasn't behind it, was it?

Inathka narrowed her eyes. Somebody was twisting the Captain's arm, and it didn't matter who. Somebody else was gonna to need to watch the ship, every millimeter, and she was just the one to do it. Sure, she was under guard–just meant she'd have to be careful is all. And if the crew with all the time in the world and suspicious to boot couldn't find out, Zandovar's people would never know.

♛

Warm sunlight filtered down on Moire's face. Just beyond her feet small waves lapped and rustled over the pebble beach, and not-yet familiar smells drifted on the breeze. The pseudo tree scent she could pick out; slightly spicy and sharp. Her head was resting on Ennis' stomach, their hands loosely clasped, and she let her breathing match his until she started to drift off to sleep.

Then voices started, carrying over the water. Shouting voices. Ennis shifted, lifting his head.

"Anybody on fire?" Moire asked drowsily.

"No smoke," Ennis sighed after a moment, and dropped back down. "Mmm. Grimaldi is taking off. Gren's watching her go." He yawned, and the arm holding her tightened.

"They can handle it," Moire agreed, and shifted position to indulge him in a long, sensuous kiss. She drifted in and out of sleep for a while, waking up again when she heard the shuttle coming in again. Seemed fast, even for Grimaldi. She opened her eyes, then resolutely shut them again. Her people were good, dammit. If she needed to know, they'd tell her. What she needed to do now was rest up, so she could pretend to be the piratical terror of the galaxy everyone on Kulvar thought she was. That kind of stupidity wore her out worse than the transit to Sequoyah.

She shifted her head. Ennis wasn't as comfy suddenly.

"Gren's headed over," he said, voice carefully calm. Moire sat up.

Gren still wasn't comfortable dealing with dirtside life, and always stepped over the driftwood at the tideline as best he could. He never stepped on the wet beach.

"Found something on the last ship," Gren said. "Guy who was doing the skin check thought it was repair debris at first."

"So what is it?"

Gren squinted at the greenish sun, then looked back at her. "Brought it down for me to take a look at, to be sure. Looks like a Koumerian-Tan reactor baffle assembly. Now I *know* it isn't from any of our ships. We've got some wrecks, sure, but they've all got working reactors or they aren't Koumerians. They found some other stuff too. Just little bits, mind. Not enough to make a ship or anything."

All restfulness was gone now, burned away in a fire of fear. "It wouldn't be." She was standing now, Ennis beside her. "Let's take a look."

"You think it is a ship?" he asked.

"Anomaly that blocks Sequoyah is uneven. Stresses'll rip your ship apart," she said, leaping between rocks in the most direct path to the cave mouth. "*Bon Accord* was lucky—one big giant node protected the ship. Plus poor speed by current standards. Still nearly didn't make it." She was half-running by now. "Ships nowadays are even more vulnerable. Faster, and multiple nodes."

The wreckage had been spread out on top of a crate. Moire turned over the pieces, examining them carefully. A piece of conduit, still connected via a bulkhead bypass to a chunk of metal, had heat discoloration and spalling from fragment impacts. A nasty, prolonged crackup, then.

"These reactors you mentioned—are they good, bad? What kind of ships have them?"

"Inner Systems," Gren said, scratching his jaw. "Don't see 'em much out in the Fringe. Small and light ships, passenger types. Not fancy or fast either. But you don't get 'em in cargo, or anything heavy."

Moire tossed the scrap of metal in her hand carelessly, keeping her face relaxed. Plenty of her people were watching her reaction from the corners of their eyes, and she didn't want to start a panic. She tilted her head towards the front of the cave, and Ennis and Gren followed her out.

"It doesn't make any sense. If it is who I think it is, why are they just throwing ships away?" Moire said, being careful to pitch her voice low.

"Because eventually one will succeed. They have a lot of ships, remember. Monopoly on colony transport. And they are ruthless enough to destroy ships and crew if it gets them what they want. What I don't know is how many attempts it will take for a ship to make it here and back in one piece."

Moire looked at Gren, who shrugged. "I wouldn't do it, not for any money. I gotta tune the nodes every other run here, that's how bad it is. Tell you one thing, they aren't telling the crew. Toren has to be beyond desperate to try this."

"What happened? Why now? Is Fleet starting to ask them awkward questions?"

Ennis looked startled, then shook his head. "No. They still need—that is, no. Besides, if something like that had happened Namur would have found a way to warn me, unless it is recent. How long ago do you think this happened?"

"If these are the first fragments, maybe a couple of weeks ago. Might have been some we missed, too, or that didn't come out of webspace. Gren, I'm sorry, but we're leaving now. I'm going to grab every canister of ammo on Kulvar that isn't nailed down, and as soon as this stupid party is over I will be back. If we were ready I wouldn't leave," Moire said, gnawing her lip. "You're in charge. I want everything and everybody underground as much as possible. Do a scan from orbit and see what pops up. Oh, and you should probably deep-orbit the extra ships. If Toren shows up for a quick look-see I want them to think we have no real presence. Got that? Kilberton will have to make the next meeting with Palmer shortly after we leave; he can pass along the message about these ships showing up in pieces."

Gren grunted. "Sure would be nice to know when they show up, but I guess sky-eyes would give it away too."

Moire looked up. "Say, that reminds me. Remember when we dropped out on top of those crabs? And you said it was just the tuning?"

"Yeah," Gren answered, looking dubious.

"See if you can come up with an early warning system. It'll have to be a web ship, probably *Frankenstein*, but just doing short hops near Sequoyah. Kilberton was saying something about a possible web pilot trainee; ask him about that too. Oh, and one other thing. We have to get rid of the prisoners."

"How are you going to do that?" Ennis asked. "Dumping them on Kulvar would bring a lot of notice, not to mention it would probably be kinder to just shoot them."

"Oh, I'll send them somewhere safe. Don't worry. I'm thinking stripped-down survival shelters, or retrofitted containers. They just have to hold atmosphere for a few hours."

"How can you be sure they'll get picked up in time?" Gren wanted to know.

Moire grinned. "I'll make it completely irresistible. Don't worry about that. Just fix up enough for every one of those bastards. And they don't have to be comfortable, either."

"Moire, what are you planning?" Ennis murmured, gently rubbing her back as Gren stumped away.

"I'm going to put Sequoyah's coordinates on the outside of the shelters," Moire said. "The secret isn't going to last. Might as well give Toren some competition."

CHAPTER 11
CHARLIE DOES THE FOXTROT

Moire eyed the dropout indicator, one hand loose on the realspace controls. "Ready, shuttle?"

"Ready as I'll ever be," Lorai said over the comm. She didn't sound like her usual happy-go-lucky self, and Moire couldn't blame her. Kulvar was enough and now sneaky spy-stuff with the shuttle on top of it. And in her case, Kilberton was back on Sequoyah attempting to put the mobile web-detector system in action so she had to dock *Raven* all by herself. Getting spoiled, she was.

The indicator blinked, Moire hit the dropout, and immediately started scoping out the possibilities on the screen. Yolanda was watching too.

"How about that three-engine rig? Big enough?"

"Yeah, but it looks rough-edge. Gotta be a clean ship. Hey, big freighter–up three an' out two. They'd never let them dock that thing on Kulvar; they'd hafta use shuttles."

"See it," Moire muttered, altering her course just a bit. "Signal?"

Yolanda stared at her screen. "Not much. What we expected."

"Shuttle free and shadowing," Moire said into the comm. The indicator pinlight for the exterior dock flickered from green to red. Yolanda Menehune was cursing under her breath, manipulating the communications console.

"Shuttle, freighter is *Daisunae Ri* with a listed dock of 2-34. Say the main shuttle is usin' it or something and ask around," Yolanda said.

"Coming in for drop." Moire eyed the approaching freighter and slowed her speed. They were in line, the freighter blocking Kulvar's sensors. "Go shuttle!" She pulled a sharp turn up and away, as if suddenly realizing how close the freighter was. There were enough crappy pilots around here it wouldn't even be noticed, and there was the shuttle, hiding in the shadow just like they'd planned. Now Lorai could pretend to be coming from the big freighter and have no connection to her piratical self. Moire nodded to Yolanda, who opened up another channel to negotiate their supposedly only dock.

This had been Ennis' idea. He was even more paranoid about Toren showing up on Sequoyah than she was, if that were possible. They needed more ammunition, medkits, all kinds of stuff that would bring unwanted attention when Zandovar was too suspicious as it was. So they had brought extra crew, none of whom had been to Kulvar before, and Ennis and

Yolanda had briefed, trained, and harangued them on how to survive and not blow cover. They would go out in separate teams, get the gear, and bring it back to the shuttle that would now be associated with the freighter *Daisunae Ri*. She hoped that wouldn't cause the freighter trouble, but really, did anyone innocent show up at Kulvar?

Ennis entered the bridge, already in his Kulvar native disguise–jacket with *Raven* insignia, boots with strange metal plates and rivets, and a black shipsuit discreetly covered by roustabout trousers and a vest with stiffened protective sections.

"You're going out with the decoys too?" Moire asked, resigned.

He grinned. "Decoys have to be noticed to work. Besides, it has to look like one of our regular supply runs."

"Huh. Ask if anybody has heavy shells; I always do."

"If I have time."

Moire rolled her eyes. "I thought you were going to do decoy shopping?"

"We need new gear for the midnite," Ennis said, his face carefully bland. "We can't go like this; Zandovar would be offended." He gestured at his current outfit.

"What's wrong with the stuff I've already got? We don't need any new gear! Besides, what you are thinking of costs a lot of money. Money better spent on bulk purchases of bloodglue," Moire grumped.

"He's right. Show up in yer grubbies, might as well not show up at all," Yolanda said. Seeing Moire's expression become more cheerful, she added pointedly, "and we already discussed this. Ya gotta go if we want to come back again, ever. So do it right and stop whining."

Moire slumped back down in the pilot's chair. "If I was a *real* pirate I could shoot you for being an insubordinate smart-ass," she grumbled.

"Ain't worried; I seen you shoot," Yolanda shouted back as she left the bridge.

"Fine. We'll look nice for our funerals," Moire said, glaring at Ennis who was shaking with suppressed laughter. "Try to find some cheap criminal party clothes, will you?"

"I'm getting substantial hazardous duty bonuses," Ennis said. "If the general fund runs out I can extend you a loan."

"Might have to take you up on that. We haven't had time to fix up any ships to sell, and all the wrecks we bring back are getting used as quarters or orbital defense. Good thing everybody is taking their pay in land or I'd really be–" She looked up, startled, as Harrington entered the bridge, followed by Inathka. "Aren't you supposed to be locked up?"

"She has a suggestion I thought you would find interesting," Harrington interjected smoothly. "Involving improving the security of this ship."

Moire narrowed her eyes. "Why now? Why not earlier?"

"'Cause I just got it workin', an' I knew you'd take it with a nose," Inathka mumbled, but she kept her head up. "Keep the govmint from gettin' in; anybody else too. Kulvar fulla pokarounds, usta be one myself."

"Yeah, I remember. Can you think of a reason why I wouldn't want you mucking with my ship, then?"

Inathka blinked, then shook her head. "But you'd *know* about it! You got me outta Zandovar's slave bin; remember *that?* Think I'd wanna go back to it? Got even more reason than you, keep them hardbodies off an' out."

Moire glanced up at Ennis. He gave Inathka a hard, appraising look. "She's correct. Most of the usefulness is in keeping the device hidden. I wouldn't advise trusting her alone just yet, but if she does the installs under supervision and we keep the controls, it should be all right."

"Great. Harrington, you just volunteered." Moire got up from the pilot's chair and stretched. Inathka seemed genuinely worried, and she would have a better idea of what to watch out for here. Ennis could double-check the work and see if they could trust her further. "I'm all for keeping this visit nice and quiet."

✵

Alan checked his weapon again, trying to remember all the rules that were new. He couldn't take his sniper rifle–Ennis said it wouldn't help here, and the other people would wonder why he had it and maybe take it away. The fabric of his new shirt was slippery, and it was hard to keep the butt of the new gun from slipping on his shoulder. If he shot it, he would have to hold it very tight. The new shirt felt good, though. Soft, and it had little gold points all over. Lots of people had new clothes for the midnite. Mostly they were black, which wasn't very interesting. It would have been even nicer with red and blue and orange.

His mother had new clothes too, but she didn't seem to like them. He wasn't sure if he liked them either. They made her look like a different person, maybe one that wasn't very nice. She had a black silk thing tied over her head and dangling down the side. The gold dragon he and the other Created had given her–she always had that. That was okay. But instead of a regular jacket she was wearing a vest that looked like it was made of dark scales, and the shirt under it didn't come up all the way. The sleeves were too short too, and he could see the white scars slashed on her arms. Moire always hid those, and he was glad. Seeing them made him feel strange.

Ennis looked like a different person too. His hair looked all wet, but still curly, and while he had a jacket, it went all the way to the floor and he didn't have a shirt at all. This must be a very strange party. Alan was glad he got to stay on the outside, with the other crew.

"Alan. Try and persuade the critter it wants to be with you." His mother was keeping her voice calm, like they had learned to do when the nerya was nervous, but he could see the muscles in her jaw flexing.

He made a soft chittering noise, in the back of his throat. Ash had taught him how. The nerya's head popped up from beneath her hair, all three eyes in front. That was good, it wasn't frightened. He chittered again, and the nerya flowed down his mother's arm and jumped to him. Alan tapped its head softly, and it cheeped.

"Good job, kid. Everybody ready? Remember–you are one of my crew, and therefore dangerous. Don't start anything, but look like it's only my explicit orders preventing you."

She turned away, and had only taken one step when the little nerya yeeped and sprang suddenly, landing spreadeagled on top of her head. The headscarf confused it, and it grumbled as it slipped until it found itself back in its preferred location, in the crook of her neck.

Alan reached for it, but it skittered away. "It doesn't want to go. If you wait it might, though."

She shook her head. "We can't be late. It had better behave itself and not run off because I am NOT going back for the little furball. Idiot nerya."

"I think it gives you a properly piratical air," Ennis said, with the kind of face that didn't look like it was laughing even though it was. "Suitably updated."

"Gaaaaah," Moire snarled, and strode out.

It wasn't the whole crew, but most of the regular ones. They moved through the corridors in a big black group, not too close. Alan could hear the instructions Ennis had given them all, repeating in his head. Observe, but don't stare. Notice what is unusual. There weren't that many people out, but he knew why already. The party was a big one, all over the dangerous parts of the station. Only very important people got to go to the party at Zandovar's place, where they were going. In the corridors he saw just a few of the ones George called the lump people, who didn't move much of anywhere and looked like they were dying.

So quiet, too. The few people who were in the corridors scrambled to get out of their way, especially if they saw Moire's face. A big man in grimy coveralls was towing several linked float pallets loaded with compressed plastifiber blocks and other reuseables, and he had to scramble to get it all to one side of the corridor.

Alan gave the man and the float pallets a quick glance as they passed. He wasn't sure what made him notice it so much. There weren't many other worker people out now. The man didn't seem like the other reusable gatherers he'd seen either. Nobody seemed to like the job, but this man didn't seem to care. The float pallets weren't completely full, but there wasn't much empty space either and he was headed in the direction of the docks, not back to the processing station. Maybe he was going to pick up from one more small ship before he stopped for the party? That would make sense. Alan relaxed, and looked around for more things to think about.

Kulvar wasn't that bad, when there wasn't yelling or fighting. He wondered why they didn't have parties more often. Did they like fighting? Alan always wanted to make anything fighting him to go away as fast as possible, even if that meant fighting back.

Now they were going past the big door that went to the upper levels that were safer. They hadn't docked up there, so they didn't have to go through this time and make the guards let them in. Alan blinked, surprised. The big door was open all the way, and while the guards were still there they were just standing around and not making people pay them. One was even talking to a woman who was dressed like an ordinary person—an ordinary person on a nice station, he amended. A slender girl with wide, mournful eyes stood behind her, tense and nervous. She kept looking at the door and then looking away.

Alan glanced back after they had passed the door, and that's when he saw the guard point to them.

"Mo—Captain." Alan tilted his head back just a little, indicating the woman who was headed their way, a grim, purposeful look on her face. The girl trailed behind, her expression even more unhappy. Moire stopped, and the woman strode right up to her. She was considerably shorter than his mother, but it was like she didn't know that.

"I'm looking for someone wearing a jacket with a black bird on it," the woman said. "Like that." she pointed at one of the crew who didn't have fancy new clothes.

"Come back later," Moire said, looking bored and annoyed. "I have no time for you now."

"My husband has been missing for nearly four years. Don't tell me to be patient! I got a message from him, from this station, and the clerk said someone with a grey jacket with a black bird sent it. It wasn't him, and nobody has seen him on this station. He said his ship was wrecked, and he was rescued ...just tell me where to find him, please."

Alan glanced at his mother, eyes wide and about to speak until he saw her make the handsign that meant "don't say anything." He felt hurt. He knew better than to say any of the secrets, like Radersent, or Sequoyah. It must be something that he didn't know was a secret? Sometimes it was hard to remember.

"She shouldn't be running around here," Ennis said in a quiet voice, his eyes flicking around. Some people, including the guards, were starting to watch. "Better hold her until we get back."

Moire nodded once, sharply. "Right. Dammit, I don't need this ... Alan, Jensen, Siguero—take them both back to the ship and secure them. Call back when you're done and don't leave until I tell you to, got that? Now let's move before anybody else gets in our way."

Alan wasn't sure what to do. Everyone said look mean, act mean out here, but he knew his mother didn't want him to hurt them. The small woman was angry, and didn't want to go and the girl was starting to cry. The two crew grabbed the woman and started to drag her away. Alan stared at the girl and hoped he looked mean.

"Move," he said, and the girl whimpered and ran to the woman. He wanted to tell her it was all right and she wasn't going to be hurt, but he couldn't out here where the real Kulvar people could hear.

He felt different being in a small group, and he watched everything even more carefully than when they left. That's why he noticed the edge of a float pallet near their dock. He walked faster, moving ahead to check it out. It was piled high with plastifiber cubes, one of which he recognized because there was a big blue piece on the side from a starch-puff bag, just like he had seen earlier. But this was only one pallet, and the man had been pulling at least three. And why was it here, instead of at the cargo hatch where the reusables always got picked up? Nobody used the personnel hatch.

He felt better when he saw their hatch open and a familiar face.

"What the–what happened?"

Alan pushed past. "She said bring them here and keep them secure. Where can we do that?"

"Why are you doing this? We just wanted to ask some questions!" the woman yelled. "Let us go!"

Now that they were on the ship they could talk. "We are helping, really!" Alan said. "We can take you to Perwaty. I think we can," he added, cautiously. "Or bring him to you."

"Where is he?" the little woman asked, staring at him intently. "Is he all right?"

"He's...at home," Alan paused, "and he isn't hurt or anything. We found him in his wrecked ship. Um, I'm not supposed to say any more. When my mom gets back she can tell you."

"But why do we have to stay here?" the girl blurted, looking frightened by the sound of her own voice.

"Because there are lots of bad people on Kulvar. You have to follow rules, and you were doing it wrong." Alan remembered he was to call in now that he was here. The comm wasn't working. He tried again, but the little screen just said unable to contact code. Was it broken? What should he do now?

Zandovar's private area was subtly and expensively decorated, sometimes with people. At the entrance a man and a woman with stunning physiques and clad only in some kind of dark nacreous paint like black pearl greeted the guests. The whites of their eyes had even been darkened somehow. The effect was eerie. Their greetings were sometimes quite physical, if the guest appeared interested.

"I guess that paint doesn't rub off," Moire muttered softly.

"Amazing stuff," Ennis agreed.

"Let's find Zandovar. The sooner we tell him how much fun we are having the sooner we can leave."

Ennis shook his head, smiling slightly. "Sorry. He won't even show until everyone is here."

"I hope everybody hurries up, then," Moire said, glancing around. "Zandovar really put on a show."

The adaptive walls, which she had last seen when Ash was dripping blood everywhere, had been changed to reflect the dark pearl theme. A wispy servant wearing shreds of dark green film like seaweed offered wreaths of dark pearlized flowers. Moire felt the nerya shift when the wreath was placed on her head, but it didn't reveal itself from underneath the black headwrap. Maybe it would, and Zandovar would be repulsed and tell them to leave?

"You look like you might be enjoying yourself a little," Ennis murmured. "Or was that a nervous twitch?"

"Momentary lapse. Won't happen again. Do we dare eat the food?"

"We should at least pretend to. You know, pick some up, wander around, drop it off after playing with it. Or feed it to the fluffball–it would probably regard any nasty additions as flavoring."

They were in the conservatory now, where the plants were backlit with something that made them fluoresce and long sheets of dark shimmering fabric hung from the cathedral ceiling. A woman in a thin dark pearl kimono was playing an instrument like a zither. A few other guests were standing in small groups, silently watching each other. Those faces which had expressions looked tense or uncomfortable.

"You know, I wasn't expecting piñatas or raucous singing, but is this really what high-class criminal parties are like?" Moire whispered. "I've been to livelier wakes."

Ennis shook his head, brow furrowed. "Maybe it's because he hasn't been in power that long...I don't know. You're right; this is odd. If he hasn't fully consolidated his standing, why hold such a public event and make it obvious? It could also be the weapons ban. They might trust Zandovar but not each other."

That made more sense. Zandovar hadn't banned all weapons inside; that would have caused a riot. Just powered weapons and guns. She was carrying a knife in her boot and another in an arm sheath, and Ennis was similarly armed. For thugs used to powered weapons, though, they probably felt half-dressed.

Another pearlized server, this time glowing white, walked gracefully by with a tray and offered it to them. It contained many small, irregular pieces each skewered by a clear red spike. Moire selected one and inspected it. It looked like deep-fried cotton swabs. Ennis had taken one that was a solid oblong decorated with random white swirls. He took a bite.

"It's a salty-sweet," he said, making a face. "Very high-class, but I've never liked them."

Moire looked at her mystery hor d'oevre and shook her head. "Come on, Gremlin–make yourself useful." She held it up near the base of her neck, and felt the little nerya shift to inspect it. When she pulled the red spike away, it was completely clean and had tiny toothmarks on it. "Hey, this is working out rather well."

More people entered the garden and started circulating. It was difficult to keep an eye on how many were present in the strange lighting. None of the faces were familiar to her.

"Let's keep moving," Moire suggested. Ennis merely nodded. "Alan should have called in by now. I wonder what happened?"

"Got distracted by something shiny?" He shook his head, ruefully. "That wasn't fair. He stays on-task when it's important, and he doesn't like it here. He'd get to the ship as fast as he could without drawing attention."

"Yeah, if what's-her-name didn't bite him." Moire fiddled with the control bracelet for the captain's earring. She tried calling the ship–no answer. Then she tried Alan's personal comm-code. Nothing there either.

"Problems?" Ennis was watching her face, intently.

"Maybe. Nobody is answering."

She tried an on-station code, just for fun. That didn't give a response either, and moving out of the garden conservatory towards the entrance made no difference. Ennis had been fiddling with his ordinary commlink, and the grim expression on his face told her he was seeing the same thing.

"Question is, is he jamming everybody or just us?" Moire murmured in a barely audible tone. More of the pearl-people were about, carrying trays or decorations, and more guests had arrived. "And why?"

"I've seen at least two apparent comm conversations going on. Could be a ploy, but it's a damn complicated one. And if it's just us, that means nothing good. No information gets to us and we can't call for backup." Ennis scanned the room. "No obvious heavies, and if the servers are carrying any weapons I'd be amazed."

Despite herself, Moire laughed. "Certainly not very large ones." She put her arm around Ennis' waist, drawing him closer, and pretended to be whispering sweet nothings in his ear. "We have a little time, then. If we hadn't met up with that woman I wouldn't be trying to call out so soon. They don't know we know yet. Ideas?"

Ennis nuzzled her ear. "Get out. Get information. We don't know the status of the people we brought or the ship. What does Zandovar want, and can we bargain with him?"

"He wants something he knows we won't give, or why bother with all this?"

Ennis frowned. "Then he'd just take it, directly. Maybe he thinks he can pressure you? You're right; it doesn't make sense. Let's see how far it goes," he said, tilting his head slightly towards the knot of security at the inner entrance door.

They drifted that direction, making innocuous small-talk. Moire was unsurprised to see one of the security personnel intercept them well before the doorway.

"Gotta stay once yer in," he said. He seemed more bored than worried. "Not gonna sweep ya every time ya feels it."

"Shureit," Ennis shrugged. "She's waitin' on dim-load, for Zandovar," he said, indicating Moire with his thumb. "They say coming, then nobody show. It heavy, right? Maybe get handoff your way, gites?"

The security goon narrowed his eyes. "Ain't no takedown. Nobody show offa yourside, no load either."

"Random, eh? Not here, not you, we just askin' where? No rough—only lookin' check the side, here. We don' go, mebbe you do us standin?" Ennis extended his hand, palm down, and the goon reached out. Moire saw the edge of a credit tab.

"Yeshure," the goon nodded, giving a greasy smile. "Sa' good."

Moire and Ennis wandered away again. She hoped her expression was suitably unconcerned.

"What the hell did you just say back there?" Moire whispered, when it was safe.

Ennis grinned. "I insinuated that they had intercepted a valuable gift to Zandovar, something you were expecting to be delivered to you by your crew, since it hadn't arrived. I bribed him to go ask our people about it."

"Cleverly *not* exposing we know we don't have comms but are expecting something to show up. Besides confirming the fact we are basically prisoners, did we learn anything else?"

"I don't think they know we're supposed to be incommunicado. When I said you had gotten the message the gift was arriving, he didn't even blink. If we're lucky, Menehune will be around when he goes and asks your people."

"Why?"

The expression in his eyes was hard, focused. She'd only seen that look when a fight was imminent. "We had a discussion about bringing Zandovar something. She was against it. Only his direct clients do that, and we don't want him thinking you want to be one. So, she'll know something is wrong. You know her better than I do; what will she do then?"

"Try and contact me," Moire said promptly. "When she can't do that, try and contact the ship, and then she'll be certain. Not much she can do to get us out, though, not without a battlegroup. We need communications. I don't suppose you've noticed any commlinks lying about?"

Ennis smiled. "We'll just have to encourage someone to drop one. How are you at being clumsy on cue?"

♔

"You're quite sure these won't be detected?" Harrington asked.

Inathka gave him a look of burning scorn. "You thinkin' a puttin' a sign up, maybe? Lookit!" She shoved one of the little devices in his face. It looked damaged and incomplete, with a few scorch marks along one side. "Anybody looksee, gonna say 'oh my, that is certainly a remote sensor' an' try an' fry it?"

"A very creditable imitation of my voice, I must say," Harrington commented, amused. "Certainly to someone of my limited experience, it looks exactly like a burnt-out component that was never removed for some reason." He stifled a sigh and removed the door control access plate.

Working with the acerbic Inathka was not a very useful pastime for him. All of the action was on Kulvar station, but there was perhaps a little *too* much action for his tastes and few opportunities for general research with the midnite going on. Since this wasn't a pleasure cruise either, he needed to make himself useful. Thus, following around an electronics specialist of dubious legality and being a glorified assistant and minder. Harrington reminded himself that he had, in fact, supported Inathka's plan so naturally the captain had thought he would make an excellent addition to its implementation. Pity he hadn't realized how deadly dull this good idea would be in action. Fortunately, they were nearly finished.

"How will you know if they work?" Harrington asked before he could stop himself.

"I put 'em in, 'zats how," Inathka mumbled, her attention focused on getting the device properly positioned and fastened in. She turned her head and glared at him. "I know my doins', ya frik nose! Wanna do it yerself?"

"No, no. Not at all. I'm just—well, let's say I'm a bit paranoid around here. I know you have far more knowledge about this than I do," he said, holding up his hands to stave off her heated protests. "That's rather my point. I was hoping there was some simple test that would demonstrate to those of limited understanding—that would be me—that everything is working according to design so I can stop worrying?"

"Yeah, yeah. Fine. Gonna wear yer jaw out all that talkifying ya do." Inathka took out the sensor datapad, muttering under her breath. She tapped quickly on the screen, efficiently setting up data nodes and test signals. Harrington watched over her shoulder, intrigued. Inathka tapped the SCAN/PROBE node. "See? Nothin' but the reg—" She broke off.

Data was streaming fast and furious over the screen of the datapad. Harrington only knew enough to be able to tell that it was a lot of data, and being sent quickly, but what kind?

"Sheeeeet." Inathka deflated. "Whadido? Looks like a core tap. Howd' I hit one a them without knowin'?"

"Can we tell which one it is?"

"Yeahh. Mmm, waitasec..."

The sound of quick footsteps ahead in the corridor made them both look up. Alan was coming towards them, his open face showing agitation. While his weapon wasn't at the ready, it wasn't slung either and Harrington felt his heart rate speed up.

"Something wrong? I thought you were part of the escort team."

Alan jerked his head, blinking. "I was, but she sent me back with the people so they stay here. It's Perwaty's family," he said, waving his hand to indicate it wasn't important. Like many of Alan's explanations, much that was in his head never made it out to the listener.

Harrington filed away his questions for later, since something was clearly bothering the boy and he didn't bother easily. "But she said, let her know when I got here and I tried but the comm says no message and nobody else knows why and Chiya said you know all about comms so can you fix it?"

He held out his comm unit to Inathka, who was still trying to process the rapid flow of speech. She accepted it automatically, glanced at it, then handed it back.

"Uh, justasec. Gotta check this thing first. Um. 'Kay?"

Alan looked distressed, but nodded. Harrington watched with amusement as Inathka carefully stepped around Alan and headed down the corridor. She had never quite figured Alan out, confused by his adult body and youthful behavior despite everyone at some point trying to explain what had happened.

"It's in the main forward hold," Inathka called back.

"May as well go with her," Harrington suggested. Alan followed. "Did you say you found Perwaty's *family?*"

"They kind of found us," Alan said. "They got the message he sent, I guess. Now she's mad at us because Mom said they have to go to the ship and wait and the girl is crying at the edges of her eyes. I *told* her Perwaty is all right," he added, aggrieved.

Inathka already had the door plate off when they got there. "One a these—inner door, hatch, or hold. Nah, this one's good." She slapped the plate back and fastened it, then opened the door, heading for the hatch with a grim expression on her face. Harrington didn't blame her. She was good at her work, and this was a flub he would never have expected from her.

Then everything happened very fast. Inathka was halfway to the hatch on the hull of the ship, next to the big cargo door. A glimpse of movement made Harrington glance to the inner wall of the hold, where a few battered storage crates remained. He had only enough time to see the man stand, realize it was not a member of the crew, see the gun in the man's hand, and open his mouth to yell a warning. He heard his own voice at the same time he saw the spreading red spot suddenly appear on her back, then another. There was no sound from the man's gun, and just as he wondered at it the violent, battering boom of Alan's weapon nearly level with his ear made him drop to his knees in pain.

The man was running. Alan's bullets hit him and he jerked, ran two more steps while collapsing, and dropped to the deck.

Harrington scrambled to his feet. His head was still ringing. When he got to her Inathka was writhing and whimpering in pain.

"Don't let him get gone, don't let..." she moaned.

"Alan has taken care of him, rather permanently," Harrington said, somewhat breathlessly. The hearing in one ear had not fully returned, and he had to turn his head to make out what she was saying. "That fellow is not going anywhere except the morgue." He did a quick assessment. "I make that three hits; two in the ribs and one in the arm that is barely worth mentioning in comparison. Anything I missed?"

Inathka managed a shaky grin. "You a medtech on side?"

"When you spend as much time as I have with this lot you pick up a great deal of combat medicine without even trying," Harrington said. He looked around until he located the emergency medkit, on the wall near the comm. "Don't go anywhere, will you?"

Alan was sweeping the hold, even opening the crates with his weapon ready. "It was just him," he called out. "And I found this." He held up a thickish, palm-sized object.

"Make sure the hatch is locked," Harrington called back as he ran to the medkit. "We don't need more of that." He snatched the kit and paused just long enough to do a shipwide alert. "Armed intruder in forward hold! Repeat, armed intruder, forward hold!"

When he got back to Inathka, Alan was standing over the dead man with a puzzled expression on his face. "I saw him before."

"Really? Where?" Harrington hastily broke out the little packets marked 'Bleeding Patch'. It wasn't nearly as good as bloodglue, but it would have to do until they could move Inathka to the med station.

"In the station, when we left to go to the party. He had a cart with reusables. And I saw some of the cart when I came in, too!"

"This has gone beyond a joke," Harrington muttered. "You have not been able to contact the captain, you say?" Alan shook his head, looking scared.

"Prolly...jamming," Inathka whispered. "Smeggers planned this...." She struggled to sit up, gasping in pain. "Hey kid, gimmee that." She pointed at the object he had found near the crates.

"I don't think you should be moving just yet," Harrington objected. She ignored him.

"'sa scanner...still sending..." She smashed her thumb down on the screen. The data that had been rolling by stopped.

Three of *Raven*'s crew burst through the open door, weapons drawn. "What the hell happened? How'd he get in? The alarm wasn't triggered."

"I imagine he bypassed the one he knew about. We had just added another that he didn't. Let's get her to medical, shall we?"

Fortunately *Raven* had recently been upgraded with a very high-quality medscanner. Harrington would have preferred an actual medtech, but this was certainly better than nothing. He followed the scanner's directions to inject the repair medium, which was a trifle more discerning about what it stuck to than bloodglue, and found some fluid packs and pain meds.

"I believe you will survive, but you may wish to get a second, trained opinion on the subject. How fortunate your attacker preferred high-velocity projectiles! I really wasn't looking forward to my first surgery."

"Me neither," Inathka said faintly.

A handful of the remaining crew had gathered in the corridor outside, watching with worried faces.

"Now what do we do?" Harrington ventured.

Ivar, a cheerful heavy-mech who had probably been left behind because he looked like a farm boy and would have never escaped notice on Kulvar, rubbed his chin. "We got barely enough people to watch all the doors. If they come at us we got a problem. We gotta get a message out somehow."

"What about the shuttle people?"

"Hangin' low, waiting for us leaving."

Harrington shook his head. "I meant can we communicate with them? Can they communicate with the station without interference?"

"Shuttle's onna ship-comm proto...procoal," Inathka said, the pain meds slurring her voice. "Maybe trynta jam, but I can ge'roun...needtha main board t'doit tho."

Ivar and Harrington exchanged glances. Inathka was badly injured, but no one else knew the communications systems well enough to do anything complicated.

"Right, then. We'll get her up to the bridge, and you fellows keep watch. We'll be in touch."

Ivar nodded, and the group moved out at a jog. Harrington turned back to Inathka, who was struggling to swing her legs down from the exam table and failing. "Will you stop that? I only just got you patched up. You'll be no use to anyone if you faint from blood loss, you know."

"Gotta...gotta get t'bridge," Inathka murmured.

"I can carry you," Alan said, hesitantly.

♛

They were starting to run out of hiding places. Not only was the party

148

getting more lively, they both had to avoid the fellow guest Ennis had surreptitiously swapped commlinks with. He'd done it real slick, too; an 'accidental' collision, a fallen commlink switched and then helpfully retrieved and returned. Moire just hoped the switch wouldn't be noticed until *Raven* was in webspace.

"Any luck?" she asked under her breath.

"Ship's still out of reach. I can get to the kiosk but it can't connect further. It's jammed, all right."

"Better try Menehune. We don't have a lot of time." Moire fiddled with the control bracelet to look up the commlink code, which the stolen unit wouldn't have. The display was flashing. "Huh. That's weird. What's a remote convo?"

Ennis stared at her. "Usually something like another ship trying to contact your comm network. Anyone we know?"

The display only showed an alphanumeric string which meant nothing to her. Shrugging, Moire activated the connection. "Roberts. Who's this?"

"Oh, thank God." It was Harrington, sounding distinctly frazzled. She thought she could hear other voices in the background–someone drunkenly cheering, and Alan wanting to talk to her. The connection was bad, with pops and hisses and blips of dead silence.

"We've been trying to reach you–we're being jammed."

"Yeah, we know. How did you figure it out? Did Yolanda get to you?"

"They called me," Yolanda's voice added. "Knew somethin' was up, but couldn't get a message out to anybody."

"Alan was trying to contact you, and then when he shot the data burglar in the hold we wanted–"

"He *what?* Who got shot?"

Ennis was now giving her very strange looks. She mouthed *trouble* and he sighed.

"Er, some fellow we found in the forward hold extracting a lot of data– webspace telemetry, I'm afraid. He didn't have much in the way of ID, and Alan dealt with him rather permanently after he shot Inathka."

Bad. Very bad. "Did he transmit anything before you got him?"

"Inathka says he sent something but she stopped it before it completed. She did manage to route our comms through the shuttle and a dodgy transmitter jumper, so at least we have that."

"Captain, what the hell's going on?" Yolanda interrupted.

"Zandovar's trying to pull something. Won't let us leave. I can't call out stationwide. Look, we got a commlink that isn't connected to us. Just in case the shuttle re-route stops working or they find a way to jam it, you'd better have that code." Moire read out the commlink information. "Any way we can sneak out?"

"Front is wired up tight,"Yolanda replied instantly. "Zandovar's heavies plus all the hardbodies of the rest of the guests. We could get everyone down here for a frontal assault and never get through the door."

"Anybody giving you funny looks? Think you can get away?"

"They'd give us funny looks and more if we all try an' leave, and we can't just leave you even if we wanted to," Yolanda snapped. "Gotta have a pilot or we're dead."

"I wasn't trying to be noble, really," Moire protested. "Can you at least get a few of you away? As many as possible. All you can do at the front is act as targets."

"Yeah, maybe a few. How we gonna get you out, Captain?"

"I'm thinking." She quickly briefed Ennis on the conversation, adding, "So we need a way out, and not the way we came in."

"Zandovar will have other exits, but they will be even more secure and harder to get to. Unless we can get some weapons or explosives, the front way is our only real option. But not a good one."

Moire looked around, hoping for inspiration. They were at the lowest level of the conservatory, behind some large shrubs with feathery leaves. The back wall was in shadow, but there was enough light to see that it was slightly convex. She looked up. That wall was featureless, with no openings, all the way up to the conservatory roof.

"I think we're near the central air shaft. See if Inathka can get a position fix on me. If you can get through the wall—we still have the plasma cutters on board, right?"

"Yeah. Inathka? Can you find her?"

"'seasy," Inathka slurred. "Service lel unner, station skin. Gezup hunnermeter. Hatch!"

"Okay, that was confusing even for you."

"I believe she was trying to say that there is an outside service hatch on a lower level, that connects to the airshaft a hundred meters below your current position," Harrington said, at his dryest. "And our recent deceased visitor had in his possession a station access card the better to break in to our ship, but now we can make use of it to open that service hatch."

"Gotta suit up," Yolanda said. "Shuttle'll get there but those things can't dock a ship."

"Better get moving," Moire said. "Someone will be expecting that operative to report back, and they might go looking if he doesn't. We'll be waiting in the conservatory."

Ennis nudged her, with a warning look. People were coming towards them, purposefully. One was the strange pale individual she had seen before. Zandovar's assistant.

"Oh crap. Zandovar wants to talk to us now."

CHAPTER 12
TRAPPED IN A COUNTRY SONG

"Yes. That is the target. Secure her and bring her to me."

Zandovar narrowed his eyes. The synthetic voice was beginning to get on his nerves—or perhaps it was the lack of inflection that made Kolpe Anders sound so arrogant.

"I have not yet received any information of value, despite the expense of the preparations. You are in no position to make demands of me."

"Her ship is here. Only a handful of crew aboard. The one you sent to retrieve the data has not reported?"

Zandovar glanced at Ghost, who consulted his datapad. "He has not returned. Databurst partially received."

"Partially?"

"The transmission did not complete. It has not resumed." Ghost looked at Anders' medical container without expression. "Ship communications continue to be electronically jammed."

"The jamming I provided you would not interfere with that signal. I designed it to only block *Raven* and Cameron from sending or receiving communications. Nothing else."

Zandovar felt a searing jolt of rage. He fought to contain it; to prevent it from becoming visible.

"I told you to jam only the ship. That could be explained away if discovered, and would give us time to...clean up, if needed. Why did you add unnecessary risk?"

"Cameron is very dangerous. She must remain out of contact until secured. The one with her also."

"They are unarmed. I have more than enough strength here to contain both of them, regardless of their abilities." Zandovar did not bother to hide the contempt in his voice. "And as I have said, I have not received what I was promised. I begin to think she is more valuable than any information you could possibly give me."

"Do you dare to think you can control her? She will destroy you." Was it possible the synthetic voice was shaking in anger? "Toren sent their best after her and they are dead. She did this to me. Moire Cameron is too dangerous to be left alive. I must have her."

An alert beeped on the medical container. Anders' medtech looked up from where he was sitting hunched against the wall and got up. "Excuse me," he mumbled, giving Zandovar furtive, terrified glances. "I must attend to my patient."

Zandovar nodded curtly. He was still very angry, and now he was angry at himself. He should never have gotten involved. Roberts, or Cameron, was a much surer thing than Anders with his vague stories of valuable secret planets and corporate intelligence. It had been a mistake to deal with him. Now, however, he needed to concentrate on salvaging whatever he could from the situation.

"Why do you do this?" It was Ghost, speaking to the medtech who was making adjustments to the medical container. Zandovar was startled. Ghost never made idle conversation, and rarely asked questions.

The medtech started, glanced at Zandovar, swallowed hard and then looked back at Ghost. "To keep him well...his histamine and adrenaline had risen too high and that can cause...discomfort and increase...risk...of implant rejection." He closed the access panel on the container and scuttled away, shoulders hunched. Ghost's eyes followed him.

"Have Roberts or any of her people attempted to leave since their arrival?"

Ghost tapped at his datapad, face immobile. "They approached the main door once. They asked a question and left."

So, it was possible the blunder had not been discovered. "Bring Captain Roberts here."

Ghost silently handed Zandovar his datapad, which never left the inner rooms, and departed. Had Ghost noticed something dangerous about the medtech? Zandovar had dismissed the man as useless except for his medical knowledge, but perhaps there was something more. Anders would certainly have preferred someone with several useful skills, wouldn't he? But Ghost would not have left now without saying something if that were the case.

"I must destroy her. It is required. You will give her to me."

"I will do nothing of the kind unless you provide the information you promised."

"Get the complete data from her ship. How much was recovered?"

Zandovar gestured. "See for yourself."

One of his people triggered the data feed. Somehow Anders could sense it; he wasn't sure how. Given his eyes were destroyed there must be a direct optic matrix translation of the code.

"There is enough to narrow the likely area. In combination with a star map the location is capable of being determined."

"Not good enough," hissed Zandovar.

The doors to the public reception area opened, and Moire Cameron and her companion entered followed by Ghost and the guards. Cameron appeared unconcerned, but that could be simply self-control. The companion, Ennis, looked annoyed but not worried.

"I am glad that you could attend this midnite," Zandovar said. "I trust your business is not greatly inconvenienced?"

"Such things take time—and an opportunity missed may provide another that was unanticipated," Cameron answered. "I have never seen anything to equal the midnite."

"Thank you," Zandovar murmured, appreciating the ambiguous answer, but piqued. Did she seem a little distracted? "I find it refreshing to occasionally mix business and pleasure."

"Is there business you wish to discuss with me?"

"Let us say, perhaps, an offer? It appears you have enemies. Enemies that are attempting to find out where you go." Cameron gave him a hard look, her attention fully engaged. She knew something, then, but not that he was the one behind it. "It may be necessary for you to expand your operations to protect them. I can provide that assistance."

"And the price?"

He made a dismissive gesture. "No price, but a share of the business. "

Cameron glanced at her partner, who shrugged. "It could work," she said, a trifle loudly. "Let's do it. But at a later time perhaps. There is much to discuss, and it would cause bad feeling among the others if I take up all of your time tonight."

"You remain at Kulvar then?" he asked, maintaining the tone of polite disinterest. This could work out well, if she did have enemies powerful enough to threaten her enterprise and cause her to join his combine. And then he could find out more, discover why she was reluctant to capture crew and perhaps redirect her efforts.

"For a few days. I am always needing to get more ammo in the forward lockbox," she said, grinning. Ennis was chuckling too, so it must be a joke between them.

"Then we are agreed," Zandovar said, giving Ghost a significant look. Ghost would see to it that Cameron's ship could not leave before certain safeguards, such as hostages, were arranged. But for now, he wanted to see how willing she truly was. It was always best to minimize the coercive factor.

They turned to leave.

"No. Stop them." Anders' synthetic voice interrupted.

To Zandovar's shock, three of his guards moved to block the doorway. His eyes narrowed. "Move away or you will be shot." They did not. He nodded at the guards nearest him, but they did not move either. They looked nervous, constantly glancing back and forth between the door and Zandovar.

"Anders, are you trying to take my place?" Yes, he should have had this stupid medical experiment shoved out an airlock the first time Anders tried to make contact. Still, it was strange that he hadn't been killed yet. He was beginning to realize, with a chill, that Anders was insane. Highly functional, but insane. There was no way for Zandovar to reason his way around this situation.

"I have no interest in your trivial criminal enterprise," Anders said. The synthetic voice managed to convey an overtone of scorn. "Had you cooperated this would not be necessary. I knew you had placed your people working for me–can you really blame me for using them to reach inside your organization in turn? Your kind is completely predictable." The medical container shifted. That was new too. He had thought the container had no self-propulsion. It faced the guards. "Watch Zandovar and the other. Take Cameron. I will tell you how to kill her. Use knives. You must work slowly, do you hear?"

Zandovar considered his options. Ghost was motionless, and of dubious use in a fight. There was a hidden weapon nearby but not close enough for him to reach before being shot himself.

"What the hell is that thing and why is it giving all the orders?" yelled Ennis. One guard had his weapon pointed at him, while two more were closing in on Cameron. "I thought you were in charge!"

"It claims to be Kolpe Anders, and he appears to have instituted some changes." Both Ennis and Cameron had shocked looks on their faces.

"But he was dead...." Cameron said, slowly backing away.

"Not completely," said Anders. "They saved enough. Make her kneel, I want to see...everything."

One of the guards reached up to her shoulder and shoved. Then the man jerked back, screaming and holding his hand. A green, hissing blur was swirling around Cameron's head. Before he could tell what it was she had scooped up the weapon the guard had dropped and was sweeping and firing.

"Everything's blown up! Get going, Yolanda! Run, run!"

Zandovar took advantage of the confusion and darted for the concealed weapon. Now Ennis had armed himself, and three of the guards were down. The medical container was flashing and beeping wildly. The medtech, wild terror on his face, flung himself on it in a futile attempt to shield it with his body. He had already been shot and in the open was getting hit again. Zandovar aimed carefully. This much, at least, he would deal with immediately.

Two shots to the container's controller and the display went dark. He ignored the medtech's screams. Taking cover behind some furniture, he looked about. Ghost was seated on the ground, arms wrapped around his knees, watching the medtech. Ennis and Cameron were dealing with the last few guards at the door. For a brief moment Zandovar thought about offering to join forces with them but dismissed it almost instantly. It was unlikely they would accept, or that he could trust them. He did not know how far Anders had compromised his organization, or who was planning to take over. He could trust Ghost, though. Ghost had no personal ambition of any kind.

"Stay in this room. Secure it, and close off the security gateways as I command. Shut the main door now." Zandovar activated the hidden door that went to his working office. From there he could do much. Weapons, and perhaps the gas bulbs he had placed in various locations. Once Ghost had sealed off areas he could activate them, and take back his empire.

Ghost waited until the room was still. He could hear the pained, sobbing whimper of the medtech, the dripping of fluid from the medical container. No one else remained, save bodies. He had never thought of them as anything else, even when they were alive. Now they were simply obstructions. He picked up his datapad. It was important and must remain with him. There were dangerous people that would try and get the data he had, and that was forbidden. He must keep it with him until things were safe again.

He had something important to do. It was hard sometimes to understand the dark shadowy memories that drifted up in his mind; they confused him. This one, finally, made more sense. It was a feeling. The medtech had it. Yes, the man that was important had given him instructions, but this took precedence. Ghost didn't even consider that fulfilling this imperative would make all others impossible.

There was a place, outside. It was where things were sent when they needed to go away completely, without a trace. A place of fire. His medtech needed to go away completely, because this place was no longer safe for him. Even Ghost understood that. So he found a float cart, loaded the bloody body of the medtech and the medical container on it, and covered it to avoid questions. No one stopped him. Zandovar always sent Ghost to do things, and no one wondered at it.

Then he reached the place, and its window of fire. The heat was like a blow when the shield door opened. The medtech was barely conscious now, but the light and heat seemed to rouse him and he moaned.

"You must go," Ghost said. "I go with you."

He would be whole again, with this healer. Who cared for his patients. That was what he had remembered. Once, someone had healed him instead of changing and twisting him, had made the pain go away instead of causing it. They would be together, and the pain would stop.

Ghost pushed the float pallet into the furnace, and followed it.

Moire peered around the corner. The corridor was empty, and she gave the all-clear handsign. Ennis moved silently to the next intersection, weapon ready. She looked back over her shoulder. Still nothing. Zandovar must still be busy with the rebellion, but how long would that last? When Ennis waved her forward, she ran.

"I wish people would have the courtesy to stay dead when we blow them up," she muttered in his ear.

Ennis grinned, baring his teeth. "Oh, Anders is dead for certain this time. I made sure to take out the life support module on that tank. Even if by some miracle Kulvar has a medical facility that can re-tank him there's no way he could reach it alive. Not with a minor war going on."

"That's the best news I've heard all day. Now how are we going to get back inside the conservatory? Are our fellow party-guests still there nibbling canapes or have they joined the more violent festivities?"

Ennis handed her the weapon he had salvaged from a dead guard. "I'll check. Don't argue; I'm more expendable and you know it."

Moire sighed. "You want to go into a room unarmed with *me* providing backup? Using a weapon I've never fired before?"

She could see the struggle in his face. They didn't have the time for this. She shoved the weapon back at him, unslung her own, and strode toward the ornate double doors of the conservatory. There was glass inset but it was so wavy and artistic it was useless for checking things out inside.

No shots when she opened the door—that was good. A few speculative gazes turned her way, and she had a brief, terrified moment where she thought some sign of the fight was visible. Then she remembered that she'd been last seen escorted away by Zandovar's personal assistant. She walked in with a suggestion of a swagger, snagged a drink from a muscular pearlized server and made sure to scan him top to bottom with an appreciative smile. Only then did she allow herself to look around and give a subtle signal behind her back for Ennis to join her.

She ignored a few hesitant efforts to get her attention, heading for the thicker greenery at the back of the conservatory. Once in the shadows, she turned. Ennis had managed to conceal both weapons under his long coat. Moire tilted her head towards the open room with a questioning glance; he nodded. Clear.

Moire tapped at the control bracelet. "Yolanda? You still there?"

"Goddammit Captain, don't yez da gain!" Her underworld accent was indecipherable, but Moire could translate purely from tone and inflection that Yolanda did not want a repeat of what had happened..

"Sorry, but things blew up in a way even Zandovar didn't anticipate. I'll tell you what happened some day if we both survive. There's a takeover attempt going on. We are back in the conservatory. Get everybody loose on the station back to the ship. Can we still get out this way?"

"Is Ennis near you?"

Puzzled, Moire glanced at him. "He's right next to me. Why?"

The section of wall near a tall palm exploded in heat and smoke.

"Need to know where ya were. Come on, Captain, we got the shuttle waiting."

One of the figures that had emerged from the hole was beckoning. It was wearing a hardbody construction suit, which in the smoke and confusion looked remarkably like battle armor. Certainly nobody in the conservatory was hanging around for a better look.

The hole opened directly into the huge central airshaft for the station.

"Ah, this brings back some memories," Moire muttered as she climbed down the ladder rope.

"This time I'm running away *with* you," Ennis commented.

It seemed to take forever to climb down to the bottom hatch. Then Moire and Ennis had to be transferred to the shuttle via emergency bags, which was more terrifying than she wanted to admit–but there wasn't time for suits. Nor was there room. The little nerya was not pleased by this mode of travel and let her know with a tight clawed grip, but she couldn't complain. Gremlin had saved their lives.

The shuttle was packed with suited people and gear. Somehow Moire wiggled through to the front controls.

"Yolanda. What's the radio chatter?" Moire eased the shuttle away from the station at regular speed. No point in looking like they were running away.

"They know somethin' goin' bad. Lotsa yelling from the ceeyo folk but not sure who they think is in charge."

"Good. Give them something to worry about besides us. Somebody keep an eye on traffic; let me know if anything looks like an intercept."

There were a few false alarms, but nothing to make her change course or velocity on the way back to *Raven*.

"Yer not botherin' to come in sneaky," commented Yolanda.

"We aren't going to be returning to Kulvar any time soon," Ennis said grimly. "Any of us."

"Even if Zandovar loses?" Moire asked.

"We can't know that unless we actually go there. Zandovar took a big hit but he didn't get where he was by being stupid or lazy. If he's gone then the new ceeyo will probably want to talk to us to see why Zandovar thought we were such a big deal. Not good."

Now they were at the ship they could speed things up. She docked as quickly as she could and ran for the bridge. Alan was there waiting for her, his face spreading in a wide smile when he saw her.

"It works *great!*" he said. "It's the best rifle ever!"

That was when she noticed he was holding the sniper rifle instead of the weapon he had when they first left the ship. Then she noticed the woman they had encountered was also there, only now she was calm and relaxed, watching Alan with a tolerant air of approval. She also was wearing a pistol in a thigh holster.

"I see you were using your initiative all over the place," Moire said, giving Yolanda a meaningful glare as she headed for the pilot's pit. She'd deal with it later.

"We did a pretend war! There were the hardbodies from all the other people standing outside, and we made it look like they were shooting each other! Well, I shot them from far away and Yolanda had some things that made noise like a gun going off."

Ah, then that explained the sniper rifle.

"Company," warned Ennis, at the scope.

"And somebody yellin' on the main channel." Yolanda looked up from the comm board, confused. "Did we take any of Zandovar's people with us?"

"We killed a bunch, but why would we want any souvenirs?" Moire was only partly paying attention at this point. A strong lineup, anywhere. Deception was called for. They had put tracers on her ship.

"They gone 'zent mental," Yolanda complained. "Now they are talking about ghosts. Give ghost back. Wha? What the hell happened back there?"

"Not our problem any more," Moire murmured, and engaged the drive.

Moire watched the readouts, feeling tired and hollow. "He'd better be there. I'm not going to wait around."

"We don't know for sure they got all the data," Ennis said, knowing what she was thinking.

"And we don't know they didn't. I wish we knew what had happened back there. How did Kolpe Anders end up on Kulvar? Yolanda said there was never any sign of a Toren presence."

Ennis shrugged. "Anders wasn't acting rational. He may have done it on his own, for his own insane reasons. Main point is, we need help to keep Toren off Sequoyah and we can't go to Kulvar to resupply. Palmer is our only link to the outside now."

"Yeah, I know. I just want to get back there and make sure everyone is all right."

"Gren knows what to do."

Moire reached for the dropout switch. "The only combat he knows about is when one of his ex-wives catches up with him." The collapsing gravity bubble dragged itchily over her bones. "Okay, we're here. Is he?"

Ennis was bent over the scope. He cursed, a sudden explosion that made her jump. "Something is here, but it looks like wreckage. Dammit, Palmer!" He spun and reached for the comm controls. "No distress beacon."

"Get back on the scope. Patch me through, I'll do the yelling. Make sure that's his ship." Moire first put out an alert to the crew. If it was him, he would need help. If not, someone might still be out there. "*Lady of Leisure*,, come in. Come in, *Lady*." She repeated the hail while Ennis scanned. Yolanda came running on the bridge.

"I can help scan," she called out.

"Do it. Ennis, you're on guns. There's a secondary screen up there too. I'm going to take us closer. Any signs?"

Ennis slung himself up the ladder. "No signal. I think it was him, though. I recognize that cargo pod. You think someone found him here? How?"

"Somebody put a snooper on our ship. They could have done the same for him. It can't have happened too long ago; we're right on time."

They continued to sweep the wreckage. The main body of the ship was in one piece, but there was a huge hole, surrounded by twisted and blackened metal. Standard core rupture. Then she saw the blast marks.

"Yep, somebody was shooting at him."

"Captain. There's a piece of wreckage that's way outside the debris field." Yolanda gave coordinates. Moire raised an eyebrow. That was significantly distant from the main body of the ship, meaning it had gotten there partially under its own power.

"See it. Let's take a look."

When they got close enough, Ennis called down, "It's his remote waldo! And there's something on it!"

Yolanda fussed with the scanner. "Looks like a spacesuit. Don't see him moving, though."

"Let's get him in. Probably injured. That makes it look like he had time to escape, anyway. Maybe he wasn't shot up here, or they would have gotten him."

Ennis went out with the crew of the runabout to recover the suited survivor. "It's Palmer," he radioed. "Seems to be breathing, but unresponsive."

"Don't hang around to take pictures. I want to get out of here."

As soon as everyone was back on board Moire set the fastest course she could back to Sequoyah. Something was wrong. Very wrong. The sick feeling in her stomach wouldn't go away.

"Looks like he took some bar-phen," Ennis said when he got back to the bridge. "He's alive and apparently unhurt, but he won't wake up until the drugs wear off. That was pretty clever of him."

"How so?"

"Only life support he had was that suit. It's not rated for extended survival. He knew his only hope was us showing up, and that we'd look for him once we saw what happened to his ship. With the bar-phen, his metabolism slows and he uses less oxygen. Plus, he gets nervous in vacuum. Prone to panic."

"I wish Fortin was here. If he overdosed we may never know what happened."

They kept a watch on him, discovering fortuitously that Mrs. Perwaty, otherwise known as Linna Ott, had once worked as a medical assistant and at least knew what she was ignorant about. Moire promoted her to ship's medic *pro tem*. Linna was still not entirely convinced they were legit, but seemed to accept that they were in fact taking her to her husband. Mostly this was due to Alan who kept telling her stories about what Perwaty had been doing. Moire just hoped he remembered not to mention exactly who, or what, Perwaty's "friend" was.

♛

A day later Linna called the bridge. "He's awake."

When Moire and Ennis entered the cabin Palmer had been given he was trying to stand up, and failing.

"He won't have reliable motor control for a day or two," Linna said, looking at the collapsed Palmer without a sign of pity on her face. "I told you what would happen. You didn't listen. You can whine to them for a change; I'm tired of it. Teach you to blow up your own spaceship," she sniffed, and left.

"She's mean," Palmer muttered. "I was thinkin' Grimaldi was hardass, but not compared to her."

"So what happened to you?" Ennis said. He lifted Palmer's shoulders while Moire his feet and they swung him back in the lower bunk.

"I'm sorry. I dunno what went wrong," Palmer muttered, not meeting their eyes. "I did it just like you said. I go to the dock, and there's the contact 'n everythin'. She got the right words. So I give her the stuff you gave me, and she hands me one a them boxes again—and that's when somebody start shootin'. Heavy load, not them popguns the night-lifters use. I duck back to get my piece, and they start ripping the dock! I dunno what happened to yer contact. She got hit pretty bad, but last I saw she was still movin'. I hear the pressure drop alarm going on-station an' I jus...I jus wanna get out, ya know? So I unclamp and kick off hard. Then I see there's this scary ship on intercept. Looked military, but it din't have no markings or numbers I could see. They start in with their big guns. *Lady* got hit. Got inta webspace before I realized the reactor control an' cooling was damaged. Kept it together for a while, but the drop I knew was gonna make it go. Rigged up a remote drop switch, got in my suit and soon as I dropped I was out the main hatch. Din't get yer cargo," he said, looking crushed and defeated.

"At least you brought us word of what happened," Moire said. Her mind was numb. The cargo they had been expecting, and desperately needed. Kulvar was gone, and now Palmer had been compromised too. "I wonder if this was Kolpe Anders too."

Ennis shook his head. "That ship on intercept sounds like Toren. They must have found out about the drop. I'm more worried about the data we sent. If that got captured, or if the data the contact was delivering, that could be bad."

"Dunno about the stuff you sent, but I got yer delivery box right here," Palmer said, brightening. "Rigged it in the suit air gear, just in case the bad guys found me somehow."

"You mean you have the data box hidden in your suit environmental controls? How?" Ennis stared at him.

"Oh, I hadda pare it down some, of course. Took a looksee with the tomoscope, makin' sure I didn't hit the security thingies, then I just milled around 'em. Took a while, bein' careful an' havin' ta run an' patch the reactor every now an' then, but it's in there!"

Ennis was already running out the door. Moire tried to smile. It was unlikely there would be anything they could use, but at least the run wasn't a complete waste.

"I dunno how I can make it up to ya, but I'll try," Palmer said.

"Not your fault I've got powerful enemies. I'm sorry you lost your ship. If we get out of all this alive I'll get you another one. We'll find something else for you to do back home. If we are going to survive this," Moire swallowed around the lump in her throat, "we need all the help we can get."

CHAPTER 13
THE DANGERS OF DIPLOMACY

She wasn't on the bridge. Or her office, or in Alan's quarters, or with Harrington and the recuperating Inathka. Ennis stood in the corridor outside Engineering, thinking. Something was seriously wrong if Moire was avoiding everybody, even him. Admittedly Palmer had brought nothing but bad news—even the messages on the data he had hidden had been less than cheering—but everything he knew of her told him she wouldn't give up when the odds were against her. She never had. So she was hiding for some other reason. Where could she remain alone? What place would she seek when she felt threatened?

He turned and jogged back to the bridge, past the pilot's pit and the realspace controls, and looked up. There wasn't any light up in the gunner's position, but the shadows were thicker than they should be. He climbed up the ladder. Moire was curled up in the chair, staring at the blank readout screens. He could see the glint of her eyes when she glanced at him, then away. There wasn't room for another person up there, so he braced himself against the lip of the access hatch and stood on the ladder.

Once his eyes adapted to the minimal light provided by readout pinlights he could see her face. She looked tired, and hard. Ennis forced himself to go still, to match the rhythm of her breathing. She hadn't snapped at him to leave but in this dangerous mood, she could. He had to get through to her without making her close up even more, or finding somewhere else to hide.

"Hungry?" he asked, after a few minutes of silence had passed.

She made a noise that could mean anything, or nothing. The silence deepened. "Do you think Fleet will come if they get your message?" she said finally.

"I don't know," he said. Wishing he could give a better answer. "A lot will depend on how quiet they think the crab war has become. They didn't give much detail with the latest summary, but there's been a noticeable decrease in attacks."

More silence, but it had a thoughtful quality. "I wonder why. It can't be just because we're talking to them, can it?"

"I keep remembering what Perwaty told us when we first found them. He said Radersent said the crab war was a mistake, and humans weren't the 'right ones', whatever that means. Maybe word is getting around among the crabs."

"How could they not know we were the wrong enemy?" Moire asked. "If the diplomacy is helping I guess we'd better show up at the rendezvous."

Ennis took a deep breath, stilling his reaction. "You were thinking of not going?"

She shifted in her seat. "I know I promised...but right now the only thing I can think of is protecting Sequoyah. We're cut off. If we don't already have it or we can't find it in the sargasso—very far away, I might add—we can't get it. I can't justify taking the time just to deliver messages for Fleet, but if it means the crabs could stop attacking altogether and Fleet can help us, that's different. A small chance. I can't count on it, though." She slammed her fist down on the armrest. "People are going to die no matter what I do. What the hell were they thinking putting me in command?"

Getting closer to the problem, now. He reminded himself again not to rush. "That you would do a better job than they would? Stop thinking we're a bunch of gullible idiots," he snapped. "Everybody who's joined up has a very good idea how dangerous this is. You've already lost people and your crew is still with you. They made their decision. Why can't you accept that?"

She drew her knees up and wrapped her arms around them. "Because I'm in charge," she said, her voice tight. "Every single one of them is important and irreplaceable. How do I choose? How *can* I choose? When choosing means somebody dies? They should at least know it was for a reason."

Something in her voice, in her words, triggered the memory. He'd buried it deep, telling himself it didn't matter any more. The person who left Fimbul, shivering in a borrowed blanket because every scrap of clothing he'd worn was contaminated, was not the person who had been born there. Who had survived there. Doing what needed to be done. That person was dead. He had survived.

How do I choose? "You find the core. Some things are bad but you do them if you have to. Like stealing. Others...you'd die, without even thinking about it, rather than do. Sometimes they aren't what you'd think they are. My foster father had built a shelter on the surface. It was hidden. You couldn't get to it without breather gear. It kept us alive. Not just because it had air and heat, but because nobody else could find it. He was old and had never been a fighter, and...and he had me to protect. About a month before the rescue I came back from the tunnels and saw tracks going towards the shelter. I always covered my trail, and my foster father was too sick to even stand, then. I never knew if that man had discovered the shelter or not, but I found him close enough to have seen it. He hadn't done anything—but I couldn't take the chance. I killed him. Dragged the body into a crevasse; went back and erased all signs of him. I never told anyone. Not my foster

163

father, not Fleet. Sometimes I wonder if I made the right choice. Maybe he had meant no harm and just was looking for a safe place himself. The tunnels were really bad then. But if he was looking for us, or told anyone ...discovery would have been death."

"Why are you telling me?" Moire asked, leaning forward.

He wasn't sure himself. He'd killed others on Fimbul but this was the one that always came back in dreams, the only one that still woke him in a chilling sweat. Ennis closed his eyes, trying to concentrate. "I think–I think it's so you will know there's one person who won't judge you for having to make those decisions. Even if that person is a murderer," he said, with an edge of bitterness.

Ennis could feel her breath on his face, then her hands. Her fingers were cold, and he covered them with his own. "I resent the implication that I would ever love a murderer," Moire said. "You can't believe everything you read in the circulars, you know."

He couldn't help the chuckle that suddenly escaped. He couldn't help reaching for her and holding her tightly, his face buried in her hair, as if she were the only source of heat on Fimbul. The warmth was back in her voice. She'd do what she had to do to save Sequoyah. Just like he would do whatever he had to do to save her.

Moire dropped out early when they reached the Sequoyah system, with the ship signal-dark. Inathka and Yolanda Menehune were both on the bridge, keeping a careful eye on the comm and scanner boards.

"No ships in-system, Captain," reported Inathka. "Somethin' hot on the big moon, but no signal. Um, got a stray power buzz dirtside."

"Note everything you see, intensity and location. You'll hand that off to Alice and wait for her to look it over in case she has questions. Yolanda?"

"All quiet. Shall I give 'em the yell?"

Moire nodded. They'd already set up a crude system for ship identification. Right now it was just specific frequencies and initial code words. They'd need something a little more sophisticated after Toren figured out where they were.

"Ding dong, Avon!" Menehune said. She glanced over her shoulder at Moire. "What the hell does that mean, anyway?"

"Sometime after the war is over I'll do a series of lectures on Ancient Stuff. It involved a thing we called a 'doorbell'. Most importantly, nobody now knows about it." Moire kept a careful eye on her scan board as they approached Sequoyah. Still nothing ship-sized. Which, considering the hulks they had in orbit when she had left, meant people had been busy.

A click from the captain's earring, and then she heard Gren's voice. "Carlos Montero is learning to make cookies from Madele."

That was the other cross-check that she hadn't told everyone about. She wouldn't land until she heard from Gren, and the first thing he said to her had to mention one of the original crew from *Ayesha*. If he didn't, that was the signal that the ground team had been compromised in some way.

"Anybody eat one and survive?"

"They aren't that bad. Well, except the batch he set on fire. How was Kulvar?"

"We set it on fire. No, really. I'll tell you about it when we get down. Short version; we're screwed. Any visitors? And why does Coyote have a hotspot now?"

She heard an audible sigh on the other end of the commlink. Gren was probably gritting his teeth and rubbing one hand over his forehead, like he always did when he was trying to keep a grip on his temper.

"I should have gone with you," he muttered. "Yeah, we had some visitors but just in pieces like before. Bigger pieces this time, and hot. Most of the reactor. Couldn't sweep up all the debris quickly, and there'll just be more coming. Figured we might as well give 'em something to find that was clearly theirs, that way if some of our stuff gets detected they'll maybe think it was just more wreckage. Crashed the reactor on Coyote with some of the other pieces."

She didn't like it, but from what Gren had said it was probably the best thing to do in their situation. Toren was going to come looking, and chances were they couldn't hide well enough for a full spectrum scan. They needed decoys.

"We gotta hide everything we've done dirtside, or give it a shield. Think you can fake a crash on top of those buried ships we've got? That could mask a lot."

He grunted. "Yeah, between me and the construction guys we should be able to."

"Get them thinking about it. I'll be down shortly."

The cave at New Houston was startlingly empty. Moire had gotten used to it being cluttered with crates and tents and supplies, and to see as it had been when she first landed on Sequoyah over eighty years ago woke old memories. She supposed they were only bad memories from her perspective–the crew of *Bon Accord* had all been alive here, sheltering in the cave, trying to fix their ship so they could go home.

Gren was waiting for them at the blast door to the underground section. They'd also managed to camouflage the door with an impressively solid wall of solid rock, the same rock the cave was made of. It looked like it had been there forever.

"What's this about setting Kulvar on fire?"

"We shot it up a little," admitted Ennis. "Our old friend Kolpe Anders was there, in a can, and working with Zandovar to grab her," he said, pointing to Moire. "When that didn't go like he wanted, he started a takeover and it was one big happy civil war when we left."

"Then we stopped by to meet with Palmer," Moire added.

Gren shot a glance at her face. "He wasn't there?"

"Oh he was there, all right. Along with his ship in several pieces, since he got attacked when he met his contact and barely made it out alive. He's in the dropship. I want Madele to take a look at him—he took some drugs to survive and he's still not back to normal. He may need some tinkering. So, I would really, really appreciate hearing only good news from your end because we are now completely cut off from civilization. I expect Toren will show up any minute now, with our luck."

Gren halted. The lights in the tunnel, clearly scavenged self-powered emergency lights from the wrecks, gave his brown skin a greenish hue.

"What the hell's going on? Why all this, right now? They are throwing ships away trying to find us."

"I don't think all of it is connected. We know Toren has some big plan in progress. We just don't know what it is," Ennis said from the shadows. "At least, Umbra isn't telling me. Somehow this planet is important to that plan, and they need it now. Toren probably also was behind the attack on Palmer." He hesitated, looking at Moire for a moment. "Umbra has been watching them for some time. My guess is Toren knows that, and has been watching them in turn. Palmer got caught in the middle."

Gren's shoulders sagged, and he turned and continued down the rock corridor. "So where are these Umbra guys and when are they gonna help out here?"

"I'm working on that," Moire said. "They have to know where to go first. How many more ships came through?"

"Gonna show you that," Gren said. He turned down a side tunnel to a room filled with screens and electronics. "Three more, one just scrap but the other two were in bigger pieces than before. We also saw this." He tapped at a small screen surrounded by the most wires and attached devices of any screen in the room. "Not sure, since we only saw the one. But if that gravitic wake thing you told us to put together is working, this ship was in webspace and it *didn't* get wrecked."

Moire stared at the blurry glow on the screen. "Dammit. Did they get picked up when they dropped out?"

Gren shook his head. "May not have dropped out here, or not close enough for us to tell. We got most scans on low power so we don't get found." He rubbed his chin. "So if they don't know where we are, how come they are sending so many ships right here?"

"Probably from what they found on *Bon Accord*," Moire said. She closed her eyes and breathed deep, remembering. "When we came here the ship was already damaged. We had to jury-rig a lot of the computers for the gravitics, and one that got scrambled was the nav log. We tried to record the data best we could, but there was so much ... I know we wrote down what we knew about the gravitic anomaly, so that survived. But the coordinates and nav data didn't. They know to look for an anomaly, but the rest is guesswork."

Gren swore. "So there's even more wrecked ships we don't even know about?"

"Probably. Look on the bright side. The more they wreck the fewer they can land here. Speaking of which, how are the prisoner transports going?"

"I don't like 'em. I know we need a lot, but I can't promise they will last the maximum exposure time. They need more tests, and—"

"We don't have the time or the people. I promise you, we are going to dump them out right at the standard approach distance of very busy stations. You've got the broadcast beacons, right? If nothing else the station people are going to remove debris from the entry lanes. They just have to be airtight for a few hours, tops." Gren sighed, and nodded. "We need to get moving. Get those containers loaded up and Kilberton on his way as soon as possible. I don't want any Toren prisoners here to be helpful when their buddies show up."

"How are you going to load up?" Ennis asked as they left the electronics room. "That could take a while, if they don't cooperate."

"We drop off the containers, and broadcast that we are stopping the food drops and they have an hour to load themselves. Then we have the trainee fighter teams go in and hunt down any stragglers with stun rounds. Whoever is in command has live ammo, just in case. None of those criminals are worth endangering my people."

By now they had reached the big main command room. Gren started calling people over and giving orders. Moire looked around. Everyone was alert, some watching her, but she didn't see any signs of panic. They actually looked like they thought they could win. It was her job to keep up that illusion as long as possible. Until the cavalry showed up or a miracle occurred.

"Hey, you want me to go round up some of those Toren pukes?" Lorai Grimaldi's expression said she was looking forward to it. "I hear we are gettin' rid of the bastards, finally."

"Maybe, but first you need to find that xenobiologist. He can get sent back with the others if he wants."

Lorai looked dubious. "I dunno, last time I talked to him he was pretty happy where he was. Might not want to go."

"He doesn't get a choice," snapped Moire. "Nobody up top except our armed teams. He can stay with us if he can make himself useful. No weapons for him, though. But before you get him, pick up our other solitary prisoner and bring him to me."

"That would be the other pilot. The one you didn't sell to Zandovar,"

Ennis said thoughtfully.

"Enver. Yes. He said he wanted to help, and I think he meant it. It's a dangerous job, but redemption doesn't come cheap. If he pulls it off, he's earned his freedom."

"What are you going to do with him?"

Moire sighed. "He's going to deliver a message for me."

❦

He had expected to be afraid. They'd given him a lightweight suit, the kind of thing a passenger or a tourist might use, not a working spacer. The station ahead would be close, if he were in a ship and not clinging to a cable fastened to a cargo container. He had to leave. If they found him here the carefully constructed story would collapse.

Enver carefully swung the bulky bag in front of him and opened it, first checking and checking again that his clip was attached. The device was clunky, awkward, and looked like it had been put together in a hurry, which it had. The man who had made it looked like some of his devices had a habit of blowing up in his face, which did not inspire confidence.

Unfolded it looked better. Working around his clip line Enver fastened the harness around him, attaching the bag as well. Nothing left behind. He checked the controls, unclipped the line, and flipped back the toggle switch to start it up.

The propulsion harness wasn't very fast, by design. There was a temporary override if he needed to avoid something quickly, but at this speed he would be more likely to be taken for random debris. He also had to figure out a safe approach. The leader–Captain Cameron–had sketched out some likely locations but she hadn't been able to give him a complete map.

He watched the asteroid with its station slowly get closer, the feeling of deep calm still enveloping him. It didn't matter any more what happened to him. He would do his best to complete his assignment, but he no longer cared about his own survival. For the first time in years he felt at peace.

At the edge of one of the medium-sized craters a string of lighted structures were visible, curving to match the edge. The one at the end was small, and there was little activity nearby. Enver adjusted his heading. The best way would probably be to come in from the back, outside edge of the crater. There was even another facility on the far side, which would fit in well with his story. He kept the jets going and followed the ground until he found some large boulders he could take cover behind. He didn't dare risk footprints where they shouldn't be, or falling and damaging his light suit. This was close enough to the outbuilding he could see other tracks, and the way was smooth.

Enver quickly took off the harness, folded the propulsion gear, and wrapped it back in the bag. He took a few precious seconds to dig a shallow hole and bury it. The dust on his suit would also be a useful mask and support for his story.

The trail of footprints led him to the linked buildings. The closest one had an airlock, but the windows were dark and it didn't look like it was used very much. The next building was larger, and he could see light. The outer door had a security scanner but it also had a regulation emergency override. Enver pulled it, knowing that it set off an alarm, and stepped inside. He glanced at the simple air gauge on his suit and grimaced. He'd cut it a bit fine. Now he really had a good excuse. Unless they had a spare tank or could recharge his, they had to let him in.

Faces appeared at the inner door window. He held up empty hands, and gestured at his helmet, shaking his head. He heard a beep; the airlock was pressurized. He took off his helmet and attempted to look embarrassed.

"This isn't the main entrance. You need to go back out and down about half a klick," a voice said on the intercom.

"I can't–I'm out of air. Look, I'm real sorry but it's only my second day on the job and the foreman sent me to the ridge to do some system checks and I got the craters mixed up. I can't get back." Enver had seen a fairly large installation near this crater, so that seemed reasonable. He hoped they wouldn't be suspicious and ask questions he couldn't answer, like the name of the company that ran it.

"They sent you out by yourself your second day? The bastards..." The door clicked and swung open. There were three people in the room, all wearing company overalls. One woman was at a desk covered with piles of sensa-paper. Looked like construction plans. Another woman was standing by the airlock controls, a pugnacious expression on her dark face, and behind her was a grinning man giving Enver a sympathetic look.

"Got the new-guy treatment, eh? They did that to me, too." He jerked his thumb at the women.

"Hey, we didn't stick you out on the surface by yourself with only a liter of air," the woman at the desk said, finally looking up. "And we wouldn't send anyone out in one of those disposable suits, either. That could get someone killed. A joke's a joke, but not if you have to fill out accident report forms."

"I'm sorry to take up your time like this. I'll be more careful next time I go out, and they should have my work suit ready for me in a day or so. Do you mind if I go back through the station entrance? I don't want to climb up the wall in this."

"You were lucky you didn't get a big hole," the pugnacious woman said. "That rock is sharper than it looks. We wouldn't let you go back in that thing. And hey, take your time. Let 'em worry about you."

"Yeah, and you can leave your suit with us! Then we could take it out, and borrow that skeleton Juana's got in her office, and see who finds it!"

the guy said, clearly delighted with his prank.

Enver finally escaped from his new-found friends after discouraging the skeleton-in-a-spacesuit joke and promising to tell them of his eventual revenge. They had given him a duffel back to store the suit in and avoid curious glances, since people didn't commonly haul suits around the inner station areas. Enver found an area with storage lockers and left the bag there. Now there was nothing to distinguish him from the other station inhabitants, and no link to the outside.

The cloud of detachment was still with him. He had to remind himself to stay alert, be suspicious. He still had work to do. Enver passed a crowd of excited people gathered around a wall screen. It was showing an outside view of a scow with a familiar-looking container being loaded on it. He'd never seen the whole container before–it had taken up a large part of the hold, with the others. There was writing on it. He waited until the vid got close enough to read the largest segment. *NASA LIVES*. There was more, but he didn't want to stay in one location too long.

First he had to find a cheap kiosk, the kind that only took credit tabs and not ID-linked accounts. Both messages went to a certain circular–one to the personal messages section, a cryptic set of words that meant nothing to him. The other was a more standard article submission. Both had been memorized.

A little of the tension in his body left when the messages were sent. Only one more thing to do. The end, the final task. He pulled up a station map. He found what he was looking for, and there was even a nearby bar.

Enver sat on a cracked plastic seat in the bar and ordered the cheapest beer on the menu. He wasn't planning on drinking much of it. He took a small sip and washed it around his mouth, then spilled some on a napkin and wiped his face with it. The rest was dribbled carefully on his boots and inside his jacket. Nothing too visible, but now he smelled like he'd been drinking for hours.

He dropped an entire credit chip in the bar vendabot pay receptacle. There would be some patrons with a much lower tab, since the 'bot didn't care who paid the bill. The rest of his money went to the charity box in front of the Lost Spacer's Memorial. He didn't need money any more, and he didn't care what the captain had said. He still had a lifetime of reparations to make. And he was now going to make things just a little worse.

The entrance to the police station was directly in front of him. Enver took a deep breath, rubbed his face with the beer-soaked napkin again, staggered in, and started throwing punches.

He regained consciousness in a restrain-board cell, hands and feet cuffed in place. His head felt like it was going to explode. They must have used a neural rod on him. His muscles were certainly spasming, and one area in the small of his back was on fire. Not as bad as he had feared. Maybe the captain had been right.

"Hey, you." A police officer was staring at him. "That's a neat trick you got there, fendi. Being drunk, but without any alcohol in your system. That must save you plenty. An' considering you don't got money, necessary."

Enver swallowed. His mouth was dry, and his tongue felt fuzzy. "I apologize for the disturbance. I hope no one was hurt."

That earned him another stare, longer this time. "Well, you were fighting like a drunk guy. Which you weren't. There some meds you need, fendi? Chem-aids for the brain?"

"No, officer. I'm afraid I had to make you arrest me. Is Chief Murayama here?"

"What the hell is this, a social call? You can just ask at the desk, yanno. Jen Soo Yi is kinda intimidating but she don't bite people, not on the first date ennyway."

Enver struggled to think around his pounding headache. "Too risky. You would have thought I was nuts, just like you do now. Listen. That ship that just dumped a crate and ran off? The crate is full of people. Alive. They were caught at a facility that creates clones. Is Chief Murayama here?"

The policeman shut his open mouth. "Uh, just a minute." He disappeared.

Enver turned his head. There was a water tube just within reach, and he drank gratefully. The pounding in his head slowed to a moderate throbbing.

"You asked for me."

Enver snapped his head around. The man standing in front of the cell was on the edge of stocky, with dark, heavy hair in a buzz cut and calm, steady eyes. Just like the captain's description.

"A little over a year ago there was an incident. A ship captain and a young man she claimed was her son, and a Toren official who claimed he was a contracted employee. She and the young man didn't have ID, so you did a gene-scan."

Murayama's face went completely still. "I remember."

Enver took another quick sip of water. His mouth was going dry again. "She sent me. She sent that container with the people. I am supposed to give you the files on them. It was too dangerous to do it any other way. It's Toren. If they hear about it, they'll kill those people–and me–rather than let it get out."

"Where is this data? You didn't have anything on you, you know. Not money, not ID, not even an entry scan from any ship in the last thirty days."

"There's a datatab embedded under my skin," Enver said softly. "It has everything on them. They created clones from non-Indexed gene data for enslavement."

"How did you find out about this?"

Enver closed his eyes. "I worked for them." Silence. He heard the bars of the cell rotate and retract. Murayama was standing with his face mere centimeters away.

"Why the hell did you bring this to me?"

"The captain told me to," Enver answered without hesitation. "I want everyone responsible punished, me included. Toren will try to stop it any way they can. The captain told me to find you." He locked gazes with Murayama. "She said you are an honest man."

✵

Ennis dropped the mug of synthetic coffee in Moire's outstretched hand, and took his own to the scan board.

"Pity you ran out of the good stuff," he commented.

Moire adjusted something on the webspace board. "Eh, this has caffeine. Good enough for me. I remember seeing the manifests for *Ayesha*. Real coffee was ten times the price of the fabricated stuff, and that was before Yolanda marked it up. Usually sold it to Inner System types that had moved to the Fringe–real spacers never developed the habit."

Ennis spun his chair around. "Speaking of Menehune, why isn't she here? You've got a pretty minimal crew this time."

"Wanted her devious mind on Sequoyah, with the troops. Besides, Kilberton is staying as the emergency exit pilot and I didn't want to listen to her complain all the way out and back."

Ennis grinned. "Like that, is it? If you don't like whining why is Inathka on board, then?"

Moire gave him a look. "Inathka is probably OK but I still want to keep an eye on her. Plus she's the best we've got for signal analysis and crab translator maintenance. That wasn't an easy decision. She's got some interesting ideas about using the hulks we have in orbit. She thinks we might be able to remote control the lot, maybe patch in some AI. That could be nice. A little robot fleet all our own, and Toren wouldn't know those ships weren't crewed."

He had to ask. "What about me?"

"I'm keeping an eye on you too."

"I mean–"

She glanced up at him with a crooked grin, then focused on her board. "I know what you mean. Yes, you would be much more useful on Sequoyah but I didn't bring you just for the pleasure of your company. You represent Fleet. Damned if I'm going to speak for all of humanity to the crabs. That's big important above-my-paygrade work and I want a scapegoat."

"I thought that was what Harrington was for."

She snorted. "I couldn't shift him with a case of thermal grenades. Same thing with Linna, since Perwaty had to come with Radersent and she's not letting him out of her sight again. Can't say I blame her." She tapped at her board again. "Here we go. Sure hope they don't keep us waiting. I want to get back as soon as possible." She flipped on the intercom. "All Hands, dropout in five. Repeat, dropout in five. Dropout is not secure. Action stations."

Ennis turned back to the board and got the scanners ready and the autoprograms set. Shortly after the announcement Alan, Inathka, and Harrington arrived on the bridge. Alan swung up to the gunner's position.

"Can I make the guns green?" came his muffled voice.

"Yes, on standby," said his long-suffering mother. "Don't shoot unless I say so. If you start another galactic war you will be grounded until the heat death of the universe."

"He's got good trigger discipline," Ennis said softly. He didn't mention that Alan hadn't always been like that. Training had helped, a lot.

"I'm just reminding him to stay that way," Moire muttered. "Okay, dropout!" She slapped the big button.

There was always a flash of signal just as the webspace bubble popped. Ennis had wondered why, and speculated that the bubble built up a realspace ripple that condensed all the radiation in a tighter space. It lasted less than a second. Then his screens cleared, and he froze, losing precious time to confusion. *Did the bubble collapse all the way?* Then he realized what the screens were telling him.

"Ships! Crab ships, over twenty of them!"

Moire swore, and kept swearing as she appeared to attack the webspace controls. He couldn't even see her hands she was moving so fast.

"Dammit, they just couldn't resist could they...twenty? I thought this crowd didn't have that many!"

Inathka tried to speak, squeaked, and tried again. "I'm gettin' the four-signal loud an' clear. Nothin' else."

"Which ship?" Moire still hadn't looked up. "What a shitty place for an emergency lineup, who the hell picked this place for a meetup..."

"All of 'em," Inathka said, at the same time as Ennis called out, "They aren't moving!"

Moire hesitated. "What?"

"None of the crab ships are moving. Even though we are."

"Holy Buddha in a bunnysuit." Moire took a deep breath, and blew it out. "Inathka. Ask them what the hell they are doing here. Diplomatic, like."

"Um, ya want I should sent the count signal back first?"

"Yeah." Moire nudged the controls. "There, we aren't moving any more. I'm still going to work up the lineup, though." Then, as the thought seemed to strike her, "Alan? Good job with the not shooting."

"There are a lot of them," Alan called down. "Why are they here?"

"A very good question," Harrington said, speaking for the first time. He was looking feverishly around the bridge, probably trying to decide where he should be watching. Too much going on too fast.

"Working on that," Inathka yelled. "All talkin' at once, an' most gibberish."

"Are the explorers here? You know, the ones we were *supposed* to meet? At least they know how to use the translator," Moire added.

Ennis was desperately trying to get more information from his scans. The ships were still in their original positions. No energy buildups or any sign of hostile intent. The types of crab ships ranged from the kinds he was most familiar with from combat, some clearly non-military like the explorer's ship had been, and two huge ships similar in size to the one Radersent had been on. The big ships were hanging back, furthest away from the translating device. There were twenty-six crab ships all told.

"Yeah, those guys are here. I'm gonna tell everybody else to shuddup."

"Diplomatically."

"Yah, whatever." Inathka was busy for a moment at her station. Ennis passed on what he had found out to Moire. She was very pale, and had never taken her hands off the webspace controls. "Hookay. Got our guys on the line. They say all here not fight."

"I like the sound of that. But why are there so many of them?"

Inathka paused. "Whaaa? I just asked 'em one question ... the explorer guys writin' a book for me. Says some ... I guess these're names? They wanna see the freaks. I mean us. Humans. More name things. This don't make sense—whaddya mean by 'see all being seen'? It's got that honorific diddle at the end too, so they important somehow."

"Witnesses?" Harrington guessed.

"What the hell are they witnessing?" Moire gritted. "They never needed them before."

Inathka was muttering to herself. "An' somma them wanna...think it's talk to you. Your name, Captain. An' the word is kinda like 'trade' but also like 'family'. I don' get it. Hostages?"

"Welcome to the wonderful world of Hsurwyn culture and communication," Harrington said. "You know, since they do seem quite firm that they don't want to shoot us, it might be wise to add Radersent to this discussion. He at least knows a little of how we do things, and may be able to explain what's going on here."

Moire nodded. "Inathka, set up a link to Radersent's quarters. Get Perwaty first and explain what's happening, and then put that line dedicated through our translator."

"Gottit. Huh. Now they say you in a war."

Ennis and Moire exchanged stunned looks.

"They've only now figured this out? The war has been going on for years," Ennis said. Was something wrong with the translator? Were these crabs from a completely different group than the ones they had been fighting?

"Nah. That's you, as in 'captain an' her people'. Not humans general-like. An' the word coming up like war, it got 'large family' and somethin' that looks like the regular 'war' but it ain't exact."

"Just me? That means—fighting Toren? Who told them that?" Now Moire sounded angry.

"Not me!" Inathka said quickly. "I never got left 'lone with it. I mean him."

"Captain?" Perwaty's voice came over the comm. "We got the signal you spliced in. Radersent's real agitated. What's happening?"

"We're real agitated too," Moire snapped. "We've got a damn crab armada we just dropped in the middle of. They seem to have gotten a good idea what's happening with us and I want to know how. I'd also like to know why they are here. Get Radersent working on it."

"Right away, Captain!"

"We need some time," Moire said. "How about giving the assembled audience that secret message? If it's translated from the original bureaucrat they may fall asleep and we can escape."

"Or it will enrage them," Ennis said before he could stop himself. "Don't worry. Umbra is the least bureaucratic institution I've ever worked with." Moire rolled her eyes. "Okay, Inathka. Tell everybody we have brought a message from a...from a much larger group of humans that also want to talk to the Hsurwyn. Do you still have it set to go?"

"Yeah." Tapping sounds, then silence. "Whaaa...they usin' that word again."

Harrington could no longer contain his curiosity. He peered over Inathka's shoulder. "Ah. And the prior communication was—yes, I see. We know they appear to have political connections between families." He glanced back at Moire. "I believe they are inquiring if you are allied with this other group of humans."

Moire looked at Ennis. "Does it matter? And how do they define an alliance? If it means not shooting at each other, sure."

"I hesitate to extrapolate from human cultures, but when there were still tribal societies on Earth it very much mattered who your allies were and if they would speak for you. The Hsurwyn have never met Umbra but they have met you. If you say you are allied with them some of your status is transferred, as it were."

"Hmm." Moire glanced at Ennis again. "Tell them yes, we are allied. I hope that won't get either of us in trouble later on."

"We can always blame the translator," Ennis said, grinning when

Inathka gave him a baleful look. "Nothing personal. This is how diplomacy works."

"Guvmint," muttered Inathka. "Righto, got the message goin'."

"Get Perwaty back," Moire said. Inathka tapped at her board, then nodded. "Perwaty, what's Radersent got to say for himself?"

"A lot, Captain. Took me a while to get him to calm down an' use small words so's me and the translator could understand. This is a really big deal. Those ships that are just watching, like the transmission you sent said? Well, they are hooked in with some kind of major crab group. The way he's saying it there's only a handful of these big leaders, and they kinda run the crab world. Okay, not so much leaders as clans, I guess. He says 'greatest-she' for those ones."

"Queen," murmured Harrington. "The clan is the queen's connections, relatives, and descendents. And sub-queens."

"Yeah, he said some a the...queens, like you said, they join up. 'Become a child' is the term he used. Anyway, they have been arguing ever since the explorers got back and told everybody what happened and getting rescued by aliens and stuff. You wouldn't believe what's been going on. So the big queens sent somebody when the explorers said we were going to show up again. To see if it was true."

"See if *what* was true?" snapped Moire. "We've been at war with the crabs for years! They knew we were aliens then. What's the big surprise? Why are we getting every crab in the quadrant wanting to show up and say hi? They used to blow up rather than let us even look at them!"

Perwaty sighed. "Yeah, I thought that was strange too. Asking Radersent gets him agitated, but I think I got a bit more now. There was that big war a long time ago, right?"

"With the Breakers," interjected Ennis. "The ones who left that gravitic mine in the sargasso."

"Yeah. So, it was a *big* war. The crabs we talk to now are the descendents of the survivors, and Radersent says they were few and "on the very edge." Not sure edge of what, but they were spending most of their time staying alive and by the time they could go home and check in, it wasn't there."

"Home?"

"Everybody else. The center of the culture, I guess. Anyway, they don't know what happened. Don't know if they won and the Breakers are gone, or if the Breakers won and could come back."

Ennis thought this out for a moment. "Wait a minute, how can they think we are these Breakers? Don't they know their own enemy?"

"They forgot, Commander. This was thousands of years ago, right? Guess a lot of these edge crabs never knew that much about them. The explorer clan, they had a few that did and preserved the knowledge. When you helped out, and they saw more, they were sure you weren't them. The explorers have high status, enough they weren't shot for talking to aliens. The crabs got paranoia about the Breakers like you wouldn't believe."

Moire sighed. She let go of the webspace controls and sat back in the pilot's chair, rubbing her eyes. "Where did I go wrong? Okay, I admit I wanted to know what started the war but this is ridiculous. We've been fighting and dying because they didn't keep their enemy identification files up to date?"

Ennis felt a chill, remembering. "That place you dropped the explorers off in their wrecked ship. That huge object. The one that was the size of a moon and was half blasted? Ask Radersent who did that."

Perwaty responded almost immediately. "You guessed it. Breakers. Oh, and he says that was on the edge. One of the few things from the old time that are still there."

Moire blinked. "That was on the *edge* of the war? Damn. Okay, maybe I believe them. I'd be hiding for years making sure the Breakers couldn't find me if they could do that. Now, back to why the crabs seem to know my personal troubles. Any luck with that?"

Perwaty chuckled. The change startled Ennis, who hadn't noticed much funny in their situation. "He was trying to help, Captain. He thinks there might be some crabs that could do something for you. He doesn't understand why you would be angry."

Moire looked skeptical. "Why would any of them want to help me? And how could they? We can't use their supplies or their weapons."

"Seems like some, the ones that believe we aren't the Breakers, don't feel right they fought us. 'course, some of them still think we *are* the Breakers, so war ain't over yet."

"Of course not, that would be too easy," sighed Moire. "Guilt, now, that's interesting."

"I get the feeling the Breakers are just about the most evil thing they can think of," Perwaty commented. "They don't want to think they were acting like 'em themselves."

"But what about—"

"Hey, all outta message," interrupted Inathka. "They all startin' ta talk at once again."

"Tell them lovely to make their acquaintance, I hope their tentacles never get munge, and I gotta go," Moire said, sitting up again and glancing over the webspace board. "Diplomatically."

"Wow."

Ennis glanced over. Inathka was looking at her screen with both eyebrows raised. "What's wrong?"

"Nothin', but the explorers got 'em to all shut up. Gonna hafta remember that one. Maybe it's cussing!" She stared at her screen again.

"Um, Captain? They wanna know when you coming back."

"Tell them I don't know. The other humans might come here, though."

"One of the large ships is in motion," Ennis reported. "Away from the rendezvous. Looks like the second one is also maneuvering."

"Is that okay?" called Alan from above.

"Moving away from us is okay," said Moire reassuringly. "They want to go home, just like we do."

"Don' think they like that answer," Inathka said. "Seem to think you should come too."

Moire swore under her breath. "Send this. I have enemies, and my people may already be fighting them. I must go back to our system and defend it. My enemy is stronger than I am. I may not come back, ever, so I ask that if the other humans come here, the Hsurwyn will listen to them."

Ennis kept a close watch on his scans. "First ship has gone into drive. Several more ships moving, all away."

"We should be doing that too," Moire said. "After this I'm looking forward to a nice relaxing war."

"Um, gotta reply," Inathka said slowly. "It's not the explorers. One of the big bugs. Seems like they just sayin' if the human ship comes without fight and speaking they will listen. But it's got this extra frequency pattern over the whole bit an' that's where the important stuff is an' I don' remember–"

"I do," Harrington said. "I think perhaps you didn't see that signal record. It was one of the first full-spectrum ones. Radersent was responding to the Captain's request when we were rescuing the explorers."

Ennis tuned out the discussion. He had a lot of crab ships to keep track of, and now was no time to get careless. The coordinate reference shifted– Moire must have started to move the ship. She was moving it slowly, though, probably to keep the crabs from panicking.

"Only ten ships still here," he reported. It was easier to keep an eye on them now that the field wasn't crowded. They really needed a better identification system to distinguish the ships. *Raven* wasn't equipped with a Fleet target identifier, and even that wouldn't have distinguished a particular ship. You didn't need to know which ship you had blown up in a fight, just that the target was gone. He should work on that... "Wait a minute. Six of them aren't moving yet. One is the explorers, one a medium size non-combat, the rest appear to be fighters."

"Terrific. Not moving, you say?"

"Captain! 'nother message. Pure garble. Lotsa 'trade family'. Can't be the explorers, they know the translate gizmo better'n that."

"Isn't that 'alliance'?" asked Harrington.

"Mebbe, but *that* ain't nothin' but noise. Pause it...the explorers jumpin' in. Askin' you ta wait."

"Why?"

Ennis spared a second to glance over. Inathka was peering hard at her screen, as if she could squeeze extra comprehension by sheer force of will.

"They lickin' smack dope from a can," she said finally. "I dunno what they want. 'kay, so that bit is alliance but why they saying be child?"

Harrington looked at the screen and scratched his head. "That does seem to be what they are saying. Hang on, what was Perwaty saying about the sub-queens? Wasn't that the way he said it? Become a child? I'm sure it sounds much more formal in the original Hsurwyn."

"Yeah, but whatabout this 'giving rock' static?"

"Get Perwaty and Radersent," Moire said flatly.

"Only the six non-moving ships remain," Ennis reported. "They have maintained their position. No energy profile changes."

"Captain?" It was Perwaty, sounding breathless. "Radersent's been explaining to me. There's one bit that I'm not sure about. He says this queen talking about rock is one of the ones who wants to live as before. That means before the big war."

"I feel slightly dissed that *we* aren't considered the big war," muttered Moire. "What does rock mean? She collects boulders?"

"I'm not sure, Captain," Perwaty said apologetically. "He gets confusing. Sounds to me kinda like a religion. They wanna live on planets, like they did before. Somehow it is important. *Really* important. He says only the great queens have planets under their control. Everybody else is on ships or, or what he calls 'big ship staying'. Station, maybe? Kinda like the Fringe, really."

Ennis heard Moire make a sort of strangled noise. "But what the hell does this have to do with *me?*"

A moment of silence, and then Perwaty replied. "You got a system, Captain. Radersent knows this and he told the others. I guess the kids told him. Well, and I see you mentioned it just now to the others. So, um, that makes you a Great Queen by their standards."

"Allow me to be the first to congratulate your Majesty," Harrington said, at his most urbane.

"Oh shut up. This is serious."

"Ooo, I see it now. That word system, it got the 'all put together as one' bit and 'planet' so that means more than one planet, yeh?" Inathka said, sounding pleased with herself. "Damn, but they got some neat ways of sayin' stuff."

The ships still hadn't moved, so Ennis glanced over his shoulder. Moire was slumped in her pilot's chair again. She looked tired.

"What. Do.They.Want. Inathka, ask them."

"Hokay. That is definitely the word for 'child' this time and no...eh, the modifier is for...future?"

"Yes, you are correct. Perhaps future generations?" Harrington said.

"They lay eggs," Perwaty said cheerfully. "We had quite the discussion about that, Radersent and me. When we were shipwrecked. He never did understand how we do it, I think. Eggs in caves, or some really secure place. It's important. Anything to do with kids is important."

Ennis blinked. Radersent had reacted strongly when told he was helping out by watching the Created. "Does this queen want a place for her eggs, then?"

"Yah! That's what it is! She wants a...a solid place. A planet, or somethin' like. Um. An she don't fight but she got friends, 'kay, allies, that do."

Suddenly the bridge was deathly silent. No one spoke or moved. The ships on Ennis' screen also were motionless.

"Do you mean if I give her someplace for her nursery she will give me crab fighters?" Moire said finally.

"I believe that is correct," Harrington said, sounding astonished himself.

"Perwaty? What does Radersent say? Is that right?"

Silence. Then he spoke. "Yes, Captain. She is asking to be your sub-queen. If you give her a planet, she will give you fighters."

CHAPTER 14
PROOF OF LIFE

Kostas started awake, momentarily disoriented. He spat and wiped the dirt and grit that had fallen on his face from the overturned tree they were hiding under. He glanced at the journeyman excavator who had had the first watch. She shook her head. No signal. Kostas sighed and went to the mouth of their hideout, covered by dangling roots. No sign of Toren, even though they knew they were out there. Somewhere.

"How long do you think they'll stay?"

"Keep your damn voice down," Kostas snarled. She winced. "It's been five days. If it's one ship doing a survey, they'll go soon." If there were more, and one stayed, things would get messy. Pity the detector couldn't tell them that.

Then again, without the webspace detector they would have been out in the open, fat and happy, blasting out signal to be detected. As it was they had just enough time to hide the gear and dig their hole. That had been the risk, taking a crew this far away from the cave, but hiding the buried ships from detection was important too. Everything that delayed Toren's realization that Sequoyah was inhabited was important.

"We've got supplies. All we have to do is sit tight until the captain comes back."

"I hope they go before that," said a new voice, carefully low. It was the bio guy, Eng. "I'm not supposed to be out here with you guys." He shuffled forward, wrapped in an equipment weather cover. The one thing they *hadn't* brought was blankets.

"Gotta have someone who knows the local plants if ya wanna plant 'em for cover," Kostas said. "Gren Forrest agreed with me. Besides, if you try anything I'll kill ya." He grinned. Eng looked pale. Kostas was kidding, mostly. Eng was all right, just a little naive, but if he stayed scared he wouldn't forget to be careful.

Sukuna poked his head in the dirt cave. "Hey. Spy-eye's got something."

Well, crap. He'd put up the spy-eye just to make sure they wouldn't get surprised, hoping it wouldn't be needed. Now what?

"Lemme see," he said, and Sukuna passed him the readout screen. She'd already marked the start time for him. He studied the readout, scowled, and ran it again. They'd placed the spy-eye on a cliff-growing tree using the runabout, which gave it a wide view across a grassy plateau. It was the best place to land a shuttle on this medium-sized island, and sure enough someone was landing on it. Kostas dialed in the focus, enough to see several people unloading crates and boxes. Two men remained, one waving to the shuttle as it headed out.

"They lookin' for us?"

"Doubt it." Kostas stabbed a finger at the screen, which he'd frozen to get a better look. "Two guys. One rifle for the both of 'em, and sidearms, see? Not expecting any human-type trouble, and not much of any other kind." He watched some more, speeding it up until the feed was showing live signal. The two Toren workers were setting up a tent, anchoring it well, and covering the rest of the equipment with tarps. Okay, all by-the-book so far. Then they left the camp, carrying packs and with the rifle in a long covered back-sling. "Whaddya think they're doin' now?" Kostas asked Eng.

"Doing a bio survey, probably. Weather, atmosphere checks, whatever they need to start planning for building." He shrugged. "Just a guess. It's what I'd do if I was dumped on a new planet. *Did* do." Eng hesitated. "They are heading north. I wish we'd had a chance to make sure the transplants are all right there. That's too near the buried ship and if they get suspicious..."

"It'll hafta do. First priority is they don't know we're here. That ship is buried deep and they don't have excavators."

They took turns watching the now-deserted camp. The two men returned shortly before dark, and a light glowed inside the tent for a few hours. When that switched off they changed the spy-eye to night view. It was not, as Sukuna admitted, very interesting.

Then they got a signal beep. Kostas wasn't sure how it worked, exactly, but a message could be encoded and compressed into a very short pulse, and only their comm devices would know it wasn't a transient solar pulse or some such. Camouflaged to blend with the environment somehow.

"Huh. No ships in orbit now," Kostas said.

Sukuna shifted, rubbing her eyes sleepily. "They're still at the camp. No sign of the shuttle."

Kostas tried to go back to sleep, but couldn't. They'd been forced to lurk in their improvised hidey-hole for nearly a week doing nothing. That, plus the fact that there wasn't enough room and he was a big man, was driving him nuts. If they could get rid of the Toren guys somehow, at least they wouldn't have to stay underground while they waited for the all-clear.

"Got an idea," he said the next morning when everyone was awake. "Wanna take a look at that camp they got."

Sukuna looked dubious. "We don't know where the shuttle is, or even that the ship is out of the system."

Kostas grinned. "That's why I wanna check the camp. The long range comm ain't light–didn't see 'em carry it when they went out. Gotta have one, though. We go in when they are out, break it so's they don't notice.

Extra insurance if they *do* notice something; can't tell their buddies about it."

Judging from the reactions, everyone was just as bored as he was and itching for action. Even Eng, who wanted to go check his damn plants. Just to be on the safe side, Kostas had Sukuna on the runabout with their comm gear including the spy-eye screen, following low and slow. They headed out as soon as the Toren men left the camp.

"Heading west, to the beach. Taking a large box, though. Sure it's not the comm?"

Kostas peered over her shoulder, and so did Eng. "Looks like a powered biosample box to me," Eng said. "If they are taking specimens on the beach they could be there all day." He sounded wistful.

"Right, in we go. Meyers and Syu, you watch the perimeter under cover. Everybody else come with me in the camp, and try to walk where I do, or on rocky bits. Don't need lots of extra footprints, gottit?"

The camp was, as expected, deserted. Kostas cast a suspicious eye but didn't see any surveillance gear. They hadn't seen any being set up, but it paid to be careful. He untucked one corner of the big tarp and examined the crates. Besides some science gear, it looked like there were enough supplies for two months for two men. Okay, probably set to stay here without shuttle contact until the big ship came back. Good.

Sukuna found the comm in the tent. Nice unit; could be useful later. Kostas opened the back, pulled out two of the flatchips, and coated the contact side carefully and evenly with molylube.

"Will that work?"

"Sure." Kostas glanced outside again. Nobody. "Learned this trick back when I was a journeyman–great practical joke. The base hydro evaporates when it heats up, and it looks like it's burned. The moly shorts out everything it's connecting. Easy to clean up, if you know it's there." He took a quick look around the tent. Nothing else had been disturbed, and he didn't see anything else worth messing with. "Let's go."

Once back in the cover of the trees, Eng whispered, "Is there time to check?" pointing north.

Their visit to the camp hadn't taken very long. Even figuring in getting back to the tree hole, they had a few hours. And it was good to be out and moving again. "Sure. Keep it quiet and no littering, gottit?"

They'd done a pretty good job with hiding this ship, he had to admit. He never would have suspected a whole Kundar-Cho medium freighter was underfoot if he hadn't buried it himself. Pity they couldn't just knock on the hatch and hide with the others inside, but that would expose the ship and who would conceal the hatch again? The plants Eng was concerned about looked all right to him, but Eng was still worried and wanted to check them all.

Kostas sighed. "That's a big area. Not gonna have time to do it yourself. All right, split up. Meyers, you go with Eng. I'll stay here with Sukuna and keep watch back the way we came. Everybody back in two hours." Good thing they had been expecting Toren, and nobody went topside without weapons. Eng just had a zapper. Cameron would probably understand taking Eng out when she heard about it, but not giving him a gun.

It was much nicer being outside in the sun instead of the damp, chilly dirt cave. Kostas found a convenient boulder to lean against and checked for movement with his long-range binoculars. The trees here had long, delicate streamers that swirled and flowed in the wind. He'd have to ask Eng what that was all about. Small flying creatures dove in and out of the foliage, making trilling noises.

"Mebbe I'll live here, when the war's over," he observed to Sukuna. "I like this place."

Sukuna rolled her eyes. "Boring. I'm gonna live wherever the first bar gets built."

"Build it yerself, then you can pick the location, right? I'm thinkin'–"

The shot cracked the air, making the flying creatures speed away and disappear. Without a word, Sukuna swerved the runabout down and around for him to jump on.

"That's where Meyers and Eng were headed. What the hell they playin' at?" Kostas muttered. He checked his pistol. If he'd been wrong about Eng Cameron would rip his head off, and he'd have to let her. But that just didn't seem right....

They rounded an outcropping and nearly ran into Meyers. He was standing with his gun still gripped and outstretched, Eng a few meters away with a stunned expression on his face. A body in a Toren uniform lay between them, a bloody hole visible in the back.

Kostas jumped off the runabout. "Get up and keep watch," he ordered Sukuna. He nudged the body over. Good thing was, he recognized him as one of the men from the camp. At least they didn't have extras wandering about they hadn't seen. Kostas rounded on Meyers. "What in the gasket-blowing everlovin' *core melt* universe were you thinking, you piss-poor excuse for a protein brick?"

"He was reaching for his comm," Meyers said in a hollow voice. "He saw Eng but Eng was busy and didn't see him and he was gonna call and we can't let them know...."

"And shooting the bastard is going to keep it a secret?" Kostas fought to keep his voice down. "Only people got weapons. You bash his head in with a rock, dump him over a cliff, now that could just be bad luck."

"I'm sorry, boss," Meyers whispered. "I screwed up."

"My fault too," Eng said. "I wasn't paying attention. I thought they were both at the beach!"

Kostas sighed. "It's done. Nothin' we can do about that now. We still gotta fix it, though. Can't leave him with a bullet hole."

The others had come running up by now, staring aghast at the scene Kostas scowled at the body, thinking. Trouble was the shot. What if the other guy had heard it? And how could they make the death look natural?

"I think I know what to do," Eng said quietly. He looked a little green. "We have to make it look like an animal attacked him."

"Yeah," Kostas said. "'Course he'd shoot at an animal, right? How ya gonna do it?"

Eng rummaged in his pack and pulled out some metal hooks that were used for anchoring lines in trees. "Messily."

It was very messy indeed. Eng wired together three of the hooks into a crude clawlike tool. Seeing how queasy he looked, Kostas offered to take over, but Eng insisted he knew how it should look. He was rather violently sick afterward, in a plastic bag to hide the evidence. Kostas took the Toren man's gun and worked the slide, ejecting a round. Just in case his buddy started a thinking habit and checked the magazine.

"I'm seeing motion," Sukuna said quickly. "To the west."

"Probably the other one," Kostas said. "Everybody take cover." He grinned. "May as well take care of him now, eh?"

He hid in the shadows of the underbrush, making plans. This one they could dump in the ocean, after taking his gear. They could lure the shuttle in with a distress call, maybe. All sorts of things they could do.

Moire propped her head in her hands, fingers running through her hair in a futile effort to stave off the massive headache that was forming. She could sense Ennis on the other side of the galley kitchen, radiating worry and conflicting loyalties.

"Still there, Captain, no change."

"Thank you, Inathka," Moire said without looking up. She was feeling pretty conflicted herself. The people she relied on for advice were all on Sequoyah, except for Ennis, and she had to make the decision now. It wasn't fair, but Ennis was the only one who could help. She just had to convince him he wasn't betraying Fleet first.

"If I tell Agurwythen to pound sand, what's the worst case scenario?"

"Agurwythen?"

"The one who wants to sublet a planet. I had Radersent do a semi-phonetic transcription. We were running out of pronouns."

That got her a faint smile. "Everybody here is dead and Toren has a perfect secret base to continue their plot, probably meaning more fighting only human-on-human this time."

Moire took a drink from her mug of cold erzatz coffee. "If I let Agurwythen take up residence and it turns out the crabs were plotting against us, worst case scenario is we are all dead, but Toren gets to fight entrenched crabs when they try to take over Sequoyah. I could certainly cope with Toren getting their faces ripped off, even if I wasn't around to see it. It would divert their attention from sabotaging Fleet, plus it wouldn't endanger any other human outposts any more than they already are."

Ennis nodded slowly. "And if Agur...whatever is telling the truth, they will fight to the last crab to defend their crèche. Even if we're all dead." He sighed, and slumped forward until his face was resting on his hands. "It just feels...as a certain former subordinate of mine would say, there isn't a form for this. Namur gave me a lot of latitude to do my job, but I am not authorized to conduct inter-species treaties!"

"You aren't making any treaties. I am. Look on the bright side. If we screw up there won't be enough left of us to court-martial. Hell, I could get a genuine mutiny going back home. There are going to be some angry people when they find out."

He gave her a hard look. "So you've decided to do it."

From the corner of her eye Moire saw Harrington peek around the doorframe, grimace, and then disappear again. "Tell me what I'm missing. All I've got is a fine assortment of bad choices. You know what we have back on the planet—a lot of eager Fringers who have never seen real combat and a bunch of defenses assembled from spit, baling wire and duct tape. I was hoping Fleet would show up sooner or later so all we'd have to do is hold out for a while—but we don't know if Palmer's contact survived or if Enver was able to get the word out. We can't count on Fleet...so I have to find a way to win now."

He sat back, suddenly looking tired. "I can't think of anything that would change our options," he admitted. "It still feels wrong. You shouldn't be making defense treaties when we can barely communicate with them. We could be making dangerous assumptions."

"Probably are." Moire shrugged. "Thing is, so are they."

"Is that supposed to cheer me up?"

"I'm not explaining it very well. I'm not a diplomat. See, we wouldn't even be having this problem if the crabs didn't desperately want to talk to us. Agurwythen didn't know there were any humans it was safe to talk to until the explorers told them, and look how fast they showed up once they did! The explorers went to a mine field because that was the only place they knew we'd show up! I'm only thinking about surviving Toren right now. You're worrying about what happens after that."

"Somebody should."

Moire smiled. "I'm not complaining. I especially like the assumption that we'll win. My point is, I believe the crabs want this to work. They'll do their damnedest and so will we, and if we have to renegotiate or clarify something later on we will."

Alan came in the galley looking worried. "I can't find Gremlin anywhere. Did you see him?"

"You should keep that furball in a cage," Moire grumbled.

"I did; it ate through the wire mesh, remember?"

A shriek came from down the corridor. It sounded like Inathka.

"Looks like someone found it, kid. Go collect it, apologize, and put it somewhere it can't escape, okay? We've got serious diplomatic stuff to do and we don't need a rampaging nerya in the middle of it."

Alan nodded and darted out the door. Ennis was looking at her with a resigned expression on his face. "Remind me. Why are we having this discussion in the galley instead of your office?"

"Because this is important. And in my experience, all the *really* important discussions happen in the kitchen." Moire got up. "Let's go see what the crab word for paperwork is."

Ennis stood and reached for her as she went past. For a moment he just held her tightly, in silence. "You have to win," he said finally, his voice thick. "Do whatever you have to do."

Moire hugged him, trying not to get choked up herself. Too many balls in the air at once, and some of them had been replaced with chainsaws. "Hey, this is all according to NASA standard procedure."

He pulled back to look at her. "Really."

"Absolutely. SOP when you run out of plan is to fly by the seat of your pants. I'm surprised that got left out of the history books."

"They always leave out the really good bits," Ennis said, following her out.

👑

They were waiting on a response from the crabs so Harrington quickly turned his attention to his notes. It was beginning to appear that the agreement was fairly well hammered out to everyone's satisfaction. It was fortunate for him that the negotiations were so intermittent, as it allowed him time to get caught up. He smiled to himself. And just when had he gotten so nonchalant concerning the first contract between humans and crabs?

It wouldn't do to get careless. He was afraid he'd done just that with his data storage, but with this side-trip wrapping up there should be a reasonable buffer for the fight with Toren. He'd intended to get a data cube or two and a transfer clip on Kulvar, but that had gone rather fruit-shaped and he was stuck with what he had brought originally. Perhaps he could go hat in hand to the crew if his reserves got low. It would be embarrassing, but he *had* to cover the war!

Moire Cameron straightened up at the console, hands at the small of her back. "That should be everything, then. They get full use of the fourth planet, we all agree to defend the solar system against any attacker, human

187

or crab, but anybody looking for trouble outside is on their own. We're responsible for telling human ships what the friendly codes are and they handle crab visitors. Agurwythen guarantees their crab allies will behave. Anything important we're leaving out?"

"Probably, but there is a limit to what can be done with point-and-grunt diplomacy," Ennis said. "And time is limited."

"Right!" Moire rubbed her hands and looked more cheerful. "Now we just have to give Agurwythen coordinates and nav guidance and we can leave."

Inathka glanced up from the console, shrugged, and started muttering into her headset. Her head snapped up again. "Radersent says not done yet."

"What?" Both Ennis and Moire stared at her.

"This deal, right? It isn't really agreed yet or something."

"But we just agreed to all the terms...are they changing their minds?" Moire looked worried. "Maybe we should just leave now. I don't like this."

"Nah, nah! Damp the core, boss. Here, you listen to him. Tell 'em, Rad."

She tapped a control on the console, and the synthetic voice of Radersent's translator sounded from the comm. "Promise of Cameron-she to Agurwythen-she spoken. Not having power. Make completed. Make circle, final. The shes see and touch, together, is final. Promise has power. Must see together. All shes."

Harrington sighed. He was going to have to condense his notes. There simply wasn't going to be enough room otherwise. Why hadn't he gotten the cube array? It hadn't been *that* expensive, and this was history!

"I don't get it," Moire said finally.

"It appears everyone who is a party to this agreement must actually meet for it to have force," Harrington explained. "Together, and see each other agreeing to it. This would match their quasi-tribal culture, what we've seen of it anyway."

"Okay, our ship or theirs?"

"Agurwythen old ways. Not ship, place of being," Radersent said. "Planet."

Moire shook her head. "No way do they get the coordinates first and sign the contract later."

"Query?"

Inathka murmured a simplified explanation of Moire's statement to the confused crab. Radersent really was doing quite well with human conversation, Harrington noted. He'd gotten better with practice, and there had been plenty of that lately.

"Not Cameron-she planet. Rock not belonging. Is here."

Moire frowned, and went over to a navigation and scanning station.

"Hmm. Yeah, there's a goodly sized rock-ice moon around the outer gas giant," she said. "Would that count as a 'planet' for crab legal purposes?"

There was a brief pause as a diagram and explanation of the proposed site was sent to Radersent.

"Good place. Say go."

Moire nodded to Inathka, who switched to the transmit circuit to the waiting crab ships.

"Need more." Radersent sounded, implausibly, embarrassed. Harrington hadn't known the synth-voice could do that.

"Now what?" Moire snapped, exasperated. "They want tea and crumpets?"

"Hsurwyn-she different all Hsurwyn." Yes, he was definitely hesitating. Was this a human characteristic Radersent had picked up? Harrington couldn't recall any other crab communicating like this. "Human-she same all human. Make Cameron-she different. Agurwythen-she, friend-she need seeing is Cameron-she."

There was a thoughtful pause on the bridge. "Well, I'm not going to suddenly grow the size of a well-fed rhinoceros," Moire commented. "I'm guessing that's not exactly what he meant."

"There is a considerable size disparity between male and female Hsurwyn," Harrington said. "If I understand him, they find our similar sizes confusing."

"And since the big one is the one in charge," Ennis said with a grin, "they would find your claim to be incredible. The only person here smaller than you is Inathka."

"Yeah, yeah, laugh it up. So what are we going to do? Bear in mind, we're all going to be in spacesuits so there's not much I can add."

"Then you will have to make the additions...outside." Harrington considered. "I have some suggestions."

It was perhaps fortunate that Moire Cameron's attention was focused on getting *Raven* to the rendezvous point and getting the dropship ready while Harrington rummaged through empty cargo bays, utility closets, and the reusables bin. He was *not* going to mention the reusables bin. It simply would not go over well. Not that the rest would either, but you really couldn't expect someone with colonial antecedents to understand the principle involved.

He was dimly aware of some other hurried project as he searched. Someone shouted "It has to be at least two and a half meters long and we need two!" No doubt it would become clear later.

Harrington's comm beeped. "Are you done?" said Ennis. "We're in orbit."

"Is Radersent suited up and available? It would be best to get his opinion before we leave, I think."

"Yes. So is Perwaty and he's got the portable translator. They're at the dock."

Harrington gathered up the voluminous folds of his creation and proceeded to the appointed location. By the time he got there Moire was present as well, suited and with a serious-looking knife strapped to the arm of her suit.

"Er. Is that quite the desired tone?" Harrington asked.

She gave him a hard look. "I'm fighting a war, and they know it. I don't know them. That's what this is all about, right? I wouldn't think much of them if they didn't have their own precautions if things go south. This way," she tapped the knife, "it's all out in the open."

"Just like Alan and his rifle will be," Ennis said dryly.

"That's different. This is symbolic. It's not like we don't have guns on the dropship, either. So what do you have to make me look properly authoritative to a crab?" Moire asked Harrington.

He held out the first item, the largest. "I modeled it on a Maori chieftain's coat," he said, leaving out that the original had been made with human scalps. "Sort of a cross between a cape and a sleeveless coat."

Moire tried it on. It certainly created a sense of increased volume, Harrington was glad to see, although it did make the captain look like a small shaggy mountain. He had attached long strips of light plastic webbing to some cargo net. Why they had a whole box of plastic webbing in the hold he had not seen fit to inquire.

"Well, at least the knife is still visible. What's that?" she pointed.

Harrington steeled himself. "For...additional height," he said, and offered the headpiece to her. It had foam padding inside to protect the helmet and he had done his best to artistically shape the back half of the remaining cylinder, but there was no getting around the fact that it had once been a beer canister.

Her expression was not propitious. "What the hell is it?"

"Regalia, Imperial, Field Expedient, one each," Ennis said with a carefully deadpan face. "You haven't seen the eyeshields yet, either. Radersent says they are traditional for these sorts of meetings. Seems in the old days the queens would be rather aggressive meeting face to face, so they had people to put blinkers up, so to speak."

Moire's shoulders sagged. "I don't believe I'm doing this." She turned to Radersent, who like always came to attention when she faced him. "Will this be acceptable?" She indicated the cloak and the headpiece. Radersent ducked his head in a human nod. "Then let's get this over with."

With all the gear, Radersent, and everybody else taking up most of the room in the dropship, Harrington struggled to get ready. He still had the sealed vid from his time on the explorer's ship, and he'd just have to hope it still could handle vacuum. It would take up precious data storage, of course, but since he couldn't take notes or make recordings with his datapad it would have to do. He'd already asked Inathka to carefully store a copy of all the communications via ship, and the remote translator made recordings by default.

He glanced up front. Moire hadn't bothered to remove the cloak and was piloting with it still in place. It was an odd juxtaposition; an image he would have to sketch. A vid still wouldn't capture the strangeness of it. Her face was intent as Ennis pointed at some feature on the rocky moon.

From the corner of a small viewport he could see the crab ships orbiting with them. The one huge one must be Agurwythen's main ship. The others were smaller, but radiated spines and other features he recognized as weapons. A cluster of even smaller ships, one for each of the crab ships, waited. As the human dropship passed, they followed. Looking forward again, Harrington saw a medium-sized crater growing larger in the front viewport. The dropship turned and slowed, curving with the crater wall. He barely felt the impact when they landed.

"Listen up, everyone. This is important." Moire Cameron was standing by the pilot's seat, looking at everyone in turn. "First, watch out for the low gravity. Don't let go of anything important or it could drift away. Next, we're going in with good intentions, but things could go sour. Always good to have backup, and that's where Alan and Linna come in. They will be stationed in the airlock. If I say run, everybody runs, got that? Be ready. *But only on my signal.* Now. I go out first. Then Perwaty and Radersent, who have escort duty with the giant lollipops. Then Ennis and Harrington. We do this ritual meeting and then leave without stopping to chat. Any questions?"

Harrington had quite a few, but sensed they would not be welcome. Especially "what happens if you, our only web pilot, gets killed?" No one said this would be a simple assignment, but he did want to live long enough to file a report about it.

The dropship airlock was technically large enough for two suited humans, but Moire in the cloak and Radersent had to go through individually. The ritual eyeshield poles looked suspiciously like repurposed cable conduit, and fortunately could be taken apart in sections. Someone had used lubricant can lids for the tops, which already had nicely crenelated edges, and had cut out a large, slightly uneven S in the middle. For Sequoyah?

Harrington came out of the airlock just as the second crab ship came in over the crater and rotated slowly, up and around until it stood on what he though would have been the tail. The dust swirled around the rough, spiny skin strangely, as if it were caught in water. The dust then drifted towards the ship, instead of down in the minimal gravity of the moon. Another huge shadow passed over them, and again a crab ship gently floated down in veils of dust.

Suited crab figures emerged from the first ship now, carrying what looked like a long, lumpy rope. They laid it carefully between their ship and the humans', then stood back. The lumps grew and thinned, forming a webbing between thin ridges that also grew out of the rope. It seemed to be forming some sort of tent. Why would they want a tent when everyone was wearing suits?

"That looks like the airlock door on Radersent's ship," Ennis said over the comm.

"Stations, everybody. They're coming out," Moire interrupted. She hefted the headpiece and with a resigned expression, carefully fitted it over her suit helmet. "The things I do to save humanity...."

Harrington could see them now, dark shapes emerging from the dust at the base of their ships. Each had one hulking figure, flanked by two smaller ones with what looked like eyeshields, and a scattering of others harder to distinguish. They moved just outside the overhang of their respective airlocks, and halted.

"Guess we go first," said Ennis, after a pause. "Radersent?"

"Great-she begins," said Radersent.

"That would be a yes," Moire said. "Here we go."

The blue primary of the system was bright yet distant, and the shadows cast by the crater walls were sharp and completely black. It gave the landscape a flattened look. The dust stirred up by their feet hung for a long time, and the plastic tape on Moire's coat was starting to stand out away from her body. Static electricity, perhaps? Harrington had to concentrate to keep his feet in contact with the ground, and to remain at the rear of the parade, so he missed when the other crabs started to cross to the strange shelter. As he got closer he could see the webbing was slightly translucent, and there was an faint orange-red glow radiating from the ribs.

"That can't be heating–it must be lights. But why so faint?" Harrington wondered.

"They don't see in the same range as we do," Ennis reminded him. "The group straight ahead–that's Agurwythen?"

"Yes. And I'm beginning to understand why she was so eager to find a permanent home," Moire said. "She may be as desperate as we are."

Harrington leaned to get a better view, and started. All of the Hsurwyn females were huge, but Agurwythen was nearly double the size of the others, mostly due to her distended middle section. She was moving awkwardly even in the light gravity, and making use of her forelimbs.

"Dear God, she's...how much longer does she have? I know they have something like eggs but there has to be a point where they must come out, don't you agree?"

"She looks like she's about to explode, yes. I hope she knows what she's doing. This must be very important to her."

Moire was now at the edge of the shadow cast by the shelter. She stepped inside. The other queens followed, Agurwythen going first. The crab-lights didn't help much, with the glare outside. Harrington tried to focus only on the gathering and slowly he was able to distinguish the participants.

It was strange. They were on an empty moon in a fairly sizable crater and yet the open-walled shelter seemed crowded. It didn't help that there were so many crabs compared to the humans.

"I guess I speak first too," Moire said. She nodded to Perwaty. "Translator channel is open?"

"Yes'm." Perwaty sounded like he had a lot on his mind.

"I am Moire Cameron, and I lead the humans of Sequoyah," Moire declared.

In unison, every crab except Agurwythen tucked their chins. Agurwythen stretched her long, narrow head out, so that it was horizontal.

"Agurwythen. She of three small. Having kinship these she." One forelimb indicated each of the fighter queens. "Agurwythen small to Cameron."

Which would mean she was declaring her alliance to Moire, Harrington realized.

Moire started to nod and then stopped, realizing the meaning was different here. "Yes," she said. There was a long pause, where nothing happened. Agurwythen was motionless. "Radersent. What happens now?"

"Cameron-she make Agurwythen-she small." Radersent's synthetic voice was barely audible.

"HOW?!"

"Put forelimb on head."

Well, that made a certain amount of sense. If big meant power, a symbolic tap on the head would make that clear. The difficulty being, even with Agurwythen's crouched position her head was still higher than Moire could reach.

Moire jumped. It was a slow jump, straight up, and just high enough for her to reach out and touch the Hsurwyn queen's head with her gauntleted hand before descending again. Harrington saw a few twitches in the assembled crabs at this unexpected event, but they maintained discipline well.

Agurwythen tilted her head up, as Harrington had seen Radersent do to Moire many times. She was moving slightly from side to side. Happydancing, a good sign.

"These she fight for Agurwythen. These she fight for Cameron."

The other queens ducked their heads again. "Okay, now what?" Moire said. "I bop them on the head too?"

"Not for making small. All she touch manipulators."

193

"That means tendrils, Captain," Perwaty added quickly.

"Ah, just a handshake for allies. Um, I don't have tendrils. And they have big heads." Moire sighed. "Let's see if this works." She lifted her arms and crossed her forearms under her chin, fingers extended.

Slowly the queens edged closer. Their movements were stiff and jerky, and Harrington guessed they were not nearly as happy as Agurwythen to be there. Still, they came. The large, heavy tendrils of the queens lifted and entwined, all in the circle.

And both of Moire's hands were entwined as well.

Now he understood what Radersent had said. It was real now. They had done it. And he had seen it all.

CHAPTER 15
HE HAS WAGED CRUEL WAR

The control room, far underneath the main cavern, appeared at first glance to be very professional. Lots of screens and readouts, efficiently arranged consoles, and no obvious dangling wires. Looking more closely Moire noticed that only a handful of the screens had the same kind of frame and some still had the bracket mounts from where they had been ripped free from their original ships.

"Are you sure it works?" she asked.

Gren shrugged. "We caught you and your new best friend coming in," he said. "Had about an hour warning before you dropped, more for them since they were taking it slow. My guess is Toren won't dare run the coupling as high as you do on that lineup, since they don't have the experience, so we should have an hour-plus when they show up."

That would give them plenty of time to get everyone underground and buttoned up, and ships in position, as long as they didn't try anything too complex. That was good. Staying underground and waiting was bad for morale.

"What about comms? You said something about capturing one of their long-range devices, right? Get any intel from that?"

"By the time we got it, Kostas had whacked the shuttle people and nobody else was transmitting much."

Moire wandered to the far end of the room. Here the ad-hoc nature of the gear was even more evident with some tools scattered about indicating the installation was still in progress. "Got the translator hooked in too. That was quick. Good job. Interfaced to the regular comms, looks like. Does Radersent have a...what the hell is this? That looks like the guts of a reader!" She pointed. Now that she looked more closely, there were two of them. The casings had been stripped off and a great deal of reconnecting had been done.

Gren rubbed his chin, glanced around, and yelled "Inathka! Get in here!" When Inathka peered around the edge of the door, he waved her impatiently in. "Captain has some questions about your project there."

"Um, it's them ships," Inathka muttered in response to her raised eyebrow. "The remotes, right? We were gonna have somebody for each one, like. Not a lotta folk with shiphandling, then we got the controls n' signal and stuff an' Alice stepped on it 'cause a crypto or somethin so I think mebbe multi-dendrite core with sub-fuzz but we sure don't got *that* in

195

the junk pile an' then I hear your kid an' them talk about that game with the ship combat an' I say hey, that's got *game* AI an' we can use that!"

"You are saying you used a reader game to imitate an advanced multi-track computing guidance system for the remote ships?" Moire said after taking a moment to parse Inathka's rush of words.

"Used two, actually. Kids ain't half mad about it. I promised I'd get 'em new ones, an' they wanna watch the battle."

Moire gave up. "Why two?"

"Game AI not so random all the time. Hadda do some bit-poking, get it to work, so we got the enemy location feed in to this one like it was someone playin' an' *that* feeds inta the other one like it was the game process an' then that goes ta the remotes. Gotta override too, if we wanna do somethin' different."

"Very...nice," Moire managed. She was *not* going to ask if it worked. "Have you had a chance to test it?"

Inathka gritted her teeth. "Can't test nothin' if I got no signal an' not supposed to move 'em," she said, looking pointedly at Gren.

"Okay, okay, that was the right thing to do," Moire said waving her hands. "Now it's different. No point in pretending nobody's home now, since we plan to pound them as soon as they show up. We'll have to reposition the ships anyway. Oh, and make sure the crabs know what's going on. We can test the transponders too that way." That part had better work. No point in having crab allies that couldn't tell the bad humans from the good humans. Even if some of the good humans were fake. "What about comms from the remote ships? It can be encoded nonsense, but there should be something or Toren will figure out they are empty."

Inathka's mouth opened in surprise, then she shut it and nodded sharply. "Oops. I'm on it."

Moire left the control room and checked out the rest of the underground facility. Every few meters she saw what Gren had complained about earlier—they'd brought back a lot of equipment from the sargasso, but it wasn't enough. Especially with the buried ships scattered over the planet, each needing its own sensor net and comms. Even here, they had barely enough vid sensors for the cave and the emergency exit. They'd only need them if the fight turned into a ground war, so it was her job to make sure it never got that far.

Kostas called in while she was walking up the long tunnel to the cave.

"Got 'em done," he said.

His voice on the commlink was weak and crackly. Moire nodded to the guards at the blast doors where the tunnel entered the cave and headed for the cave entrance, where the signal would be better.

"Where are you now? Did you let them know?"

"On *Raven*. Heading in. Yeah, they told 'em and I guess they dropped down that minute. I hope they got some kinda sealer for those tunnels, though. They aren't gonna hold atmosphere and if they are gonna put their babies in there...."

Moire grinned. Kostas had gone from red-faced fury when he was told to build some tunnels on the rock world for the crabs, to worried concern when he learned what the crabs would be using the tunnels for. He still had flashes of paranoia, but they all did. "They have that goop they use for their hull repair, or something similar," she said. "Better than plasticrete. Thanks for doing this on short notice. I know you would rather be back here doing the junior commando thing."

He laughed. "Hey, I ran out of Toren grubs. Wish I could be sure I got 'em all, but they didn't leave me a list."

"I just wish you could have captured one or two instead of killing them," Moire said dryly. "We could use more information."

"Mebbe. Outfit like that, the ones that know anything won't tell you. Not without getting nasty with 'em," Kostas said, sounding doubtful.

Moire sighed. "You're probably right. Did you find anything useful?"

"Nope. 'Cept for the long-range comm. It was all standard exploration kit. Well, and we got their shuttle which is handy."

Kostas signed off, and Moire went back to worrying. No word from Ennis, which meant he was busy. Still would have been nice to hear his voice. There was too much to think about, too many things that could go wrong. The crab fighters hadn't arrived yet. People were starting to get stressed and snappish, herself included. She kept thinking there was something she had missed, and she probably had. Gren had done some drills and dry runs before they had returned from the crab rendezvous, so it shouldn't be anything major. But in war, little things could get you killed just as dead as big ones.

The greenish sun was setting over the bay facing the cave entrance, and the deep amber light was filtering through the huge trunks of the pseudotrees growing in the shallows. Moire called in to let Gren know where she was, and then she found a convenient boulder and watched the sun go down. *It's going to be messy. Remember you're doing this for a reason.*

The stars began to come out and the last light drained from the sky. Then one of the bright lights got larger, and moved, and not long after the long dark shape of the shuttle came in on the quiet whine of engines. She watched it land inside the cave, then got up and walked over.

Ennis was the first out. He looked worn and tired, but his eyes changed when he saw her.

"Everything with guns has ammo," he said, wrapping his arms around her and holding her close. "Maybe only five rounds, but ammo. I feel like I moved an entire reload ship by hand."

"You probably did. I wish...."

He pulled back, looking at her. "What?"

"Nothing. We can't go back to the sargasso; it would take too long. I know this. But when you tell me five rounds per gun it sets off the panic alarm."

"It's not all of them. Just a few."

"Oh, well then. The war's won!"

She could feel his laugh before she heard it. "They'll never know what hit them." A silence, then, "Have you told Kilberton?"

Moire sighed. "No. I kept hoping Fleet would show. He'll want to stay, but it's him or me."

"You've had Palmer doing the webspace detection runs, why not him?"

"That's all short hops, close to this system. The anomaly doesn't kick in there. Palmer doesn't have the skill, and he knows that." Moire grinned. "Besides, he wants to stay for the fight."

Ennis shook his head. "Of course. What was I thinking?"

"Come on. You haven't seen the latest Inathka invention," Moire said, tugging his arm. "Proof positive that computer games lead to violence."

Her comm buzzed, in alert mode. "Multiple blips inbound," Gren said breathlessly.

They ran for the control room. More people in the corridors; Gren must have hit the alert. The control room was crowded too, with all the positions manned. Even Inathka was crouched over the game-powered remote interface.

"What do we have?" said Moire.

"Three blips. They are pretty faint. Could be wreckage."

Moire peered at the screen. "They are off the main vector, though. You retuned *Frankenstein* for human ships, right? How much overlap with crab drives?"

Gren paused, thinking. "Yeah, could be. Not much overlap, but we got the whole damn gravitic grid on that ship wired up now. Think it's the crab fighters?"

"No reason for Toren to come in from that direction, and the speed's very low. I warned them to do just that. When will they get here?"

"Approximately four hours," Alice said, her voice calm. She'd designed the signal system, so she would know.

"We've got time, even if it is Toren. Sound the alert again if more show up, or if they change their speed. We'll treat it like a live drill for now." Moire glanced around the room. "Stay sharp, people. For all we know Palmer kicked the detector comp and that's the invasion." She glanced at Ennis. "Guess we'd better go find Kilberton now."

She hadn't expected the discussion to go well, and it didn't.

"Look," she said tiredly, after half an hour of argument. "You won't be running away. I only want you to go into drive if Toren somehow wins. We hid our people pretty well and they might not find them. You'd be going to get help. Fleet apparently never got our messages. You can tell them what happened, and you are the only other experienced web pilot for this route. You'll get them here faster."

Kilberton had his arms crossed across his chest and a stubborn expression set on his face. "I should not be leaving just when things are going badly. This will take a ship away from the few we have to use. How can you ask me to watch and do nothing?"

"You're the only backup we have," Ennis said curtly. "That's not nothing. I'd have picked you even if you weren't the only one. You are calm and have good judgment in a crisis. If we lose here, it could still get worse if Fleet doesn't know what happened. Do you want Toren repeating this elsewhere?"

Kilberton shook his head.

"You'll also be the last chance out for anyone who has changed their mind," Moire said. "I know you want to help. This is what I need you to do."

Kilberton sighed. "I do not wish to go," he said softly. "But if you require it, I will."

"Thank you. I know it won't be easy. Better get your stuff together; we'll be leaving for *Raven* in less than an hour. Ennis can get you the coordinates to some reliable Fleet locations."

Kilberton nodded and left.

"How many took up your evacuation offer?" Ennis asked.

"Just a handful. Plus some of the Created, the ones I could persuade. I'm glad Gip Farouz is staying. He can keep the rest out from underfoot." Moire looked at him. "We'll be going out hot soon. Got everything you need?"

He smiled. "Everything important."

She smiled back. "Me too."

There were echoes from shouting voices in the cavern. Moire sighed and resumed her preflight inspection of the attack ship. It was the second iteration, and she was getting jittery again. Where the hell was Kilberton? The shuttle with the evacuees had already left. It would be nice to have a web pilot for them.

A bleep in her ear alerted her that a priority channel was being piped through. She'd switched to the captain's earring for comms. "Latest web alert, Captain. Same three ships, no change in speed."

"Thanks. Has Palmer changed to the shorter runs?"

"Yes, Captain. Less than an hour round trip."

That was good. Palmer could only send the data when he was on the Sequoyah end of his loop, and there was a danger they could miss the invasion if the attackers came in fast.

Those blips had better be the crab fighters. Otherwise their entire planetary defense consisted of one attack ship, *Raven*, and a handful of modified sublight freighters most of which were controlled by a computer game. Moire stopped, closed her eyes, and took a deep breath. She had to be calm. Be calm for her crew. Her people, dammit. A whole planet with people, and how had that happened?

"Join the exploration teams, it will be fun, they said. Discover new worlds, they said. No mention of defending a renegade colony with nothing but rubber bands and rocks," Moire muttered. She took another deep breath. The blips had to be the crabs. They had time. This was just an abundance of caution and not, repeat not, reason to panic.

Kilberton had still not shown up. Moire gritted her teeth and fiddled with the control bracelet to get someone to hunt him down.

"Captain!"

Someone was calling from across the cave. She looked up. Kilberton and Yolanda Menehune were walking quickly her direction.

"Where the hell have you been? You should already be on board," Moire snapped.

"Got somethin' to ask you," Yolanda said. Then Moire noticed they were holding hands. Tightly.

Moire blinked. Well, it hadn't exactly been a big secret but she hadn't considered it any of her business. Looked like it was. Somehow.

"You want to go with him?" she asked, rapidly running through all the things Yolanda would have been doing dirtside, and who could cover for her.

"Think I'd run when the heat's coming down? We just...we were gonna..."

"We are agreed in this," Kilberton interrupted Yolanda's outburst. "She will stay here and I will go to the ship—but we wish to be married first."

No, she hadn't been expecting this. "Um, you both know I'm a bit out of date on this kind of thing, but I thought the usual procedure was to sign a cohab contract these days. Mammachandra even has the retina scan and verification chip rig too, so all you'd need are witnesses."

Yolanda gave Kilberton a look of resigned affection. "He got religion. Priests don't hold with do-it-yerself."

Kilberton nodded. "They do, however, recognize emergency ceremonies performed by traditional figures of authority, if no priests can be found. Judges, for example. Or ship captains."

"Aha." Moire looked at them both. "I don't have any objection. But I thought that ship captain thing was only when they were in command of a ship, at sea and such."

"Yer in command of the whole damn planet, Captain, that's gotta count."

"I wish you'd stop saying that," Moire sighed. She saw the textcard in Kilberton's hand. "Those the official words?" He nodded and handed it to her. "Hang on a sec."

She jogged around to the front of the attack ship and climbed in. Ennis was in the copilot's seat and looked up as she entered.

"Time to go?"

"Slight detour," Moire said, checking the rear vid and then toggling the back door and ramp. "Do an all-hands for me, will you? Everyone who isn't in the command center to the cave. Including Radersent. Time he got to see some incomprehensible alien ceremony for a change."

"What?"

"Kilberton and Menehune want to get hitched." She walked out the back and stood at the top of the ramp, and motioned Kilberton and Menehune up. A trickle of people started to come out from the back cave entrance, looking puzzled. When they saw her they headed her way.

"Er, Captain?" Yolanda asked, with a dubious expression on her face. "We just need you ta say the words."

"Oh, I will. But back in *my* day, people got married by making promises in front of everybody who would have to put up with them later. None of this signing a textsheet in Harvey's office and sending it to a records depot nonsense. And if we're standing on a ship during the proceedings that should satisfy any legal nitpickers." She waited until there was a good crowd, held up a hand for silence, and started in.

The vows were sufficiently similar to what she remembered that she didn't stumble too noticeably. When she finished, Yolanda was staring at her, looking a little stunned.

Moire grinned. "Kiss, or it isn't legal."

While her two newly married crewmembers complied with their captain's order, Moire looked at the sea of watching faces. The older ones had a distant look, remembering. Carlos Montero was smiling with vague benevolence. There was Radersent, all suited up and apparently having everything explained to him by Perwaty who was pointing to his own wife, while holding her with the other arm. Everyone, for just a moment, had forgotten the pending war, which was why she had done it this way.

"So, do you think it's legal?" Moire murmured to Ennis under the growing noise of celebration.

"This isn't an official colony of any description, and you are the recognized legal commanding authority of those present," Ennis said. "For all practical purposes, and until you import lawyers, yes."

Now she could hear music. She'd better make sure everything was still going according to her last information, before the party really got started. She tapped at the control bracelet.

"What's the incoming status, Control?"

"Palmer hasn't dropped out yet, Captain. Hey, we sent a feed of the wedding from the surveillance vids in the cave to the offsites, I hope that was OK? I thought they'd want to know, everybody likes them both..." Alice hesitated.

"Yeah, sure. Good idea. Sorry you have to stay down there. We'll have a bigger party later, when nobody is shooting at us."

Alice laughed. "That will motivate everyone—Palmer's in. Analyzing data now." Moire heard a sharply indrawn breath, followed by muffled conversation. She could hear Gren's voice, and it sounded tense.

"What is it? Have the blips changed speed?"

"No, Captain. That is, we still see signal from three webspace objects with their original vector." From the corner of her eye, Moire saw Ennis focus his attention on her, his face grim. He could tell something was wrong, just as she could. "We are...we are seeing multiple signals. From the expected human space direction."

"Speed?"

More murmured conversation. "Fast. Faster than the first ones. If we've got it right, they should all be arriving around the same time. Around an hour. That's to dropout, and then there'd be realspace travel to get here."

Moire walked inside the attack ship, where no one could see her face. "Dammit! If the crabs don't show up first we're going to have a lot of fun explaining things in the middle of a fight. I'm sending Radersent back. Get him to record a message that we can send the instant they show up. If you can, pipe it through one of the remote ships. No need to give away our position from the beginning. How many?"

"I-I can't tell," Alice said. "I'm sorry, but the resolution isn't good enough. More than five."

Crap, crap, crap.

"What is it?" asked Ennis. His face was carefully neutral but his eyes were intense.

"Toren. Coming in fast. They must be desperate, or stupid. Alice can't tell if the crab fighters will get here before them. We've got maybe an hour before contact with the enemy."

They stood at the top of the ramp and looked out at the crowd, holding each other close. Everyone was happy now, and she was going to have to stop it cold. But not just yet. They had a little time, before she had to tell them. Just a few minutes more. So they could remember, later, what they were fighting for.

✹

Kostas climbed up the rocky slope and stood on an outcrop, breathing heavily. If the damn island had any large expanses of flat surface, he hadn't found 'em. He always seemed to be going up or down a steep hill, and the little extra bit of gravity didn't help much either, especially not with the gear he was carrying.

Alan's dark head peeked over the edge, and he joined Kostas in one agile motion, never standing fully upright. Guess that was the right way to do it, if there were bad guys around waiting to shoot a good target like someone standing on a high outcrop. Kostas shrugged, accepting his laziness.

"What about this place? Better?"

Alan looked around, careful and serious. "Yes. I can cover the whole slope to the exit, and the flanking positions."

"Right. Everybody dig in!" Kostas called down the slope. The rest of the team spread out to their assigned places and started unpacking. They were the only fighters outside on the surface, and even if things went bad it would be a while before the fight came to them. They were to defend the escape hatch and make sure it stayed clear. Kostas would have preferred a more active role, but since he didn't know how to fly a ship the only other choice was to stay underground in the tunnels and there wasn't much for him to do there, either.

Kostas turned and dropped his pack. Might as well get comfortable; they were in for a long wait. Alan had already set up his sniper rifle on its stand and was checking the area through the scope. Kostas fought down a surge of worry. Alan ought to be inside, with the rest of the children and Created. The captain had been very blunt about it. She, Commander Ennis, and Alan were the only defenders who had any training at all in real combat skills. "We've got plenty of talented amateurs and bar brawlers, but enthusiasm doesn't substitute for training," she'd said. "I don't like it any more than you do, but it wasn't my idea. Toren trained him to be a killer. Too damn bad we're going to use that against them. He's got the skill, but he doesn't have adult judgment. That's your job. As long as he's in the fight and armed, you stick with him. He'll listen to you."

His conscience still gave him trouble, even when he reminded himself this was the last line of defense and probably the safest place for anybody. He sat down and leaned against his pack, making sure his scope was handy. Time to check in.

"Kostas to Control."

"Hey there." Alice's voice always had a little smile in it, at least to him. He smiled back.

"That your idea of a proper military greetin', gumdrop?"

He heard her sigh over the comm. "What's your report, dear?"

"We're in position. You can start the war now. Oh, and we're out of supplies."

"Very funny," Alice said in a reproving voice. "I packed your food myself, you serial liar. Hang on a sec—gonna check the short-range." There was a pause, then she said "Go to the short comms. You're close enough to the repeater there, and less chance of them picking you up. Keep it light though, even now. We probably won't be contacting you until they are in low orbit, OK?"

Kostas looked up and saw Alan staring at him with a burning question in his eyes. "Any word from out there?"

"Nobody has shown up. Captain and the Commander are in position." Kostas gave Alan a thumb's-up and a wink. "Oh, and Gren wanted me to tell you—they can't find that foggy maintenance guy, Carlos Montero. He's wandered off before and forgotten to tell anyone or call in, but keep an eye out. He could be inside, but we don't know for sure."

"I saw him in the cave for the wedding party," Kostas said. "We'll let you know if he shows up. Bit of a hike for an old guy like him, so's not likely."

He signed off, and prepared to be bored. It wasn't a bad place for a lookout. The sun was mostly behind them, another good tactical decision. The big trees of the cave bay didn't grow here so he could see out to the islands on the far horizon. One of them had a buried ship but he couldn't make out which it was. The water was a deep slate-blue, rippled with small waves. Small twisted bushes grew in the cracks and crannies of the rocks. Kostas thought he recognized some of them from the camouflage landscaping Eng had done. He wondered where the xenobiologist was, and if he'd had to be tranquilized yet. Nobody was happy about Toren coming, but Eng was terrified.

The comm alert woke him from a light doze. He'd have to be careful about that. It was getting too warm and the sound of waves was relaxing.

He reached for the commlink, but it wasn't blinking. Where was the alert coming from?

Kostas felt a sudden wave of cold over his skin. It was coming from the captured long-range comm. A stranger's voice, faint and distorted by distance, came through. The damn Toren idiot didn't say anything useful, just someone's name, but it was enough. The enemy was in-system.

He crept to the edge of the outcrop and whistled through his fingers, once. When everyone's eyes were on him, he held out his hand in the construction signal for "secure for detonation." Kostas closed his eyes, thinking of his wife and daughter underground. *Daughters*, counting Aurora. *Only way Toren gets to 'em is through me.* Better still, Toren should do any dying that needed doing. Bastards had it coming, three times over.

On the main deck of *Raven* Ennis checked that the remote sensor buoy was still sending back its bursts of data. He had salted the area with some scraps of wreckage, just in case, but the data bursts would also hide the fact that it was a functioning device. Both *Raven* and the attack ship were relying on the buoy for sensor data since they were hiding out in what passed for an asteroid belt in the Sequoyah system. Fortunately both ships were not large. The belt was thin and patchy, and he wasn't planning on staying hidden for very long–just enough to be able to sneak up on the Toren ships. All ten of them.

He shook his head, swearing quietly to himself. Ten ships. Ten fully crewed, functional Toren ships. They must be pushing their colonization plans as fast as they would go, given the first surviving ship could not have had very long to report back. Maybe they had this fleet prepared and waiting? It seemed like a waste of resources, but Toren had the resources to waste.

They weren't expecting a fight here, he reminded himself. The most recent information they had was Sequoyah was completely uninhabited and undeveloped. They would notice the robot ships, of course. No attempt had been made to hide them, just outside the orbit of the three moons. The robo-ships hadn't been detected yet, he knew, since he was monitoring the frequency used by the Toren exploration team long-range comms. All he'd heard so far were routine attempts to make contact with the Toren ground team. Nobody sounded particularly worried. Yet.

He glanced over his shoulder at the pilot's position. Palmer was leaning back in his chair, looking like he was asleep. Ennis knew he wasn't. They'd been lucky to get him back in time to grab him for ship handling. His web piloting skills might not be that hot, but nobody questioned his ability to make a ship behave in realspace while dodging debris. Lorai Grimaldi had been quite emphatic about that, Ennis remembered with a grin.

Since *Raven* was a private commercial vessel in its previous life, it didn't have a command jumpseat. For the moment Ennis was running the signals board, but as soon as things got heavy he would be needed at the guns. It was going to be interesting, being Sequoyan Admiral from the gunnery chair, but there was no other way. All the other ship commanders had their orders. He would have to give guidance from the limited information patched in to his position.

Suddenly he noticed the contact attempts had stopped. The lead ship had slowed its velocity as well.

"They're on to us," he called out to Palmer.

Palmer sat up. "Took 'em long enough. Can I do it now?"

"Not yet. They know something's wrong but not that it's dangerous. We've only got a few tricks and we can't waste them." Palmer sighed. There was a flurry of signal, all encrypted, between the Toren ships. Then a signal in the clear. "Yep, they know someone's here ahead of them. They're hailing the robo-ships. Standard request for identification." The Toren ships were not identifying themselves, which was not standard at all. Ennis listened with only half an ear, instead trying to locate the ship doing the hailing. It was probably the command ship, and he wanted to make sure it got priority on the target list.

Then he heard Moire's voice on the comm. It was a recording, sent from the fake flagship they called the goat, and it meant the ground control had decided the Toren ships had gotten close enough. *This is Moire Cameron. All invading Toren ships are ordered to leave this system immediately. Norstar Fleet is aware of your actions and has these coordinates—and we have other allies. This will never be a safe place for you. Any movement other than out of system will be considered a hostile act.* It was strange to hear her, with her ship silent near his. He didn't even know her exact position in the asteroid field.

The transmission cut off. The Toren ship attempted further communications, but there was no reply. The defenders had all agreed there was no point, beyond strategic deception, in talking with Toren.

"They sayin' anything?" Palmer asked.

"Nothing unexpected. Surrender or die, Fleet won't help you, et cetera." Ennis shrugged. "What else can they say?"

Palmer studied a readout. "They're still goin' in, but slower. *Now* can I do it? What if tail-end-charlie decides to run away?"

"Not yet. Why would they run? They have us outnumbered. Even if they knew about these ships they have us outnumbered." Ennis watched his own screen. "Robo-ships are moving. It's starting." This was the plan, he reminded himself. This is the way it was supposed to work. The ships were empty. Nobody would die on them, even if they blew up. The old instincts, however, said ships meant people and that those ships were going to be destroyed.

"I'm going to my station now," Ennis said, standing and setting the comms to feed up to the gunnery display. "I'm pretty sure the command ship is the second or third—those ones," he said, indicating on Palmer's display. "Those are identical to military ship profiles. These are probably freighters, and I don't know about that one. It doesn't fit any type I'm familiar with. The one hanging back is a commercial light freighter. The military ships, if they have the standard weapons, will have an area just behind and below the dorsal section where it is difficult to aim the guns. Fleet can do it, but we train for that. Never let this ship get along the front centerline—that's where the targeting computers are optimized."

Palmer nodded. "Lemmee guess, not yet?"

Ennis grinned. "First the robo-ships, then us, *then* you can do it. But wait for my signal!"

"Least I get ta do *somethin'* now," Palmer muttered.

The robo-ships were fully engaged by the Toren front ships. Ennis did a quick sweep of the readouts while strapping in to the gunner's chair and making sure his shipsuit was sealed. Given their positions, they must be taking a tremendous amount of fire. One appeared to be damaged so badly it could no longer move. Still no sign that Toren knew they were fakes. He watched the screen carefully while he did his pre-checks, wincing when he saw every single robo-ship jog just a bit in the same direction. Something must have twitched in the ad-hoc controller, but if it happened again Toren might notice—and figure it out.

The Toren ships were now as spread out as they were likely to be until the visible threat was dealt with. It was time.

"Move out!" Ennis yelled. "Get us between that first freighter and the third ship in the line!"

Palmer never needed to be told to move fast. The freighter was closest, so Ennis took as many shots as he could until the suspected command ship was in range. Now that they were out in the open, he signaled Control dirtside and gave them his quick assessment of the various Toren ships they were facing.

"One remote ship is completely unresponsive," Control replied. "Another has severe damage and limited mobility. The rest are only slightly damaged. Toren is using one of their standard encryption schemas. I've put it on the second nav channel. There's a one-minute delay since we don't have their gear to decrypt with."

"Better than nothing," Ennis grunted, trying to get a lock on the third Toren ship. He knew where the reactor was on that ship, and a lucky shot would render it useless. He could see Moire's ship on the scanner now. She was weaving through the front of the Toren fleet, skimming low over the ships so if the others fired they would be just as likely to hit each other rather than her.

It was all chaos now. He could only focus on his guns, switching occasionally to the decrypted Toren channel to gauge their reaction. He felt *Raven* shudder, taking a hit. Palmer would have to deal with it. The Toren voices had an edge of unfocused panic. They'd gotten that part right, anyway. Ennis listened carefully now, until he started to hear signs of a growing understanding. That was dangerous.

"Palmer!" he yelled. "Time to do it!"

"WOOHOO!" came the answering yell.

Ennis grinned. Another scan of the display...only two of the robo-ships were still capable of moving. *Frankenstein* was coming out of the shadow of Sequoyah to its last-ditch defensive position. Moire had scored a direct hit on the second ship and encouraged more friendly fire on the third, but the Toren warships were still very much in action.

Then he saw the flash indicating a large energy burst from the position of the hindmost ship. Palmer's pet project, the missile hidden in old wreckage, had scored the first complete hit of the war.

"Yes!" Palmer screamed. "I knew they wouldn't scan their own wreckage! Wish I had a hunnert of 'em!"

"They'd figure it out after the first fifty or so," Ennis said.

"Yeah, yeah, but it'd be fun!"

As he had hoped, the surprise attack where there was no enemy ship threw Toren into confusion again. Unfortunately, that was pretty much the last of the clever ideas the Sequoyah defenders had. Everything else would have to be done the hard way.

"Time for missiles," he sent on the defender's frequency.

"Was that Palmer's toy that just went up?" said Moire. The relief of hearing her voice was like water in the desert. She sounded busy, but not desperate. Well, she never had, if he remembered correctly from their days on *Canaveral*. Even when she should.

"Looks like he got first blood. Let's mop up, shall we?"

She laughed, and then things got busy. The ship she had been firing on drifted slowly, as if it no longer had the ability to maneuver. Then he saw two large bays opening up.

"Look alive, they've got fighters or something coming out!" Ennis yelled.

"We're showing multiple ships on scanner," Control said.

"Yes, I see them," Moire snapped.

"Ships are entering the system now, from the other arrival point," Control continued.

Well, it was nice that the crab fighters had shown up finally. Ennis felt a rush of relief. Now they could get something done.

"Hey, they are firing on our ships!" someone said. It sounded like the pilot of *Frankenstein*.

"Control, did the welcome message get sent?"

"Yes!"

Ennis swore. "Well send it again! Oh crap ..." A large crab fighting ship was bearing down on him. "Somebody left out the important bit about who the friendlies are!"

CHAPTER 16
ANACREON IN HEAVEN

Moire skimmed close around the surface of a damaged Toren freighter, dodging fire. She heard Ennis yelling something about the crabs shooting the wrong ships. She'd been so busy with her own fights she hadn't even noticed their arrival.

"Send it again!" Ennis yelled. "I didn't get a damn thing, so they sure won't!"

Moire switched the comm to pick up Control. " We're sending it the same way you're getting this," Alice snapped. "We see the signal from Radersent too. I don't know why it isn't working!"

"Don't run translator signal through the encoder," Moire said. "You're probably stripping out some of the higher frequency data."

"Encoder is hardwired, I'll have to reroute—"

"Just do it! We need to get those crab fighter shooting at the right targets."

More chatter, and Moire had to shut down the Control link. They could raise her if they really needed to, and she had enough to worry about. Such as the tragic lack of ship-killing missiles. They'd used up the few they had, and the remaining ordnance couldn't penetrate to reactor cores. The best they could do now was take out the engines and that required a lot more precision and luck. Why had Toren sent so many ships, anyway?

She had the feeling the freighter wasn't going anywhere soon. It was moving but not in a way that indicated it could maneuver, and she'd already taken out all the guns on one side and the big ones on the other. There were other targets requiring her attention, and too many Toren fighters giving her all of theirs. She'd taken some hits but nothing significant, no doubt due to the lack of combat experience the Toren pilots had. You couldn't learn everything in a simulator.

Wreckage had increased—most of it, unfortunately, from their remote ships. It slowed her down, but also gave her something to hide behind now and then. New target, new target...who was shooting at her most? The ship that had been third in the original formation seemed to fit that description. She also didn't like the way it had moved back from the main fight and let the others take most of the damage. That sounded like the Toren higher-ups were aboard.

She wished she could hear Ennis yelling about something, so she would know he was alive.

There was her target, and right coming up to it from the other direction were three crab fighters. Had Control managed to get the message out by now, so they knew which side they were supposed to be on? Only one way to be sure.

Moire swung about and cut across the crab ship's line of approach. This put her in line for the forward connection of the engine nacelles on the Toren ship, and she toggled the heavy shells. Moire fired four times and then pulled up to avoid the defensive fire. Heavy shells would have enough visual impact the crabs could see it, especially in the infrared. She dodged and spun behind a chunk of wreckage, intending to make sure where everyone was before she tried it again.

Now only one crab was forward of her. The other two were behind and in flanking positions, showing no indication of attacking her. "Looks like I just got some wingmen," Moire muttered. Now, how was she going to tell them what to do and why? They hadn't even considered that possibility. Well, point and grunt had gotten them this far, point and shoot should be even easier. She hoped that the message from Control had done the trick and not her four-shot signal.

She accelerated out from behind the wreckage for another attack run. Sure enough, the two crabs were following her, staggered-ragged. Moire aimed for another engine to spread the love around. Hopefully her two new friends would understand that was the desired target. She kept one eye on the crab fighters as she pulled away again, and contacted Control.

"I've got crab helpers now," Moire reported. "Did you get through? Do we have any live comms with them?"

"Only with the main ships," Alice said. "Fighters don't have translators. Latest arrival doesn't have much experience with it, so we have a lot of confusion. Don't have any crab comm gear for Radersent either."

"Terrific." They *had* to do a better job with their communications for the next war. This was ridiculous. Why bother having alien allies if you couldn't tell them what to do?

"Hey, Ennis. What's it look like?"

"Too many of them can still move—at least five. We have to change that or we're dead." He sounded tired. "Control, set the remotes that aren't moving to Last Call—but make sure the crabs know to stay away."

Moire flipped her attack ship over and went after the keel gun on the Toren ship. It was firing accurately enough she had all she could do to dodge. One of her crab fighters wasn't so lucky. "Control. Status on the ships launched from enemy ship #2?"

"Tracking six targets. Data to command ship. They are moving between originating ship and enemy ship #3. They have not engaged."

"Looks like a variant of our latest intra-system fighter," Ennis commented. "Standard load is two missiles, plus heavy cannons forward and a light cannon aft. Can just kiss the top of the atmosphere, but no further."

Moire sighed. So that's where all the missiles were. The enemy had them.

"Wait a minute, I'm seeing some strange behavior from the back half of the convoy. They are holding or pulling back," said Ennis, sounding interested. "I wonder why?"

"They don't have as much in the way of weaponry as the front ships," Moire said. "Control, confirm that crab main ships are closest to them?"

"Confirmed," Alice said. Her voice was thoughtful.

"They're spooked!" Ennis yelled. "They never faced crabs in combat—they are running! Control, get one of those main ships to move flanking enemy ship #6, the light commercial freighter. Have the other maintain course, and if they can get there maintain position between enemy ship #3 and Sequoyah."

Moire raised her eyebrows. Unconventional, but it could start a stampede. She thought further, and frowned. Panic was desirable, but not a stampede. If any of them escaped into webspace they would bring a *much* better prepared fleet back with them, and the defenders would have very little left to counter them with.

"We can't let any of them leave," she said. "They need to be crippled or killed."

"Got it," Ennis said tersely. After a moment, he snapped, "Attack ship and *Raven* on remaining forward Toren military ship. *Frankenstein* and any remaining ships with movement attack the rear with the help of one crab main ship. Crab fighters attack the Toren fighters. Control, get the word to the allies. Primary objective is still to defend the planet, but keeping the enemy here is a close second. Execute!"

Moire swung around for another run at her designated target. It made sense—*Raven* and the attack ship were much better choices to face down warships, instead of the repurposed freighters like *Frankenstein*—but that didn't make it easy or fun. Getting the big crab ships out of the gravy was also smart, since panic could cut both ways. Better to have them hunt multiple terrified targets.

The lower guns were still firing, but with a slower repetition that told her they had been damaged. Another run could take them out entirely. As she made her run she caught motion from the corner of her eye. A new, darker patch on the underside, and just when she understood what was happening her scope picked up the approach of the no longer motionless Toren fighters. They were coming straight for her. Moire dodged to put the bulk of the ship and then a freighter between them, and hoped her crab shadow would follow.

"Toren ship, launching shuttles!" she called out on the comm. "Enemy fighters defending. They're trying for a landing!"

Ennis swore. "What mental midget is in command there? What good will that do? They can't possibly have enough people to hold a whole planet."

The shuttles were going all-out, direct for Sequoyah below. Moire squinted at the outline of the islands just visible on the twilight edge, since the darkside was nearest to them, trying to orient herself. Then she froze. The shuttles, and their fighter escorts, knew exactly where they were going. Moire fought the sudden sick feeling. Toren wasn't trying to force a beachhead on the whole planet, just one specific location.

"Brace for impact, Control. They found you."

Carlos Montero was confused. There had been a party, he was sure of that. Everyone was happy, and while he was happy too he didn't like crowds very much. He'd just assumed the big war wasn't coming for some reason, and decided to have a nap in the warm sun. When he woke up it was dark. He went for a walk along the beach to admire the light of the moons on the water and get some fresh night air before going back inside. There were songs his grandmother had sung about sweet night air and moonlight, in the old tongue, and he wanted to see if it would be like that on this different world. Then it got cold and he went back, but all the people were gone and so was the captain's ship. Even the door inside was hidden and closed.

It would be better not to make a fuss. Eventually the door would open again and people would come back to the cave and he could simply...merge back, like he'd always been there. Carlos didn't want to trouble anyone, or get in trouble himself. That was when he got noticed, and that often was uncomfortable. It was still cold, though, and he couldn't find anything to keep warm in so he decided to keep walking. It was clear, with none of the horrible smelly plants, and he liked the sound of water trickling and rustling on the shore. He went far, farther than he'd ever gone before.

Even though he was walking it was still cold outside, so cold he was relieved when he saw a group of people ahead and waved, walking faster so they would see him and not leave. He didn't recognize any of them. He didn't think much of it; there were so many new people all the time. They were surprised to see him, he could tell. They didn't yell at him, not at first. That made him wonder. Then—then he knew they didn't belong on Sequoyah. The captain would yell when she was angry at him, but she never tied him up, or hit him. These must be the ones they were supposed to fight. It was confusing. Wasn't the party because the fighting was done? So much happened when he wasn't paying attention. Maybe this was a different fight.

It didn't really matter, in the end. The important thing was the captain would be angry about this. Very angry. The strangers wanted him to show the way in. They'd hurt him, hard, to make him say yes. He remembered that sort of thing from Nova Curacha, that was why he left. Stay on a ship, fewer gangs there. He had been confused by gangs too. Why would they never leave him alone?

This new gang was talking amongst themselves, about him. Carlos didn't want to tell them anything. But gangs didn't work that way, they'd kill him or hurt him so bad he would say something he shouldn't and it was hard to remember what you shouldn't say when the pain was bad. So first, he had to make them think he was telling them something they wanted. Then he had to find a way to hurt *them*, to make them stop.

He sighed, feeling gloomy. Even when he was young he had never been good at fighting, and he was tied up and injured too. It didn't matter, though. This was his fault so he had to make it better. Not let them use him to hurt the people here.

"Thought it over?" said the leader. Carlos hadn't heard him, he'd been thinking so hard, and he gasped in fright. The leader smiled, but it didn't reach his eyes. "Yeah, you're in the deep shit. Only thing that will keep you alive is showing us the way in, and we don't *need* you for that. It would be quicker if you helped, sure. Maybe we'd be grateful. Maybe. But your buddies are getting nulled one way or another, so why be a hero for nothing?" The leader glanced at him again, shrugged, and chambered a round in his pistol.

Carlos started to babble. He let it happen, knowing it would make the strangers think he would agree. "Bbbut..I..I'm lost! 's why I'm out here, an...and I thought you were coming f-for me, and the *chupalitros* come out soon!"

"The what?" said a dark woman. She was holding a large wrench, meaningfully.

"They are...they fly in the night. Warm things draw them, living things. It is true our blood poisons them, but by then you are dead, no?" Carlos shuddered, remembering when the flying thing had collided with his face. Without any harm to either, but if he remembered being frightened it would show, and they might not believe, but they would wonder.

"So let's get inside where it's safe, then."

"I don't know where I am!" Carlos wailed, as loudly as he dared. It was true enough, even though he wasn't really lost. He could follow the beach back and find the cave, but then they would too.

"Keep it down," snarled the woman, and hit him in the ribs with the wrench. Carlos felt something snap, and a sharp stab of pain. He sobbed.

"D'ya mind not killing him just yet?" the leader said sourly. "I think he's feeling more cooperative, aren't ya, beb?"

He couldn't speak around the pain, so he just nodded. The leader went

213

to one knee beside him, holding out a handheld display. It showed a rough scanner outline of the island. There was a white circle on the island, but it wasn't where the cave was. "We know your boss is sending signals from here. It is just up the slope from this position. Memory coming back?"

Carlos thought hard, staring at the display. The signal came from there. They didn't send signal where the tunnel was, so the bad people couldn't find them. The tall woman who knew so much about comms had found a way to fool them, make it seem like that was where they were. So, the people were safe for now. But he could see the beginnings of dawn, and if he didn't lead the strangers away they would see his footprints and maybe follow them back, and then they would find the cave.

"I know where I am now," Carlos whispered. The pain had retreated to a dull, constant ache that spiked whenever he took a breath. "There is...there is a back entrance near here. Hidden."

The leader stared at him. "So, show us."

"I need the light, to see around it!" Carlos pleaded. "It is disguised, I tell you, and only once I saw it. Up there," he nodded with his head. "On the hillside."

They argued some more. As he had hoped, they did not want to use bright handlights that might give away their position. Even they had noticed daylight was approaching, so it would not add that much time to wait. The leader decided they should at least climb the hill near the beach, which they could do in the dawn light and would give them more cover. They untied Carlos' legs and helped him, not gently, up the slope.

The trick was to find the right time. Carlos had seen a flash of light in the sky. The fight was coming closer now. He didn't know how these people had evaded detection, but he was sure someone would know ships were coming down. There were defenses for that, and he had helped build them.

They were now standing on a flat, sand-dusted bluff overlooking the beach. Large flat rocks were scattered over the surface. He recognized the one he was looking for, but let his eyes wander over it as if looking for another. The pain was bad, but he made it appear even worse, as if he could barely walk.

"In...in my pocket," Carlos gasped. "Metal plate. Has a datachip." Rough hands searched him, holding out what looked like a baffle for HyVar medium power regulator. It *was* a baffle for a HyVar medium power regulator. "You have to...hold it over...sensor. Black rock with...with a white line. Or maybe two. I can't remember...." If he was too specific, they would kill him now. If there was a chance he still had information, they would wait. Carlos limped around as if he were looking for the sensor rock, ending with one foot against the certain rock slab. The strangers, convinced that he was barely mobile, spread out to look.

His nerves were stretched to the point of snapping. It had to happen. Before they became suspicious that he had lied to them.

Then he felt it, a low, shuddering vibration in the rock. He shuffled back, trying to look amazed, and shouted, "That's it! You found it!" Then he turned and ran.

They were shooting at him now, of course. He counted under his breath, keeping the count even when a bullet slammed into his back. He could still run, not very fast but he didn't want to run fast they had to follow him and come to the place, the place they all must be, at the proper time.

His vision was going dark around the edges now, but he still had a little viewport to the world and he could see the cleft in the rock wall ahead, carefully matching the stone around it. More than big enough for a man to enter, but that was not its purpose. Carlos started shouting, to make the lie more real. "Help, help, they are behind me!"

He felt his ears pop as the air pressure changed. Just a little further now. The gun door was open, the shells already on the way. And when they left the firing tube, the vent tunnel they were in would be filled with fire. Another shot hit him, on the hip, and he fell. It didn't matter, the strangers were too far down the tunnel to escape in time. Carlos smiled. He would kill a few of the enemy, even though he was not a fighter, and maybe the captain would not be quite so angry with him now.

The first gust of air rushed over him as the world went dark, and he was no longer cold.

✦

Ennis stared at his scanner screen, hoping Moire was mistaken. She wasn't. The pattern was unmistakable—fighter escorts defending troop transport shuttles. The only bright side was the move had positively identified the Toren command ship.

"I'm the only one who can fight in atmosphere," Moire said. "Sorry, but it looks like you'll have to take care of this one."

"That crab cruiser is backing me up. Go take care of business."

Control broke in, voice rough with a thin layer of panic. "Enemy signal intercepted, from the surface! I thought you said the shuttles hadn't landed yet!"

A silence, then Moire spoke. "The ones I'm seeing have barely reached the atmosphere. It is possible Toren managed to get one one in with stealth countermeasures. They do supply Fleet, you know."

"Was it encrypted? What were they talking about?" Ennis asked, keeping a weather eye on the continuing battle. Moire was streaking away on an intercept with the fighters, along with a handful of crab ships.

"Something about being on fire," Control responded, sounding confused. "It was just a fragment. Sent in the clear. They weren't happy

215

about it. It was a few minutes after we started ground defenses."

Ennis raised an eyebrow. Had the stealth shuttle been shot down, perhaps? A bit lucky if they hadn't been aiming at it. That was now Moire's problem. He had his own work to do.

As if they didn't have enough to worry about, *Raven* was getting low on ammunition. Ennis focused on making every shot count, which meant Palmer was so busy dodging fire and wreckage he had no energy to make his usual smart remarks. They had to think of something else, soon, or their luck would run out in a big way.

Ennis glanced at the screen and tapped it to get the status on the friendly ships. The crab ships didn't have a status, unfortunately. One of the dead robo-ships was not far away, a drifting hulk—but the indicator for the Last Call option, something that Gren and his crew had rigged, was still green. They had a weapon but no way to aim it.

"Hey Palmer! Think you can get that Toren ship to chase us past that wreck?"

"Maybe," Palmer gasped. "Dunno if we'll live to tell about it."

"Do what you can," Ennis ordered. "I'll see if I can get the crabs to push them our way."

He got on the comm with Control, trying to figure out a simple and easily translated set of instructions to send. Move closer and harass, but don't just sit there and take damage. It would take time, first to tell Radersent and then for him to explain the crazy human idea to the crabs. He could confirm with the crab cruiser directly if what they were doing worked. Maybe.

It was even harder to get a lock on a target now with Palmer's wild maneuvers. Ennis felt the ship shudder, taking hits. Something was beeping insistently. He just hoped it wasn't the reactor overload alarm.

The crab ship was starting to move now. It had an effect, all right. The Toren command ship redoubled its rate of fire on *Raven* and moved to intercept. Clearly they would rather fight their way through a small human ship than a crab cruiser. Palmer spun the ship away, as if planning to head for the planet below, then skimmed around behind the wreck, using it as a shield.

"I think I got 'em, I think I got—"

The wreck reactor detonated. The energy blast blinded their sensors temporarily, but he didn't need them to know something large had hit *Raven*. The impact slammed him hard against the chair harness, slamming his head against a screen mount. Ennis touched his head, wincing, and saw red on his hand when he pulled it away.

"Palmer! Status!"

"Shit. We got holed bad! Um, looks like we lost pressure pretty much everywhere except here. Oh, and Cargo Bay 3, not that it does us any goo...DAMMIT! Engines dead. I sure hope we got that guy." Palmer started muttering and banging.

"It'd be shredding us now if it could," Ennis said. The scanner screens were starting to clear. "That was a bit close."

"Hey, you said make 'em chase us," Palmer snapped.

Of course the sensors nearest to the Toren command ship were destroyed in the blast. Ennis could tell by the way the detection field changed that they were drifting away from the impact point, and rotating. He just had to wait until his working sensors got in position. He waited impatiently, tensing for the next hit. It didn't come.

Then he saw why. The Toren ship had a large, blackened hole in its side. They also appeared to have lost engines, and none of the surviving guns could be brought to bear on them.

Ennis relayed the good news to Palmer.

"Woulda been nice to hammer 'em flat, but this'll do," Palmer allowed. "I ain't complaining. Well, I am but not about that. Stupid alarm is getting' on my nerves."

Ennis checked his partial scanner. The fight was still going on, but in areas far from where they were. It wasn't as if he could do much up there with the ship dead, and they were down to the last few shells anyway. He unstrapped and swung down to the main deck.

The emergency pressure doors had deployed outside the regular ones to the bridge entrance. Now he could hear the alarm Palmer had mentioned. It was shrill, loud, and grating. It was also, he discovered, on the other side of the emergency pressure doors.

"Hownell can we hear it then?" Palmer wanted to know. "Ain't no air to speak of there."

"Vibrating through the walls," Ennis said. "Looks like we're stuck with it. Any luck with the engines?"

"Nope. Prolly floatin' out there with the rest of the wreckage, I'm guessing. Got some trim jets for docking, though. Won't get us much, but better than nothing."

Ennis went over to the main scan board. Apparently the other crab cruiser was doing an excellent job keeping the remaining freighters spooked. The cruiser nearest them had figured out the Toren ship was unable to move and was staying just out of range while sending their version of missiles. The Toren crew were good with countermeasures, but it was just a matter of time. He blinked. Were they actually winning?

He studied the disposition of the remaining friendly ships. "It looks like *Frankenstein* is going to pass by soon. If they can, I'll have them pick us up."

"In suits?" Palmer asked, dubious.

"The whole ship. Mfume, Gren's sub, is on board to help with the weird gravitics and he knows how to do a ship tow configuration. Plus, we still have a few working guns and they could use the firepower."

"Better'n sitting out here all lonely like," agreed Palmer.

Frankenstein was able and willing, and in a very short time *Raven* was tucked inside the hollow ribs of the back end of the modified freighter. Ennis stayed down on the bridge, counting on enough warning from *Frankenstein* to get to the gunner's chair at need. He wanted to make sure they weren't missing anything in the chaos.

One of the spooked freighters had been destroyed, so the crab allies had earned a notch. Unfortunately the remaining Toren ships were also adding things up. The freighter that was now the furthest out had changed course, and it looked like it was headed out of the Sequoyah system. Not good.

"Is that ship trying to leave?" Ennis asked, pointing. "If so, we have to stop it."

Palmer leaned over his shoulder and cursed. "Yeah, that's a webspace runup for somewhere human. I wish..." his voice trailed off. "Hell, what am I saying? *Frankenstein* is set up for it!" He darted for the emergency locker, rotating the latch and slapping the fasteners loose with impatience. "Ain't nobody getting' there fast enough to stop 'em in realspace. I got an idea but I gotta use *Frankenstein* to make it work, OK?" He pulled out one of the evac suits. They were stronger than a shipsuit and had almost an hour of oxygen, but they weren't what Ennis would choose for outside work. Especially not in the middle of a war, but Palmer looked determined.

"You're going to chase that ship in *webspace?*" Ennis asked, incredulous.

"That's the plan. I got lots a time tracing incoming. Know what it feels like. Think I can take 'em out. Yer gonna have ta trust me. It needs doin', you know it does." Palmer had the suit on now and had the helmet, ready to seal.

Ennis thought furiously. Yes, the ship had to be stopped. *Frankenstein* was the least armed ship left and could be spared. "What if some of the others try it?"

"I can see 'em, remember? Get 'em the same way."

Ennis nodded sharply. "Do it. I have to stay here, though. Drop *Raven* before you go."

He alerted *Frankenstein* while Palmer finished getting the suit sealed up. Getting Palmer off the bridge was the hardest part, since there wasn't an airlock. Ennis put up his shipsuit cover, just in case, and they managed to wedge the pressure doors open just enough for Palmer to wiggle through. Ennis wasn't sure he had made it out safely until he saw the dark ribs of *Frankenstein* sliding away.

So. Now he was alone on a dead ship, not that it mattered since he doubted he could fly it even if the engines were working. Still, there was a war on. He had to find something useful to do. He turned back to the sensor board, and searched for Moire's ship while he listened to the comm.

She had to stay cool even though she felt like screaming. There was only one of her and making stupid mistakes would get her, and everybody else killed. Too many fighters for her to get to the shuttles at first, even with the crabs helping. The shuttles got a good head start. Now she was entering the atmosphere, so it was just her and the shuttles. They had weapons, but she had maneuverability and speed. And weapons.

The comm beeped, a direct channel. Probably not good news, since that was dirtside.

"I see we've got company," said Gren. "Letting you know I'm picking Door Number Three."

Moire felt her stomach twist. That was the code meaning he was sending people out to fight. They had hoped it wouldn't come to this but they had planned anyway. She hadn't held up her end of the bargain. Enemy forces were landing, and Gren had authority dirtside. He was right, but she didn't have to like it. *Alan is down there.*

And then Control had let her know Palmer was chasing a Toren ship that had gone into webspace. Ennis' call. It had looked for a moment like they might win, but now? She shook her head. Stop the shuttles. Keep the ground war from getting dug in. All by herself. No, she did have one asset she could call on now.

Lorai Grimaldi was standing by with the captured Toren shuttle.

"Time to cause trouble," Moire said on the comm.

"Hot damn, thought this war gonna pass me by. Whaddya want me to do?"

"Wait for the first couple to pass by your position. Merge in with the rest, start yelling and screaming and flying like you are having seizures. Mess up the formation. Oh, and do some low skips over the water if you can."

Lorai just laughed. It was her idea originally, and if they could pull it off she would be insufferable.

The shuttles were heading for New Houston, all right. They had spread out, knowing she was on their tail. Still, a few were careless and bunched together. Moire squeezed the trigger on the lead shuttle of a group of three and pulled up sharply before they could get a bead on *her*. She looked back and smiled. Her target had disintegrated, and one of the two following had gotten a face full of debris. It was leaking smoke, slowing, and not holding steady. Might make it, but she needed to deal with the others first.

The rest of the shuttles had scattered completely by now, and they were firing on her. Didn't matter—she knew where they were going. Moire pushed the attack craft as fast as it could go, and thumbed the comm.

"Knock, knock."

There were three clicks in response. Moire slowed, loitering behind the mass of the island of Bon Accord waiting for the shuttles to show up.

Specks on the scope became specks in the distance. She accelerated again, low and straight on, blending in visually with the island in the background. Their scopes would pick her up, if they were paying proper attention, but the shuttles didn't have targeting computers. She fired as soon as she had range, tearing through their formation, flipping up and around to dive through again, doing as much damage as she could.

That's when a new shuttle joined in, pilot shrieking on the main Toren channel in terror and desperation. Moire pretended to chase Lorai for a bit, then switched to a real target that looked shaky. Lorai was flying low over the inter-island water, shallower than the deep sea, in a strange semicircle that would dip for a moment, then suddenly jerk up, as if she were having trouble maintaining altitude.

Moire chased her target in the same area, firing from above. A darker patch of water, almost like a shadow, had become visible. She dived, the shuttle desperately skimmed the water hoping she could not follow so closely—and the dark shadow erupted from the water. She whistled, awed by the size of the thing. It was at least as long as the shuttle was, black and sleek. She'd never seen one of the water creatures so clearly before. It struck the shuttle, bone-tipped tentacles lashing at the hull, and both creature and shuttle fell into the water in a fountain of water and spray.

Still too many shuttles in the air, but now they never went close to the water. Certainly made it easier for her to shoot them. Lorai was still doing her crazed-with-fear act, now with live ammo. Since the other shuttles had let her get close, it was effective. The Toren pilots weren't stupid, unfortunately, and when Moire saw some weapons turning to train on Lorai, she toggle the comm again.

"Knockitoff, knockitoff," Moire snapped. Lorai sped off, zipping low over an area she knew, but the Toren folks didn't, was too shallow for the huge sea creatures.

Moire did another fast pass over the beach, swearing. There were fewer targets in the air, but not because they'd been shot down. Some of the shuttles had landed.

"Control. Beachhead on Red Sector. Two down." She skimmed the hillside, coming up and over to give the landed shuttles enough heavy sustained fire to make them unflyable. She didn't see any people on the ground, but they had probably scattered as soon as the hatch opened. She took out a few more still in the air, including the limping, wounded shuttle she'd hit earlier, but by then the rest were down. There was nothing much for her to do except call out the landing locations and blow up the actual shuttles.

She tried not to think about what would happen next. The shuttles had landed almost a hundred trained, armed Toren troops. At least they wouldn't be going anywhere else. Time to get back up in the dark and the rest of the fight.

Ennis' voice came over the comm once she switched it to the general ship channel, still directing the battle. Moire frowned. She'd thought he'd been with *Frankenstein* before, when *Raven* lost engine power—but then she remembered where *Frankenstein* had gone. That meant he was still up there in a ship that was drifting. By himself.

♛

So far it hadn't been too bad. There'd been a certain amount of drift and rotation once *Frankenstein* had let go, and in the interests of keeping up the appearance of a wreck Ennis had not attempted to change that. Besides, he still only had one side of sensors and the rotation made sure nobody was sneaking up on him.

It sounded like there were still two holdout ships, but the crab cruisers were making up for their late arrival. It could just be a protracted mopping up. He should be making notes for the inevitable report.

"*Raven*, come in."

Ennis sat up. That was Moire's voice. Where was she? The scope didn't show anything.

"Where do you keep the coffee on this ship? I need to stay awake."

She laughed, and he smiled, feeling shaky. A near-run thing, from start to finish. But Moire was laughing and alive, so it had been worth it all.

"We're out, remember? Are you OK up there?"

Up there? "I just remembered I can't get to the galley anyway. No air. How about you? I heard you were busy."

"Yeah." She didn't sound happy about it. "I did what I could. Good thing the fighters couldn't follow down to the deck or we'd have twice as many of the bastards to deal with dirtside." She paused. "Did the crabs get the rest of the fighters?"

"They got most of the ones escorting the shuttles," Ennis said, fiddling with the scanner resolution. "I saw a few around the command ship before it got taken out, but I don't know what happened to them." His screen was showing him things he didn't want to see, and his stomach tightened. "Never mind. I think I found them. Or they found me."

"On my way."

Ennis had the sinking feeling they had somehow figured out he was the one sending the commands. There had to be plenty of transmissions from other damaged ships yet there they were, homing in on him. To make matters worse, there were only three shells left assuming they would be considerate enough to attack on his good side.

"Don't dawdle," he managed. He opened another channel to Control. "Any chance of getting some crab help here? I've got enemy inbound."

"Crabs lost a lot of fighters," Control responded, sounding ragged. "I'll pass it along but I doubt the cruisers can get there in time."

221

Terrific. Well, if he was going to get shot at he should at least *try* to shoot back. Ennis took a last look at the scanner screen and headed for the gunner's chair. It wasn't long before the first shells hit. He was blind that direction, and had to wait, sweating, for the scanners to pick up anything useful. Alarms were shrilling, so something that hadn't been damaged before was damaged now. Most of the ship was dead anyway, but the fighters wouldn't know that.

The Toren fighters swung into view. Three of them. Ennis wasted one precious shell by undercompensating for the new rate of rotation, but then got a hit. The last shell was a miss. No reason to stay here now. Where the hell was Moire?

He unbuckled the harness and reached for the handhold to swing himself out and down to the deck below. Suddenly the section of hull near the gunner's chair buckled and broke, spewing metal and slamming him against the bulkhead in the explosion. Somehow by instinct he kept his grip on the handhold, despite the pain. Everything hurt, but especially his left leg. His hearing was damaged too, because he could feel the wind of escaping air but everything was silent.

Down. Down was where the emergency suits were. Where the comm was. He tried to climb down the ladder, but any attempt to move his left leg was so painful he was in danger of blacking out. He looked down. A jagged spike of metal had impaled him, just above the knee.

The metal spike was still attached to the hull, and there was no way for him to cut it off. He had only seconds before lack of air or blood loss made him lose consciousness. Ennis gritted his teeth and jerked his leg free. He screamed, and let go of the handhold. He landed on the deck hard, dimly sensed snapping feelings in his body adding to the raging agony already there. Somehow he managed to pull himself up to the control that shut the hatch to the gunner's position. It wasn't airtight, but it would slow the loss of atmosphere.

Every control board had blinking red lights. More metal wreckage strewed the bridge, torn loose when the shell hit. He didn't feel any wind now. Ennis tried to walk but fell with another scream. He elbow-crawled his way to the emergency locker, knocking away debris that covered the door. One suit was ruined, sliced through. The one remaining had a small hole. He could patch that.

First he had to do something about his leg. He cut free some fabric from the damaged suit, using a sharp piece of metal, and used a piece of cable to hold it in place. Putting the good suit on was agony, especially where it contacted his injured leg. He remembered to put a patch on the hole before crawling to the comm panel.

"I'm hit!" he yelled. "Losing pressure." Ennis shook his head to clear his blurred vision. The scanner screen...was it still working? He blinked again.

Another section of sensors had gone dead. Only a sliver of screen was still active. Something was traversing it, but he couldn't tell who or how many.

His head was ringing. It gradually resolved to emergency alarms, and he realized his hearing was coming back. Someone far away was calling his name. Moire, on the comm.

"Ennis! Dammit, come in! *Ennis!*"

"I'm here," he managed, and coughed. "Mostly."

"Can you hold out for a bit? Still got two..." she paused, "make that one to deal with."

"I'm suited up. Stuck on the bridge. It took two of us to open the door to get Palmer out, and I'm messed up."

"How bad?"

"I can't walk." That didn't sound quite right, so he repeated it. The words were thicker somehow. Talking tired him out.

"Ennis. Listen to me. Put your helmet on. I'll come and get you."

Emergency suits only had ordinary comms, without encryption. Toren would be able to hear. Bad idea. He tried to explain but Moire wasn't listening. Arguing tired him too, so he put the helmet on and sealed it.

Slowly his vision cleared, and so did his mind. Lack of oxygen had nearly gotten him. He still felt very weak, and tried not to think about why he couldn't feel his left leg any more. He fumbled with the suit comm.

"I'm thinking again," Ennis said.

Moire gave a short, shaky laugh. "Had me worried. Stand by."

He shifted until he could lean against a wall, and waited. Moire would be able to see better than he could the best way to get in. He wondered what she would do if she couldn't dock her ship.

Ennis woke from a light doze to find her kneeling beside him, suited, shaking his shoulder.

"We've got to get moving. Control thinks there may be a few more Toren fighters unaccounted for. Battlespace is such a mess with debris it's hard to tell." She pulled his arm over her shoulder and lifted. Ennis couldn't suppress the groan. "Sorry. Let's get you out of here."

Ennis concentrated on moving his one working leg, breathing, and not screaming. They rounded a corner and he saw Moire had taken advantage of the battle damage to back the attack ship up and drop the ramp inside, both easing his passage and anchoring the ships together. She dragged him in, raised the ramp, and when the pressure returned opened the forward compartment.

"We'd better check your damage," she said, helping him to a reclineable seat. "You don't look good."

Getting the suit off was even more painful than getting it on. The look on her face told him how bad it was. Moire snatched the medical kit and opened two packets of blood glue, one after the other, without even checking if the first one was holding. Then she opened a third one.

"The leg of your suit was full of blood," she said quietly. "You need medical attention."

"I'm not arguing," Ennis replied, weakly. "I just don't know where to get it. Dirtside is under attack and buttoned up, and I doubt Toren will help."

"Better keep moving or we'll need even more," Moire said, looking grim. She dropped in the pilot's seat. "Area's still clear. Checking the long-range...hmm, that's interesting. Or really, really bad news."

"Don't keep me in suspense," Ennis murmured. "Stress is bad for your health."

Moire snorted. "Two more blips on screen. Outsystem, bound in. Why can't Toren take a hint?"

"It could be Palmer, with the ship he was chasing," Ennis said.

"Not Palmer. No transponder code. Not crabs either, wrong direction. Hey, Control, expecting any visitors? Two unknown ships approaching."

There was a pause, a long one. Moire exchanged a worried glance with Ennis, who shrugged.

"Captain?" Alice at Control sounded dazed. "They are transmitting on both signal levels."

"Say again?"

"They are sending crab translator code as well as our regular signal. They demand identification of all ships."

"It's Fleet," Ennis whispered, when he finally understood. "Fleet made it." He closed his eyes.

"Captain, they want to talk to you," Alice said. "It's *Boorda* and *Temaire*, Captain Prees in command."

Ennis started. "*Temaire?* Who is in command of that ship?"

"Why?" Moire asked.

"*Boorda* is the main ship. It's old, probably the only hull of its class left. *Temaire* is brand new, a corvette. I know someone who was up for a command on one."

Moire relayed the question. "Name's Shabata. Sounds vaguely familiar," she said thoughtfully.

"I need to talk to her! Quickly, before Prees starts giving orders!"

Moire tossed him a commlink, looking puzzled.

"Captain? Shall I tell them you're contacting them?" Alice wanted to know

"No. Tell them you are still fighting on the surface and she is not available," Ennis said quickly.

Moire raised an eyebrow. "What are you plotting?" she asked.

"Nele Shabata is a personal friend. Fleet will have plenty of medical help, but I don't want them to get ideas about grabbing you."

"She's enough of a friend she'd pretend she hadn't seen me?" Moire had a dubious expression.

"I won't try her that far. No, but she'll help and she knows who I'm working for these days. Switch it to external."

Moire shook her head, but toggled the comm.

Ennis had to fight to keep his concentration. It was harder and harder to keep his eyes open, and he could barely hold the commlink.

"This is Commander Byron Ennis. I need to speak to Captain Shabata."

It took a few repeats before *Temaire* picked up, and then another request before he got Shabata personally.

"Ennis, what the hell have you been getting up to here?" was the first thing she said.

"I'm glad to see you too, Nele," he said, faintly. "Need a medevac."

"You are aware *Boorda* has a fully staffed medbay, and I have a few corpsmen, correct?"

"Umbra business. I'll brief you as much as I can. The ship I'm in is needed elsewhere. Still fighting."

"Which reminds me, I'd better have Control tell our crab allies the new visitors are friendly," muttered Moire. "We don't need any diplomatic setbacks now."

Shabata sighed over the comm. "Very well. I'm expecting a really good story, 'Ron."

Ennis let the commlink fall from his hand. All his strength was gone. Awareness faded in and out, mercifully he was unconscious when Moire moved him from the forward compartment. Perhaps not completely, for he distinctly remembered warm lips against his cold ones before the sound of a door closing, the ramp opening, and heavy feet and strange voices beside him.

It was, he decided, a good memory to have before passing out.

CHAPTER 17
A WORLD MADE NEW

Kostas tried to hide the groaning noises he made going up the slope, but Alan heard them anyway.

"Why did you do that, back there? You pushed me away and got in the way when that man shot at us. Didn't it hurt?"

A laugh and a groan, mixed together. "Damn right it hurt. Just like the other two holes I got." Kostas looked back the way they had come, his eyes sad. "Ain't complainin'. Could a been worse."

Some of the people with them had died, fighting. He kept thinking they would get up again, just like in the training he'd had back in the Place. The Toren place. He liked these people. How could they just die? And if they knew they could die fighting, why didn't they run away and hide?

"If it hurt why did you do it?"

"Wouldn't hurt near as bad as it would if you got shot and your mother found out," Kostas puffed, wincing as they reached the top of the ridge. Alan checked, no movement below and no hiding places either. It was safe to walk down.

"She wouldn't hurt you, would she?"

"Didn't say she'd hurt me, son."

Alan was going to ask more, but then they saw the dark shuttle on the beach. The one they'd been told to find. The comm had said a signal came from here, so the people fighting outside, the ones that were still alive and could walk, went there.

He watched carefully as the others checked the shuttle. He was glad when it was empty. Then someone shouted, and they went to look.

"Hey, they sneaked in but wore this stupid knit hat!" The woman held it up, grinning.

It was orange, with holes in it, and he recognized it. "That's Montero's hat!" Alan said, surprised. "Why did they have it?" Then he remembered. Carlos Montero was missing when Toren came, and people were worried. "Maybe he's here somewhere."

Kostas nodded, but his face looked hard. Wouldn't it be good to find Montero?

They found some footprints in the dirt, and scuff marks going up another hill. Alan kept watching for the Toren people from the shuttle, but he didn't see anyone.

"The comm relay is close, but the tracks lead away from it," Kostas said.

"What were they headed for?"

Alan could smell smoke now, and it was getting stronger. Now he could see a black hole in the rock, and big black mark in front of it...and strange black lumps, some outside the hole. They looked...wrong.

They were people. Burned people, some with bones coming through. The smell made him feel sick. One was collapsed near a comm unit.

"The exhaust vent? They can't have thought they'd get in that way, they ain't that dumb." Kostas peered in the dark hole. "More inside. Maybe somebody told 'em that was a way in."

One of the others came up and looked in too. "That don't make no sense. They aren't open unless the guns fire, an' then they real visible with all the smoke."

"Yeah. Unless somebody knew to wait. Just before the first gun fired." Alan stared at Kostas. One tear was tracking down the side of his face. "Some foggy guy who knew damn well where we put the vents and how they worked."

When he understood, Alan started to cry too. It couldn't be real. "Montero...went down there?" Kostas just nodded. "No! I want him to come back! *Why did he do it?*"

Kostas wiped his face. "Because he got brave when he had to. Those bastards musta caught him, forced him to help. So he helped 'em right into a furnace."

"But why can't he be alive?"

"Because he didn't have a choice. Help the bad guys kill us, or die fighting. You gonna say he did the wrong thing?"

Alan slowly shook his head, but his thoughts kept crying *I want him back!*

They didn't stay much longer, which was good. He didn't want to see the bodies any more, or think that one of them was Montero. Someone talked on the comm and told the people in the cave, and they could go back. And he did, and he tried to sleep but the fighting and the screams he remembered kept waking him up again. Then he heard the noise that meant one of the smaller ships was coming in, and he ran to the cave.

People had said his mother was OK and he'd heard her voice, but it wasn't the same as seeing her. It made him feel everything would be made better. Even Montero. She looked tired, and there was blood on her clothes.

"It's not mine, kid," she said when he ran up to her. Her face looked like pain, though. He wanted to make it go away. It frightened him to see his mother like that. Maybe...maybe she couldn't make this better.

"Then how—"

"I don't want to talk about it," she whispered, and hugged him tight.

♛

The uniform was stiff with newness, and possibly confusion on the part of the fabricator who had made it. Moire sighed internally. Here she was, surrendering just like she was supposed to, and all she was getting was a big steaming helping of hurry up and wait. Precisely how many accused mutineers were on the docket anyway?

Finally the doors opened. An older man with thinning black hair entered, wearing the insignia of the legal division of Fleet. He gave Moire a steady look, without expression.

"Lieutenant, you are out of uniform."

"Sir, with respect, this is the correct uniform for a United States Air Force Captain. Unless I have been discharged without my knowledge, that is my current rank."

A very, very small quiver disturbed the corner of his mouth. "Ah, I thought I would enjoy this case. I am Colonel del Sor. I will be your representative in these proceedings. I will admit to some curiosity how you managed to find such an antique uniform."

"Newly fabricated, sir, from memory and an illustrated children's encyclopedia. The history section."

"Of course."

He escorted her, with her guard, to a small room. The guard remained outside. Moire was impressed. Carriers did not usually have a lot of empty rooms, and del Sor had not even had to kick anybody out.

"I have been reviewing your case, insofar as the files have been made available to me. I understand a great deal has happened since, but we are only concerned with your actions aboard *Canaveral* before and during the mutiny."

"I am not wearing this uniform as a joke, sir. I was under orders given to me decades before the keel of *Canaveral* was even laid. It was due to those orders that I took the actions I did."

Del Sor sat back, his dark eyes lidded. "Tell me more."

She had more time than she had expected to prepare with del Sor. He made elliptical comments to the effect that they were waiting for the various members of the court-martial board, which didn't make sense. She had sent her message to Fleet with *Boorda* once the Sequoyah system had been secured and all the Toren ships and people dealt with. They had agreed on the location to meet months ago. Why was this still getting arranged?

She hadn't expected it to be fun. It hadn't been enjoyable nearly having to sneak away to avoid being kidnapped by her own people so she couldn't go. And once the court-martial started Ennis was there, sometimes even in the room as a witness, and she could only permit herself to glance at him. To do anything else would put him in danger, but it was hard when she saw him still painfully limping. She didn't even dare ask about the extent of his injuries.

Fleet's case was very straightforward and strong. No one disputed the reality of the mutiny. Moire did not dispute that she piloted the ship for the mutineers. Everything else del Sor challenged and argued, even introducing some highly interesting tape she hadn't known existed from her confrontation with Soliyah, defending Hallin's life. There was a definite reaction on the board to that information.

Then, after several days of this, the court-martial recessed suddenly in the middle of a session without explanation. Del Sor told her nothing, but she could tell he was also confused. Moire was even more surprised when less than an hour later she was summoned to the bridge. It resembled a recently-stirred hornet's nest, and the captain appeared on the point of an aneurysm.

"Did you tell them where to find us?" he yelled the instant she appeared on deck, stabbing a finger at her.

Moire blinked. "I don't understand, sir. Who are you referring to?"

The captain now had his dark face inches from hers. "The crab carrier that appeared just off my port bow," he said, his voice now dangerously calm. "It's not alone, and they are asking, I am informed, for *you*."

Well, at least they were talking. "Sir, I didn't know myself where they were taking me when I met the courier at Cullen. How could I possibly pass on information I didn't have?" She didn't mention her instant suspicion, that a certain specialized ship that *could* determine heading and destination had probably been hanging around Cullen when she left. But where had the carrier come from? Her allies didn't have one. Had Gren decided to pull some diplomatic strings? It didn't seem like him.

"Captain Baxter, the crab ships are maintaining protocol," Ennis' voice made her turn her head sharply. "One of the escorting ships is from the explorer clan, and they do not participate in hostile actions. I also recognize a cruiser that fought in the recent action around Sequoyah."

Ah. Perhaps the diplomatic string-pulling had been on the crab side. And wasn't it handy the way Ennis was passing her useful information right out in the open?

"Why do they want to talk to me?" Moire asked.

Ennis conferred with a busy group around a console, then straightened with a wince. "It appears that certain elements that had been suspicious are now convinced that the humans of Sequoyah are what they claim to be, and wish to discuss...it isn't quite an alliance, but something more than diplomatic relations." He gave her a bland look.

"I left Gre...I left people in charge. Why aren't they talking to them? I'm out of the loop now."

"Not according to them. A queen remains in authority until defeated in battle—you won—or a properly designated heir is elevated—the individual you refer to is male. They will accept communication from you through him, but not from him alone."

Hmm. Maybe she'd have to run things from the brig. And she'd been looking forward to a break from all the responsibility, too. Or she could convince someone like...oh, Mammachandra to step up as queen. She even had a female heir, too.

"Sir, I recommend that we delay. Inform them she is here but unable to speak with them at the moment," Ennis said to the captain. Moire narrowed a look at Ennis, and he gave a minute nod. The reason why she couldn't talk right now would be glossed over. She had a bad feeling if the crabs understood she was essentially a prisoner things wouldn't be so friendly any more.

The message sent and the crabs apparently agreeing to wait, Moire was escorted off the bridge and back to her secured quarters. Three days passed without any news, or even progress on the court-martial. On the fourth day del Sol came to see her, bursting with curiosity.

"A courier has just arrived with a high-ranking officer aboard. The board is meeting now with her."

Moire stared at him. "We've been waiting all this time for someone to show up for the court-martial? I thought they would want to deal with the crab situation first."

Del Sor spread his hands. "I would concur. I only inform you because it does involve the board. This is highly irregular, but you seem to have that effect on people. I have every hope this will be a very satisfactory case to end my career with."

"I hope, sir, that being involved with me hasn't put your career at risk?" Moire asked, feeling guilty. She hadn't helped Ennis much either in that direction. She hadn't *meant* to cause trouble.

"I do not believe so, but the court-martial has not concluded, true? No, I would have retired three years ago if not for the war. And it appears due to your actions," he gave a courtly nod, "the war is, if not officially ended, no longer active."

Moire sat back, considering what he had said. Had they really stopped the war, just because she took pity on a shipwrecked crab long ago?

"I hope you have a very enjoyable retirement," she said. Everybody should have a nice retirement. Including her.

"I believe I shall," del Sor agreed. "I have an interest in comparative constitutional theory, and the opportunities to do research on that topic are somewhat limited in Fleet. Perhaps also–" the annunciator at the door beeped. More marines, and an officer, stood outside.

"Board is reconvening, sir."

Del Sor raised an eyebrow at Moire as they went to leave.

The seating for the officers of the board was now crowded with a new addition, a stone-faced general. Otherwise the room was sparsely filled.

.

.

None of the witnesses or supporting staff were present, even the marine guards were posted outside the room. Moire and del Sor were the only non-board members in the room.

Highly irregular. Del Sor did not let any reaction show on his face, and Moire did her best to follow his example. They hadn't decided to shoot her out of hand for being a pain in the neck and attracting crabs, had they?

"I am General Gast," the newcomer stated. "These proceedings are now classified State Necessity, codeword PANGOLIN. No one in this room is permitted to communicate what will be discussed in this room prior to the conclusion of this board. FarCom has determined that current need supersedes the normal progression of this court-martial. No criticism of the conduct of this board or the reasons for convening it are expressed or implied by this action. The individual known variously as Moire Cameron of the former United States Air Force, alias Ann Sayres of the Tabrizi Mercenary Force and Fleet Command, alias Ren Roberts, has assumed a crucial position of authority recognized by the Allied Hsurwyn Moieties, an authority recognized of no other human organization."

I didn't assume *anything!* Moire fumed. *I didn't have a choice! It was an accident! The translator didn't work right!*

"Given the overriding priority of ending the current state of war between humans and the AHM, I have been ordered to make arrangements to restore Moire Cameron's freedom to resume her responsibilities as the recognized authority of the Sequoyah system and commander in fact of its forces, with the understanding that Sequoyah will in good faith and action promote and encourage peace between the warring parties. With regard to the matter before this board," the general said, looking directly at Moire, "It is my considered opinion that Moire Cameron did in fact assist the mutineers of *Canaveral.* However, I am convinced that diligent legal counsel," she looked at del Sor, "would have a reasonable chance of success of proving that such assistance was conditional on no loss of life, that this condition was enforced, and that Moire Cameron had valid reason to think both that she was not in Fleet chain of command and that her life and the lives of others were in danger if she confided in it. I propose the following: that this board dissolve itself with a verdict of No Finding, but that Moire Cameron in consequence of her actions be permanently barred from the Sol system."

Moire's mind was a white roar of confusion. They were letting her go? That was it? She'd never really thought about returning to Earth. Never thought she'd survive long enough for that to even be possible.

An elbow in her side jarred her attention back to the present. "What is your response?" del Sor whispered. Right. She had to agree to it. For a moment she toyed with the idea of turning it down, but her conscience won out. This wasn't about her.

Moire rose. "I accept the proposal of the board."

She didn't even try to follow the rest as the court-martial wrapped up. Her part was over, and del Sor would let her know if she needed to say anything. She was so tired...and all she'd done was sit in a room.

The board stood, and she and del Sor stood too. The general did not leave the room immediately, but strode with precision before Moire and executed a perfect, knife-edge salute. Without thinking, Moire returned it, astounded. General Gast turned on her heel and left without a word. *What the hell?*

Alone in the room with del Sor, Moire turned to him and asked, "Did I just miss something?"

Del Sor permitted himself a smile. "The legal ramifications may not have been immediately apparent to a non-specialist. The general's actions were correct protocol for the representative of Fleet greeting a head of state."

Moire sat down again, hard. "Excuse me?" Was it too late to call the board back?

"It is diplomatically expedient for both sides in this conflict to have a third party with which to conduct negotiations. I believe in your time there were still tiny vestigial states on Earth that retained autonomy, mostly for the legal convenience of other, much larger states."

I'm Lichtenstein in space. I should have read the fine print.

"I suspect they will be wanting you to reassure the local crab flotilla that you will be dealing with them next," he continued. "It would definitely be a courtesy to Captain Baxter if you could persuade them to leave, and perhaps meet somewhere else?"

"I would like to request the assistance of Commander Ennis, who has worked with Sequoyah and the crabs previously," Moire said, her head in her hands. If she didn't have someone to complain to soon, she would explode.

"That should present no difficulty." Del Sor extended his hand. "If you will permit the informality, since I am not aware of the title that should be used to address the head of Sequoyah. It was my very great honor to represent you."

Moire shook his hand. "Colonel del Sor, the honor was mine."

There was blessed silence after he left, and she remained at the table purely from lack of energy to move. Presumably she could leave at any time now, if she could get a seat on a courier. Or were scruffy heads of state allowed on couriers?

The door opened, but she didn't raise her head. A mug was placed in front of her, full of something hot. "They were out of coffee," said Ennis.

She looked up at his too-pale face, still thinner than she liked. "Sit down before you fall over," she snapped. "You look like you should still be in medical care." In a softer voice, "How are you?"

He sat down beside her stiffly, placing his own mug on the table. "It's not as bad as it looks. My past come back to haunt me," he said ruefully. "The injury was not the main problem. Extensive nerve damage usually heals with the right protocols, but not when there is existing, also extensive radiation damage. They had to use a large prosthetic web to work around it. I'm still...adjusting." They sat for a moment, companionably silent. "They didn't tell me much about what happened at the end. Only that the Toren ships and prisoners were taken away by Fleet."

Moire sighed, sipping her drink. It was some kind of smoky tea. "It took us a while to get all the ground troops," she said, rubbing her forehead. "We lost too many getting there. Thirty-two, was the last count. A few still missing. We found enough of Carlos Montero to identify, though. Ships—you saw what happened there, nothing changed after you left. No, you didn't see Palmer return. He's full of himself, of course, getting that last ship like he did. The crabs—*Remaining Shard* was the cruiser that took on the Toren command ship, it lost most of its fighters and took damage but they got it repaired pretty quick. *Honor Glowing* lost 30 percent of its complement and only minor damage. One of the shuttles crashed near the cave entrance and knocked down part of a psuedotree, they are still cleaning that up."

He nodded. "What about you? I was told to go and assist Sequoyah, but what does that mean? What did the board decide? I notice the guards are gone. Were you acquitted?"

"They made me stay in charge," Moire said gloomily. "That's punishment enough. No, FarCom came in and stepped on the court-martial so they could use Sequoyah as a buffer state. Why me? I never, ever wanted command and now I'm officially in charge of the whole damn system, according to Fleet *and* the crabs."

"You are taking care of your people. Even the ones with tentacles on their faces," Ennis said, smiling. "Which reminds me. I should return this now." He held out the enameled NASA pin, her pledge to him that she would return. Moire held it, turning it in the light. Remembering everything it had been, the people she had known. The promises, old promises, she had made. And fulfilled.

Pity more promises had to be made to do it. But that seemed to be the only way to get things done any more.

"All right, let's go talk to the crabs." She held out a hand to help him up. He took it, and held it.

"Yes, let's talk to the crabs."

There was time with Ennis while that was going on, so she didn't mind the delays and confusion. Somehow everything she had to do now seemed possible when he was there. But then it was done, and she was suited up one more time, and she heard the warbling whistle on the ship's intercom and the voice announcing "Sequoyah, departing," and she had to leave. Walking down the corridor to the hatch, past lines of Fleet officers and enlisted at attention, to where the dark familiar suited shapes of the Hsurwyn...*her* Hsurwyn waited to welcome her to their ship. To take her home.

Ensign Wernicki had not seen so much excitement since Lambert Station. She still didn't know why she got transferred all the way out to the new border outpost, but except for the difficulty in getting current trid shows she didn't really mind. It was very by-the-book with lots of rules, and that always made it easier for her.

Strangely enough, the excitement was because of Commander Ennis and that was funny because things had been more exciting than she liked when he was on Lambert Station too. He seemed to bring trouble, but she liked him anyway. He tried hard not to yell at her, and she appreciated that. Only this time he wasn't her superior officer, he was just waiting for transport. Waiting for transport from *crabs!* She'd been with him when they got to shoot at crabs, on Lambert.

Wernicki frowned. Okay, maybe Sequoyah wasn't all crabs but crabs *lived* there, right next to humans! She'd heard stories they were all pirates, and had a mystical web drive, and all sorts of strange things. Commander Ennis was very brave to be taking a posting there. Liaison, he'd said. He'd been there before, so maybe it wasn't so bad. Mostly if he wasn't in his quarters he would be watching the viewscreens, not saying anything. Some of the others whispered he had been sent by Umbra to find out the secret drive. He seemed to think he'd be staying there for a long time, years and years. That distressed Wernicki. If it was hard to get trid out here, still in the human sector, it would be even harder out there. He wouldn't even be able to get mail from his friends very often. She hoped he had friends. Otherwise it would be too lonely to think about.

Now something had come. It was scary, thinking she had to communicate with a crab ship right outside the outpost, but they did everything like they were supposed to, and the machine that translated worked just like the manual said too. Wernicki wasn't quite sure she believed it really was talking to them. A thought occurred, a fresh source of terror. Would actual crabs come on to the outpost itself?

"Tell them I am ready to leave," a voice said, and she jumped. Commander Ennis had come up behind her and she hadn't head him.

"Yessir. Um, now, sir? Won't you need a suit?"

He smiled. "This is *Bright Choosing*, the first human-Hsurwyn hybrid ship. It has human and Hsurwyn sections for the crew." Ennis pointed at the exterior vid console. "Take a look, it's worth it."

She brought up the display for the sensor nearest the approaching ship, and gasped. Human ships were mostly smooth, crab ships had spines. This ship had a surface that...swirled. Curving things like tendrils extended from the surface, so that was *sort* of like crab ships, but they had small bright lights at the tips. If it was in shadow, the ship would look like a cluster of stars.

"Oh, that's pretty!"

He smiled, but didn't say anything. He was focused on the ship with a strange, hungry look in his eyes.

"Ship is docked, sir," Wernicki said after a moment. She wondered if the commander of the outpost would have guards ready.

"On my way," said Commander Ennis. "Take care, Wernicki."

"Thank you, sir," she said, her smile faltering as she saw him limp away. He had never mentioned what had happened, and she hadn't dared to ask. She hoped he would be all right by himself.

She stewed for the remainder of her shift, which wasn't that long, and when she was relieved stuck her chin out and made a decision. Commander Ennis was nice. Okay, maybe not *nice* but a good officer and he shouldn't think nobody cared he was being sent all the way away from everything *normal*. She would say goodbye.

He had already cleared out of his quarters. The ship hadn't left yet, so with some trepidation Wernicki made her way down to the main dock, the only one the big ship would fit. No crabs, not that she could see anyway, just some cargo handlers moving some crates and baggage. She caught a glimpse of a familiar dark head and hurried to catch up. He was heading for the personnel hatch, and entered with a quick step, carrying a large bag.

Wernicki skidded to a stop. People were already there, inside. Not crabs. A woman with short brown hair grinning at Commander Ennis, and a young man that looked like her, and grim, silent Commander Ennis had dropped his bag and was hugging both of them like he would never let them go. They seemed happy to see him, too. Then they turned to go in the ship, the young man picking up the heavy bag as if it were empty. He saw her, and waved. Wernicki waved back, relieved. Commander Ennis wasn't going to be lonely after all. In fact, she realized as she went back to the main part of the outpost, he looked like he was going home.

The End

ABOUT THE AUTHOR

Sabrina Chase was originally trained as a Mad Scientist, but due to a tragic lack of available lairs at the time of graduation fell into low company and started working in the software industry. She lives in the Pacific Northwest and is owned by two cats.

Further sordid details may or may not be available at her website, chaseadventures.com

Made in the USA
Middletown, DE
30 August 2024

60023881R00136